CLAIRE DELACROIX

The Warrior

WARNER BOOKS

NEW YORK   BOSTON

Cover design by Diane Luger
Cover illustration by Alan Ayers
Hand lettering by David Gatti
Book design by Giorgetta Bell McRee

Warner Books

Time Warner Book Group
1271 Avenue of the Americas
New York, NY 10020
Visit our Web site at www.twbookmark.com

Printed in the United States of America

First Paperback Printing: March 2004

10 9 8 7 6 5 4 3 2 1

For Mary O'Gara,
with thanks.

Prologue

Inverfyre, Scotland—November 1390

*H*is father had been right.

Every step Michael took into the forests of Scotland made it more impossible to evade the astonishing truth. He had always assumed that his father's tales of Scotland had been whimsy, heavily embellished with a nostalgia that his mother would find appealing. Gawain Lammergeier was not above stretching the truth, especially when his tall tales prompted Evangeline's laughter.

But all of those tales had been true. The land was so beautiful as to leave Michael breathless, and it could be as mercilessly cruel as a beauteous woman with a heart of ice. What he had not expected was his growing sense that these lands were not quite earthly. He might have stepped into the domain of the fey. Michael was uneasy with this awareness, for he had never heeded such tales and knew not what the rules of this land might be.

There had been frost this morning when his company awakened, and all the trees were etched with silver filigree so fine as to rival the work of a master jeweler. The sky was a blue so bright as to hurt one's gaze, but the shadows in the forest yielded their secrets to none. Michael surveyed his surroundings constantly as they rode, unable to dissuade himself of the conviction that they were being watched.

And not by mortal eyes.

Certainly not by friendly eyes.

He urged the party onward, fighting to ignore the oppressive feeling that the forest disapproved of his intrusion. He was the seventh son of Magnus Armstrong, the heir of Inverfyre, the warrior destined to fulfill an old prophecy, and the son of the greatest thief in Christendom besides.

Fortune would not dare deny him his due.

Or so he told himself.

At least, Michael was not alone. Tarsuinn had been invited to join this journey, his half-sister Rosamunde had not, but they both rode behind him all the same. (He knew that he should have anticipated that Rosamunde would have her way.) Sebastien and Fernando, two good friends from Sicily who had proclaimed themselves in dire need of an adventure, accompanied him as well. A dozen stalwart men from his father's household and ship comprised the rest of the group that had sailed north.

Michael might have stolen his father's vessel—a feat he did not doubt his father savored—but he was not fool enough to embark on a quest without information. He had commanded the crew to drop anchor at the Lammergeier stronghold of Ravensmuir to seek the counsel of his uncle, Merlyn. But Merlyn and his wife Ysabella had been away—in lieu of Merlyn's counsel, Michael's cousins Tynan and Roland had insisted upon accompanying the party to Inverfyre, along with their trio of squires.

The company comprised more than twenty in all, but the

sound of their passing was almost naught. The young squires had ceased their chattering as soon as the shadow of the woods closed around them. By the time Stirling had fallen into the forgotten distance, none of them dared to make so much as a whistle.

Just the day before, Michael would have counted it a blessing if Rosamunde and Tynan could have ceased their bickering over every inconsequential detail. On this day, he had the urge to provoke them, if only to hear mortal voices at normal volume. He felt that they trod close to a sleeping demon whom they dared not awaken.

Yet not all slumbered, for something surveyed their progress. Michael halted suddenly and knew without glancing back that the rest of his party stopped behind him. Stillness settled on all sides, the shadows seemed impenetrable, the cold of pending winter chilled his marrow. The forest breathed on all sides, watching, waiting.

He shivered involuntarily and his heart quailed. It seemed suddenly to be tremendous folly that had brought him here, that he could never accomplish his objective, that he had made a fatal error.

Nonsense! He would not be defeated by silence!

"Are there wolves in these woods?" Michael demanded of his cousin.

Tynan shrugged. "There are wolves in all the forests of Christendom. They are not more numerous here."

"Are they more malicious?" Rosamunde asked as she eased her steed closer to the pair.

Tynan snorted. "Have you amiable wolves in the south?"

Rosamunde lifted her chin and glared at her cousin. "Are they especially vicious in this barbaric land?"

"All predators are vicious, particularly those willing to

prey upon men." Tynan turned to scan the forest, excluding Rosamunde with his manner.

Michael did not miss the hot glance his half-sister cast at their inattentive cousin.

Rosamunde was a willful beauty, unused to any man failing to show interest in her charms. Michael and Rosamunde were of an age, but Tynan was some eight years their senior. Further, he was tall and dark and given to dismissing Rosamunde in a manner she clearly did not appreciate.

"What observes our progress, then?" Michael asked.

Tynan smiled. "I could tell you a thousand tales of ghosts and specters, each and every one of them purportedly true. One seldom feels alone in our woods, though I never have felt another presence so strongly."

It was on Michael's lips to ask how close they were to Inverfyre, but a cloaked figure stepped out of the forest ahead of them and silenced his query before it was uttered.

He saw her and he knew, he *knew* with unwavering certainty that he stood already upon his hereditary holding.

But how could he be so certain? They had passed no boundary marker, indeed they were not even upon the road.

He blinked and looked again at this unexpected figure. Indeed, he could not have said that this soul truly stepped from anywhere—it was more that the figure had appeared where it had not been before. He might have thought that he imagined its presence, but Rosamunde whispered a prayer and crossed herself. Tynan lifted a hand to stay him, suddenly as watchful and silent as a predator himself. Roland caught his breath, as if he bit back a warning.

Michael understood then that they, too, felt the uncanny power of this stranger.

"Do you shirk what you cannot see, heir of Magnus Armstrong?" the figure shouted, her voice revealing her gender.

"Or is the blood of Magnus' lineage so diminished that his heir has not the boldness of a babe?"

Tarsuinn gasped. "God in heaven, it cannot be."

"Who is she?" Michael demanded.

"An old crone of the woods. I thought her dead years past." Tarsuinn peered at the distant figure, shaking his head as he marveled. "But it is she. This one was of aid to your parents once, though she is unpredictable. I advise caution, my lord." He eased his steed forward and raised his voice. "Adaira? Do you yet occupy these woods?"

"Tarsuinn Falconer," she replied haughtily. "I would know your voice in any land, though the birds have spoken of your pending return."

This made little sense to Michael, but before he could ask, the crone lifted one hand. She pointed a gnarled finger toward the clouds. Four birds cried and flew overhead as if she had summoned them. Their distinctive silhouette made the company gasp.

"Peregrines!" Tarsuinn whispered in awe, craning his neck to follow the course of the birds.

Another trio followed, crying as they flew. One had a fresh kill and the others tormented it, trying to steal the meat.

They were all snared by the sight and Michael knew his heart was not the sole one to soar with the birds. His forebears had made their fortune by training and selling the finest peregrines in all of Christendom. When his mother had been forced to leave Inverfyre, the peregrines' numbers had been diminished to scarcity.

But nigh on twenty years had swelled their numbers, just as all had fervently hoped. These birds seemed uncommonly vigorous and he took encouragement at the majesty of their flight.

Tarsuinn, son of the old falconer, smiled and tears shone in his eyes. "How many, Adaira?" he demanded, his words husky with hope. Indeed, he had come to Inverfyre despite his age in the hope that he might see the cliffs thick with his beloved birds. "How many have returned?"

"The falcons are plentiful in numbers at Inverfyre again, Tarsuinn Falconer. They tell me that they await your hand. Long has the alliance betwixt the peregrines and the blood of Magnus Armstrong prospered, after all."

Tarsuinn's delight was nigh tangible. "My lord, this is the finest news for which we might have hoped . . ."

Adaira's voice hardened. "I have no business with you on this day, Tarsuinn Falconer, and the falcons have not waited so long that they cannot wait longer. It is the boy I have come to greet."

Michael felt the hair rise on the back of his neck when she pointed a calloused finger at him. How could she know who he was? Tynan, Roland and Rosamunde eased their steeds to his one side, Sebastien and Fernando to the other, but Michael raised his hand to stay them.

"This matter is mine to resolve." He urged his destrier to step forward alone. It was a magnificent black stallion, granted to him by his father upon his eighteenth birthday— along with the seal of Inverfyre that reposed in his purse. Lucifer was afraid of naught, tall and strong, and just the sight of him made men halt to stare.

But the old woman stood her ground as Michael approached. Strangely, her eyes seemed to glow within the shadows cast by her hood. "Aye, boy, I come to parley with you and you alone."

"And I am here. Say what you must."

When he halted the steed several paces from her, she cackled with laughter. "Are afeared, boy? You will not recapture Inverfyre if you cannot even approach an old woman!"

One of the squires snickered, but Michael was already swinging from his saddle. He cast the reins aside with impatience and doffed his gloves. Tynan said something cautionary but Michael strode away, making his way directly to the crone. She was smaller than he had guessed, the top of her hood below the middle of his chest. She watched him approach, her eyes gleaming, though he only saw why they shone so oddly when she suddenly cast back her hood.

Her gaze was veiled with the pale blue sheen of cataracts. Her tanned skin was as wrinkled as old leather, her features so shrunken that the flesh was tautly stretched over her bones. Her teeth were gone, her hair as white as fresh snow, her pose defiant. He recoiled and she laughed beneath her breath.

"What is your name, boy?"

"You seem to know as much already."

"Tell me!"

"I am Michael Lammergeier, son of Gawain Lammergeier and Evangeline Armstrong, Laird of Inverfyre."

She chuckled. "You are not laird yet."

"I have the seal and the bloodright . . ."

"And there are others who occupy your lands, others who are not creatures of the forest."

Michael had expected as much. His mother had told him a hundred times of the avarice of the MacLaren clan and their lust for Inverfyre. "Do you come to curse me or to warn me?"

Her smile softened, as did her voice. "Not I, Magnus. Not I."

He shook his head, thinking her wits addled. "I am not Magnus, but Michael, as I just told you . . ."

Adaira interrupted him. "You are Magnus Armstrong, just as you are the seventh son born in succession from him. Make no mistake, Michael Lammergeier, the spark of Magnus resides within you and his debts sit upon your shoulders."

"I do not think so." Michael took a step back from this woman who was obviously mad.

She granted him a look so quelling that he halted against his own will, then she beckoned.

He found himself leaning closer, drawn by some compulsion he could not name, half-certain she would tell him something that would be of merit in his quest.

Instead she caught the back of his neck in her hand, her gesture quick and her grip strong. Before he could protest, she pressed her ancient lips to his in a parody of a kiss. Her tongue was between his teeth, its invasion as skillful and revolting as that of a snake slipping into a lair.

He made to pull away but froze when a curious sense overcame him. He was remembering, remembering events that were not his to remember.

The scene of a richly appointed hall unfurled in his own thoughts. He was within the hide of a man garbed like a king, a man who was him but not him, and a glorious maiden was seated at his left. Her hair was of chestnut hue, her complexion was creamy, her waist narrow and her eyes a fathomless blue. She turned to him, her gaze filled with adoration, and smiled so sweetly that his heart nigh broke. He saw himself raise a hand to her nape, felt the silk of her hair around his fingers as he pulled her closer, tasted the sweet honey of her lips as he kissed her deeply.

That kiss melted into this kiss and Michael realized what he did.

He tore his lips away from the crone's and felt himself trembling.

"What witchery is this you do?" he demanded, his words hoarse. To his horror, the crone's smile was tinged with his recollection of the sweet smile of the maiden, the blue of her clouded eyes reminded him all too well of the maiden's clear loving gaze.

Michael wiped his lips with disgust, then spat out the taste of the crone. He made to step back, but her hands locked again around his neck. "Release me, witch!" he cried, even as he fought against her unholy grip.

"Another," Adaira whispered, her voice as low and velvety as a ripe maiden's. Indeed, Michael knew that if he closed his eyes, he would err again, he would think this crone the maiden he remembered loving with all his heart and soul.

But Michael had never loved a woman thus. He had never known a woman who looked like that maiden, he had certainly never loved a damsel with such vigor that his heart ached so at the very sight of her. This was some trick! He fought Adaira's wickedly strong grasp, but her lips closed over his all the same.

And the witchery worked its darkness again. He tasted the sweetness of honey and the tang of wine on the lips of his damsel, felt the ripeness of her naked breast beneath his hand. He saw that the demoiselle and he had retired to a richly draped bed, a bed unknown to him. Her hair was unbound, hanging thick to her waist, her flesh was fair, her nipples rosy. She was perfection, she was his love, she was his mate.

"Magnus," she whispered with awe as her playful fingers closed around his erection. She giggled when he caught his breath, as merry a sound as he had ever heard. Michael thought his heart would burst with the fullness of his love for her.

For a woman he had never seen before.

Sorcery!

He broke the embrace with an effort and glared at the old woman. "You are a witch, bent on driving me to madness," Michael accused in a low voice. "Why? What accusation would you make against me?"

Adaira smiled. "You will remember all, Magnus, in time."

"I am not Magnus . . ."

She turned then, her head lifting suddenly like a doe who hears the hunter. Then she seized his hand, her other hand fumbling beneath her cloak. Michael struggled to break free of her merciless grip, but she had an unholy strength.

"It was not my intent to betray you, Magnus, never that," she declared in a low voice. "Still I love you, with all my heart and soul, as I did centuries past, as I loved you on the night that you betrayed me."

"I have never—"

"We must seize this chance to make matters come aright."

"The chance for what? What is this nonsense you utter?"

"Still I love you," she insisted, then lifted an ancient dagger high in her hand.

"No!" Michael cried out and took a step back, certain the madwoman meant him ill. He heard the consternation of his men behind him. He fought her with renewed vigor, but to no avail. She held fast, her grip as strong as a demon's.

"What do you fear of me?" she whispered, hurt in her tone. "I offer you aid, no more than that. You will need this."

She turned her hand, offering him the blade, even as two arrows soared past Michael's shoulder and tore violently into her chest. Her body jerked as she fell back, her grip upon him loosing only now.

"No!" Michael shouted, appalled that he had misunderstood her, shocked that he had been responsible for such an error. He caught her in his arms as she collapsed and watched helplessly as the blood flowed from her.

He glanced back to find the members of his party pale-faced, their expressions shocked. Sebastien and Fernando both held their bows at the ready.

"She meant me no ill!" Michael shouted in dismay. Later he would marvel at the root of his certainty, but in that moment, he knew without doubt.

He heard footsteps approaching, saw Sebastien lean down beside him. "I am sorry, my lord. I thought . . ."

"I know, I know. The error was mine," Michael whispered, unable to explain his sorrow. Sebastien stepped away. Michael saw him raise a hand to halt the others, but he cared solely for Adaira.

Adaira's wounds were fatal, that much was clear. She knew it, as well, for there was resignation in the set of her lips.

The dagger tumbled from her feeble grip and she raised a trembling hand to his face. Her odd gaze seemed fixed upon him, nay, it seemed she could see directly to his soul.

"Another betrayal," she murmured with a shake of her head. "Beware, my love, for the treachery wrought must all be repaid."

"It was an accident . . ." Michael began, but she shook her head.

"There are no accidents in truth. And in a sense, I am relieved. This life has been long and arduous, each day painful in your absence." She sighed and smiled, her fingertip shaking as she touched his face. "I have missed you, love."

Michael did not know what to say. He could not explain the deep well of grief that opened within him.

"Remember me well, Magnus Armstrong," she whispered. "Remember that it was not my intent to betray you on this day, though I feared matters would come to this. I had to see you one last time, despite the price." She shook her head. "The gods will have their jest, after all."

Tears began to run from her eyes as Michael watched helplessly. Her fingers traced the lines of his face as if she would know the look of him despite her blindness.

She was mad, that much was clear, and an utter stranger, but still his heart tightened. It seemed to him that he had had many painful partings like this, though he knew he had not.

"I love you, Magnus," she said, her voice no stronger than a breath. "I love you with all my heart for all time."

Michael saw her die, he witnessed the moment that life left her being. Indeed, he could have had no doubt of it. Just as the old woman's eyes closed and her lips stilled, a light seemed to flood her face and he saw again the features of that young beautiful maiden.

On impulse, he bent, compelled by some nameless urge to press his lips to the maiden's lips one last time. The vision abruptly faded and he found only the dead crone's lips beneath his own.

Shaken, Michael laid her on the ground and took an unsteady step back. As he stared at her, a tumult of memories loosed in his mind that he was certain were not his own. Throughout them all rode that maiden, her smile tightening his chausses and making his heart pound.

He glanced back to his companions, seeking some hint that he was not the only one affected, but they regarded him with uncertainty.

As rightly they should. He did not know what had possessed him. Michael bent and impulsively claimed the unusual dagger, shoving it into his belt, as he sought the words that would return matters to how they had been.

He did not have long to think. The silence of the forest was rent suddenly with shouts. A tattered army of vagabonds leapt out of the shadows, blades flashing. His party was assaulted on all sides by a nameless and innumerable foe.

Sebastien shouted and loosed another arrow into the throng of attackers. Tynan roared and unsheathed his blade; the horses neighed and reared. Roland's blade rang out as it met that of one attacker. Rosamunde drove her dagger into the face of another assailant.

Michael was the last to draw his blade, Adaira's whimsy like cobwebs in his thoughts. He had no doubt that this was but the first of many battles, part of the greater war that would be required to reclaim what was his own.

He bellowed commands and his men formed a circle around him. Blades swung and blood flowed, the watchful peace of the forest shattered by the warfare of men. They were upon the soil of Inverfyre, Michael could feel it in his very feet, and he would either die or triumph upon these lands.

His fate coursed through his very veins.

And through the years ahead, a maiden smiled benignly in Michael's newfound memories, encouraging him, loving him, welcoming him home. She buoyed him when his spirit might have faltered and each time he unsheathed his blade, he swore to serve her proudly. He knew he would never forget this beauty, a conjured dream who had claimed his heart without saying a word.

Indeed, had he listened to his heart, he would have recalled that she was his destiny.

It would be more than eighteen years before Michael glimpsed her again, eighteen years of memories and yearning, eighteen years in which he measured each damsel against her memory. She would be wrought taller, more fair, but with the same blue eyes and the same mysterious smile. He would be older, with silver at his temples and experience on his blade. He would be known as the Hawk of Inverfyre by then for his talent in seizing a moment of opportunity to claim a victory.

And the Hawk would steal the sole prize he desired, a deed that befitted the son of a thief he had always been and the ruthless predator he had become.

It would be a long eighteen years.

I

Abernye, Scotland—March 1409

Does a hare know when the hawk's gaze lands upon it?

Aileen knew the moment the stranger spied her. She first glimpsed him from the top of the stairs, but was so unsettled to find his gaze upon her that she immediately looked away. She feigned undue concentration upon her descent to the raucous hall.

The hair on the back of her neck prickled and her face burned under the weight of his regard, though she knew he would soon glance elsewhere.

Curiosity could only compel so long a perusal, especially for so plain a maiden as she knew herself to be. She held her head high and crossed the hall to the high table, fighting her desire to turn and look.

"Such a notorious guest!" whispered a maid as she arranged the skirts of Aileen's new stepmother, Blanche. This was yet another kirtle that Aileen had not seen before, the silken cloth richly gleaming in the light of the torches. It was trimmed with fur that must be ermine, and embroidered with gold.

Whatever Blanche had expected when she seduced Aileen's father, she could not have anticipated the simple austerity of Abernye, with its pastures and sheep and rough hall. From whence had the coin come for yet another kirtle? Aileen did not imagine it had been Blanche's own purse.

Though her stepmother had been rumored to have a fat dowry, it was the treasury of Abernye that seemed to pay for all her fripperies.

"The Hawk is said to have killed a thousand men to claim Inverfyre," confided another maid on Blanche's opposite side, her hands just as busy as her tongue.

Aileen's fears were momentarily forgotten. Their guest was the Hawk of Inverfyre? She knew his name and repute, of course—who did not? She struggled to suppress her urge to glance his way.

"It is said that he stole it from its rightful lords, slaughtering those who opposed him, and without remorse!" the first maid added gleefully.

"He is a thief."

"A murderer without morals."

Blanche's eyes gleamed with interest as she openly watched their guest. She was finely wrought, this prize fetched from the English court, her pretty features and delicate build making Aileen feel all the more tall and ungainly.

"All this and handsome, too," Blanche murmured with satisfaction. "What fortune brings us such an intriguing guest! I forbid you all to mention such rumors in his presence."

At that, Aileen could not help but steal a glance, certain the Hawk's attention would be diverted.

She sorely miscalculated. The man in question watched

her avidly. She should have demurely dropped her gaze, she should have looked away, but Aileen could not. She found herself snared by his bright gaze, helpless as the proverbial hare. Indeed, her heart nigh stopped and her mouth went dry, though not simply because of his looks.

The Hawk was tall, his shoulders were broad, his hair was dark with a touch of silver at the temples. He was tanned to a golden hue that spoke of vitality and he moved with a warrior's resolve. He was handsome, that much could not have been denied. There was an ease about him, a grace uncommon in the fighting men of Abernye although beguilingly male all the same.

Yet he was a warrior, of that Aileen had no doubt. This man had made choices, he had swung his blade, he had decided who would live and who would die.

He did not appear to be burdened by regrets.

He was garbed in blackest midnight, a hue so dark as to draw the light of the hall and devour it. His boots were high and similarly dark, his tabard was devoid of insignia or embroidery. She decided that he would not be a man who favored embellishment. Three cohorts flanked him, warriors just as fearsome and just as darkly garbed, though there was no doubt in Aileen's thoughts who ruled them all.

She stifled a shiver, shocked to her marrow that she was still the focus of the Hawk's attention. It was the intensity of his regard, the fixedness of it that put Aileen in mind of his namesake, the predatory hawk. He was so still that she was certain he neither blinked nor breathed, his gaze so intent that he might have been touching her.

Even as she felt a desire to cross the floor to his side, Aileen understood instinctively that this man was dangerous. A thousand prickles raced over her flesh and her color rose hotly. She held her ground but still she could not demurely look away.

"I heard that his own peregrines are trained to hunt men," the first maid whispered. "That they tear out the very hearts of their prey, and that when he looses them from Inverfyre's towers, the skies turn dark with their many wings."

"Fool! It is the *eyes* of his enemies that the birds devour!"

The corner of the Hawk's lips quirked, offering Aileen the barest ghost of what might have been a smile. He could not have heard the nonsense repeated by the maids, for he was too far away, but his expression was so knowing that she wondered. Her heart thumped with painful vigor, yet still she could not avert her gaze.

He savored her predicament, her awareness of him, her inability to behave as she should. Aileen knew this. Indeed, the air seemed to crackle between them, as if they were old adversaries met again.

But they were not. Aileen had never met this man before.

All the same, she was not some shy maiden unafraid to speak her thoughts. Aileen lifted her chin and held his gaze with defiance, even as the rumors of his deeds echoed around her, and his smile broadened ever so slightly.

Perhaps he savored his own dark repute.

Perhaps he did not care about her own reputation. Aileen's pulse quickened at the prospect.

"You know, of course, that he is the spawn of a family who made their livelihood in the theft and sale of religious relics," the first maid clucked.

"Unholy vermin!" breathed the second, though her tone was not as scathing as it could have been. "I heard that his desires cannot be denied."

They giggled together at this morsel. "His blade purportedly cannot be turned aside," continued the first, "and he refuses to be denied whatsoever he seeks."

"Yet he cringes from no deed, no matter how foul, if it will see him sated." The maids sighed in unison and Blanche's dark brows arched high with interest.

Why had the Hawk come to Abernye? Aileen had a dark premonition in that breathless moment, though her good sense dismissed the possibility with ease. No men came to her father's hall to hunt her hand any longer. He must be making a jest by feigning fascination with her, the icy daughter of the Laird of Abernye.

That realization made it simple for Aileen to turn away, even as her wretched heart sank. The Hawk's companions laughed loudly and she was convinced it was at her expense.

Aileen knew that she was old for a maiden, she was tall, she was plain of face, she was outspoken. She knew that she had recoiled from a man's kiss too often for her distaste to not be noted. She had had her faults so oft recounted that she knew them as well as a clerk knows the debts in his accounts.

The Hawk was cruel beyond belief to mock her in her father's hall. Aileen added "rude" to the list of his dubious attributes and fairly marched in her haste to reach the far end of the high table. She would sit away from the viper her father had been so foolish as to wed, she would eat with haste and then retire.

The pair of Blanche's women nudged each other as Aileen passed, no doubt noting her high color. "So, even your frosty womb can still recognize a man," the first maid whispered with a malice that made the other cackle.

"Do not set your ambitions so high, dear Aileen, lest you die of disappointment," added the second. They laughed together, these two evil old crones, though Aileen gave them a look so sharp it might have left a bleeding wound.

Her father's new wife, of course, did not defend her from her servants' insolence. Stepdaughter and stepmother had long past dispensed with pleasantries and Aileen tried to avoid any discussion with her father's new bride.

She felt compelled to be polite, though Blanche did not apparently feel the same obligation. Aileen had no doubt that Blanche would have had her cast from the gates if that lady had not feared that the laird himself might object.

Aileen was not certain he would. Her father was so smitten that it seemed Blanche could not err in his estimation.

"Our guest had best sit directly beside me," Blanche said smoothly, stroking the spot Aileen's father usually occupied.

Aileen halted, shocked that her stepmother would be so bold. She knew she should leave the matter be, but guessed that her father would not protest such an uncommon breach of protocol. "Father will be displeased by such uncommon arrangements," she said simply, though she longed to say more.

Blanche smiled with a confidence that made Aileen's blood boil. "He will not deny my will."

"But surely a laird should be shown respect in his own hall?" Aileen demanded. "Surely it would be unwise to show such a warm welcome to a man of such dark repute, especially when his mission here is unclear?"

Blanche sniffed, her gaze cold. "When I have need of your counsel, Daughter, I shall ask for it."

Aileen let her gaze drop to Blanche's slender waist. They were nigh the same age, daughter and second bride. "You surely know as I do, Blanche, that you are not my mother in truth."

"Unfortunately for you," Blanche whispered, her accent

suddenly more pronounced. "For you are burdened with, how do you say, the *taint* of your mother's blood."

"She possessed no taint!"

Blanche's dark eyes narrowed and she might have said something vicious, but Aileen's father cleared his throat, revealing his unexpected proximity. He halted behind his wife, looking hale and hearty for all his years. Blanche turned one of her honeyed smiles upon him and Aileen was disappointed to see how her father fairly glowed.

"What is this I hear of you seating our guest at your very side?" Aileen's father asked, his manner genial as ever. Aileen was certain, however, that she could detect a similar uncertainty in their guest's motives.

Her father had taught her when to be suspicious, after all.

"One would not wish to insult such a powerful guest, Nigel," Blanche cooed. When Aileen's father did not immediately agree, Blanche dropped her voice beguilingly. "You may be certain that I will offer compense for your inconvenience later, my lord." She ran a fingertip up his arm and licked her lips so overtly that Aileen felt obliged to glance away. The maids giggled.

The Lord of Abernye flushed. "Of course, Blanche. Whatsoever you desire is my will." He ceded to his new wife's demand as readily as that, much to Aileen's disgust, looking more like a besotted boy than a man of fifty summers. Her father was a large and genial man, increasingly cursed to see the good in the hearts of others at the expense of being blind to their flaws.

Blanche stood testimony to that.

Aileen addressed her own toe, driven by this exchange to remind her father of all he had once claimed to believe. "Forgive me, Father, but I am confused. Is it so that even if your guest comes with no stated intent or invitation, even if he travels beyond far for no apparent purpose, even if he is the most dreaded man in Christendom, Blanche must not be denied her whim in courting his favor?"

Blanche granted Aileen a look fit to curdle milk.

"Aileen, you see danger in no more than shadows," her father said heartily. "A man's repute is not the fullness of him."

"It was you who counseled me that smoke oft warns of a flame," Aileen reminded him quietly and her father had the grace to color.

"This is not the same, Aileen . . ."

Aileen continued, feeling a strange compulsion to warn her father. She could not dismiss the sense of foreboding she had had when she held the Hawk's gaze. "Father, this man, rumored to be both violent and reclusive, has ridden across all of Scotland to visit Abernye, unannounced and uninvited. Why? He is neither liege nor vassal to you, his lands do not abut ours, and further, the spring weather is unruly."

Aileen heard her voice rise slightly in the face of her father's discomfiture and Blanche's resolve. "You do not hunt, so he cannot be seeking trade for his famed peregrines. You have naught that such a man might wish to buy and no associations held in common. I find his presence most suspicious, even if you do not, and I do so by the lessons you yourself taught to me!"

Aileen felt a sudden heat at her back and her heart sank to her toes. The false welcome that claimed her father's expression and the sudden brightness of Blanche's eyes told her more than she wished to know.

A man touched the back of her waist with a heavy fingertip and she stiffened in outrage at his familiarity. Aileen knew, she *knew* who stood there, and she knew too that he had overheard every word of protest she had uttered.

"I see that my reputation has preceded me," the Hawk murmured for her ears alone and Aileen felt herself flush scarlet at the intimacy of his tone.

Worse, she liked the low rich timbre of his voice and dared not glance in his direction when he stood so close behind her. She strove to give every appearance of ignoring him, though her flesh was all a-tingle. She would be scolded later for her rudeness, she knew it well, though in this moment she wished she might simply disappear.

Sadly, she could not flee, not with the weight of the Hawk's fingers on her back. His touch seemed to sear her flesh, even through the thick woolen kirtle that she wore.

"Good evening, Laird of Abernye," the Hawk said, seemingly untroubled that Aileen ignored him. His words were uttered slowly as if he pondered the import of each word—or sought to beguile his audience. "I am most honored by your hospitality to myself and my companions."

Instead of demanding a reason for the Hawk's arrival, Aileen's father smiled like a fool. "A Christian host cannot do enough for a guest." He inclined his head slightly. "I apologize for my daughter. She is cursed to be outspoken."

Before the Hawk could reply—if indeed he had any intent of doing so—Blanche summoned his attention to herself. "*Bienvenue, monsieur,*" she said, offering her hand with the coy gesture Aileen so despised.

The Hawk stepped forward to bend over Blanche's hand, Aileen's back chilling when his hand was lifted away. "*Enchanté,*" he murmured, his accent perfect to Aileen's rustic ears.

Aileen eyed him covertly, reluctantly acknowledging that he was more handsome close at hand. The hard planes of his features seemed softer when she could see the glint in his eye.

She took a step back, hoping to ease away, but the Hawk's hand landed upon her elbow so surely that she was halted in place.

Blanche smiled and, typically, her accent became more evident as she sought to charm. "*S'il vous plaît*, you must sit with me. It is not often that we have guests from afar, and I know that I shall savor the tales of your adventures." She patted the place to her right.

Aileen's father's lips tightened with a displeasure he could not fully hide, though whether it was the prospect of being parted from his bride or the breach of protocol that troubled him more was unclear.

"It would be more fitting if I sat further down the board," the Hawk suggested, his tone as smooth as Blanche's had been.

"But . . ."

"My motives could well be misinterpreted if I sat in the laird's rightful place. And I would not cause gossip for the Lady of Abernye, not after such a gracious welcome." The Hawk's tone was so firm, his argument so sound, that Blanche could not have possibly protested.

Aileen was shocked to find him express the precise objections she felt, albeit more eloquently.

"But, of course." Blanche smiled tightly, knowing she had lost, and Aileen felt a twinge of admiration for their guest.

Her goodwill was not destined to last, for her father beamed. "As we are equal beneath the king's eye, I must insist that you call me Nigel, Nigel Urquhart."

Aileen gaped at her father, marveling that he would put himself on such intimate terms with this man of whom he knew so little. Perhaps his wits had been addled in truth when her mother died!

"Michael Lammergeier. You must call me Michael in your turn."

The men shook hands and Aileen dared linger no longer. She would say more, more that would be regretted, and she was best to depart.

She turned to deliberately lift the Hawk's fingertips from her elbow. "If you will excuse me," she murmured, hoping to slip away while the trio basked in mutual—and undeserved—admiration.

But the Hawk did not release her elbow. Indeed the grip of his fingers tightened, compelling Aileen to look at him. He was watching her again, his avid gaze all the more potent at such close range. His eyes were green, a clear piercing green, his lashes dark and thick for a man.

Aileen could not fully draw a breath and her flesh tingled beneath his touch.

"I fear we have not been introduced," he murmured, that tentative smile melting her resistance.

"I am merely Aileen," she managed to say, feeling as lacking in graces as Blanche oft insisted she was.

"*Enchanté, encore.*" The Hawk let his hand slide down her forearm and captured her fingers. His hand was warm and gentle for all its size and strength. He fair engulfed her fingers in his, and she was not a small woman.

His gaze locked with Aileen's as he lifted her hand to his lips. Her heart skipped a beat. His lips were firm and dry against her knuckles, his very touch making her swallow.

Something flickered to life within Aileen, something she had never felt before, but which she might be tempted to call desire.

What a fool she was to respond to the Hawk's touch!

Her father cleared his throat. "Aileen is my daughter."

The Hawk remained solemn. Aileen felt he studied her,

though she could not have guessed why. He did not readily release her hand, and his thumb began to move slowly across her flesh. It was a seductive move, one that put uncommon thoughts into her head.

"You cannot be the same daughter of Abernye reputed to be skilled with a bow?" the Hawk asked, his manner that of one truly interested.

"The very same," Aileen said proudly, but Blanche spoke in the same moment and spoke more loudly.

"She pursues such inappropriate deeds no longer. I have put an end to such foolery."

"Aileen learns finally to embroider!" her father crowed with pride. "Blanche reports that she makes fine progress."

The Hawk's expression was so conspiratorial that Aileen knew she had failed to hide her feelings about this change. "And which task do you prefer?" he asked quietly.

As intriguing as his manner was, Aileen knew that this was an alliance that would be folly to pursue.

She spoke sharply, more sharply than she had intended. "It matters little, as the choice is not mine to make." She pulled her hand abruptly from his. "How pleasant to make your acquaintance," she said, her crisp tone implying otherwise. "Welcome to Abernye." She inclined her head and would have stepped away, but the Hawk halted her with his words.

"Perhaps I might rely upon your hospitality, Aileen."

Her name sounded like a caress upon his tongue, the sound enough to make her step falter. Aileen paused and glanced to him, seeing in his eyes that he was well aware of the impact of his voice upon her.

"I fear I lose my bearings in this keep," he said, apparently confiding in her. "Though I would not presume to burden the laird and lady with a matter so mundane as my orientation, I would greatly appreciate your assistance."

"Our hall is not so large and complicated as that," Aileen said with a cool smile. She pointed helpfully to the two portals to the hall. "But two corridors are there, one leading to the kitchens and one to the stables." She met the Hawk's knowing gaze. "I should think a man's nose could tell him which was which. Indeed, I would have anticipated that a man of your reputed cunning would have oriented himself quite readily."

"Aileen!" Blanche whispered.

Some comment began to rumble in her father's chest, but Aileen held the Hawk's gaze, daring him to argue the matter with her.

That smile touched his lips for a heartbeat, then it was gone. "Perhaps you might take pity upon a man with such a poor sense of smell, then." He spoke politely, but there was a thread of steel in his words.

Aileen saw his resolve. She knew that she would not evade this deed readily. She did not need to glance her father's way to feel the press of his insistence that she act in a hospitable manner. Indeed, she had the sense that the Hawk had cornered her as neatly and deliberately as he had evaded Blanche's choice of seating.

There was a glint in his eyes, almost a challenge. He had heard what she had recounted of his deeds—did he taunt her for questioning his motives? She could not deny that she would like to prove to this man that she was not afraid of him.

"If you insist, of course, I can only comply." Aileen smiled with a grace her mother would have applauded.

The Hawk left her no time to change her thinking. He folded his fingers around her elbow and held her so fast

against his side that she could fairly feel the pound of his
heart. She was dismayed to realize how she liked the heat of
him against her, the solidity of his muscles against her hand.
The top of her head came only to his shoulder and that in itself was a rare delight. He bowed his head to her father and
Blanche, then fairly pushed Aileen across the hall.

"Perhaps we should begin at the gates," he said with a resolve that brooked no dissent.

Two hundred gazes followed their course, the whispers
beginning in the rear. Aileen walked with her back as
straight as a blade, knowing full well that Blanche's women
would tease her about her supposed marital ambitions. They
were so confident that she had none, that even she knew her
chances of a good match to be nil.

There was something exciting about being chosen by
such a dangerous rogue, even for a matter as perfunctory as
granting him a tour of the keep. Indeed, Aileen's heart
skipped with the heat of his presence.

At least until they passed his companions, one of whom
winked boldly at Aileen. Another gave a lecherous whistle
that made her color rise.

"Ignore them," the Hawk counseled softly.

Aileen resolved in that moment to ensure that no taint
could be cast upon this excursion, that no rumor could cast
shame upon her father. She might not be marriageable, she
might be rumored to be cold, she might carry the repute of
madness, but she would not earn an undeserved reputation
as a harlot either. She would keep their course in the light
and the company of others, and ensure that this man culti-
vated no interest in her meager charms by sparing him no
more attention than she would grant a hungry hound.

"Aye, it would be better to begin at the gates to ensure

that you are not confused," she said, ensuring that the Hawk did not miss her condescension. She pulled her arm from his grip then marched out of the hall ahead of him.

"Do you oft have this trouble with unfamiliar abodes?" she asked, as if he were the most dim-witted man that ever she had met. "I would think it a most inconvenient affliction for one who reputedly makes his way by raiding and pillaging."

The Hawk let her precede him, though she heard him strolling behind her. "Is that the rumor of my deeds?" he asked mildly.

The hall's sounds faded as the shadows of the quiet corridor enfolded them. To Aileen's dismay, there were no other souls in what was commonly a busy corridor. She hastened her pace, but the Hawk caught her elbow in a casual grip, slowing her steps to match his.

"Oh, that and more," Aileen ascertained with an insouciance she did not feel. She was aware of his heat as she had not been before, aware of his fingers wrapped around her upper arm and their proximity to her breast.

He could probably feel the wild dance of her pulse, he could probably smell her skin as clearly as she smelled his. She waited for fear to seize her throat as it customarily did when she was alone with a man, but this time, her terror was absent.

Why? Did this man have no amorous intent?

His thumb caressed the back of her arm and belied any such thought. Still Aileen did not fear him, though she granted first his hand and then him an arch glance.

"You might become cold," he said with apparent innocence, though his eyes glinted with intent.

"I am most hale," she insisted, putting an increment of

space between them. He let her do so, easing his grip slightly.

"Tell me what else is rumored."

"Why?" Aileen cast him a mutinous glance. "So you can hold these half-truths against me? Blanche would love to hear that I had so compromised my father's hospitality." She tossed her braid over her shoulder. "Ask a more willing maiden to sate your vanity about your own repute."

That beguiling smile touched his lips again. "Might I conclude that you and your father's bride are not compatible?"

Aileen slanted him a glance so rueful that even in the flickering light of the sole torch, it should have answered his every question. He chuckled. If she had thought the timbre of his voice intriguing, the rich echo of his merriment was even more so.

Aileen knew that she was too clever by half to find such a man alluring and yet, some foolish part of her was tempted to know more of him. How would such a man kiss? Her gaze rose to his firm lips and her heart leapt, though the twinkle she found in his green eyes made her spin away.

If he mocked her, she gave him fodder for his jest. Why was she intrigued by this man? Surely, she should fear him above all others?

But this was the first time she had been alone with a man other than her father and felt no terror. She felt only a strange excitement that seemed to make her blood dance in her very veins.

She quickened her pace again, breathing a sigh of relief as the light of the bailey came into view ahead. "You are in a fine mood for a man whose wits are so addled that he cannot follow corridors as well wrought as these," she charged.

"Indeed, I am," he acknowledged. "It is the finest mood

I have known for nigh twenty years. Would you care to celebrate the occasion with me?"

Aileen glanced to him, mystified by his meaning.

He arched a dark brow, which made him look diabolical.
"You said 'half-truths,' lady mine."

"I am not your lady!"

"A mere slip of the tongue," he murmured, his gaze
dropping to her lips. It was as if he had read her thoughts.

Aileen blushed crimson, though she struggled to maintain her outraged manner. "Of course, I said half-truth. All
rumor is half-truth."

"Yet few acknowledge as much." His voice was dark, seductive, and Aileen was sorely tempted to lean closer to him
though she knew that would be a foolhardy deed. He would
take advantage of weakness before she had a chance to cor-
rect her mistake.

"It is only sensible to make conclusions upon evidence,"
she said, her words falling more quickly than was her wont.

"Indeed, it is."

The Hawk's tone was complimentary. Though Aileen
was not averse to an acknowledgment of her intellect, she
was again certain that he teased her. She pivoted to shake a
finger at him. "Do not begin to pour some nonsense in my
ears . . ."

"Do you realize that you are the first in decades to find
me only half-guilty, Aileen?"

While she wondered what to make of that, he moved
closer. She could see the glint of his eyes, she could feel the
intensity of his gaze and found herself helpless to step away.
Indeed, she had no desire to flee. The cold of the stone floor
permeated her leather slippers. Surely that was what made
her nipples tighten, what made her shiver so deliciously,

what made her lick her lips as if she hungered for some forbidden morsel.

"Then, perhaps you should change your behavior so that it does not lend itself so readily to rumor," she said, her words uncommonly breathless.

"Or, perhaps I should reward the rare lady who thinks well of me." He held her elbow fast, but his other hand rose slowly to cup her chin.

The gentle warmth of his touch turned Aileen's protests to naught. Had he sought to subdue her, to force his desire upon her, she would have fought him tooth and nail, but she could hardly protest such a gentle seduction.

Not when his touch felt so wondrous.

Not when she was so curious as to where it would lead.

Not when she was without fear in such circumstance for the first time in all her days. Perhaps she had passed some threshold, she did not care, she yearned only to know what a man's embrace was like. Oh, she knew she should flee his touch, she knew she should shun his scheme, but she was snared in unfamiliar desire, her own wits addled by his sure touch. Surely he would claim no more than a kiss? Surely it would not hurt to *know*?

The Hawk eased her back against the wall and Aileen found her breasts against his chest, his thumb moving across her chin in a caress that threatened to melt her very bones. Heat rose within her as well as a desire she had never felt before. Her gaze fell to his lips and yearning quickened within her, even as he watched and waited.

"I did not know that the despoiling of maidens was among your crimes," she whispered.

"It is not," the Hawk said with reassuring resolve. Aileen parted her lips, knowing she should protest his familiarity, but found no words upon her tongue.

She had no chance to summon any. The Hawk's mouth closed over hers with such determination that she understood this kiss had been his objective all along. He coaxed her to join the embrace, his lips cajoling her, his grip firm but not rough. His fingers slid into her braid, cupping her nape, holding her captive to the pleasure he seemed determined to grant.

Aileen was lost. She had never felt such a delightful languor, never yearned for more of what she could not name. She parted her lips to him without intending to do so. His tongue slipped between her teeth as he made a low growl of satisfaction. She felt the hardness of him against her, felt the thunder of his own pulse when her hands landed upon his neck, and thrilled that she summoned a response from him. His hand tightened in her hair as he lifted her to her toes, his own desire as fervent as her own. His other hand slid around her waist, catching her close, his fingers fanned across the back of her waist.

He deepened his kiss and the oddest thought came to Aileen.

A memory unfolded in her mind, a recollection of another passionate kiss so shared. Though Aileen knew she had never been kissed with such possessive ardor, that she had never been touched by this man, a curious certainty grew in her thoughts. She had the odd conviction that they were lovers met again, that they had so embraced a thousand times before, that his heart was as familiar to her as her own.

It made no sense, yet this notion grew in her thoughts, seemingly fed by the power of his kiss. It pushed her doubts from its path, it dominated her knowledge of who she was and who she embraced. She saw them entwined nude together, as she knew they had not been, yet was convinced that this was a memory of her own.

It seemed some fey being had taken possession of her body and soul, and that the truth she knew—that this enigmatic warrior stole a kiss from her in her father's abode—faded like a whisper on the wind. It was replaced by a strange urgency, a need to feast upon this man's lips, a lust to lift her skirts and welcome his heat within her once again.

She wanted to welcome and celebrate his return.

Her arms twined around the Hawk's neck, and Aileen kissed him with a wantonness she had never known that she could feel. She was caught on a tide of desire that she could not stay. She wound her fingers into his hair and drew him boldly closer, wanting more, wanting all the pleasure that he could grant.

To Aileen's shame, it was the Hawk who broke their embrace. He put an arm's length between them with an obvious effort. They both breathed quickly and his eyes glittered like stars.

"Magnus," Aileen whispered, awe in her voice and no clear sense of why she had said such a thing in her thoughts.

His expression turned wary. "What did you say?"

"Magnus," she repeated, unable to explain her compulsion to address him thus. "You are Magnus Armstrong returned and I welcome you." She reached to touch his cheek in a gesture of affection from a source she could not name, but he stepped abruptly away.

"My name is Michael," the Hawk said harshly. "Do you confuse me with another of your lovers?"

She flushed. "Of course not!" Aileen averted her face, ashamed to have to confess such a thing aloud. "There has been no man who has touched me as you just have."

He stepped closer, his hand rising to her jaw. He tipped her face so he looked into her eyes. Aileen returned his regard unflinchingly, willing him to see that she told no lie.

"Then why?" he asked more quietly, so quietly that she almost thought he knew the answer.

"I had a vision ... almost a memory. It was most strange." Before his obvious skepticism, Aileen's confession faltered and fell silent. She thought of the accusations against her mother, the rumor that she too would go mad in time, and bit back her words. Silence stretched long between them, the corridor suddenly cold as it had not been moments before.

"There are no visions, Aileen," the Hawk said.

She glanced up, stung by his tone, and his eyes narrowed, as if to warn her.

"None," he repeated. "Do not succumb to such madness."

"My mother was not mad!" Aileen declared and pulled away from his grip.

"I speak of you, not your dame." The Hawk glared at her, then he pivoted and marched down the corridor with nary a backward glance.

He left Aileen standing alone, her body screaming for something she could not name, her thoughts filled with confusion. She shivered as he stepped through the portal to the bailey, shivered in the cold she had only begun to feel.

Then the Hawk was gone, the corridor as silent as if he had never been in her presence. And still Aileen stood there, lips afire, heart filled with trepidation that alien thoughts had evicted her own. She touched her burning lips with marveling fingers and tried to recall if she had ever heard tell that the Hawk of Inverfyre was a sorcerer.

This could not be madness. No, it was witchery wrought apurpose by the Hawk. Aileen could only hope the effects of his potent kiss were fleeting, for she had certainly been beguiled.

II

The Hawk paced the stables of Abernye behind the four raven-black stallions, breathing deeply of the chill air and trying to drive the heat from his blood. He was consumed with the recollection of Aileen's kiss, a kiss that should not have seared his lips so, a kiss that had exceeded his every expectation.

If Aileen Urquhart of Abernye was as icy as the North Sea, then it would seem those waters had known an incredible thaw. This lady's kiss had him simmering to his very toes. It had been fortuitous that he had even been capable of stepping away from her, for her embrace had roused every fiber of his being.

But Magnus! She had called him *Magnus*. The Hawk stifled a shiver and paced the width of the stables with new vigor. He could see her yet: her long braid the hue of strong honey, her eyes even more blue than those of the phantom maiden who had long haunted his dreams. Indeed, they were so blue that he could have willingly drowned in their sapphire depths. Aileen was as slender as a young tree, yet possessed of curves that tempted his touch. He had felt strength in her grip, a vigor uncommon among maidens who spent days in leisure.

Or at embroidery. He smiled despite himself.

The keen edge of Aileen's speech was no liability, to his thinking, for forthrightness was the sign of a trustworthy soul. He liked that she was devoid of feminine wiles, and seemed most sharp of wit. The Hawk liked that she spoke her thoughts even when she was uncertain of his intent. He liked that she was bold, despite her obvious fear of him.

Mere moments in her company and she had awakened a fire within him, a lust to claim her that far exceeded any desire he had felt before.

He wanted her.

He needed her.

Aileen of Abernye alone would suffice as his wife.

"Tell me the demoiselle was not such a fool as to spurn your charms," Sebastien teased, laughter in his tone.

The Hawk pivoted to find three of his comrades loitering watchfully in the entry to the stables. They were never far, these men who had proven to be more loyal than any laird had the right to expect, and they moved as silently as shadows. The other three of his six stalwart cohorts had remained at Inverfyre, guarding the Hawk's hard-won prize in his absence.

In but a week, such vigilance would no longer be necessary.

"Did she not return to the hall?" the Hawk demanded, suddenly fearful for his lady's fate.

Sebastien's smile flashed in the shadows. "She returned—flushed, disheveled and alone. I guessed you to be responsible."

The Hawk released the breath he had not realized he was holding.

Ahearn stepped out of the shadows, his lips curved in a smirk. "Are you smitten, my lord?" he teased.

The Hawk granted him a glance that should have silenced him, but that rogue only laughed.

"Does the old curse make itself known, finally?" Ahearn asked.

"There is no curse," the Hawk said flatly. "Thus no nonsense to make itself known, now or ever."

Sebastien arched a brow. "You believed it once."

The Hawk's heart clenched, but he dismissed the notion before it could fully form in his thoughts. "For a heartbeat and no longer. There is no curse, there is no old tale. I am not Magnus Armstrong and he is not me."

"Even though your victories are much the same?" Ahearn mused.

"Righteousness is on my side," the Hawk insisted, "and the blood of champions courses through my veins—these are my links with my forebear and no more."

The men smiled and exchanged glances. "If you so insist, it must be so," Sebastien ceded. He nudged Alasdair, and the wiry, blond Scot shrugged as if he too would dismiss such whimsy.

The Hawk turned his back upon his men and paced anew, shocked to realize that Aileen's kiss still sizzled upon his mouth. He licked his lips surreptitiously, tasting her again, and desire raged.

When he had heard about the Laird of Abernye's unwed daughter, with her taste for archery and her sharp tongue, he had expected to find an ancient miss devoid of charm.

He would not acknowledge the way his interest had redoubled when he had heard the maiden's age.

His every expectation had been proven wrong, for he had instead met a demoiselle who had captured his attention at first glimpse. He liked that Aileen had been so eloquent in describing his crimes. There would be no secrets between them this way. She knew of him, she was unafraid to express her disapproval, yet she melted beneath his caress. Theirs would be an honest yet fiery match.

Perfect.

When the Hawk pivoted to pace back toward his men, he found Sebastien's gaze upon him. Sebastien's dark charm and relentless pursuit of pleasure had been responsible for the disheveling of many a maiden over the years. "It is time enough that you learned some skill from the Master of Love, my friend," that man declared. "There was not time enough for you to have finished what you had begun, that much was clear . . ."

"Ha!" snorted Ahearn, that handsome Irishman as smitten with his own charms as many of the women they had met. "Mind who you call the Master of Love in my company."

"You leave women so disappointed that they are compelled to come to me for consolation," Sebastien retorted. He held his hand over his heart. "It is a burden that only a man of honor could assume."

"Then why have you taken the task?" Ahearn demanded with a roll of his eyes. He gave the Hawk a playful nudge. "Time enough that you engaged in such play, is what I say. I began to fear that I had pledged my blade to a monk." He shuddered in mock horror at the prospect, then chuckled along with Sebastien.

The Hawk did not smile, nor did Alasdair who was of a far more serious temperament than these two.

"Her father is displeased," Alasdair noted grimly. He had not moved from the portal and now folded his arms across his chest. "There will be trouble for us all if she appears thus again."

"She will not," the Hawk said with resolve.

Ahearn feigned a pout. "Surely you cannot have tired of the charms of women so quickly as that?"

"Surely you would not spurn the first woman to catch your eye so quickly as that?" Sebastien protested.

"Of course not," the Hawk said, his plan clear. "On this night, I will claim a bride."

Stunned silence filled the stables and the Hawk almost smiled.

"Marriage?" Ahearn gasped and shuddered elaborately, the very word anathema to him.

"I knew it well," Sebastien murmured. "I knew the moment his gaze fell upon her. She is that old crone . . ."

Ahearn brightened. "The tale recounts that they recognize each other upon sight, that the flame is kindled like that." He snapped his fingers.

"Do not repeat such folly!" the Hawk retorted sharply. "She is an alluring maiden, one that I intend to wed, no more than that." In the face of his men's doubts, the Hawk continued. "It would be irrational to believe such whimsy. I know myself to be a supremely rational man. Is it so uncommon that a man of my age should choose to take a bride?"

"It is uncommon enough that you should give a care for women," Ahearn commented wryly.

"I thought the sole reason we left Inverfyre was to lull the MacLarens into believing us content and complacent," Alasdair observed.

Ahearn nodded agreement. "Aye, to coax them to greater confidence afore we make our final assault." His expression turned thoughtful. "Or is that plan to change now that you will have a bride to sate?"

"So we planned and so we will do," the Hawk affirmed.

"My taking of a bride changes nothing, save that it will only encourage the MacLarens' confidence further."

Sebastien smiled, his manner mischievous. "So, it was but coincidence that you claimed no bride until you found one young enough that she might be Adaira reborn?"

The Hawk granted him a quelling glance. "Inverfyre was not secured."

"It still is not," Alasdair insisted. "We are but days from reclaiming its very heart! Would you bring a woman into the midst of this battle? Would you compromise all for the sake of your desire?"

"He can do naught else," Sebastien whispered. "She is the mate to his soul."

"He could claim a bride in a month," Ahearn retorted. "The lass will not spoil in so short a time as that!"

"I claim a young bride because I have need of sons, and I claim this one because she pleases me," the Hawk declared, his voice rising with an anxiety he would not name. "There is no old tale at work here, and there is no threat to our scheme! Where is your confidence in my leadership? Is it so thin as that?"

"I would not have you distracted now, when victory is so close." Alasdair shoved a hand through his hair with dissatisfaction. "God forbid that we should lose this war for the sake of your prick," he muttered, then turned away. Ahearn hooted with laughter, but the Hawk did not share the jest.

He angrily pursued the Scot, catching Alasdair's shoulder and forcing him to turn. "Her presence will persuade them further that my ambitions are sated. The choice is a good strategic one."

The mercenary held the Hawk's gaze for a charged moment, then bowed his head. "I pray it shall be so, my lord," he murmured.

"I know that it will be," the Hawk said. "Our scheme cannot be thwarted at this late date."

Ahearn cleared his throat. "All the same, I feel compelled to observe that there is no need to actually wed the maiden."

"You could simply steal her," Sebastien suggested cheerfully.

"Or partake of the feast she offers while all others sleep," Ahearn added with a grin. "It would be so much less complicated, my lord." The pair nodded to each other, in perfect agreement as to the proper place of women in a man's life.

"A stolen or illicit coupling would only create difficulties betwixt her father and myself," the Hawk said and Alasdair nodded in grim agreement. "Marriage it will be and the ceremony will be this night. We shall return to Inverfyre with time enough to prepare for the assault on the new moon."

Recognizing his tone, the fighting men stepped forward, their expressions solemn. Over the years, they had come to understand that though their comments were welcome while various strategies were discussed, the Hawk did not change his mind once his choice was made.

"What are we to do?" Ahearn asked, his playful manner dismissed.

"See to the ale, if you will." The Hawk quickly considered the tasks to be accomplished and chose the man with the appropriate skills for each one. "No doubt some wench in the kitchens can be distracted long enough to suit your purpose. I hope that you have brought an herb that will be of use in this."

Ahearn nodded with confidence and headed for his saddlebag. "I have brought the very herb that will be of aid."

"No doubt you intended it for some prank upon the rest of us," Sebastien said and Ahearn chuckled.

"A devious mind has its place, as you can see."

Ignoring this exchange, the Hawk indicated Sebastien.

"Fetch the priest to the chapel at midnight, and see that he makes no sound to alert the keep." That man nodded curtly.

"Alasdair, I would bid you secure the doors to the chapel, lest we be disturbed during the festivities themselves."

That man nodded in his turn.

"And I assume the gatekeeper will grant you no argument."

Alasdair nodded. "The gates are as good as ours, my lord."

"Good. Ahearn, ensure that the horses are ready, if you will. We ride forth immediately after the nuptial vows are exchanged. With Fortune beside us, we may not be pursued before the morn."

"By then it will be too late," murmured Ahearn with a wink. "The match will be made and consummated."

Sebastien cleared his throat pointedly. "But will you not have need of a bride, my lord?"

The Hawk allowed himself a smile of anticipation. "I shall fetch the lady myself."

The men nodded and departed, leaving the Hawk to ponder his choice. On this night, Aileen of Abernye would become his own. The prospect gave him more pleasure than any conquest had in a long time. He felt a flicker of uncertainty, for Inverfyre was not yet completely won, but pushed it aside. His wife would be safe, because he would ensure that she was so.

Instinct had never served him wrong and it told him without doubt that this was the sole woman he should wed. The nonsense of an old tale was of no import to his decision at all.

The ale tasted sour to Aileen that night so she put hers aside. Perhaps it was simply that she did not wish to purge the taste of the Hawk's kiss from her lips.

The conversation flowed around and over her, so much nonsense in her ears as it never was. She still simmered, still yearned, still did not know what she wanted.

All the same, Aileen feared that she knew the source of her discomfiture well enough. Indeed, she glanced down the high table and unwittingly caught the Hawk's gaze, and heat flooded her.

His gaze was brooding and she had the eerie sense again that he could read her thoughts. After a moment, he lifted his cup to her, though whether in salute or mockery she could not guess. Aileen looked away as her face burned.

Clearly, she was unwell.

Blanche granted her stepdaughter a smug glance. "Your color is high this night, Aileen," she called down the table, her gesture coaxing Aileen's complexion to an even more rosy hue as every soul took a look.

"Have you seen, how do you say, a ghost?" She turned to the Hawk, reaching over her husband to tap the Hawk's forearm with her fingertips. "Her mother claimed to speak with spirits and ghosts. Of course, we have long waited for the same madness to appear in the girl."

"Blanche," Nigel protested. "Mhairi had the Sight."

"*S'il vous plaît*, Nigel, you must cease this talk." Blanche pouted prettily. "Only ignorant peasants believe such superstitions. Although it is painful, you must accept your wife's weakness. This is what a man must do, *non*?"

Aileen's father flushed, his expression grim when Blanche appealed again to their guest.

"Do you not agree?"

The castellan whispered something to Aileen's father and that man rose abruptly to his feet, though Blanche barely noted his murmured excuses or his departure.

The Hawk shrugged, his gaze unswerving from Aileen. "I

was raised in Sicily," he said quietly. "I learned there that many matters in this world are not readily explained."

"Ah, but talking with the dead!" Blanche rolled her eyes and laughed. "What could this be but madness? The woman was *folle!*"

The Hawk did not share in the jest. "I would not presume to judge a woman, not only deceased and mourned, but unknown to me, as well."

It was apparent to Aileen that the Hawk counted Blanche in the same company as himself and she was touched that he so defended her much-maligned mother.

She could not fully hide her smile of pleasure and knew he noticed her response, for his eyes gleamed.

Then he arched a brow and Aileen feared that he anticipated a reward from her. There was but one way to ensure the man could not addle her wits further.

Aileen pushed to her feet and cleared her throat with purpose. "Clearly my color is high because I am unwell," she said firmly. She forced a smile. "I must have caught an ague. Please excuse me."

"Of course." Blanche flicked her hand in the same way that she dismissed her servants. She placed a hand upon the Hawk's arm with unwarranted familiarity, clearly pleased that they were more or less alone at the high table together.

"The mother was mad," she whispered loudly. "It was, how do you say, *une tragédie*, all the more so because none of them will acknowledge the truth of it." She sighed and smiled, then fluttered her lashes at their guest. "Of course, my lineage is impeccable."

Aileen turned her back upon the cooing pair and crossed the hall. She was well aware of the gazes and whispers that followed her as she ascended to the solar, but she had no care for gossip. One gaze—and she knew well whose it was—

bore into her back, but she refused to acknowledge it and
him.

Sicily. That might explain some of the mystery of this
man. It certainly explained his dark-haired and dark-eyed
companion, if not the others.

And perhaps his necromancy. Was Sicily not said to be a
breeding ground for witchery and magic? If a man was to
learn in any corner of Christendom how to infect the
thoughts of others, it would be there, Aileen was certain of it.

But she was a sensible woman of the country. She would
drink a hot posset and sleep deeply this night. That would
purge the Hawk of Inverfyre and his sorcery from her
thoughts. That would destroy the memory of his infernally
tempting kiss!

Some errant sound startled Aileen to wakefulness in the
deep hours of the night. Her eyes flew open.

Intruders! This was the first thought that she had, yet it
seemed that all was as it should be. The ladies' chamber was
dark, for clouds hid the moon and the braziers had burned
down to coals. The rhythmic breathing of the women around
her filled her ears. It seemed that a higher number of them
than usual snored this night.

Aileen took a steadying breath. Had her fright been
wrought of no more than a bad dream?

All seemed tranquil, and indeed, she could not have
named the sound that had roused her. No shouts rent the air,
and there apparently was not another soul awake. Aileen
peered into the shadows and was certain that she discerned
the lump of Blanche in her own bed, two of her women sharing the mattress with her.

The others lay on pallets around the great draped bed, as
did Aileen. Blanche had a dozen women who waited upon

her. Aileen had had one, but when that elderly nursemaid had passed away during her mother's last days, she had not chosen another.

If her father's new bride did not fret for the weight of his purse, Aileen would. Each soul housed within these walls had to be fed and clothed and shod, after all. Abernye's sheep could not be shorn weekly simply to sate the new lady's lust for the trappings of a wealth Abernye did not possess.

As her fears eased, Aileen found she could not sleep. In the middle of the night, one's worries tend to take on a force of their own, and thus so did hers. Aileen's thoughts churned, restless, and she began to fret that Blanche would see her father impoverished. The prospect made sleep impossible.

Blanche would see Nigel destitute, his spirit broken. She would leave him starving and garbed in rags, she would take every trinket from Abernye. She would take Abernye itself, down to the last morsel of bread. Aileen could envision Blanche plucking it from her father's hand, from his very mouth. She would laugh as she left him for another richer man, she would grind his shattered heart beneath her heel . . .

Aileen heard a stealthy footstep.

She caught her breath and listened. A second step sounded upon the wooden floor. Whisper-quiet, it would never have been discerned by one lost to dreams. All the same, it was weighty. The slow creak of the floor could mean nothing else.

A man was in the ladies' chamber!

Aileen's heart began to flutter. She lay upon her side on her pallet, not daring to move even as her thoughts flew. Hers was the last in a row of pallets occupied by sleeping women, and even as she wondered what to do, the sound came again from behind her.

Aileen strained her ears, struggling to locate the intruder

precisely. Was this a thief come in the night for her step-mother's gems? Or did one of the maids have a lover? Possi-bilities abounded, but in Aileen's heart, she knew who lurked behind her.

And she feared the Hawk's intent. Perhaps Blanche had invited him to visit her.

Perhaps he had invited himself.

She could not decide what to do, what she could do to deter him. She had no weapon and she knew that he would be far stronger than she.

The silence stretched long, no other step sounding. Where had he gone? Had he left? Had he merely come to view his prey?

In the end, she could not tolerate the uncertainty. There was only one way to see whether he had left, without alarm-ing him that she witnessed his presence if indeed he was still in the chamber.

Aileen sighed deeply and nestled into her linens, as if soundly asleep.

She heard nothing.

She pretended to snore.

Still there was not a sound.

Slowly then, she rolled over, eyes closed, feigning that she moved in her sleep.

Nothing echoed in the chamber.

She was half-certain that he had left, as quietly as he had come, though she could not guess his scheme in so doing. All the same, she waited, breathing deeply as if lost to dreams.

The footstep did not sound again.

Aileen waited and breathed and curtailed her desperate desire to look with only the greatest difficulty. The mo-ments stretched out to eternity. She could have screamed in vexation.

When she could bear it no longer, she opened her eyes the barest slit.

Her eyes widened in astonishment, for she stared directly at the Hawk of Inverfyre's wicked smile. He lay beside her, fully garbed, the length of an arm between them.

Aileen made a most odd gurgling sound, so astonished was she. She should have heard him breathing! She should have felt his heat! He quickly unfastened his cloak as she gaped mutely at him, and new fear helped her find her voice. She made to yelp but the sound never passed her lips.

He moved with lightning speed, his gloved hand clamping over her mouth and his weight settling atop her. She bit his hand, futilely finding only the leather between her teeth, and knew then why he had worn the gloves.

That he had schemed some fate for her—for her!—awakened her terror.

Aileen struggled, cursing the fact that the other women had left a space around her, due to her own lie that she was ill. She could not even kick one to wakefulness and it was the fault of none but herself! She fought her assailant, knowing all the while that her efforts were hopeless.

He bent and placed his lips against her ear. Aileen's heart thudded so loudly that she feared she would not hear whatsoever he said. He braced his weight over her, pinning her in place but not crushing her.

A traitorous pulse within her quickened.

"They will not awaken," he said with confidence. His breath tickled against her ear in a most distracting way and she felt her blood heat with unwelcome desire at the low rumble of his voice. "The ale was tainted this night with an herb that induces sleep." He kissed Aileen's temple with a familiarity undeserved. "I should have known that you, lady mine, would defy expectation and not drink the ale."

Aileen made a sound of protest beneath the weight of his glove.

"On the other hand, it poses a greater challenge for you to be awake . . . and I greatly savor a challenge." He kissed her earlobe with leisure then, sending heat coursing through her. Aileen trembled beneath his sure touch, then struggled anew, as much against her own response as his confidence. She felt the sign of his own ardor against her belly and froze in terror.

"There are two courses open to us, Aileen," he murmured with an ease that the lady in question did not think the situation deserved. "One, far more pleasant, requires your cooperation in leaving this chamber quietly. We shall simply walk to the portal, you and I, in a most civilized manner."

She shook her head with vigor.

"I thought you might not cede to that." He sighed, as if her reluctance was inexplicable.

The most notorious brigand in Christendom, and he expected her to calmly accompany him to some nameless fate! Aileen wished she could have bitten his hand in truth.

"The other scheme I leave to your imagination." He bent and his words fanned her ear, sending a thousand unwelcome shivers over her flesh. "We shall celebrate our union this night, you and I, of that you may be assured."

Aileen's blood ran cold. She knew then that the Hawk meant to rape her. If he did not so indulge here in the ladies' chamber, then the deed would occur somewhere in her father's abode. She knew that he would show her no mercy and that her life in the aftermath of his deed would not be worth living.

It is one matter to be a plain maiden unwanted by any man, and quite another to be despoiled. Aileen's virginity and her father's name were the only assets she could offer a potential spouse—the loss of her chastity would eliminate her father's endorsement, as well. She had no doubt that her father would cast her out of his home once he knew the truth, for he was a man of high principles.

Like any man of sense, he would deem her rape to be her own fault.

How dare the Hawk do this to her? Aileen looked into the glint of her assailant's eyes and felt determination rise within her. The Hawk might mean to steal the last hope she had, but she would fight him with all the strength she possessed.

Even if she was doomed to lose. He seemed to be waiting, so Aileen bit his glove fiercely to give him her answer. The deed must have taken him by surprise for she felt some flesh between her teeth. He muttered something and she struggled with new vigor. She managed to free one arm from his grip and gave his hair a tug that must have hurt.

He swore beneath his breath, caught her face in his hand, then kissed her grimly.

His move was unexpected, so aggressive that no tenderness could be found within it. Aileen screamed, and he swallowed the sound with ease, then what had happened earlier repeated itself.

Almost.

A vine appeared in Aileen's thoughts: no, two vines entangled tightly together and growing into the infinite distance. The vines wound around each other, one rife with thorns and one burdened with flowers.

They were a hazel and a honeysuckle, Aileen knew this though she could not imagine how. She knew little of plants and had never heeded her mother's lessons. But these she knew, with eerie certainty.

The two were so entangled that it was not easy to see where one ended and the other began. Aileen understood that they could not have been separated without threatening the survival of either or both. Yet entangled thus, they thrived.

The plants coiled, opening into a tunnel of green as tall as Aileen. In her mind's eye, she stepped into this verdant corridor and peered into the tangle of leaves and branches as she walked down it. She saw the Hawk and herself, half-hidden in the vines, their limbs as entwined as the branches themselves. Then beyond, further down a corridor of shadows, she spied a warrior she knew to be Magnus Armstrong, his hand clasped in that of a maiden with blue eyes and long dark hair.

Anna. Aileen knew the woman's name, though she knew not how. The tangle of growth bent then, like a corridor that turned a corner, and she could see no further along its length.

The Hawk's lips burned against her own and Aileen again understood the origin of these alien thoughts. He would cast a spell upon her! She fought to evade the Hawk's touch. He deepened his kiss and the vision claimed Aileen in a grip as fierce as his determination to possess her.

Aileen saw herself, the thorned vine knotted around her ankles. She saw the Hawk holding her in a passionate embrace, much like this one, but as if she stood outside of her own skin. As he kissed her, the hazel grew around them both. It was followed by the honeysuckle vine, growing with unholy haste, surrounding them so that they were locked in an eternal embrace. The creamy honeysuckle flowers blossomed in abundance, hiding the hazel's thorns, perfuming the air with a heady sweetness.

Aileen was shocked numb.

Was this her destiny?

Was the Hawk her fate?

Or did he simply try to persuade her to accept his dark scheme?

The Hawk lifted his head, his gaze searching hers even as the vision was dispersed like mist beneath the morning sun.

"Sorcerer!" she spat and that was all it took.

He abruptly braced himself upon his elbows and Aileen tasted the prospect of freedom. She fought anew, but he shoved a wad of leather into her mouth. He wound a length of cloth over it and knotted that behind her head, rendering her mute.

Aileen choked in outrage over this and the poison he had poured into her thoughts, but he moved deftly to complete his work. He pinned her legs beneath the weight of his own. He held her hands above her head in one hand, his grip relentless. She fought, but to no avail.

It seemed he had lied about despoiling maidens, for he clearly had experience in performing such foul deeds. He cast aside Aileen's bedlinens, then grasped her chemise by the neck and tore it from her body. It was old and thin, and the cloth barely whimpered as it was shredded.

His leather tabard was cold against her bare flesh, the chill of his mail sent shivers from each point they touched. Aileen closed her eyes, knowing what must come next.

To her astonishment, he grasped her tight against him, her back against his chest. He rolled over, away from the women. She felt fur beneath herself and man above, and braced for her last chance to defend herself against his rape.

But she was rolled within the fur, rolled over and over until she was swathed and fully trapped. It was his cloak, she realized belatedly, cut full and lined with fur. The fur was warm, uncommonly soft and thick.

And it rendered her helpless. The Hawk bent over her, knotting rope around her in a lattice, securing her into his cloak. She was bound into the cloak from neck to foot. His deed stilled Aileen's struggles and left her only able to thump her bound feet against the floor.

She did so, with vigor, but the layers of fur ensured that she made no sound.

She glared at her captor and wriggled in her bonds, fearing what fate he had planned for her. She hated how well he had planned his assault and how successful it had been.

He leaned closer and whispered in her ear. "I would have you be silent."

Aileen growled and thumped her feet, unwilling to make his foul deed easier.

The Hawk's eyes gleamed and he put his lips to her ear, his words dark and dangerous. "Know this, lady mine. There are a thousand rumors of my wickedness, and lest you imagine otherwise, I am guilty of every crime."

His fingertip stroked her cheek, then he turned her face so she could see the determination in his eyes. "And if you are so foolish as to betray me, I shall hunt you down and wring your neck with mine own hands." He held her gaze and Aileen did not doubt that he told her the truth. "I have no intent to kill you, but you clearly aim to change my thinking. I would suggest you desist."

He left her there then, trussed like a package of pelts to be shipped south and trembling in fear. Aileen loathed that there was so little she could do about her state. She quietly rolled in an attempt to escape, but only hit the wall with a muffled thump. She tried to angle herself toward the door, but the fur was so thick that she could scarcely bend.

Meanwhile, the Hawk crouched beside her pallet, untroubled by her efforts. Aileen watched him when she knew herself trapped. In all honesty, she was somewhat more reassured to be a bundle than a naked wench beneath him.

She could not be raped in her current state, though that might prove to be a small mercy.

Hope rose within her that she might have another chance to evade his desire. His threat echoed in her thoughts, meanwhile, making her very heart tremble.

As she fretted, he spread her chemise before him with care, the white linen fairly glowing in the darkness. He doffed his glove and cut his thumb without a flinch, letting the blood drip to stain the linen. Aileen was mystified as to his intent.

The Hawk was, however, disinclined to confide in her. He returned his knife to its scabbard and sucked the side of his thumb to stanch the bleeding, even as he pushed her chemise into his belt. He glanced toward her, the pure mischief in his expression so startling that her heart leapt.

She struggled as he approached her, but he donned his gloves, picked her up and cast her over his shoulder with appalling ease. He left the ladies' chamber silently and moved with speed to his destination.

Wherever it might be.

III

As they crossed the hall and took the corridor leading to the gates—passing many intimate chambers that could have been utilized for a quick rape—Aileen's thoughts flew. It seemed that she was being kidnapped.

But why?

Did the Hawk imagine her father to be so wealthy that he would pay a rich ransom for her return? If so, he should have stolen Blanche, for Nigel would have sold his soul for her return!

It would suit Blanche, Aileen suddenly realized, to not only be rid of her stepdaughter but be rid of Aileen to such a man as this. Had they made a wager at the board after Aileen retired? Perhaps Blanche had even summoned the Hawk to do this deed!

Aileen's father might think it a fine solution to his woes in finding his daughter a spouse, particularly if Blanche presented the matter to him as artfully as she could argue her way. Perhaps she had even seen fit to aid the Hawk in polluting the ale to ensure that his crime might more readily succeed.

And what would be Aileen's fate? She had no illusions that an honorable match would come of this inauspicious beginning, nor did she imagine that a plain maiden like herself would hold the gaze of a man like the Hawk. She was bound like goods because she would be treated like goods.

She was being carried into concubinage, at best. Perhaps the Hawk would savor Aileen for a while, perhaps she would merely be given to his men to divert them. It was a cruel punishment for one known to find a man's touch abhorrent, perhaps a jest that a rough warrior would find amusing.

Aileen shuddered at the prospect. It would destroy her spirit to be used as a whore and discarded. She had need of a scheme to ensure her own survival.

But what could she do?

Aileen was swung upright so abruptly that she felt dizzy. Though she was set upon her feet, the padding of fur gave her no sure footing. When she toppled, the Hawk caught her fast before him. She saw, with some surprise, that they were in the chapel. Two candles were burning on the altar, and Abernye's priest stood rumpled before her.

One of the Hawk's men had clearly roused Father Gilchrist from his bed and held him fast. The felon was garbed in armor and dark clothing, just like his laird. He was a grim-looking man, swarthy of complexion and black of hair, his eyes so dark as to be fathomless. He winked at her, a rogue much enamored with his own appeal.

Or one anticipating his chance to sample her. Aileen looked to the priest, sickened by her circumstance.

Father Gilchrist looked to be bleary with sleep. Aileen guessed that he had partaken heavily of the tainted ale, though his eyes widened at the sight of her. He was an older man, unafraid to speak his thoughts, and generally sharp of tongue.

Perhaps he might aid her!

"What blasphemy is this?" he demanded.

"Quiet, Father," growled the Hawk's man. Aileen saw the glint of the man's blade touch the priest's side and understood that this was no jest.

Father Gilchrist swallowed then, his gaze flicking between his captor and the man that now unknotted the cloth that gagged Aileen. Another of the Hawk's men stood in the shadows, guarding the door, his expression grim and his hand on the hilt of his blade. He was dark-haired, as well, tall and blue of eye. He also wore dark garb like the Hawk— they were men dressed to do foul deeds in the midst of the night.

When Aileen's gag was unbound, she lost no time in spitting out the leather within her mouth. She barely had a chance to lick her lips before the Hawk's gloved hand closed over her mouth with surety. She made an indignant sound of protest but he merely tightened his grip upon her.

"Begin, Father," he said. "We have no time to waste."

The priest straightened and gave her captor a sharp glance. "It is imperative that the parties both be willing."

"We are both willing," the Hawk said with resolve.

Aileen guessed then what he meant to do. She twisted against him, unable to understand why he would compel her to wed him, and anxious to halt the ceremony.

"I hardly think . . ." the priest said, then paused to frown at the blade that prodded his ribs anew. He fixed a stern eye upon Aileen's captor. "The lady clearly is not willing."

"Umph!" Aileen nodded in emphatic agreement to that.

"Then perhaps the lady does not understand her own best interests," the Hawk said smoothly.

Aileen would have gladly argued that assertion and the priest clearly made note of her flashing eyes. He made to protest, but the Hawk released his grip upon her waist. White flashed before her eyes and the priest instinctively caught the object tossed at him.

It was Aileen's chemise. And there was blood upon it, blood where the blood of a woman's broken maidenhead would fall. The blood was yet wet, of course.

Father Gilchrist realized what he held and dropped it immediately.

Aileen saw the look in the priest's eyes and knew that he believed that she had been raped. She felt doubly ill then, for she understood that the Hawk had cornered her again. If he abandoned her now, nothing she said could take the stain from her name. If he claimed her, she could not imagine her existence.

She was left with no good choices.

The other two men began to chuckle. "I thought you took overlong, my lord," said the one by the door, his manner teasing.

The other winked at Aileen again. "The Hawk of Inverfyre leaves no detail to chance."

"Certainly not," the Hawk lied easily, though Aileen supposed that would be a minor crime to a man of his ilk.

"The garment is torn," Father Gilchrist insisted with vigor. "The lady was not willing."

"Yet the deed is done all the same," the Hawk said with such confidence that none would doubt him. Aileen loathed him in that moment with all her heart and soul. How dare he damage her reputation? "Surely what is of import is that I would treat her with honor from this moment forward."

"With honor?" Father Gilchrist sputtered. "What mockery is this? You cannot imagine that I will be persuaded that you would treat the daughter of my patron with any dignity after you have raped her! I would be a fool to cede her hand to you!"

"And you think her fate much improved to remain here, soiled as she is? How many suitors do you think will come for her now?" The Hawk's tone was derisive. "You are a fool to think that you—or she—have a choice."

The priest frowned. "Why do you wed her?"

"Perhaps I am smitten."

The Hawk's men laughed and Aileen felt her face heat. The Hawk, though, did not laugh. Indeed, he must have granted his men a stern glance for they abruptly sobered.

Father Gilchrist regarded the Hawk with skepticism. "Her father will provide no dowry or lands, given your deed."

"I have no need of whatsoever he would give." The Hawk tightened his grip upon Aileen. "I already possess the sole prize of Abernye."

The certainty in his tone fairly took Aileen's breath away, though she could not imagine that he meant his words.

His breath stirred her hair suddenly and unexpected humor tinged his next words. "And perhaps Aileen will be less inclined to kill me when next we meet abed, if she is my lady wife. Women have a fondness for such formalities, I am told."

"I will call for aid and foil your scheme," Father Gilchrist argued.

"I would advise against that." The Hawk's tone turned as grim as the expressions of his men. "It will be the last sound you make on this earth."

"You would not kill a priest in the sanctuary of a church!"

Aileen might have agreed before she heard the coldness of the Hawk's reply. "I have done worse before and likely will do worse again," he said and Aileen shivered, remembering his threat just moments before.

"I will take her, either way," the Hawk continued with resolve. "Would you deny your laird's daughter the honor of a marital bond, or do you dispatch her to the uncertain life of a concubine?"

Father Gilchrist clearly wanted to deny this man his will, but Aileen saw the blade of the Hawk's man dig deep enough to make the priest flinch. A trickle of blood stained the priest's undyed robe. The gazes of priest and would-be bride met, their fear tangible.

"My lady? I shall not do this thing without your assent, even if they do kill me for it." The priest who had baptized Aileen eighteen years before now studied her.

The knife against Father Gilchrist's side gleamed evilly. These men would kill him and Aileen knew it. And as much as she might have preferred, there was truth in the Hawk's claim: she would have more rights as his wife than as his whore.

Further, she might have the chance of escape once they left this chapel. He had planned this deed well, for she truly had no choice but to cede to him, for the moment.

Aileen nodded once, without enthusiasm. At least, she would not have the blood of a priest upon her hands—nor would it be on the hands of her spouse. Their lives would be bound together from this night onward, be it for better or for worse.

Let the Hawk imagine that she was amenable to that. There would be time aplenty for vengeance after he was persuaded that he could trust her.

Aileen never remembered the words of her wedding service. She assumed they were the usual ones, for the Hawk showed no displeasure with the ritual they were granted.

What she remembered was the tightness of the bonds

around her, the conviction in the words her new spouse uttered so close by her ear, the smoothness of his leather glove against her lips.

And his kiss to seal the match.

She remembered how he turned her face to his, she remembered how he warned her quietly not to scream, she remembered how he had coaxed her participation in their ritual kiss. She remembered that she had no fear of his touch—on the contrary, she hungered for the brush of his lips across hers. She remembered how an uncommon heat filled her veins, how his touch awakened a thousand apparent memories.

Most disconcertingly, she would always recall how utterly certain she was that what they had just done was *right*.

Then he had trussed the gag across her mouth anew, his expression inscrutable, and she feared that she had fallen into the hands of the devil himself.

In no time at all, they were riding. The black stallions had been saddled and waiting in the shadows outside Abernye's walls, so dark as to be shadows themselves. The last of the Hawk's men had been waiting there, the reins in his grip, the stallions stamping in their impatience to gallop.

The gate of Abernye had stood open, against all conventions. When they passed beneath the portcullis, Aileen saw the gatekeeper hale enough, snoring with his mouth open in his gatehouse.

At least, he was not dead. Aileen told herself to be grateful for small mercies.

She realized that all had been prepared with chilling precision. Aileen understood then that she should not underestimate her new spouse's ability to anticipate any event—much less, to plan for it.

She would need all her wits to escape this man alive.

The Hawk's men set their spurs to their steeds with nary a word between them, as if such thievery were habitual among them. She supposed it must be and feared anew what household she had been compelled to join.

The Hawk's company closed ranks around him, their ebony horses moving like the night wind. Aileen was trapped before the Hawk, bound and silent, the fluid movement of the horse forcing her against her husband's heat.

Husband.

Over the Hawk's shoulder, Aileen watched the waning moon rise over the squat towers of Abernye. Those familiar towers diminished in the dark shadow of distance until they were swallowed by the hills and lost to her forever.

It was then that the truth chilled her blood. She was bound to this notorious warrior forevermore. She shivered then, despite the wealth of fur around her, and her husband caught her closer. He looked down at her then, his handsome features wreathed in shadows, and Aileen knew she saw him smile.

The Hawk's scheme, it seemed, proceeded precisely as he had planned.

Thus far.

Aileen was his and his alone.

The Hawk was triumphant in his success. His plan had been executed perfectly. The miles fell behind them with no hint of pursuit and every step made him more certain that they would reach Inverfyre unchallenged.

And there, there, he and Aileen would have a true nuptial night to celebrate. He could scarce wait.

His bride sat stiffly before him for long hours that night, defying the Hawk's every expectation. He had anticipated maidenly tears, but his bride had not shed a single one. He had feared an unholy fight in the chapel—or worse, her refusal to comply—but Aileen had agreed so readily that he was convinced that their thoughts were as one.

Matters began most well.

When she finally slept, he pulled her weight against him more fully. The night was silent save for the hoofbeats of their galloping steeds. Wilderness surrounded them on all sides, for Abernye was far to the north. The Hawk unknotted the gag and eased it from his lady's lips.

She did not awaken. There was a mark upon her flesh from the binding and he caressed it tenderly, regretting that he had trusted her as little as he had. No doubt she would have simply taken his hand and agreed if he had asked, if he had not been so fearful of her refusal.

He loosed the bonds that bound her, leaving her wrapped solely in the warmth of his cloak with his arm fast around her waist. The cloak fluttered in the wind and she started to sudden wakefulness, no doubt because of the chill that touched her flesh.

He might have expected a sweet confession, or that she would have nestled close against him again in contentment, but Aileen straightened. She wasted no time on pleasantries, her tongue running quickly across her lips as she glanced at the darkness around them.

"I assume that we are so far afield that no one could hear any cry for aid that I was fool enough to utter," she said.

The Hawk nodded assent, startled by the bitterness in her tone. Her conclusion was true, though it was not the sole reason he had loosed her fetters.

The lady stretched slightly, then gathered the cloak more closely about herself. "And presumably you believe that I am not so addle-pated as to leap from the back of a racing steed?"

The Hawk pulled her closer with proprietary ease. "Your wits are sufficiently keen that a man might cut himself upon them, lady mine."

She glanced up then, her gaze bright despite the darkness. He had the sense that she feared that he mocked her, so he held her gaze.

"I like that you are clever," he said, sensing her doubt.

She frowned and eyed his company with undisguised curiosity. The wind lifted blond tendrils of her hair and drove them against his chest, the feminine softness of them feeding the Hawk's possessive instincts. Ah, to be abed at Inverfyre already!

"Did Blanche concoct this scheme with you?" she asked, her tone mild.

"Blanche?" The Hawk knew that his astonishment showed.

His bride's lips tightened. "My stepmother would like to be rid of me." Her mutinous glance flicked to him. "She would like even more to grant me to a man of such notorious repute that I might be raped and left dead in a ditch."

The Hawk perceived somewhat belatedly that his threat, intending only to ensure her silence, had been given greater credence than he had anticipated.

"I made no scheme with your stepmother," he insisted. "And it is not my intent that your days end so poorly as that."

She granted him a glance so dubious that the Hawk knew not what to say in his own defense. "What then is your scheme for me?"

"You are my lady wife. You will sit upon my left hand in my abode, bear my sons and honor my hall with your presence. Surely you cannot imagine that I desire other than this?"

Aileen made a small skeptical sound, then closed her eyes to end their conversation. The Hawk knew from her breathing that she did not sleep.

He did not know what to say to ease her concerns, indeed, he could not have named what those concerns might be. He knew that it was right that they should be wedded. He knew that Aileen was the wife for him.

He suddenly feared, however, that the lady was somewhat less persuaded of this truth than he.

The Hawk pondered his course until the eastern sky turned rosy. He indicated to his companions that they should leave the road, and the four steeds trotted into the forest, merging with the shadows of the woods. A river gurgled ahead, and the Hawk let his steed pick their path toward the water. The stallion halted with his front hooves in the course of the river, then bent his head to drink.

The Hawk dismounted, lifting his bride into his arms, and left the other men to dismount and water their steeds. He seized his saddlebag, then carried her into the woods, feeling her stiffen with every pace he took.

Indeed, she caught her breath in a consternation that vexed him mightily.

"Yesterday, you did not fear me," he reminded her with some irritation. "Yesterday, you welcomed my kiss. Indeed, you encouraged it."

Her eyes flashed. "I had never been kissed afore!"

"Then you show an innate talent that bodes well, lady mine."

"Had I guessed your wicked scheme, I would not have surrendered to your kiss," Aileen retorted, color staining her cheeks. "You will *not* insist that this circumstance is my own fault!"

"No, I will not." He set her upon her feet, dropped the bag and bent to rummage within it. They were within a hollow, shielded from the view of the others yet sheltered by the steep incline of the land around them.

The ground was thick with brambles beneath the tall trees, and it was no accident he had chosen this spot. He felt her restlessness, fairly tasted her urge to flee and knew himself to be responsible.

Instead of the triumphant suitor, he felt a knave.

He heard Aileen take a step, then saw that she hastily pulled her foot back. When he glanced up at her face, her arms were folded across her chest, the voluminous cape wrapped around her, and her eyes were snapping with sapphire fire. Her hair had spilled from her braid and the sunlight had entwined itself within its length. He had a yearning again to touch her, but knew that would only feed her fear.

"Yet again you scheme with surety. No soul alive would be witless enough to try to flee barefoot through such bracken," she said, clearly irked with him.

The Hawk merely nodded again, then offered her a white linen chemise of his own and a pair of dark chausses. "It is hardly feminine garb, but it is the best that can be managed afore we reach Inverfyre." He granted her a glance. "You will appreciate that I did not ride to Abernye with the intent of claiming a bride."

"What changed your plan?" she asked, her annoyance clear.

He stepped forward and caught her chin in his hand. "This did." He brushed his lips quickly across hers and heard her catch her breath. It was but the barest taste of her, but enough to make his desire rage.

She shivered beneath his embrace, unable to hide her intuitive response to his touch, and he knew again the sense of his command over himself slipping away. He repeated his gesture, unable to resist the softness of her lips. He wanted to bed her on his cloak, here in the forest, not a dozen paces away from his men.

The woman wrought a madness within him with her kiss, a madness he would welcome when they were alone together.

As they were not yet.

Reluctantly, the Hawk broke their embrace and stepped back. He sealed her lips with his thumb and held her gaze. "Or perhaps I should say that you did."

The lady's lips twisted wryly. "No man has ever lost his wits over desire for me."

The Hawk nigh smiled. "I count myself fortunate that these hills are full of blind men."

Aileen took a step away from him, her wariness such that he let her go. "You will turn your back," she insisted, twin spots of color staining her cheeks. "For you are not blind and I will not relieve myself beneath your eye."

The Hawk straightened, giving her a stern look that spoke volumes.

"Where would I run?" she demanded, flinging out one hand. "Where would I hide that four warriors could not find me?"

Her frustration made him recall an old jest that what a woman desired most was her own will. Was his lady annoyed with him because he had granted her no choice in this? But how could he have done so? Though he was not averse to risk, he had been in no mood to risk losing her.

And he would not lose her now. The Hawk turned so he

could see her from the corner of his eye, folded his arms across his chest and waited.

"Will you not turn further away?"

The Hawk shook his head. "No." He met her outraged gaze. "Or I watch you openly."

The lady inhaled sharply, her eyes sparkling in her indignation. She was infinitely desirable in her fury. "You are a barbarian," she muttered and he grinned.

"You are fetching when you are irked. Calm yourself, lady mine, or we shall consummate our match here and now."

Aileen glared at him. She pivoted without another word, lifted his cloak so it did not brush the ground, and squatted.

Content that there was indeed no chance she could get far even if she did try to flee, the Hawk watched the sky turn blue overhead. It would be a bright day, and one in which they would have to move carefully so as to avoid being noticed. He was tempted to whistle, for he was much encouraged that the lady cared enough about his presence to be annoyed with him.

His mother, after all, had long said that hate and love are but a whisker apart.

A moment later, the Hawk felt the weight of his fur-lined cloak pressed against his arm. His heart thumped with the import of that—his bride was nude and near his very side.

"I cannot keep it from the forest floor while I dress," Aileen said. "Please do not look." He accepted its burden, knowing she would not welcome his urge to gaze fully upon her. He examined the cloak's hem with apparent interest, fully aware that Aileen was not two paces away from him and that his imagination had probably not done her justice.

He ached to look. The shadows in the lady's chambers

had hidden her too well, to his thinking, and he was cursedly curious. A mere glance would have sated him—perhaps not, but that was what he told himself. He knew that in her current mood, though, she might despise him forever for stealing a glance.

She doubtless thought he had stolen too much already.

All the same, he heard the draw of every lace, even over the thunder of his heart. He heard the slide of linen against her bare flesh and believed his gallantry was hard won. He noted the flick of her hair as she pulled it from the chemise.

"Have you a comb?"

"A wooden one, unfit for a lady," he said by way of apology, but retrieved it from his saddlebag all the same. He could not keep himself from watching as she shook out her golden tresses. Her hair fell to her waist and was more curly than he had expected, its tangled mass inviting his hands to trail through its length.

His chausses fit her snugly through the buttocks, emphasizing her curves, and she had rolled the hems up for they were too long. She had pushed up the sleeves of the chemise and tied the neck lace tightly in an attempt to disguise her charms. The morning sunlight, though, silhouetted the curve of her breasts beneath the linen, and the sight tightened the Hawk's own chausses.

Aileen noted his glance and quirked a brow as she braided her hair, securing its glory once again. "Your garb is not so large as to be overwhelming. It has long been said that I am a woman wrought cursedly tall."

The Hawk snorted. "Tiny women are oft sickly or too coy in their manner." He slanted her a telling glance. "I cannot fathom why a man would take such a creature like your stepmother to his bed."

Aileen froze in the midst of knotting the tether for her braid. "You did not find her alluring?"

He arched a skeptical brow. "I would not turn my back upon such a viper, not if I had any token of value she desired."

The lady's smile was all the more beguiling for being unexpected. The Hawk lifted his hand, intending to touch her cheek as he marveled, but she abruptly sobered.

Her manner changed as if she recalled that she had no reason to smile.

Or as if she feared his touch. He swung the cloak around her shoulders again, and deliberately fastened it at her neck. He lingered over the task, reveling in the scent of her and the softness of her so close at hand.

She watched him with that same wariness in her eyes. "Is our match no more than a jest between you and your fellows?"

He met her gaze in surprise. "We exchanged vows, and a vow is not to be broken. I intend this to be a marriage in truth, lady mine."

She licked her lips, clearly choosing her words with care, and her gaze flicked away from his. Still she voiced the question that plagued her and he admired her determination. "Will you beat me?" She swallowed. "I know a man has the right . . ."

If this was her fear, he would see it dismissed this very moment!

"Never," the Hawk declared with such resolve that she could not doubt his intent. "No man of merit beats a woman."

There was a welcome glint of amusement in her eye, though still she did not smile. "But I have heard that you are not a man of merit."

He chuckled despite himself. "Nonetheless, I pledge this to you."

She tilted her head to regard him. "And of what value is your pledge, then, if you are not a man of merit?"

The Hawk sobered. "It is of every value, and I shall prove it to you. Indeed, lady mine, I shall prove to you that the evidence of your eyes is more compelling than the rumor gathered by your ears."

She studied him, her expression inscrutable, and he could not keep himself from asking. "I thought you wished to wed and be away from Abernye," he suggested cautiously. "I thought you did not find my touch offensive."

"I thought a man asked a woman's father for her hand."

"The end is the same, lady mine," he reminded her. "And there is no delay in this. I have little taste for loitering when my decision is clear."

"And what of my decision?" she murmured. Before he could reply, she sighed and glanced into the forest, a small frown marring her brows. Resignation claimed her then, and her shoulders drooped, though he never would have imagined that she would surrender any battle so readily.

"I forget myself. If you do not intend to beat me, then I suppose my lot is more fortunate than that of most women. One way or the other, we shall make a match of this, I suppose." Aileen granted him a smile so sad it fair tore his heart in two. "I should have liked to have been courted, but God knows, I must be content with what has been granted to me. A thousand women would likely be pleased to take my place."

The Hawk feared she might weep, but his wife brushed past him then and headed back to the horses, stepping with care around the worst of the brambles. The Hawk watched her, feeling more a cur than ever he had.

A courtship, to his thinking, could be arranged.
Especially if the prize was his lady's favor.

Aileen cursed herself for the remainder of the day. What impetuousness had claimed her, that she had matched wits with the man? It was too tempting by half to talk to him, especially when he spoke to her as if she was someone possessed of intellect. Yet each time she bantered with him, she revealed more of herself and undoubtedly dissuaded him of the notion that she was passive and amenable.

And trustworthy. Aileen gritted her teeth at her own susceptibility to the man's charm. She could not take the words back: she could only hope that she was more successful in future.

How keen were the Hawk's wits? She suspected they were sharp indeed. How attentive was he? Would he even notice if her manner changed? Many men took little note of women, much less of their changes of temperament.

Aileen feared this man might, for he seemed most observant. All the same, she had to try to hide her intent to escape from him. She had to remember to act meek and agreeable, regardless of what he said or did.

It would not be easily done. His was a dangerous allure, that much was clear. There was something about the Hawk that tempted her to speak her thoughts in truth. Perhaps it was his lack of censure for her words, perhaps it was that half-smile or the way her heart leapt when he looked at her with a mischievous gleam in his eyes. She liked his pledge to not beat her—and worse, she believed it.

It was nonsense, of course, but Aileen almost thought him a gallant knight bent upon winning her affections. She almost believed that he wished to make a marriage in truth.

Then why the sorcery? And why did he deny it? It could be no accident that he no longer forced his kiss upon her.

What of his reputation, and his own threats? He must be behaving other than he was, as well, in an attempt to gain *her* trust. Aileen dared not be beguiled. She had to escape him, and do so before he enchanted her completely.

Aileen's scheme grew more clear as they rode persistently south. Every day, by her reasoning, they traveled closer to the king's own court. If she could only escape the Hawk, she could make her way to Stirling and throw herself at the mercy of the king. Surely a bishop would take her pledge that her match with the Hawk had never been consummated, surely someone would believe her.

She could not imagine that any honest soul would give credence to the Hawk's view, or that no one would defend her against such a man as he.

She knew that a dispensation could be had from Rome for a match unconsummated or one made between a man and woman too closely related. She was not a cousin of the Hawk, sadly, so the argument of consanguinity would not aid her. She was certain, though, that she had heard once of a woman abducted who had seen her match dissolved.

All she had to do was escape. Evasion of four men bent on observing her would not be readily done. Worse, she saw that the Hawk was by nature wary. They halted seldom and only for short periods, and she had no respite even when the Hawk slept. There were always two men awake, and at least one watched her exclusively while the other stood guard.

The party rode through the forest when they traveled during the day, and Aileen was certain that they circled around villages and keeps where awkward questions might have been asked. Sometimes she smelled a distant woodfire, though she gave no hint that her blood quickened at the presence of others who might lend her aid.

She might have to wait to escape until they reached Inverfyre, which was certain to be little more than a circle of men's tents. By then, the Hawk would trust her fully.

She would make certain of it.

IV

On the second night after they had left Abernye, the Hawk took guard and watched the moon wane from last quarter. There was only a sliver of it left and anticipation quickened his pulse. He sensed that his men were increasingly tense as the final battle with the MacLaren clan drew near. He, too, was impatient to see the matter resolved, especially now that he had a bride.

It was time to fill Inverfyre with children and laughter, instead of talk of war and fear of pillage.

It was time to claim the last piece of Magnus Armstrong's original holding of Inverfyre. The MacLaren clan still held the original site of the first keep and chapel. They launched their assaults from there, they had built a wooden keep of sorts there, and the Hawk was prepared to possess what was rightfully his own.

He watched his bride sleep as the night slipped away, then roused the company just before the sky brightened. The men saddled their horses with gruff haste, their breath fogging the morning air. The lady made no complaint, as the Hawk was beginning to expect of her, and swung into his saddle at his gesture.

He admired her lithe grace when her gaze was averted and regretted that there was yet another matter that must wait. He would court her abed, not pounce upon her in the forest.

Even if the waiting killed him.

They made good time, but halted in midmorning and hid themselves in the woods. The men were restless and unlikely to sleep at this hour, though it was treacherous to continue. The further south they rode, the more dense the settlements and the more likely they would encounter a shepherd before they even realized a town was near.

The Hawk sat back on his heels beside his wife and strove to put her at ease. "I must apologize, lady mine, for years of battle have dulled my manners," he said, keeping his voice low. "I have failed to introduce you to my men."

She sniffed, her eyes flashing with disdain before she managed to compose her expression. "It is of no import."

"I forget how to bow," Alasdair said with a grin.

"Ah, I shall remind you how to greet a lady," Ahearn declared with a smile for Aileen. The lady regarded him with appropriate wariness, to the Hawk's thinking.

"This," the Hawk said, gesturing to Ahearn, "is the most notorious rogue in our company." The tall, dark-haired man rose and bowed deeply, untroubled by this introduction. "Ahearn O'Donnell is an ostler by trade, a warrior by necessity and a seducer of women by inclination."

Aileen sniffed, though she said nothing.

"I have a way with herbs, as well, my lady, if ever you have a wound in need of healing," Ahearn said as he gallantly kissed the back of Aileen's hand.

"How intriguing," she said. "And where would you have learned such a skill?"

"From my old aunt, who had a talent with such matters."

"Ha! He will grant you a potion that will have you upon your back," Sebastien snorted. "A man of such dubious charm has need of nefarious tricks to coax maidens to his bed."

"I consider myself warned," the lady said.

"Ahearn is also a vigilant trickster," the Hawk counseled. "Should you find a frog in your boot, you can readily name the man responsible."

"I am innocent of all such deeds!" Ahearn declared, and the men roared disbelief as one.

"As you might have gleaned, Sebastien takes exception to Ahearn's reputed success with women, for he regards himself as the paragon in that endeavor," the Hawk continued.

"How many dark-haired children grace your hall, my lord?" Aileen asked softly and the Hawk did not know what to say. She granted him a knowing glance that made him feel a fool for never wondering about the fruit of his men's encounters.

Meanwhile, the Sicilian bowed gracefully and bent low over Aileen's hand. His dark hair tumbled over his brow and his eyes gleamed. "It is my splendid good fortune to make your acquaintance, Lady Aileen."

"As apparently, it is mine." A polite smile touched the lady's lips.

"Sebastien and his comrade, Fernando, have been my stalwart companions since childhood. They accompanied me to Inverfyre eighteen years ago."

"Fernando?"

"He remains at Inverfyre," the Hawk said.

"You will know him by his moustache," Sebastien said, making a twirling gesture with his fingers that prompted the men's laughter.

"He loves it more than a woman!" Ahearn declared.

"He loves it more than his own prick," Alasdair muttered and they chuckled as one.

"We are in the presence of a lady!" the Hawk reminded them sternly and apologies were granted. Aileen did not appear to be overly shocked.

Hawk liked the snap in her eyes, though, and yearned anew for his chamber at Inverfyre. He was prepared to spend many hours upon that plump mattress coaxing his bride's smile.

He gestured now to the last man who had accompanied him. "And finally, Alasdair Fergusson, a valiant warrior and archer, come from the Hebrides to pledge his prowess to me."

The fair-haired Scot rose and bowed in his turn. His sleeves were pushed up and the woad-stained tattoo that wound around his arm was visible, though Aileen did not seem to be troubled by the sight of it. The Hawk supposed that she might be accustomed to this practice, as he had not been, since it was common for Gaelic men from the Isles and Highlands to mark their flesh thus.

"I came to hunt relics and pursue adventure upon the seas," Alasdair told her, "but sadly, the Hawk has surrendered such trade."

The Hawk felt his wife's quick glance but by the time he looked down at her, she studied her hands meekly. "You could have pledged yourself to my half-sister Rosamunde instead," he noted. "She is reputed to have an uncommon talent for the family trade."

Sebastien laughed. "Talent? She is a veritable queen of the pirates and looters upon the seas!"

"Indeed?" Ahearn looked intrigued by this detail.

"And a woman of such beauty as to steal your breath

away," Sebastien affirmed. "Ah, Rosamunde! She was the first to lay claim to my heart."

"Yet you have never invited her to Inverfyre," Ahearn said to the Hawk. He made a face of mock dismay. "I thought you were fond of us, my lord."

"Rosamunde would make minced meat of you," the Hawk said with a smile and Sebastien chuckled in agreement. "She is a warrior of rare impatience. You may have your wish, for all of that, for she may deign to visit at midsummer."

Ahearn pretended to swoon at the prospect, while Sebastien groaned. "My heart could not bear the injury," he moaned, then winked for Aileen.

"No woman can be a warrior of competence!" Alasdair scoffed. "You must remember her as being more talented than she is."

"I think not," the Hawk said softly.

"I would never pledge my blade to a woman," Alasdair snorted. His eyes gleamed as he turned to the silent Aileen and the Hawk knew that Alasdair would try to provoke her. He watched with interest. "Is it true that the daughter of the Laird of Abernye has skill with a bow?"

His manner was challenging and the Hawk noted how his bride's shoulders stiffened. "What do you think? I am but a woman, after all," she said finally, an edge to her tone that told him what such docility had cost her.

"Are the tales true?" Alasdair demanded. He pulled his bow from over his shoulder and offered it to Aileen. "Can a woman truly hit a mark?"

The Hawk straightened in his turn, for he would never have granted his captive a weapon. He felt Aileen's quickening, as a peregrine will tense when she spies meat, and he knew then that she was indeed skilled with a bow.

Alasdair fairly shoved the bow and an arrow toward her, his manner mocking. The lady hesitated, though her urge to seize the bow was tangible.

"Show him wrong, lady mine," the Hawk urged in an undertone.

She granted him a glance so bright that he flinched, then rose and took the bow. He saw the way her hand curved lovingly around it, saw the ease with which she fitted the arrow and drew back the bowstring. Her posture was perfect, but she dropped her shoulder at the last moment. When she released the arrow, it drove itself into the ground. The fleche, in passing, grazed her inner arm so fiercely that it bled.

Alasdair hooted with laughter and the other men chuckled. The Hawk, though, was sober, for he guessed that his bride had deliberately shown her talents to be less than they were. It could be no accident that she fixed her gaze determinedly upon her feet. He examined her wound, which she insisted was of no import, and bound a piece of clean linen around it himself.

He met her gaze then, finding assessment in her blue eyes. She clearly wondered whether she had fooled him and the Hawk bit back his smile. In truth, he was intrigued that his wife was so anxious for him to underestimate her skills.

What scheme did his lady concoct?

Aileen saw no one other than the Hawk and his men for three days, and this, she knew, was contrived. She knew by the sun that they rode more or less directly south, away from the verdant plains around Abernye and through the wild Highlands. The Hawk did not try to kiss her again, and she found herself more cross with him than she might have expected.

The Hawk had spoken aright of Ahearn, as the trickster of

the company. Never a day passed without a jest—of which Ahearn consistently swore innocence, his eyes sparkling all the while: on one morn, there was indeed a frog within Sebastien's boot; on another, the contents of Alasdair's saddlebag had been scattered far and wide—by pixies, according to Ahearn.

They could have been a merry company of knights, had Aileen not known of their nefarious repute. She dared not be seduced by these men's charms—or more particularly, the charms of her husband.

The Hawk was as courteous as a courtier could be, under such circumstance. He ensured that she had a few moments to herself several times a day, to tend to needs she would keep private. He let her eat first, waiting to use his cup and knife after she was done, holding her gaze as he sipped from the same spot as she had. When he aided her to mount and dismount, he oft managed to give her a slight caress on the shoulder or the back of her waist. The Hawk always found her a soft bed of cedar branches or similar for her bed.

It was clear that Aileen's husband meant to win her favor. Indeed, had she not known that he was a sorcerer, had she not only heard of his dark repute but had him vouch for it himself, she might have trusted this man.

At night, she recalled her last vision and shivered at the thought of being bound to this man for all time, a vine of thorns holding her fast to his side.

The Hawk was not one to speak overmuch, but when he did, he was temperate and fair. The respect his men obviously held for him said much of his treatment of them, in Aileen's opinion.

But then, they were a company of rogues themselves. Aileen told herself to remember that critical detail. To her thinking, they could not reach his humble holding of Inverfyre soon enough.

On the fourth morning, Aileen awakened to find Alasdair saddled to depart. He rode off with great haste and she failed to hide her curiosity from the Hawk's bright gaze.

"Is something amiss?" she asked, hoping she contrived a look of innocence.

"No."

"Are we close to Inverfyre, then?"

"Why?" It seemed to Aileen that there was a measure of assessment in the Hawk's gaze, as if he had already guessed her thoughts.

"My father often sends a runner when he is close to home, to ensure that the hall is made ready for his return," she admitted. "I thought perhaps you did the same."

"Perhaps I do. But Inverfyre is not that close, lady mine."

Indeed, it was not. They rode hard all that day long, so relentlessly that Aileen's buttocks ached. The sun had disappeared and she was hoping they would take a respite just as a high-walled keep finally came into view, its tower silhouetted against the star-flecked sky.

Aileen was certain that they would circumnavigate this fortress, as they had avoided all others. Indeed, the sight of it persuaded her that they would ride much longer before halting and she sighed disappointment. She was surprised they had come near enough to this one to glimpse it so clearly.

But the Hawk took the road directly to the keep's gates, his men riding openly behind him. A standard was raised above the gatehouse as they rode closer, a red banner with a black hawk upon it. A shout rose from the outer walls and the men behind her shouted a greeting in return.

Aileen's heart fairly sank to her toes.

"Inverfyre?" she asked weakly. She had expected a circle of tents, perhaps a timbered hall or crude settlement. This formidable fortress fair took her breath away. Escape from within these high walls would not be readily accomplished!

"No other," the Hawk said with undisguised satisfaction. He gave her waist a squeeze. "Welcome home, lady mine."

The Hawk had quickly guessed that his lady was not so resigned to her fate as she appeared to be. Her gaze flicked too quickly to the road, her nose twitched too readily at the hint of woodsmoke, her interest in their direction was too avid to be disguised.

Her passive and acquiescent manner upon this journey was utterly at odds with the fiery maiden who had so ably listed the threats he brought to her father's keep, not to mention the feisty demoiselle who had fought his abduction with such strength. It made no sense that she accepted her fate with such complacency. Further, he knew that she had feigned incompetence with Alasdair's bow.

Aileen had a scheme, unless the Hawk missed his guess, and the prospect pleased him enormously.

He had told no lie when he had declared that he liked her keen wits. There was no better way, in his estimation, to win each other's trust and admiration than to attempt to foil each other's competing schemes.

His was to seduce her and coax her love for him. Hers—well, her plan was not clear as yet but it would become so. He viewed this as a contest of wills, and the Hawk was well accustomed to winning contests.

He would win this one, of that he had no doubt.

He saw to her every comfort as they traveled. He stole no more kisses from her, though he yearned to do so. He felt her shiver when he caressed her shoulder or hand and knew she was not so resistant to his caresses as she would like him to believe.

And on this night, all would come to fruition. The prospect of a night abed with his bride had kept the Hawk awake too much of late. He was more than prepared to court her final favors all the night long if necessary.

But the Hawk's courtship was doomed to wait. Ewen met their party at the gates, his countenance so sober that the Hawk understood immediately that something was amiss.

"We have captured another, my laird," he said. "The vermin tried to scale the walls, but we ensured his failure." Ewen sneered as he delivered this news, his contempt for the MacLaren clan more than clear.

But then, his hatred had a deep root.

The Hawk cursed the timing of his rivals. He was suddenly concerned that he had brought Aileen here too soon, that his haste to possess her might put her in danger. He felt her recoil, but knew he had not the time to put her fears at ease.

This matter had to be resolved with all haste. The spy might be persuaded to speak this night, and might provide some gleaning of Dubhglas MacLaren's intent.

"I shall come immediately," he said, then dismounted and lifted Aileen down. The portcullis closed behind them with a clang and the gates were barred. To his relief, there was a full contingent of sentries upon the walls, and the gate was well guarded.

"Who scaled your walls?" Aileen asked as the Hawk urged her toward the keep.

"It is not of import," he said flatly, having no intent of discussing military matters with his wife. He would not have her fear for her security.

He was sufficiently concerned for them both. He hastened

her toward the hall. Only when the last vestige of Inverfyre was secure in his grip would he sleep easily.

Aileen's eyes flashed, the first sign of passion from her in days. The Hawk cursed Fortune that she should awaken to her true nature now, just when he had to abandon her.

"I think it is of import," she argued. "And as lady of the keep, I believe I should know . . ."

"You will know what I choose to have you know," the Hawk retorted. He kept a firm grip upon her elbow as he hurried her through the hall.

Servants halted to stare, more than one stifling a smile. He knew that Aileen's uncommon garb had been noted and feared that her place in his household would be misconstrued.

"My lady wife," he called to them by way of explanation, not slowing his pace to properly introduce her. Aileen struggled against his grip, which only would feed their speculative whispers. "Behave yourself," he bade her in an undertone. "This is not the time to defy me."

Aileen granted him a look of such fury that he longed to kiss her. "I am not a poorly trained hound that can be bidden to follow your will," she muttered.

"Sadly not, for a disobedient hound can be whipped."

She abruptly pulled away from him, her eyes wide, and he knew he had chosen the wrong words. "You granted your pledge to me," she reminded him, a thread of fear in her voice.

"So I did. You need not make me regret it with such haste." The Hawk fairly shoved Aileen up the narrow staircase to the chambers above, though she fought his every step.

The Hawk looked back to the company in his hall with apparent confidence. "Sadly, my lady wife is too tired from our journey to accept your congratulations on our marriage," he said to them. "On the morrow, she will undoubtedly be much restored."

Aileen took advantage of his diverted attention to pivot and pummel her fists against his chest. The Hawk grasped both of her elbows to compel her up the stairs.

A low whistle carried over the company and Guinevere sauntered toward the Hawk and Aileen. She smirked. "Truly, Hawk, why would you ride a week to find a wench so unwilling?" She propped a hand upon her hips, the pose showing her curves to advantage. "There are many here who would be glad to welcome your attentions."

"I am not a whore who must do your bidding to earn a paltry coin," Aileen fairly spat. "Though many of those in your household appear to ply that trade."

The Hawk glared at her, ignoring Guinevere. "You must be tired after our journey, lady mine," he said, willing her to agree.

The lady did no such thing. "I will not meekly do your bidding," Aileen insisted with undisguised defiance. "Not afore you tell me who has been captured and why."

"I cannot tell you what I do not know and I will not tell you what I choose to keep secret." He compelled her toward the stairs, leaving Guinevere behind and well aware of the many souls observing this dissent. "Hasten yourself to bed!"

Aileen paled, though her eyes glittered with new anger. "I will not hasten to be raped!"

"Trust me, rape is not my intent," the Hawk whispered.

She caught her breath in trepidation. "Then what?"

"I had imagined we might meet amiably abed."

"I doubt as much . . ." she began to scoff, but the Hawk bent and kissed her thoroughly. He aimed to reassure her with his touch as he had failed to do with his words.

Truly, he had forgotten the challenge of women. He was

gentle, cajoling, though he did not turn away. She shook like a spring leaf in the wind, but seemed powerless to fight her response to his touch. The Hawk delighted when she gave a small sigh of surrender, then leaned into his kiss. Her lips softened and the resistance melted from her hands, which had been braced against his shoulders. Now, she twined them around his neck.

He heard the company applaud when he finally lifted his head, but noted only that Aileen was unsteady on her feet. A whistle echoed over the company, and he did not doubt that Guinevere mocked him. The Hawk did not care. Aileen's eyes were glazed and she seemed disoriented. He suddenly feared what she would say.

"I saw . . ." she began to whisper.

"No! You saw nothing." The Hawk interrupted her with resolve, having no patience for more talk of visions. He would not let her speak of this here, not where the company might overhear her and begin to whisper that she was mad.

The lady's chin lifted with determination. "I saw . . ."

"You will ascend the stairs willingly or I shall cast you over my shoulder again and carry you," he muttered through his teeth, letting her see his determination. "And I will suffer no talk of visions this night. The choice, lady mine, is yours."

His manner seemed to dismiss her dream-like manner. Aileen glanced back at the rapt servants and made a sound of frustration.

She met his gaze, her eyes snapping anew. "You have a most irksome tendency to insist upon your way alone, my lord," she whispered hotly.

The Hawk smiled. "You will find that my way is not always so loathsome as you tend to assume."

Aileen's gaze lingered on his lips for a breathless moment. The Hawk bent to ensure his meaning was not misconstrued and kissed her ear with leisure. She shuddered to her very toes, then turned and marched up the stairs before him, her stature as proud as that of a queen.

At the first landing, she hesitated, but the Hawk urged her on. There was but one door on the second and last landing, and he threw it open.

"I trust your chambers will suit," he said, knowing the room was far finer than the lady's chamber that Blanche shared with all her women. His wife would have no cold pallet upon the floor for her nightly rest, but a curtained and pillared bed, hung with the most costly of weavings.

Aileen granted him a mutinous glance before she preceded him into the chamber at the summit of the tower. She might well be convinced that he meant to rape her this night, but he liked that she did not balk before her worst fear. Hers was a courageous heart, one that he knew would partner well with his own.

And he heartily anticipated proving Aileen's foul expectations of him to be wrong. He would seduce her, not force her, so that they both found the summit of pleasure. The prospect made his blood thunder in his ears.

Aileen was nigh dizzy from the visions inflicted upon her and the ardor of the Hawk's kiss. She stumbled across the chamber and clutched the sill of the window, willing her feet to steady. Her heart was galloping and she took a deep breath afore she turned to face her taciturn spouse.

He watched her, impassive, a thousand secrets hidden in his thoughts.

But Aileen had glimpsed a few of them. She still could not make sense of the rapid sequence of images she had seen, much less her intuitive understanding of them. She had seen herself in a dozen guises—as a crippled boy, as a young girl, as a babe, as a crone, as a peregrine, as a young mother, as a grieving widow—and for each glimpse of herself, she had seen another soul, a partner, who she knew was the Hawk.

How could she be so certain of such a thing? Aileen could not guess, nor could she shake her conviction.

Clearly, the power of his sorcery knew no bounds. He watched her, his eyes gleaming, and Aileen feared suddenly for her fate in his keep. Was this madness that tinged her thoughts? Was this uncertainty of what lurked within her own mind what her mother had endured?

She gripped the sill and stared out into the darkened bailey, desperate to compose herself afore he embraced her again. A shadow slipped over the walls and she caught its movement from the periphery of her vision. She turned and peered into the darkness, but it was gone, so surely that it might not have been there at all.

Was this the progression of the madness? Would she see things with her eyes open that were not there in truth? What did this man do to her that so dissolved her wits?

Aileen had watched hawks hunt and knew they harried their prey before they made their kill. She shivered in fear. The hawk only pounced once the hare was tired and its strength was fading. Aileen dared not let her husband guess how weakened her defenses—and her wits—had become. She must demand something of him, as if she was the one who launched an assault.

But what?

As the Hawk watched, his bride pivoted to face him again. He admired how she squared her shoulders, even in her trepidation, facing her fears of his intent with courage.

Indeed, she sauntered across the chamber, openly appraising its contents. She trailed her fingertips across the linens on the bed, clearly choosing her words, then halted beside one of its pillars.

"I thought you had not come to Abernye to hunt for a bride," she said, granting him a look so filled with challenge that he was tempted to let the MacLaren spy rot all the night long in the dungeon.

"I did not."

"Then why is this chamber prepared?" She arched a brow. "Have you a wife already, whose acquaintance I have yet to make?"

"No. I have never wed until now. I knew, though, that one day I would find the woman I would take to wife." He smiled, hoping to reassure her. "I am a man who claims his desire without delay, lady mine, so I wished to have all prepared for this day."

She averted her face, but her caressing fingers revealed that she was impressed by the chamber. The Hawk knew he should leave, but he could not resist the opportunity to grant her one small kiss, a kiss to keep her warm until his return.

A kiss to encourage him to not linger long in the dungeon. He caught Aileen's shoulder and spun her to face him, touching his lips to hers before she could protest.

As always, she stiffened slightly at his touch, but when he persisted, she softened. In a trio of heartbeats, the fire was kindled between them. Her hands were on his chest and she was on her toes, straining to taste him more fully. He locked his hands around her waist and lifted her against him, liking well that there was no pretense between them in this.

When he lifted his lips from hers, his heart pounding in his ears, she tilted her head to regard him. "Tell me one thing," she asked softly, even as she took a step away from him.

"You have only to ask."

"Will you always use the visions to disorient me?" Aileen folded her arms across her chest to regard him.

The Hawk shook his head and took a step back in his turn. He spoke with resolve. "I have told you that there are no visions."

Her expression hardened. "If you desire a match in truth, then there must be honesty between us, at least in this chamber."

"I have inflicted no visions upon you," the Hawk insisted, his voice low. He dared not agree with her, not after his earlier experience with Adaira had so shaken the confidence of his men in his leadership. Not now, not when a mere three days stood between him and triumph. He would not jeopardize their support.

"But of course there are!" she retorted. "You have forced strange thoughts into mine every time we have kissed. When I would resist you, you plant memories in my thoughts that persuade me to accept you as my destiny. At least, have the grace to admit it!"

"I do not!"

"You most certainly do!" Her eyes flashed. "Do not deny that you used your kiss to confuse me in my father's hall that I might be more readily captured!"

The Hawk held his wife's gaze stubbornly, letting her see his conviction. "I do deny it. I used my kiss to ease my desire for the woman beneath me, and perhaps to surprise a demoiselle to silence."

"Your sorcery is foul enough, but to protest it is even more foul."

"If there is sorcery here, it is no more beneath my command than the rising of the sun each morn."

They glared at each other, each as convinced of their view as the other. Aileen clearly sought some evidence in his expression that he lied, but the Hawk knew she would find no hint of guile.

So determined was she that he found himself curious. "What appears in your visions?"

She granted him a scathing glance. "Now, you would give them credence?"

"Now, I would understand what we confront."

She shook her head and walked across the room, then turned to face him, her eyes glinting. "So, you might find me mad. Is that to be my fate? To be locked away as a madwoman? What advantage do you hope to gain in this?"

"I ask only so that I might understand what you fear."

Aileen glared at him for an eternity, then she shook her head. "You must know what I see."

"If I did, then I would not ask!"

She propped her hands upon her hips, her pose defiant. "I see you and me, but in other lives, it seems. You were Magnus, and I was the true love you rejected. Anna was her name. Since and before that, we were together also, but something went awry in that life." Her words faltered. "It is a most strange sensation, to see these people and recognize who they are, knowing all the while that they are strangers to me. I cannot fathom how you inflict this upon me."

"I am not responsible," he said gently, though the very words made her eyes flash. The Hawk fought to find an alternative explanation. "Perhaps it is maidenly whimsy to find the root of everlasting love in a hasty match?"

Aileen shook her head, impatient with the very suggestion. "I am not whimsical! The visions are clear." She granted him a shrewd glance, though it was her words that shocked him. "You fight my assertion so vehemently. I would wager that either you lie to me or you know more of this matter than you would admit."

The Hawk recoiled. "Nonsense!"

But Aileen was not so readily dissuaded as that. "You argue overmuch," she accused softly, crossing the floor toward him. Her manner was intent, like a huntress who knows she has spied her prey. "You know more of this matter than you would confess to me."

"And I have responsibilities, duties of greater import than this futile discussion," the Hawk said flatly, then turned to depart.

"Liar!" Aileen cried. "You lied when you said you desired a true marriage. Marriage is wrought of honesty—"

"And life is filled with treachery." He glanced back at his wife's fury and desire nigh took him to his knees.

He had to leave immediately, or he would not leave at all. Cursing the fact that a spy had been caught on this night of nights, the Hawk closed the door and turned the key in the lock.

"Cur! You leave to avoid answering me!" Aileen shouted. He heard her jiggle the latch without success and then what might have been her foot collided with the oaken door. He winced, but turned on his heel to descend.

His nuptial night, the Hawk had to admit, had not begun overly well.

But until he persuaded her that he was not the demon she believed him to be, the Hawk dared not trust his wife. The sooner he began this unpleasant task, the sooner he would be done, the sooner he could return to Aileen and their bed. His footsteps hastened seemingly of their own accord.

If nothing else, Aileen was passive and compliant no longer. Truth be told, he would willingly brave any scars just to see her eyes flash with such passion abed.

Aye, and the Hawk would ensure that she was too busy to talk of visions and destiny. That prospect restored his smile.

*   *   *

At the original site of Inverfyre, Dubhglas MacLaren worried the scarred flesh where his eye had once been. A rare smile touched his lips as he considered the news that had come to him this night. He rose from the board in his hall and stood outside the burned wreckage of the chapel, the wind tousling his hair as he gazed upon the splendor of the new Inverfyre.

Soon, it would be his own.

Hopefully, his man now captive inside Inverfyre would discover the location of the *Titulus Croce*, for Dubhglas would need the relic to be invested as Laird of Inverfyre. His possession of it would prove the legitimacy of his claim to the common people, but the Hawk had never shown it. He had to hold it, and it had to be in that fortress.

The moon would be new three nights hence. His smile broadened. Dubhglas could wait three more nights, after having waited almost forty years for vengeance. He could wait three more nights to claim everything the Hawk of Inverfyre had built, all the wealth he had amassed, and even the bride the Hawk had claimed.

Perhaps he would keep the Hawk captive long enough to let that man watch every MacLaren man savor his new wife.

Perhaps the wench would spawn an heir with MacLaren blood in his veins.

Dubhglas could barely suppress his glee at the prospect. It would all be his—title, holding and heir—for he had no doubt of his triumph. The Hawk would not guess that he had been betrayed.

Not until it was too late.

V

*S*coundrel and cur!

Aileen spun in fury to survey her shadowed prison. There
was nothing that infuriated her more than lies. How dare the
Hawk lie to her about his own witchery?

She was trapped, Aileen knew it. And she was deeply
afraid. A curse upon her own inability to hold her tongue in
the company of this man!

She slowly walked the perimeter of the room. There was
a window on every wall save the one with the oaken door. Although shutters were latched over all but one of the windows,
a cold wind whistled through their crevices.

Aileen paused at the open window. She took a heartening
breath of the chill air, but drew back when she spied the
Hawk striding across the bailey below. Her blood quickened
as she followed his silhouette. He was well-wrought, this
husband of hers.

What or who had they captured? The Hawk conferred
with his men there in the shadows, oblivious to her regard,
and she wondered what transpired at Inverfyre. There were

more men than the three they had traveled with, perhaps another three in that same somber garb.

The troop of men turned as one, their path taking them quickly out of Aileen's view. She moved to another window, then another, but could catch no further glimpse of them from her aerie.

It was fitting to imagine that she occupied an aerie. Was the Laird of Inverfyre not reputed to be a hawk himself, not unlike the hunting hawks in which he traded so successfully? She knew that she had heard such a rumor, even at so distant an abode as her father's hall.

She did indeed have a perch like that of an eagle's nest. This chamber appeared to be at the summit of a tower which rose over a large stone keep. She noted (with some craning of her neck) that there was another row of windows between her own and the ground far below.

The keep was roughly square and the tower was built from the corner opposite the gatehouse. The hall appeared to comprise not only the base of the tower, but most of the wall extending to her right. There were battlements atop it, which extended fully around the square. To the left were kitchens and stables, and Aileen saw the silhouettes of tethered horses within the bailey.

There was no chapel, or at least, she could spy no cross on any roof. Should that have surprised her as much as it did? Aileen feared not.

Beyond the walls of the inner bailey was another ring of fortified walls, all wrought of stone and smooth of surface. There was not a speck of moss upon these stones. Indeed, the keep might have been conjured into being merely the day before, so oddly new did it appear to be. A river wrapped itself around the point where the tower was located, and the terrain plunged downward from the protective walls. She would not be able to discern much more until daylight.

Aileen turned to survey the room. It was sufficiently illuminated that she could see that there was solely the bed within it.

To be sure, it was a massive bed, cornered with great pillars and hung with thick curtains, its mattress piled with coverlets, cushions and furs.

But it was a bed.

Was she to be the Hawk's captive, kept solely to sate his lust or provide his heir? Men claimed wives for many a reason, but Aileen was woman enough to dislike that her spouse's expectation might be solely for her womb's fruit. Perhaps if she had been born a beauty, she might have years ago made her peace with being desired for her looks alone.

As it was, the prospect irked Aileen. Her old nursemaid would have said that she should have been glad to be desired at all, for a wench with a sharp tongue, a plain face and a small dowry cannot set her expectations too high.

Aileen sighed and leaned against the window sill. She had long been convinced that a man would have to feel affection for her to take her to wife. In lieu of lust, in lieu of her already faded youth and fertility, she had expected love or naught at all.

Yet now she was a sorcerer's captive instead.

Why had the Hawk not stolen some witless beauty? Why had he not seized some foolish lassie, who would have been glad of such a fate? Sadly, the Hawk had left her naught with which to injure him when he came to claim her maidenhead.

Doubtless that had been his scheme. The man seemed to plan for every eventuality with fearsome ease, and was all the more frightening for his ability to hide his every thought.

Aileen shivered and cast a glance of trepidation over her

shoulder to the silent bailey. What fate did the prisoner meet now? And how long before the Hawk came to have his due of her?

She did not doubt that he would deal with her next.

Aileen paced the chamber, leaving the shutters open so that the cold kept her awake. Still the Hawk did not come.

She watched the sliver of the moon rise higher, watched the spill of its silver light across Inverfyre's formidable walls.

Still the Hawk did not come.

She unbound her hair and shook it loose, running her fingers through it as she watched the sentries endlessly walk the circuit of the high walls.

Still the Hawk did not come.

She took off his chemise and chausses, half-certain that the garments were grimy enough to stand in the corner on their own. She enfolded herself in the fur-lined cloak, fretting about what he would make of her choice to wear only this.

Still the Hawk did not come.

Aileen eyed the bed, inviting and plump and undoubtedly warm, then turned her back upon it to watch the moon. She counted stars. She paced the chamber again and again, but still the Hawk did not come.

She tried the latch upon the door though she already knew it was fastened against her. She pressed her ear to the door, straining to hear some sound from the hall below, and thought she could discern the echo of contented snoring.

Still the Hawk did not come.

She dared to feel the bed and discovered that the mattress was plumper and softer than she had dared to imagine. She yawned, feeling the ache of a long day's ride in her buttocks. There were wolf pelts upon the bed, their thickness tempting her to snuggle beneath them. She pushed away from the lure of the bed to pace anew and still the Hawk did not come.

She stood at the window until she was certain she had frozen in place.

She turned slowly then, considered the bed, and resolved that the Hawk could have his way with her while she slept. She was too exhausted to be vigilant any longer.

Aileen dropped the cloak as she crossed the chamber, climbed into the bed, and fell asleep nigh as soon as her head hit the pillow.

The Hawk came to his wife's chamber shortly after that, and gazed long upon his sleeping bride. He had not the heart to wake her, though, and did not wish to startle her. He was exhausted by the prisoner's stubborn refusal to reveal anything and vexed by his own refusal to endorse torture.

He tucked her more fully beneath the pelts and kissed her brow lightly. She nestled more deeply into her bed and he thought that perhaps she smiled.

The possibility cheered him.

He left her reluctantly and locked the door after himself, descending to the chamber below on quiet feet.

A courtship, it seemed to him, would be best pursued while the lady was awake.

A ray of sunlight awakened Aileen when it landed surely upon her face.

She sat up, astounded to find herself still alone, and quickly checked the mattress to see whether her spouse had sampled her while she slept. She had slept like a corpse, dreamlessly and deeply, so exhausted had she been. Anything could have happened during the night and Aileen suspected that she would not have awakened.

There was no blood on the linens and she was reassured. She was restless, though, certain that her maidenhead would not be long intact. She explored the chamber in the morning sunlight and discovered that there were hooks upon the posts of the bed. She found a linen chemise of such fine weave it fair stole her breath away. It was a lady's garment, finely embroidered around the neck, and if not left for her use, then she would claim it anyway.

Had it been here the night before? She could not have said.

She donned the chemise, and the sheepskin boots left beside the bed. The shearling lined them still, and they enclosed her legs to the knees in soft warmth. Their soles were of leather and they looked both newly wrought and sturdy. They fit her perfectly.

Had they been fashioned while she slept? Had the Hawk conjured them with a spell? Or did the Hawk's sorcery allow him to foretell the size of his bride's feet?

Hung from another hook and nigh obscured by the drapes was a simply cut woman's gown of woad-dyed wool. Aileen accepted this gift, her spirits bolstered by the fact that blue was a hue which favored her well.

Had the Hawk chosen this color specifically for her? Aileen smiled to note that the hem had been let down—a fold line lingered where the new kirtle had been hemmed afore. His sorcery was not infallible, then! That was most encouraging.

A fur-lined tabard lurked behind the gown, its silken exterior lush with embroidery. It fitted over her hips and laced snugly through the waist.

Aileen was delighted. Though she had neither stockings, bath nor jewel, she felt garbed richly indeed.

She threw open the remaining shutters, running from one

to the next. She had heard water the night before and now could spy the river far below the tower. It was partly hidden by the gorse clinging to the steep slope that tumbled down from the high wall. On the opposite bank, hills rose sharply, trees clinging to their precipices. Aileen recognized this as a defensible site.

She crossed the chamber again and looked over the bailey. She spied now a jumble of huts between the walls of the keep, the village of Inverfyre. She spied a mill upon the river, its wheel turning merrily, and heard the distant laughter of children.

Her lips twisted. Dark-haired children, perhaps, who did not know their fathers' names?

Undoubtedly, the lands were too wild for the village to be outside the walls completely. The country certainly looked untamed. The dark green of the conifers became more sparse in the distance, with those trees with barren branches gradually becoming dominant. She could spy a ribbon of bright new green, probably the course of the river that leaped below her windows, winding its way downward through the hills.

This keep sat on the cusp of the north. Aileen imagined that on a clear day, she might be able to see all the way to Stirling, to the lands held by the king and his forebears. Her heart ached with unexpected loneliness, for this land was wild and unfamiliar, as unlike the verdant valley of Abernye as any place could be, and the refuge of the king's court seemed so far away.

A rattle at the door made her jump. She spun to confront whoever came, not knowing what to expect and having nothing with which to defend herself.

She did not expect the rosy-cheeked young woman who peeked around the edge of the door. "Good morning to you, my lady Aileen!" The woman, a few years younger than

Aileen, smiled pertly, then bustled into the chamber. She seemed untroubled that Aileen gave no reply.

She was not so slender as Aileen—indeed, she was quite buxom. Her hair was a reddish hue and her eyes were such a dark brown that her lashes seemed to be wrought of gold. She set down a steaming bucket of water with a thump, placing a bowl beside it and several cloths as she briefly rubbed her back. She appeared on the verge of laughter, her eyes twinkling in a most merry way. Her expectant and welcoming manner coaxed an answering smile from Aileen.

"I had hoped that you were yet sleeping, so as you could have a hot wash upon awakening," she said, then shook her head. "It is a filthy business, riding in haste for days and nights on end, and one can only expect such foolery from men. Even if you are not black and blue from his lairdship's pace, you might favor a good hot rub."

"Indeed," Aileen managed to say. "Your thoughtfulness is most welcome."

"And you all dressed for the fair, as my mother would say, with nary a scrub behind your ears." She winked even as she scolded Aileen. "From whence have you come, Lady Aileen? What would your mother have to say about your deeds this morn?"

Aileen smiled despite myself. "My mother would have said little, but my nursemaid would have tweaked my ear."

"And rightly so!"

"But I was too impatient to linger abed."

"Aye, and a healthy urge is that. I have no respect for women who lie abed all the day long." She clucked her tongue. "I told his lairdship that you would be cold, that I did, but he insisted 'twould not be safe to be leaving a brazier burning here with none to watch it. There is sense in that, even if all in the kitchens were certain he would warm your bed himself!" There was no malice in her manner and she laughed outright when Aileen blushed. "I will not be asking after your sleep on the night of your nuptials, upon that you can rely."

She gestured impatiently to the bucket. "Do you mean to leave the water turn cold? Ignoring a courtesy is as good as spitting in the eye of the benevolent one, that is what my mother used to say, and she had more sense than most."

Aileen quickly unlaced the tabard that she had only recently fastened. "Forgive my rudeness, but who are you?"

The maid laughed, which made her ample bosom bounce merrily. "Nissa Macdonald I am, and you are Aileen Urquhart of Abernye sure as I know my own name." She snapped her fingers. "Come, come, shed that garb. Though it was surely meant for you, it will be all the warmer once you are clean."

"Was it meant for me?" Aileen asked.

"Ah yes, indeed." Nissa nodded. "His lairdship had a number of us stitching into the night so as you would have garb for this day."

This was most intriguing. Aileen had not guessed her spouse was so thoughtful—or perhaps he only wanted her garbed more suitably to meet his household. Certainly, he was a man who left no detail to chance. The water was yet blessedly hot and the soap Nissa had brought had a pleasant scent.

"Make it ourselves, we do," she acknowledged when Aileen complimented her upon it. "And there is enough of it that a body need not be cautious with its use."

With that, she worked up a sumptuous lather upon Aileen's skin and set to rubbing her. Aileen's flesh was quickly pink from her rough cloth. Indeed, Nissa scrubbed her back with such a vengeance that she could not remain silent.

"I would be clean, not devoid of flesh!" she protested.

Nissa laughed again. "You do not have so many bruises as I feared. My laird must have been careful with his prize." She pinched Aileen's buttocks then, playful and irreverent.

Aileen did not know how to respond. She had never known such ready familiarity from servants before.

Nissa seemed to guess as much, for her sure gestures faltered. She nibbled on her lip in her uncertainty. "Did I do something amiss, my lady? You might have guessed that I have never served a noblewoman, for I have only ever served at Inverfyre."

"Are there no noblewomen here?"

"Some women come from the village to serve and a few of us live here, but there are no ladies."

Aileen was startled by this, then realized she should have expected little else in an abode of fighting men. She smiled and decided she might as well be honest. "Truth be told, I have never been pinched by a maid afore, Nissa. You surprised me."

Nissa flushed crimson and apologized profusely. She knotted her hands together, the very image of contrition. "You must tell me, my lady, when I err." She glanced up, sincerity in her eyes. "I should like to serve you well."

"I will," Aileen agreed, touched by the girl's earnest manner. "Though I must admit that I am not accustomed to having my own maid either. We shall find our way together."

They shared a smile and Aileen realized she might glean a good bit of information from this talkative maid, far more certainly than her spouse was likely to share.

Here was the opportunity she had not even realized she sought!

*   *   *

Aileen rubbed herself all over with the dry cloth as she considered how best to ask what she wanted to know. "You seem fond of your laird," she finally said, keeping her tone neutral.

"And why not?" Nissa hastened to dry Aileen's back.

"He is oft called the Hawk. That might leave a soul afeared."

"Though not a bold bride raised in Abernye and said to be skilled with a bow," Nissa teased, then leaned closer when Aileen glanced up. "It is said that when my laird claimed Inverfyre, he attacked his opponents with the ruthlessness and cunning of a hawk. Many are the tales of his victories, though there is not a one of them fit for a lady faint of heart."

"But why Inverfyre if it was so hard won? Could he not have set his ambitions upon another holding?"

"Inverfyre was rightfully his own." Nissa nodded. "Aye, his mother, Evangeline, was the daughter of the sixth son of the founder of Inverfyre. Though Lady Evangeline was driven from her abode, she vowed she would return with her son to claim his birthright." Nissa smiled with pride. "He did not wait for his mother, not our laird: nay, he claimed his due with his own blade and rightly so. He is a warrior valiant and true."

Aileen laced her tabard. "Is the keep newly built then?"

"Of course! For eighteen years, there have been stonemasons from over the sea by the dozen, laboring even as the holding was regained, and they are not yet done."

She guided Aileen to the window and pointed. "The walls were wrought first: indeed, when I came to serve in this hall, there was no hall. We all slept beneath wooden canopies in the bailey, while the sentries paced the top of the battlements. One never knew when the cursed MacLarens would rally and attack. That was only six years past." She gathered up the cloths with satisfaction. "And now, just as the prophecy predicted, peace has come to Inverfyre."

"What prophecy?"

It was apparent that Nissa had been waiting to be asked. She beamed before reciting the verse.

"When the seventh son of Inverfyre,
Saves his legacy from intrigue and mire,
Only then shall glorious Inverfyre,
Reflect in full its first laird's desire.

"And the current laird is indeed the seventh son born in the line of Magnus Armstrong," she continued, even as Aileen's heart nigh stopped in recognition of that name.

She spun to face the maid. "Not Magnus Armstrong!" she cried. This was the name that had filled her thoughts when the Hawk kissed her. "The founder of Inverfyre was Magnus Armstrong?"

"Indeed, he was. I see that you have heard tell of his exploits. Now, there was a man who spawned a hundred tales." Nissa smacked her lips with satisfaction. "Though the most wicked of them all was the tale of his wives."

Aileen folded her arms across her chest, disliking the maid's salacious tone but oddly certain that the circumstances of the brides of this Magnus might reflect upon her own. "He had more than one?"

Nissa laughed with glee. "He had a dozen!"

"So many?"

"At first he was said to have unfortunate luck with his brides, but in time, other tales were told."

"Such as?"

Nissa glanced furtively to the door. Aileen's curiosity was

fed by this sudden fear of discovery. Nissa pointed out the window. "Those cliffs opposite the river were that first bride's dowry lands, those cliffs thick with the nests of peregrines. Though she died in a year, Magnus never surrendered those lands to her family."

Aileen shrugged. "There is little scandalous in that. Warfaring men do as much all the time."

Nissa's eyes gleamed. "But even warfaring men do not eat their brides."

Aileen stepped back from the maid. "What nonsense is this?"

"It was said that Magnus ate his brides, every one of them." Nissa nodded.

Aileen could not keep from grimacing though she was skeptical. "You cannot mean that he truly ate them? Surely this is but a fanciful tale?"

"Aye, but he did. He locked them in a high chamber, not unlike this one, and forbade any others to visit them. He fattened them for a year and a day, and then he had them dressed in the richest finery. They thought the consummation of their match had come, and perhaps it did. Few knew what happened in that chamber, save that the bride never survived the night."

"No!"

"It was said that he wrung their necks, as if they were no more than chickens. It was said that he would have the cook aid him in the butchering and that the floors of the chamber—which none saw but himself and the cook—were stained red with the blood of his brides."

"That cannot be!" Aileen strode away from the maid in disgust. "I will not listen to such whimsy!"

"They disappeared, did they not?" Nissa insisted, her words low and hot. "It was not so much that they died, my lady. There was never a trace left of any of his wives. There were no witnesses of their demises. A coffin would appear in the chapel the next morn, and no more was said."

Aileen's bile rose at this gruesome tale, despite the vigor of the sunlight and her own certainty that it could not be true.

"It is told that a handmaid said that she had peeked within one coffin and seen naught but bones and a heart, a heart still beating, red with blood."

"This is nonsense."

"Aye? Then why were the coffins nailed closed after that?"

"There could be a hundred reasons. You cannot know such details so many years later. The tale has been embellished, Nissa, any fool can see as much. These are no more than fanciful stories to entertain . . ."

Nissa's eyes brightened. "Believe what you must, but I believe that Magnus devoured his brides, in stews and soups and sauces. He sucked the marrow from their bones; he ate every morsel but their hearts. And then he buried them, out there—" she pointed out one window "—and kept their dowries when he claimed another bride for his own."

Aileen followed her gesture. "There is a line of trees there, beyond the outer walls."

"Aye, great old trees, twelve great old trees, trees that unfurled from the hearts of these sorry women. The sole thing that halted his deeds was his own demise."

"Surely not!" Aileen made a skeptical snort. "Admit the truth to me, Nissa, admit that this is some tale concocted in the hall after too much ale has been consumed."

"Is it? Explain to me then who planted these trees?"

"Some soul who made a jest upon the laird, no doubt, just as you jest upon me."

Nissa held up a warning finger. "They are trees that no

soul planted, by the tales told 'round the fire. They are trees that sprouted suddenly from the earth, half as tall as a man one morning when they had not been there the night before. They grew, each of them, on the eve of the nuptials of the next bride, as if to warn her of what lay ahead."

"But . . ."

"They are strange trees, that much is certain. They whisper in the wind even when there is no wind. It is said that they grew from the women's beating hearts, that they stand witness to the crimes of Magnus Armstrong. It is said that they will turn red, as red as blood, when his penance has finally been served."

Aileen stifled a shiver. The morning seemed somewhat less bright than it had just moments before. "Then you tell me that Inverfyre is built twice upon blood—the blood of these women and the blood of the Hawk's enemies."

"Indeed so. Old crimes have been done in this place and great tales have been spawned here . . ." Nissa stepped away, abruptly falling silent. "But, of course, you do not believe in such whimsy."

The maid turned to leave, but Aileen caught her sleeve. "Show me the proof of it, Nissa. Persuade me. Show me these whispering trees." She told herself that she made the suggestion for no better reason than to leave this chamber, but in truth, she was intrigued by this gruesome tale.

The maid hesitated. "The laird said as you should remain in your chamber this day."

Aileen smiled coolly, for she was determined to not be as biddable as a hound. "A woman should not cede everything to a man simply because he anticipates as much. Am I not the Lady of Inverfyre now?"

Indecision warred in the girl's eyes for only a moment, then she nodded with resolve. "I will take you there," she agreed. "I cannot imagine that my laird would be displeased that you are curious about your new abode."

"I will go to the chapel first and hear the mass, then I will break my fast," Aileen said, having no intent of altering her usual routine. She glanced up to find the maid watching her. "What is it? Surely you hear the mass daily?"

"We have no chapel, my lady."

"That is not of import. Summon the priest and he can bless a space."

"We have no priest, my lady."

Aileen stared at the girl. She had never heard of a keep without a priest. "Surely this is not true. You must have a priest!"

"One came from Stirling several times a year until three years past."

"And then?" Aileen prompted when Nissa hesitated.

"And then he was murdered, my lady, and there has never been another." Nissa pivoted and left the chamber, clearly assuming Aileen would follow.

Aileen left her high prison, her thoughts spinning. If there was no priest, then no sacraments were being offered to the people of Inverfyre. Surely the Hawk was not so wicked as to condemn those beneath his care to hell?

But then Aileen recalled how the Hawk's men treated the priest of Abernye. They were unholy warriors, that much was clear. Annoyance rose within Aileen. How could the Hawk have so little regard for the souls of those beneath his hand, even if he spurned the faith himself? Trust a man of his repute to have no sense of his responsibility! Perhaps there was some good she could achieve in this place!

Aileen gritted her teeth. Though she had no certainty what the Hawk planned for her and she did not believe Nissa's ominous tale, she had no intent of waiting patiently in that chamber for a year and day to learn the worst.

Indeed, the Hawk might well regret bringing her to Inverfyre.

The kitchens were busy, and redolent of freshly baked bread and roasting meat. Two boys followed the dictate of the cook, moving hastily to prepare the meat for the spit. The cook himself was plump—always a good portent for the fare, in Aileen's father's words—and spared a smile for her, though he clearly had much to accomplish. There were surprisingly few women at work in the kitchens.

Though the servants clearly would have preferred her to eat in the hall, Aileen insisted upon remaining in the cheer of the kitchen. She was seated in a corner with a large piece of dark bread and a comb of honey, an ample napkin, a cup of ale and a knife. She murmured a prayer herself and was content with her feast. Indeed, she was ravenous and ate every morsel, though normally the bread would have been too generous a cut.

A trio of women sat together near the fire, murmuring and giggling to each other. Their hair hung loose and their kirtles were not laced demurely at the neck. It appeared that they had used carmine upon their reddened lips and cheeks. They were pretty women, though their manner was less decorous than Aileen might have preferred.

She guessed what task they performed to earn their keep, and supposed she should not have been surprised to find harlots in a hall filled with warriors. The one with hair as dark as ebony watched Aileen openly, her eyes filled with malice and amusement. "I do not care how vexed Fernando becomes," she told her companions gaily, one eye upon Aileen. "I shall oust him without regret each and every time the Hawk crooks his finger at me."

The women giggled, sparing covert glances for Aileen, who ignored them.

"That is only Guinevere," Nissa whispered. "Pay her no heed, my lady."

Aileen realized that this was the whore who had challenged the Hawk the night before.

"She likes naught better than to set people at odds." The girl wrinkled her nose. "She will have decided to dislike you already, my lady, for she greatly fancies the Hawk."

Guinevere arched a brow, as if well aware of what the maid confided, then bared her teeth in a mock growl. Her companions laughed lustily at her antics, though Aileen concentrated upon her meal.

She was not surprised that the Hawk had a whore and had no intention of doing anything about the matter. He would need the woman's consolation after Aileen was gone.

Had she been staying, or wed happily, Guinevere would have faced a much less tolerant Aileen.

The sole thing that troubled her in this kitchen, Aileen decided, was the floor. The rushes cast there were dark with grease, and she felt she could smell their filth. The matter was made worse by the dozen dogs that lingered underfoot: some kept their watchful gazes fixed on the meat being prepared while others burrowed in the old rushes. They found many a morsel and bone hidden there, their foraging too successful for Aileen's taste.

In future, she would be hard-pressed to eat much that came from these kitchens, however savory the smell. She could not keep silent about the matter, and indeed, it gave her an idea. It could not hurt to prove herself so irksome that the Hawk might willingly discard her—or at least, might not pursue her when she escaped.

Aileen cleared her throat. "Are the dogs always in the kitchens, Nissa?"

The maid nodded and grimaced, her own opinion of this clear. "Aye, my lady."

Aileen finished her ale, resolved to make at least one change in her new home. She was Lady of Inverfyre and the kitchens fell beneath her jurisdiction.

She would remind the Hawk as much if he was vexed.

A slender older man halted before Aileen and bowed his head. "Good morning, my lady. I am Gregory, the castellan of Inverfyre, and most delighted to welcome you to your new abode. I trust that all is suitable?"

It was intended to be a polite inquiry and Aileen knew as much, but she dared not lose the opportunity. "Indeed, Inverfyre is a marvelous keep, and I must salute you for its fine state."

Gregory smiled and made to depart.

"But I wonder, Gregory, when the rushes in the kitchen and hall were last changed?" Aileen smiled with all the sweetness she could summon when he glanced at her. "Although many change them once a year, my mother always favored a monthly sweep to discourage vermin. I confess that I favor her scheme, perhaps because it is what I learned to expect."

The castellan's nostrils flared as he straightened, and Aileen was certain he did not appreciate her interference in what he perceived to be his domain. His very manner annoyed Aileen, for he should have made a token acknowledgment of Aileen's status.

Unless the Hawk had forbidden his servants to show her any concession. Aileen straightened and returned the castellan's regard unflinchingly.

"I shall ask my lord as to his preference," he said coolly and she doubted he would do any such thing.

"You know mine," Aileen said with resolve. "Please have the hall swept and the rushes replaced before the midday meal. I will not suffer vermin in my abode, and neither, I am certain, will my laird husband."

Gregory smiled thinly. "With respect, my lady, Inverfyre is not Abernye. We have always managed matters thus and acknowledgment of custom is key to a well-administered keep."

"With respect, Gregory, habit does not make a practice right. And indeed, Inverfyre is clearly bereft of noblewomen. One cannot expect a warrior to tend to the details of maintaining a gracious hall, though I have no doubt my husband intends for me to take such a responsibility. Why else would he have wed at all?" She smiled so that Gregory could not deny her without looking like a disobedient cur.

She heard Nissa hold her breath, and noted the girl's eyes widen with awe. Aileen had no doubt that the castellan still would ask for the Hawk's agreement and dared not imagine what might result from that.

Gregory cleared his throat and bowed. "As you wish, my lady," he said tightly, then turned to depart.

Aileen resolved to finish what she had begun. If the Hawk was going to be furious with her, he might as well have good cause.

"And Gregory," she called after the castellan. The man paused and glanced back warily, clearly anxious to be away from her demands. "Though I know this to be an abode of hunting and fighting men, I cannot suffer dogs in the kitchens. They too oft carry vermin, and their presence underfoot complicates the labor of those in the kitchens who already work overhard. In future, the dogs are welcome in the hall and in the stables only." Aileen held the castellan's gaze, letting him see her determination.

"My lord greatly indulges his hunting hounds," he said with care.

Aileen let her smile broaden. "And he is welcome to do so in the stables. See to the matter immediately, if you please, Gregory."

Gregory could not summon a word of either protest or agreement, so startled was he. He merely bowed and departed, his neck as red as a morning sky. Aileen doubted that he had ever been challenged by a woman before.

"My thanks to you, Lady Aileen," the cook declared, waving his wooden spoon with a flourish. "I trip over these hungry hounds all the day long and fear to break my very neck."

"Hounds have no place in the kitchens," Aileen reiterated firmly.

The cook grinned. "Indeed, they do not. I will not wait for Gregory's edict, for the Lady of Inverfyre has spoken." He gestured to a pair of boys and waved to the dogs. "See the hounds out to the bailey, and say that it is by my lady's command if any question your deeds."

One boy took a bowl of scraps, another roused the dogs, and the hounds willingly followed the bowl, their noses in the air.

Nissa smiled and Aileen felt a certain satisfaction in improving the state of her husband's holding, even if the three whores wrinkled their noses and left the kitchen in disdain.

Perhaps she would see the hall rid of them, too. The prospect made Aileen smile.

VI

$\mathcal{A}$ stout older woman, the sole female in the kitchen other than Nissa and Aileen, nodded with undisguised satisfaction at Aileen's edict. She seized a broom and began to clear the floor. She swept the rushes with such vigor that the stone floor was quickly visible.

"Time enough we had a lady in this hall," she said with resolve. "Time enough these boys learned to be men." She wielded her broom like a weapon, halting only to incline her head respectfully when she reached Aileen. "We shall see the rushes all replaced before midday, my lady, upon that you can rely."

"I thank you."

The woman hesitated before returning to her labor, her uncertain manner revealing that she had a request.

"What do you desire of me?" Aileen asked kindly. "And tell me first what is your name?"

"Gunna is my name, my lady. I saw you pray, meaning no disrespect, and I would ask you whether there is any scheme to bring a priest again to Inverfyre."

"Of course we must have a priest," Aileen said firmly.

"How many souls make their homes in the village and keep proper?"

"A hundred in the village, my lady, fewer in the hall."

"I shall speak to my laird husband about the matter, Gunna." Aileen's heart quivered at the prospect, but she forced a smile. "You might offer a prayer to my success. I may need such aid."

"I will do so. I thank you, my lady." Gunna took her broom to the floor with enthusiasm.

Her meal complete, Aileen rose to leave the kitchen, Nissa fast by her side. In that moment, the boys hefted the hind of meat over the fire, fitting the ends of the spit into the iron brace inside the fireplace. The cook bade them stoke the fire and the flames left high, licking the fat of the meat.

The smell of burning fat and the crackle of the meat braising made Aileen's bile rise as always it did. She pivoted, sickened, and hastened from the kitchen, fearing she would be ill. The revulsion within her made her own flesh crawl and she could not be far enough from that cursed sound.

"My lady? Are you ill?" Nissa demanded, her footsteps quick behind her.

"It is nothing, Nissa. I simply cannot tolerate the sound and smell of browning meat." Aileen shrugged and smiled. "It is folly, I know, but it sickens me and always has. I do not know why or how it might be changed."

The maid regarded her with consideration. "How odd," she said. "I never heard of a soul being troubled by that until I came to Inverfyre."

"Indeed?" Aileen commented only to be polite, embarrassed as always by this ridiculous aversion.

"Indeed. My laird himself leaves the kitchens when the

meat first sizzles over the fire. Though he grants no explanation, his expression is much as your own."

Aileen glanced to the girl in surprise.

"All know of it, my lady, just as all will know that you share his dislike." Nissa smiled. "Perhaps it is a portent that your match is particularly well-made."

Aileen found herself somewhat cheered that her affliction might not be so uncommon as she had always believed. "Perhaps."

The maid's eyes glowed as she matched her steps to Aileen's. "A priest would be most welcome, my lady. Gunna's niece is two summers of age and still in need of a christening."

Aileen halted in horror. "No!"

Nissa nodded sadly.

"This is appalling!" Aileen marched through the hall, outraged that the Hawk should show so little regard for his people. To her delight, the rushes in the hall were being swept out, as well. She waved cheerfully to a sullen Gregory, then continued on her way. "I *must* persuade him to summon a priest. Come, Nissa, you vowed to show me these trees."

The maid's smile faded immediately. "I think it a poor notion, my lady. Perhaps you speak aright and it is folly, after all."

Aileen paused to glance at the girl. "But just moments ago, you insisted it to be true."

The girl flushed and wrung her hands together. "Perhaps I spoke in haste. It is cold, my lady. Let me show you more of the keep instead."

"The trees, Nissa. I will see the trees." Aileen smiled encouragement. "I am from a more northern clime than this. A bitter wind will not deter me." She turned and crossed the hall, waiting for the maid to follow.

Nissa did so, if hesitantly, and Aileen wondered what had so suddenly shaken the girl's conviction.

The wind was bitter even in the bailey, and a late frost broke beneath their boots as they walked. Nissa had become remarkably quiet and Aileen wondered whether she had oft been rebuked for her garrulous tongue.

Perhaps she regretted recounting as much as she had.

They approached the gates and Aileen braced herself for a confrontation. Had the Hawk not decreed that she should remain in her chamber?

To her surprise, she and Nissa were permitted through the gates of the inner walls with nary a comment, though much watchfulness. From afar, Aileen could see that the sentries jested with each other, as men do, but they fell silent as the women drew near. Aileen heard not a word clearly and could not have said whether they spoke Gaelic, Norman French or another tongue.

She felt the weight of their gazes even long after they passed, especially when she glanced back to find that two of the Hawk's companions had joined them. The villagers drew away from Aileen's course, more than a few of them exchanging whispers as they observed her passing.

The watchful manner of all these souls did not explain Aileen's sense that her every move was being closely observed. She felt beneath a possessive eye and her color rose slightly with each step, for she could guess whose eye followed her progress. For one accustomed to being unworthy of much interest, this sense made Aileen unnaturally aware of her every move.

There was a group of men with hooded and tethered

hunting birds in the outer bailey. Curious, for this training was said to be the root of Inverfyre's fortunes, Aileen paused to watch the older man who clearly was in charge.

Though he was tending to portliness, his every move was agile and experienced. His hair was silvered and he spoke with authority to the men working with him. He unhooded the bird upon his one fist, then cast a dead rabbit through the air with his other hand. Blood flew from the carcass, the rabbit obviously freshly killed.

Nissa grimaced and made a sound of distaste. The peregrine, though, watched avidly, its eyes gleaming. It seemed to Aileen that the man sang softly to it. The bird cried out as the man launched it from his fist with an inaudible command. The bird flew, pounced upon the meat, then took flight, heading away from its captor.

The tether upon the bird's ankle could not be denied, though. The man pulled the defiant bird to him by the leash, his pace relentless and firm, his command echoing through the air. The bird was not anxious to surrender its prize, even when it flapped right above his fist.

But the falconer claimed the rabbit, hooded the peregrine, then gave the bird a morsel. He sang to it softly. Aileen could see the tension in the creature, the lust to finish what it had begun, even as it was taught what it must do instead.

The falconer then turned his gaze upon Aileen, his expression oddly knowing. Aileen had the sense that he recognized her, though she had never seen him before, and the hair prickled on the back of her neck.

"It is an unnatural business, training a wild creature to do man's will," Nissa muttered.

"What of hounds? Or horses?" Aileen asked mildly. "Or even children?"

Nissa laughed.

Aileen turned and followed the maid, her thoughts churning. Was she being allowed her lead, as the falcon was allowed to fly to the end of its tether? Doubtless there was a finite distance she would be allowed to go without interference.

The outer gates were clearly not that limit. The women passed through them without comment from the sentries and Aileen eyed the hills before her. To the right and the left, the land folded upon itself with greater vigor than had been visible from above. She could not perceive the narrow valley that the leaping river followed downward.

There was only the barest glimmer of a distant spire perched upon another hill. Had the spy who had been captured scaling Inverfyre's walls come from there? If so, these were the Hawk's foes, and they might be willing to assist her.

But first, she would have to escape.

The wind whipped 'round the women as they reached the corner of the wall, its nimble fingers snatching at their cloaks and burrowing beneath their layers of garb. The twelve trees, too, were larger than Aileen had guessed. The river roiled behind them, the ground falling away in an undulating line that echoed the river's path.

The trees stood in a perfect line, so closely planted that there was but two paces between them. Their barren branches stretched like black fingers toward the sky, knotting and tangling with each other like a high hedge. There was something ominous about them, and indeed, Nissa halted and refused to go closer.

Aileen approached the trees alone. There was an eerie stillness in this place. It was not the usual silence of the wilderness. It seemed that all held its breath here, though Aileen could not guess what these trees anticipated. Even the river's gurgle was muted, perhaps by some trick of the land's curve, perhaps by sorcery.

She could hear only the whisper of leaves overhead, though the tree branches were bare. It was a whispering akin to women gossiping at the back of a church and the sound sent shivers down Aileen's spine. She thought again of the visions that the Hawk had poured into her thoughts, the two vines twining with each other so thoroughly that they could never be separated.

Aileen swallowed, not liking how tenuous her grasp upon her wits seemed to be. It was not possible for trees to whisper, for Nissa's tale to be true, for another to infect one's thoughts with his own.

She strode closer to the trees, determined to put these whimsies to rest. The bark of each tree was silver and smooth, unlike the bark of any tree that ever she had seen. It was more like pewter flesh than bark. Aileen laid a hand upon one tree, wanting to prove its texture to be like that of any other tree, but it felt warm.

Foolery! Her fingers were merely chilled by the wind. She wrapped both hands around the trunk, determined to find the wood no warmer than it should have been.

A pulse beat beneath her palms.

Aileen snatched her hands away and took a hasty step back. Her breath came in haste, her fear that she dreamed while awake grew with every moment. She surveyed the line of trees and saw then that there were more than twelve.

Aye, there was a small one at the end of the line, so small that she had not discerned it from her chamber. It too was a silvery tree, though it was no taller than her waist.

Thirteen. Aileen counted them again but it was the thirteenth, of that there was no doubt. A lump rose in her throat, for true to Nissa's tale, there had been nuptials just days before.

Aileen's own nuptials.

This must be a jest! She strode boldly to the young tree, her heart thundering at its portent. There was not a footprint before her own. The icy filigree of the frost was shattered around the trunk, as if the tree had thrust itself through the earth. It must have done so the night before, or perhaps this very morn after the frost had fallen.

Impossible!

But the evidence was before Aileen's own eyes. She snatched at the tree and found it solidly rooted to the spot. She doubted then all she knew to be true. She feared that her mother truly had been mad and that she, Aileen, had inherited the taint herself.

She was losing her wits in this place.

Aileen spun to face Nissa, hoping the maid had played some trick upon her. The maid's level gaze confessed nothing, but it was not her expression that made Aileen's own heart clench.

It was the presence of the Hawk of Inverfyre himself, standing tall and silent beside the maid. His dark cloak lifted in the wind, his arms were folded across his chest. His gaze was fixed upon Aileen, his expression grim.

Aileen fancied then that she could hear the echo of thirteen hot pulses close behind her. Their pace was urgent, as if they beat a warning to the new bride. He had tricked her, captured her, would rape her. He sought to drive her mad. Perhaps in a year and a day, he too would have a fancy for sucking the marrow of her bones.

Aileen's mouth went dry. Part of her insisted that Nissa's tale was madness, but still there was the tree . . . and the resonance in her own thoughts, the name that came more readily to her lips than her spouse's given name.

Magnus.

"Leave us, Nissa," the Hawk said firmly. She did not so much as hesitate, this servant who had seemed so kindly. She turned immediately upon her heel, marched back to the gates and abandoned Aileen to whatever fate this man would decree.

Aileen tasted her morning meal anew as he said not a word. Nissa's footfalls, crunching on the new frost, faded to nothing. Her form disappeared through the darkness of Inverfyre's outer gates.

Then there was solely the steam of breath between husband and wife. The Hawk watched her, his expression inscrutable. Did he know already that she had pronounced an order in his hall? Though she had anticipated his disapproval, she had not thought to face it in such solitude.

The silence pressed against Aileen's ears until she could bear it no longer. Though it seemed weak to be the first to speak, she surrendered to this contest of wills.

"I hear that your forebear had uncommon taste in brides," she said finally with an audacity she did not feel. Indeed, she tossed her hair over her shoulder, as if untroubled by tales, trees or spouse. Aileen's fingers latched on to the small tree and she clutched it, as if it alone would keep her upon her feet.

"It has long been said that we had much in common, Magnus Armstrong and I," the Hawk said.

"Because you claimed Inverfyre by force, not caring for the price?"

"Among other deeds."

Aileen stifled a shiver. "It would seem an expensive matter to claim bride after bride, when surely just one, well treated, would suffice."

That half-smile tugged at the Hawk's lips, softening his features and making him yet more handsome. Aileen reminded herself not to be beguiled.

"Do you suggest that a man should not lay claim to what he desires most?"

"I suggest a man should be moderate in his desires, all the better that they might ultimately be sated. It seems a lesson neither you nor Magnus were inclined to learn."

He smiled truly then, as if he found his bride an amusing diversion. "Do you give me counsel, Wife?"

"That would depend upon your intent. What do you desire of me?"

"I desire what all men desire of their wives, as I have told you afore. Indeed, it seems we linger overlong in sating that desire." His gaze slid over Aileen and her face heated beneath his appreciative perusal.

"Do not lie to me! There may be a thousand reasons why you have chosen to wed me, but desire for me cannot be one of them."

"Can it not?" he murmured, his voice like silken velvet. Aileen saw his gaze darken, she saw the confidence in his smile.

She saw the Hawk take a step toward her, then another. There was intent in his every pace, intent that sent terror dancing along her veins. No man had ever looked at Aileen thus and she was frightened by the portent of his desire. So bright was her fear that she did not remember her own plan to either win his trust or his disgust. She did not wait to see what he would do.

She fled.

There was but one direction in which she had a chance to

elude a larger and faster captor, one route upon which she would be pursued by him alone and not his sentries, falcons and hunting hounds. Aileen turned her back upon the keep and its high gates. She leapt into the gully of the river, forded its coursing waters and dove into the shadows of the forest.

Like the hare, her sole chance lay beneath the undergrowth of the forest, within the tangled brambles where a hawk could not fly.

Her husband swore. Aileen gained the far bank breathlessly, ducked into the forest and ran.

The forest seemed to favor Aileen's quest, for the brambles fairly parted before her. Aileen glanced back once and could not discern the path she had taken, though it was clear before her. She heard the Hawk curse with vehemence, but his voice was more distant than she had expected.

Did he simply try to trick her into slowing her pace? She would have expected as much of him, would have expected him to step out from behind a tree into her path and snatch her up in his talons.

Aileen ran faster. She thought of the distant tower and knew it to be her best destination. She wasted precious moments glancing back through the trees to study the walls and tower of Inverfyre to guess her position relative to the neighboring tower.

Aileen had been in the forest afore and knew how to set a straight course. She fixed her gaze upon a large tree that was located in the direction she wished to go, and made her way toward it. The brambles fought her passage now, but she did not sway from her objective.

That was the way of becoming lost.

Once she reached the large tree, she drew an invisible

line betwixt it and the ford of the river that she could still see through the forest's shadows. She pivoted then and imagined that line stretching out in the opposite direction until it reached another distinctive tree.

Aileen's father had taught her this means of crossing a woods and it worked without fail. The trick lay solely in choosing a tree each time that was sufficiently distinctive from each side that it could not be confused with another. She knew that she must be able to recognize the previous tree or two to plan her ongoing course.

The sounds of the Hawk's pursuit faded with every step Aileen took. Gradually, she became convinced that he had abandoned the chase, for the moment, and slowed her pace from a run to a quick walk.

Only the sounds of the forest, the agitation of her breathing and her own furtive footfalls echoed around her. The sun climbed higher, but with Fortune upon her side, Aileen knew she would be at the hearth of that neighboring tower by nightfall.

She also knew that this would be her sole chance to escape her husband's hand. If she failed, she would never be granted leave from that tower chamber again.

The very prospect quickened her pace.

The Hawk could not believe his own eyes. His lady wife was gone, as completely as if she had been swallowed whole by the forest, or taken captive by the fey. He hunted with diligence but found not a trace of her.

His fear grew with every moment. What would Dubhglas MacLaren do to Aileen, if he managed to seize her? The prospect was terrifying, for Dubhglas was without remorse.

Scratched by a thousand brambles, the Hawk shouted to

those at the gatehouse. He called for hounds and horses, and set nigh every soul in Inverfyre to finding his wife.

He cared not what they whispered in the kitchens, he cared not if they said he was driven nigh mad with desire. He knew a fear to his very marrow, a fear that he could lose far more this day than his bride. He had frightened her and now he feared that she would pay the price of his error.

The Hawk would not rest until Aileen was safe within Inverfyre's walls again.

The woods surrounding Inverfyre had the advantage of being of mixed kinds of trees. Aileen chose a kind of silver-barked tree for each of her points, as their bark could be readily spied at a distance. They also seemed relatively uncommon in this woods.

They seemed to glimmer, even beneath that day's overcast skies. It was only after Aileen had walked for a goodly measure of time that she realized these were similar trees to those thirteen that grew outside Inverfyre's walls. She shivered, knowing herself to be fanciful, and laid her hand upon the next one to prove her whimsy wrong.

The bark was warm, as it should not have been.

Aileen pulled her hand away hastily, not wanting to feel that eerie pulse beneath her palm again. She halted and listened, for the forest was filled with an uncommon, watchful silence.

She could still hear the gurgle of the river. She wondered whether this river curled back upon itself, for she should have left it far behind by now. There was a strange hut in the clearing before her. She peered ahead into the forest and could not spy the walls of that neighboring keep. It could not be as close as she had hoped.

Indeed, she could still discern the walls of Inverfyre

through the trees behind her and almost hear the shouts of its sentries. She was perhaps a third of the way between the keeps.

Aileen frowned, for she had not come far at all.

What jest was this?

She studied the hut, for it seemed almost to glow in this afternoon light, as if it tempted her to look more fully upon it. Aileen could not imagine why. It was uncommon, for it was wrought of living trees, but humble and neglected. The boughs of trees looked to have been coaxed over years to bend into roof and walls, though they were as deadened as the slumbering forest surrounding her.

Aileen spared it little more than an impatient glance, for she guessed it to be abandoned. She noted that the sun was just past zenith, seeing its glow through the clouds. She had walked all morning, yet still was not far from where she had fled the Hawk.

She must have traveled in circles, despite her caution.

Aileen resolved to be more diligent in marking her course, so that she did not make such an error again. She took a good look at the tree that she meant to use as her marker, noting the burl in the wood from a branch that had been broken. She fixed her gaze upon another silver tree, one with a gnarled branch that had grown in a low curve, as if it had been bent under the weight of a very plump bird.

That one could not be confused with another!

Nissa was slinging a bucket of slops from the kitchen when Ahearn stepped into her path. His appearance should have improved her unhappy mood, but instead she was impatient with him. She narrowly averted spilling the bucket's contents on his shining black boots and granted him a quelling glance as a result.

Typically, he was undeterred. This rogue was as mischievous as they came and his eyes danced with wicked merriment. He was taller than she and powerfully built, cursedly handsome and just as audacious. Ahearn was well known as the trickster of Inverfyre, for he could never resist making a practical joke.

And Nissa knew that she had been his accomplice too often.

"Well?" he demanded with characteristic enthusiasm as he matched his steps to hers. "Did you tell her that old tale?"

"I did," she admitted glumly.

Ahearn's eyes sparkled. "And? Did she believe you? Was she frightened? No one can spin a tale as you do, Nissa!" He dropped his voice and leaned down, his breath tickling Nissa's ear. "I heard that she insisted upon seeing the trees for herself." He chortled. "Surely she was terrified when she spied the small one!"

"She was startled, to be sure." She granted her companion a dark glance. "I did not know that you meant to put a young tree there."

"Was it amusing beyond belief?" Ahearn fairly danced in his glee. "I wish I could have witnessed her response!"

"It was cruel," Nissa said, her voice flat. Ahearn gaped at her, but she nodded with resolve. "It was a mean jest and I am ashamed that I had a part in it."

"Nissa! My partner and cohort, my confidante and partner, how can you say these things?"

Nissa set the bucket down so abruptly that it nearly landed on Ahearn's toe, but she did not care. She confronted him, not troubling to hide her displeasure. "I should not have done this, not at your behest. You were only seeking to make mischief."

"Of course, I sought to make mischief! Nissa, life is too

short to be grim. Should we all be so dour as the Hawk himself?" Ahearn made his sour face, which normally prompted Nissa's laughter. On this day, she felt no urge to smile.

She hefted her bucket anew and continued on her way. "I have no time for your foolery," she said. "I have a mind to tell my laird of your wickedness."

"You would not!"

"I might."

"You will not do so, or I shall condemn you, as well." Ahearn strode after Nissa when she did not halt, seizing the bucket from her grip to slow her departure.

"Give me that!"

"I will not." The mercenary swung the bucket behind himself, its contents swirling dangerously close to the lip as he did so.

"Spill it and I will be scolded!"

"Pledge to me that you will not tell the Hawk of this." Ahearn grimaced. "He seems to have little humor regarding his lady wife."

"I will not. Give me the bucket."

"Are you not the Nissa I know and adore?" Ahearn demanded, giving her a thorough scrutiny. "Hmmmm. You have the same curly hair of the same feisty hue. Same sparkling eyes. Same pert nose. Same winsome smile." He winked devilishly. "Same delightful curves."

"Give me that bucket," Nissa insisted, knowing her cheeks were flushed.

"Are you not the same Nissa who stitched Alasdair's chausses so cunningly after he collapsed drunk, ensuring that he could neither don them the next morn nor figure out why? Are you not the same Nissa who laughed herself to the point of illness with me over his confusion?"

Nissa colored with guilt. "I am. Give me that bucket."

Ahearn swung the bucket beguilingly close to her, then beyond her grasp again. "Are you not the same Nissa who aided me to lock Reinhard in the dungeon by delivering a false missive from his lady love in the village? Are you not the maid who chortled with me at his disappointment that she was not there?"

"I am, to my eternal shame."

"Are you not the Nissa who cut away half of Fernando's moustache one night while he slept too deeply?"

"It was me, to be sure, for you could never have wielded the knife in your own besotted state."

"You did it for me." He clutched his heart in mock delight at this and his manner only infuriated Nissa all the more.

Was every matter a jest to Ahearn, even her foolish yearning for his affection?

She glared at him. "I did it because you have a gilded tongue, to be sure."

Ahearn cast the handle of the bucket from one hand to the other, each of its leaps through the air terrifying Nissa that it would spill and she would have to answer for it. He kept it just out of her reach and just shy of spilling. "Are we not old partners, Nissa? Are we not two of a kind? Are we not comrades in making Inverfyre a more merry place?"

"No, we are not, not any longer."

"I thought you loved me." He teased her with this claim, making a pout of disappointment. The words made her heart clench even though she knew they meant nothing to him. "Nissa, how shall I continue without your admiration?" He pretended to be heartbroken and Nissa barely stifled the urge to slap him.

Oh, she had been smitten with Ahearn since the day she had arrived at Inverfyre, since the day he had persuaded her to aid in playing some trick upon the cook. She had fallen in love with his dancing eyes and his carefree manner, his wicked smile and merry laughter. She had even foolishly imagined that he might take romantic note of her if she helped him make mischief.

No longer. Had her lady not reminded her that a man should not be granted his desire simply because he asked for it? Nissa had granted Ahearn his every request—but one—for six years and to no avail. He would grant her nothing, save a chance to lose her chastity and be shamed forever.

It was not enough.

At least her lady vowed to teach her the skill of a proper maid. Nissa grew no younger and she had a dream of wedding a man who would give her sons and small home of her own.

Ahearn's approving smile would no longer suffice.

"Come along," he coaxed, his charm as thickly spread as butter on the king's bread. "Tell me, Nissa, tell me what happened. Do you not wish to collect the kiss I promised to render to you?" He tickled her beneath the chin with one fingertip. "I know that you desire a kiss from me more than any other treasure in Christendom." And the knave smiled with cursed confidence.

Nissa folded her arms across her chest. "I told my lady the tale as you requested. I do not think she believed it." She took a deep breath, well aware that she had never questioned Ahearn's humor afore. "And I do not think it was amusing to tease her thus. This was wrong, Ahearn."

"What?" The mercenary gasped in mock dismay, then clutched his heart as if she had dealt him a lethal wound. "Say this is not so! Say that you do not doubt my schemes!"

"I like her," Nissa declared and took advantage of his astonishment to reclaim her bucket with a savage gesture. "I will not make mischief upon my lady again." She turned her back upon this handsome rogue who had so oft and so readily cajoled her aid, and marched away. "And I will tell my laird of your deed, if it suits me to do so."

"But Nissa!" Ahearn cried. "You have not collected the kiss that was your due!"

Nissa glanced back, hardening her heart to Ahearn's appeal. Just a day past she *had* yearned for a kiss from him, however mockingly bestowed, but she did not like how she felt after teasing the Lady Aileen with that dark tale. She did not like how the lady had paled when she spied that small tree, planted with cunning by Ahearn.

"I have no interest in your kisses," she said haughtily. "Perhaps another maid will welcome the boon owed to me."

She savored Ahearn's shock for a heady moment, then lifted her chin and turned away.

"Such mastery in the courtship of a woman," Sebastien declared from further back in the corridor, his words brimming with laughter. "You must tell me, Ahearn, how you so readily coax a reluctant maiden to your view. Indeed, I can see that I have desperate need of your expertise and counsel."

"Shut your mouth, fool," Ahearn growled.

The sound of Sebastien's merry laughter made Nissa smile herself, though this time, Ahearn did not share in the jest. Indeed, she heard him swear as she never had before. His boots echoed on the stones, fading to silence as he strode hastily in the opposite direction. Nissa glanced back, fearing she had spurned him too harshly.

But Sebastien winked encouragingly from where he leaned in the shadows and his whisper carried to Nissa's ears. "Well done, little Nissa. He will think of you more this night than ever he has before. Indeed, he may be haunted by that kiss he did not claim."

Though that had not been her intention, it was a marvel for Nissa to think of Ahearn haunted by her. The very prospect put a bounce in her step. "I doubt as much, Sebastien," she said gaily. "Ahearn's memory for women is short indeed."

Sebastien did not reply, though his smile broadened. Nissa continued on her way, her heart lighter than it had been.

Perhaps her lady would aid her to find a good husband. She had heard that ladies oft ensured good matches for their maids and it seemed to Nissa that the Lady Aileen would show such concern for a maid she favored. Had she not been worried for Gunna's unbaptized niece?

Nissa had best learn promptly all the lady tried to teach her and thus earn the lady's favor. She could ask the laird if all those fine kirtles that his mother had brought should be lengthened for his lady wife.

There was naught more pleasing for a lady than to have garb that fit and flattered, Nissa was certain, and the Lady Evangeline had an eye for a beauteous kirtle. Lady Aileen had been so pleased with merely one garment this morning, that she would be speechless when she saw them all.

She was clever with a needle, Nissa was. Indeed, there were few who turned a seam as artfully as she. She could aid her lady in that and perhaps, oh perhaps, earn Lady Aileen's favor.

Nissa would not consider, not for a moment, what Ahearn would say when she wed another man. Doubtless, he would not care.

She blinked back tears and shifted the bucket to her other

hand. She would not care what Ahearn thought, not any longer.

The sky was darkening and large flakes of snow had begun to fall when Aileen halted next. She was breathing heavily and had perspired mightily in her haste to reach Inverfyre's neighbor, though there was yet no sign of its sentries in the woods. Was the distant keep so poorly guarded as that?

She heard dogs in the woods behind her, and the hoof-beats of horses, as well as the shouts of men. Aileen laid her hand upon her target tree when she stood alongside it, then circled it, anxiously seeking her next mark.

The next silver tree upon her course had a distinctive branch, bent low. It looked as if it had grown beneath a heavy burden.

Aileen's heart clenched. She glanced to the tree upon which she rested her hand and saw the scar upon it, the burl from a lost branch.

Its pulse thumped beneath her hand.

Aileen stepped back in dismay, and heard the gurgle of the river. This could not be! She quickly spied the strange hut again and her heart sank to her toes.

She had made no progress.

She had trodden two circles in the forest.

Aileen buried her face in her hands, felt the fullness of her exhaustion, then looked again. Her eyes did not deceive her. She was returned to precisely the same locale.

Worse, night was falling with a vengeance. Dread touched her heart. What folly it would be to find herself lost in the woods at night! She had slept beneath the pelts of wolves the night before and did not believe that they were the last of their kind hereabouts. No woods in Scotland had been purged of all its wolves, and these woods were wild indeed.

Aileen heard the mournful howl of just such a predator in the distance and shivered at her own recklessness. She was not far enough on her course to be certain that she would make that other keep afore nightfall. She had not escaped her husband, yet she was outside Inverfyre's walls and might not survive the night.

Unless she retraced her steps and begged for leniency.

Aileen's lips set. She would not surrender to the Hawk's will so readily as that. If she was a falcon being trained to savor the lead, she would fight that training for as long as she had the strength to do so.

But how could this have happened? How could she have made such an error in orientation, not just once but twice? How could her father's counsel have so betrayed her? Aileen looked up into the thick swirl of falling snow, fought her frustrated tears, and understood a simple truth.

Her grandmother had had the Sight. Her mother had been said to be mad, but Aileen remembered how her mother had known things she had no means to know. Aileen herself had been born to the caul and her grandmother had watched her avidly in her early years for some hint that she too bore this blessing and curse. But she had never had the slightest foreknowledge of any event.

Until the Hawk had kissed her.

What if the Hawk's touch had only awakened what already lay dormant within Aileen?

The prospect made her mouth go dry. Aileen would have preferred that the Sight had never awakened in her, for she had seen the toll it could demand. She was her mother's daughter, though, so knew better than to spit in the eye of the Fates. Some enchantment guided her path this day. She had been forced back to this hut, time and again, because she was being fed some morsel of which she had need.

She could repeat her mother's error and spurn what she was granted, though she knew the price of that. Aileen stared at the hut, recalling full well how her mother had railed against the burden of the Sight.

Mhairi had lost. Aileen could fight the force that turned her steps this way, as her mother had fought the burden of the Sight, but it was a battle no mortal could win. The sole way to keep her sanity was to cease to fight the power that sought to claim her.

She had to surrender to it.

Aileen straightened, the tree pulsing beneath the weight of her hand, and accepted the burden she was offered. She ceased to seek a means of escape from this hut, she acquiesced to the Sight, and abandoned all pricks of reason.

Reason possessed no map to this territory, after all.

VII

*W*ith each step that Aileen took toward the strange hut, an aged crone named Adaira claimed more of her thoughts. Indeed, Adaira was Aileen and Aileen was Adaira. Aileen had been Adaira when last she donned mortal flesh. Aileen knew that strange fact to be unassailably true.

A mere week before, Aileen would have fought such apparent nonsense with every fiber of her being. Now she knew that it was utterly natural that her footsteps returned unerringly to this hut, for this hut had been her sanctuary when she had been Adaira.

And before that, as well. Ah yes, Anna had huddled here, slandered and spurned and hunted, centuries ago. And there was yet another wraith in the corner, a wraith whose features Aileen could not discern and whose portion of the tale was as yet unclear to her.

It would come. Aileen knew this with utter certainty.

Indeed, she had only to ask to remember. This land, these trees, this hut, had all been infused with memories by herself for her own use. It was her own repository of the past, a memory palace left to endure.

Aileen flattened her hands against the walls of the hut and summoned its myriad tales. She closed her eyes and leaned her brow upon the living walls, gasping at the vigor with which strangely familiar thoughts invaded her own. She sensed relief, she sensed that her arrival had been long awaited and was even overdue.

And then she looked, knowing she could resolve nothing until she knew the truth.

A scene in the forest took shape in her memory and Aileen knew it was this very forest in which she stood. She saw Adaira, so long alone and wretched; no, she was Adaira, striding through the forest to greet the Hawk on his arrival at Inverfyre.

She felt the bittersweet ache in the old woman's heart when the Hawk's party rode into view. Adaira's delight to have lived to see her love again mingled with despair that he was far younger than she. Her joy was entangled with the realization that their debt would not be resolved in that lifetime, that time and forgetfulness were allied against them.

Aileen felt a tear upon her own cheek even as she heard Adaira call out in summons.

Aileen's pulse thundered as the Hawk dismounted, then strode toward her. It was more than foreknowledge, more than recognition, for he was a man who would have snared her eye in any circumstance. She smiled that she found him less attractive in his youth than she did now, shook her head when she sought a hint of his confidence in the stance of his younger self.

Then she tasted the kiss Adaira had forced upon him. She nigh felt his lips soften in reluctant acquiescence and her heart swelled with yearning for him. Aileen savored the kiss, letting Adaira claim her, letting the majestic love she felt for Magnus and the Hawk well up. She felt Adaira try to pry open the Hawk's own memories, try to compel a vision upon him so that he remembered the history between them before it was too late.

She succeeded, but only just. She saw understanding in his eyes, recollection and fear, a reaction with which Aileen could sympathize.

Adaira parted her lips to explain, but there was no time. Aileen saw the arrows coming, and Adaira did not duck their impact. She bared her teeth as they tore into her breast, the pain far exceeding any expectation. Death caught Adaira in his cold clutches and Aileen saw the anguish in the Hawk's eyes before she slipped from Adaira's skin.

Aileen watched from outside that shell of flesh as Adaira died and Aileen's vision glazed with tears at the grief between the two. She lingered, watching the Hawk's despair, his tenderness, his confusion.

Even as she wept for the death of a woman she had not known in this life, for a love fated to go awry, Aileen spread her hands against the walls of the hut, greedy for more. She knew that this was a gift she had left to herself.

To remember was the key, she saw that already.

No wonder she had been drawn to this spot—she had planted the seed in her own thoughts, perhaps turned the very forest to her own will. As Adaira, Aileen knew she had understood many arcane secrets she would never know again.

Aileen peered past that painful parting to a thousand moments in the past. She trembled at the extent of the labyrinth she had entered and yet knew that she alone could find the thread of sense within it. Aileen had been chosen; no, she had chosen to come.

She and the Hawk had been fated to be lovers.

This fantastical tale was blessedly simple, so clear that a

babe could understand it. Aileen understood that the Hawk had wed her because he could wed no other. He had sought her out, though he might well deny it; he had searched for the woman who carried Adaira's spark within her. That was how he had known from a mere glimpse, from a kiss, that Aileen was the wife he must possess.

And his kiss, perhaps by some old contract they two had made, had awakened her own memories of what stood between them. Her challenge was not to evade him, but to win his heart for her own.

The Hawk was her destiny and she was his.

When her hands fell away from the wall, Aileen was trembling and dizzy with all she had seen. There were yet a thousand questions unanswered, though she doubted she had the strength to draw more from this hut without repose. She felt that she had run a hundred miles, and indeed, she had walked far this day.

A sense of urgency plagued her. Aileen had so much to discover, a certainty that there was precious little time to do it, and the Hawk did not believe. Her first course would have to be to persuade him of the truth, for surely they could accomplish more together than apart.

Aileen opened her eyes, fearful yet filled with purpose, and found the snow falling thickly around herself. The sky was dark, the forest around her swathed in a thick layer of fresh white snow. She swallowed and stepped shakily away from the hut, then gasped to find the Hawk not a dozen paces away.

He stood on the periphery of the clearing, his gaze fixed upon her, the reins of his black steed trailing in the snow. Her heart soared, for she half-imagined that she had summoned him to her side by will alone.

Then Aileen saw that the Hawk was displeased. Of course, he was unaware of the revelation she now clutched to her heart, and she had fled from him. He stood straight and tall, his expression inscrutable. His eyes were narrowed and his posture was stiff.

Beneath his steady regard, the conviction wrought by Aileen's vision, the certainty that they were destined to be together, faltered.

"Are you a sorceress?" he asked, his words carrying to her on the white cloud of his breath.

Aileen, her knees weak, shook her head, not understanding his meaning.

He indicated the hut behind her and she turned, her eyes widening in shock. The branches that made the walls and roof of the hut had burst into new leaf since her arrival. Their winter-deadened branches were now dressed in the brilliant green leaves of spring, even as the snow fell thickly around the hut.

She took an unsteady step back. "I did not do this!"

"I fear you did."

Aileen knew the law sufficiently to realize that he had the right to condemn her for sorcery. She knew the fate of witches and the prospect of being burned struck fear to her very marrow. She could almost hear the crackling of skin touched by flame.

She took a deep breath, then faced her spouse anew, hastily confessing what she knew. "I did not do this willingly, for I have never had magical powers of any kind. I must confess, though, that since we met, some such power seems to have awakened within me. I cannot command it, but I do not believe it means ill to either you or myself."

She swallowed, disliking that she could not guess his reaction from his expression. "I know no more than this, I swear it to you." Aileen held the Hawk's gaze, needing his guarantee and hating that her voice faltered. "Do you mean to have me burned, my lord?"

The pause between them was charged, the brightness of his gaze fairly stealing the breath from Aileen's chest.

Then the Hawk strode toward her and took her hand within his. "No," he said, conviction resonating in that single word. Aileen's heart jumped when he kissed her cold palm, his caress sending heat over her flesh. He met her gaze and his voice turned husky. "I am too relieved to find you hale, lady mine, to dispatch you hastily from my side."

Aileen's heart thumped and her knees weakened in her relief. Was it possible that he became more impassive when his emotions threatened to shake his composure? "You feared for me," she guessed.

"I protect all of those beneath my hand," the Hawk said and that ghost of a smile touched his lips. "Even those who would evade that protection."

Aileen parted her lips to apologize, but a wolf howled in the distance, interrupting her. She eased closer to her spouse without a second thought and his arm slipped around her waist. The stallion stamped, impatient to be safely within Inverfyre's walls again.

"There are many predators in Inverfyre's woods," he murmured against her hair, "and I would not see you fall prey to any of them."

His very manner encouraged Aileen. Surely, if she touched him, she might awaken the memories within him, as Adaira had done? Was this not the wager they had wrought?

There was but one way to know. Aileen tipped her head back to meet his steady gaze. She tentatively reached out to touch the Hawk's jaw with her fingertips, letting her fingers trail over the stubble of a day's growth of whiskers, and he did not move away. She licked her lips, noting how he hungrily watched her gesture.

Still he neither pounced upon her nor stepped away.

"Do you include yourself in the company of predators?" she whispered.

He smiled then, not a fleeting smile but one that clung to his lips. "There are those who have suggested as much."

Her heart thundering, Aileen stretched to her toes and brushed her lips across his cheek. "I am persuaded otherwise, husband mine," was all she had time to whisper before his mouth closed demandingly over hers.

The Hawk wanted more, far more, than he had had thus far of his lady wife, and her willing kiss dismissed his caution. Relief added urgency to his embrace. He kissed her with a vengeance, unable to halt when she softened to him.

He had feared to lose her in this woods, either to her flight or to ravenous wolves or the wicked MacLaren clan, and could only admit the depth of his terror now that she was safely in his embrace. The lady welcomed his touch with an enthusiasm that reassured him fully. His blood quickened when she parted her lips to his kiss and desire fairly roared when she arched against him.

Never yet had she greeted him with such ardor and, though he could not guess the root of this response, neither did he care. He was content to partake of the feast she offered.

He wanted to partake of it now.

But no, he would give her what she had asked of him. First, he would court her. Indeed, she might have fled because she was fearful of their first coupling. Who could guess what she had been told of the deed? A courtship alone would win her heart for his own. Though he yearned to hasten, he let her set the pace.

After a languid and promising kiss, Aileen pulled her lips from his. The Hawk let her do so, though he did not release her from his embrace. She was flushed, her breathing quick, her eyes sparkling and her lips reddened. He thought her more beguiling than any woman he had ever seen.

She glanced down and must have seen the evidence of his erection for she blushed crimson. He flicked a telling glance at the hut and her color deepened with understanding.

"Surely, a crude hut in the forest does not suit your ardor," she said, so charmingly breathless that he yearned to kiss her again.

"Surely it matters less where one seeks pleasure than with whom." He traced the curve of her cheek with his fingertip, loving how her eyes darkened.

The lady smiled, the fairest encouragement he could have had. He forgot the wolves and the falling shadows of night, he forgot the restlessness of his steed. There was naught but his lady wife and her sweet kisses.

The Hawk caught Aileen in his embrace again, swinging her into his arms as he kissed her. He carried her into the old hut, intent upon tasting more of the pleasure suddenly roused between them. It was warm here, warmer than it should have been, though perhaps it was the lady's passion alone that heated his blood.

He knew precisely what he would do.

Aileen caught her breath when the Hawk broke his kiss and she realized she lay upon her back, her spouse braced on his elbow above her. She made to sit up, but the weight of his hand upon her waist halted her.

"Perhaps we should take advantage of the first time in days we have been alone together," he suggested.

"I know not what to do," she whispered.

"Do whatsoever you desire to do," he counseled.

Aileen swallowed, but he held her gaze, willing her to trust him. This would all be new to her, and he wanted her to find pleasure. He slowly slid his hand over her ribs, savoring the curve of every bone. She parted her lips, perhaps to speak, but his fingers cupped her breast and she fell silent with a small gasp.

Powerless to resist her, the Hawk kissed his bride anew. Even through the tabard, kirtle and chemise, he could feel her response, could feel her nipple bead beneath his caress. He coaxed her participation, tasting and teasing. Heat raged within him, commanding him to conquer and claim her for all time, but he fought its urgency. He let her set the pace, let the kiss be long and languid.

Finally, he lifted his head and regarded her. She smiled shyly at him, her eyes sparkling with pleasure. "Tell me something of yourself," she urged in a whisper. "Tell me something I have not heard from others."

The Hawk chuckled. So snared was he in his wife's allure that he confessed something he had never intended to confess. "There is a kernel of truth in your challenge of last evening. I know more of these visions than I implied."

The lady's eyes lit with a pleasure that made his heart sing.

"When first I came to Inverfyre," he continued quietly, "I met an old crone, a woman named Adaira who lived in these woods."

"Adaira," Aileen whispered, then nodded approval.

The Hawk refused to give much weight to her acceptance of this name, for she could not have known it. He slid his hand beneath her nape, cradling her against his heat as his other hand slid beneath her skirts. He eased beneath the hem of her chemise, felt the warmth of her knee beneath his hand. The softness of her bare flesh nigh made him forget what he had intended to tell her.

"You knew her?"

"I but met her the once. It was said that she lived in this hut. She, too, spoke of visions," he said, leaving his own memories of the tale aside. "So, you are not the first to have such notions at Inverfyre."

"What happened to her?"

"She died," he said simply, thinking the details unworthy of her attention.

"I envisioned that I was her and she was me," Aileen whispered, apparently more excited by his words than his caress. "Just as you and Magnus are one and the same."

The Hawk frowned, not having intended to divert her attention so fully from their lovemaking. He felt the passion cool between them and fought to recapture what had promised to be a pleasurable interval afore it was fully lost.

"I think such thoughts do not deserve our consideration, particularly in this moment." The Hawk stroked the soft curve of her breast and though she shivered, his lady still was too concerned with whimsy for his preference.

"I disagree." Aileen placed her hands upon his shoulders, compelling him to look into her eyes. Their fathomless blue reminded him of the maiden who had haunted him, the maiden who had been awakened by Adaira's kiss, and the Hawk felt a certain uneasiness. "There is an old curse at work at Inverfyre, one that governs much . . ."

He interrupted her sharply. "No, there is not."

"Yes, there is," she insisted. She tapped his chest with a fingertip. "And it commands the fates of both you and me. It serves nothing to deny this truth . . ."

"No such folly commands me."

Aileen studied him, then her lips set stubbornly. "Heed what I am telling you, for it is of import: there is a spell cast upon you and me . . ."

The Hawk slid his thumb across Aileen's nipple, his patience with this tale exhausted. Her words faltered and fell silent, her eyes widened, but she did not pull away. He moved his hand down over her stomach, feeling the skin become softer and softer, knowing the target he sought.

The lady did not seem to. His fingers slipped between her thighs and she gasped, even as she arched her back toward him.

"Let us see what the spell makes of this," he murmured before he claimed her lips anew.

The Hawk found it bewitching that Aileen responded so keenly to his kisses. Passion was all new to her, that much was evident, and he was not surprised that a laird's sole daughter should have been kept chaste.

He was surprised at the protectiveness that her innocence roused in him, no less by his own urge to coax her passion to a flame, to savor it himself. He kissed her because he could not have denied himself the sweet softness of her lips, the tiny gasps she uttered when his touch surprised her, the astonishment and pleasure in her wide blue gaze.

He was shocked when she welcomed him so readily, astonished when her hands closed over his shoulders. He was enflamed when she parted her lips beneath his, shocked and delighted when her tongue tentatively touched his, astounded when she shyly parted her thighs to his questing fingers. There was naught but Aileen for the Hawk, naught but the fire they roused between them.

Though he had intended solely to awaken her, her passionate response meant that he could no longer cease his caress. Her own ardor dismissed his chivalry. He touched her more boldly when she knotted her fingers into his hair and urged him onward.

Her kiss grew more demanding, her hips began to move, at first slowly then with greater vigor. He knew only the taste of her kiss, the smell of her arousal. He wanted to sample every morsel of her flesh. She was wet and restless with her desire, she moaned into his kiss, she writhed beneath him with an urgency that boded well indeed for the marital bed.

When Aileen reached the summit of her pleasure beneath his hand, the Hawk felt nigh as triumphant as she looked. She shuddered from head to toe and flushed scarlet as she gasped, her fist knotted with painful vigor in his hair. He did not care. Her eyes opened wide, their hue a brilliant sapphire, and he found himself grinning at her amazement.

His courtship proceeded well, to his thinking.

Then the lady spoke.

"Your old falconer, the one who was training peregrines this morn," Aileen whispered, licking her lips in dismay.

The Hawk's victorious mood was shattered so surely that it might never have been. He pulled away slightly. This was not the moment, in his opinion, for his lady to speak of those men pledged to serve him. "You must mean Tarsuinn."

"Tarsuinn," she murmured, as if she tried the name upon her tongue. She closed her eyes and murmured it again, her manner most strange.

The Hawk felt a strange prickling, the sense of someone walking on his grave. He would not have this moment soiled! He bent to kiss his bride again but she averted her face, a frown puckering her brow.

"Tarsuinn. He has a wound upon his shoulder, a scar from

an old wound that was stitched closed." She touched her own right shoulder and met the Hawk's gaze.

"How could you know such a thing?" he demanded, fearing suddenly that some hook had been baited with this tempting maiden. Already there was one spy in his dungeon, a spy captured at a cursedly important time. The Hawk got to his feet, his manner turning cold. "Did your father have spies within my hall?"

"No!"

"Then how can you know of a mark on the flesh of my falconer? You have never been to Inverfyre and you cannot know Tarsuinn, who has not left it since afore you were born."

"I saw it . . ."

"No." The Hawk dismissed this explanation as unworthy of consideration. He paced the small hut, thinking furiously, even as his innards turned cold.

"Nissa," he concluded with certainty. "She gives much credence to these old tales. Indeed, she gathers them. Did she tell of this?"

"No, no, she did not." Aileen shook her head with vigor. "I saw it in my vision." She met his gaze steadily. "I swear it to you that this is so."

To his own dismay, the Hawk was tempted to believe his wife.

Perhaps he simply fell prey to his wife's charms too readily.

"Then, how? Explain yourself, and know that I do not take kindly to deception."

"I do not deceive you!" Aileen was outraged, or feigned it well. She bounded to her feet in turn and shook a finger at him. As irked as he was with her insistence upon this foolery, the Hawk had to admire that the lady was unafraid to challenge him. "It was your kiss that first poured this poison into my thoughts!"

"So you say."

"So I *know*. We must decipher the meaning of these visions and solve the riddle to put it to rest."

The Hawk shook his head. "I refuse to believe such nonsense. There are no visions."

"And I refuse to suffer your obstinacy," his wife retorted, glaring at him. "We shall resolve this matter together or I shall leave."

Fear clutched the Hawk's heart. In his determination to assert his claim over her, he chose the wrong words to soften her stance. "You cannot leave. We are wedded. That pledge is eternal before man and God."

She held his gaze stubbornly. "If my visions are not valid, if they are not to be acknowledged, then I will be said to be mad." Her eyes glinted and he thought of the rumors Blanche had muttered about Aileen's mother. "I refuse to surrender my wits to marriage. No man is worth madness."

"You will surrender more if you venture away from here without my protection," the Hawk retorted. "You are clever enough to know that the world has no place for you if you leave my side. You will have to beg, or whore yourself, or steal."

"Having my wits and my reputation might be compense enough!" She flung out a hand in frustration. "And I would not have to travel far to earn coin as a whore. Your own hall abounds with whores!"

"Men have need of gratification." The Hawk dismissed this concern with a gesture. "Ours is a company of warriors and these women abide here by their own choice."

Aileen snorted. "My mother never was compelled to suffer whores within Abernye's hall. Their presence challenges your assertion that you mean to make a marriage in truth. Would you have whores play nursemaid to your children?"

The Hawk was appalled. "No!"

"No decent women will serve in your hall in its current state. No vassals will entrust their daughters to my training." Aileen shook a finger at him. "My mother always said that distance cools a man's ardor, and fewer bastards in the hall keep coin in the laird's treasury. You could do me the courtesy of dispatching the whores to the village."

The Hawk did not care to be threatened, though there was merit in her request. He folded his arms across his chest and regarded his lady wife, taking no trouble to hide his anger. "Do you threaten me, if I do not comply? I forbid you to leave Inverfyre without my accompaniment or permission."

Aileen glared at him, a rebellious light in her eyes that should have made him cautious.

Instead, he spoke more foolery, so fearful was he of losing her.

He stepped forward until they stood toe to toe, and gathered her untied chemise in his fist. He lifted her onto her toes, though she did not so much as blink. "Leave," he threatened softly, "and you need not return. I shall spurn you forever."

"You need not make the prospect so tempting," she said, her teeth gritted in her anger. "Indeed, I cannot imagine why I would desire to remain with a man who thought so little of my counsel, especially when I tell him what he knows to be right!"

They glared at each other for a charged moment, and the Hawk considered shaking her until her very bones rattled. How vexing this woman could be! She was right, though he was sufficiently irked that he could not admit as much.

Then, to his astonishment, Aileen took a deep breath and glanced down at his fist in her chemise. "We have made this error afore," she said quietly and he knew immediately that it was true.

She laid her hand atop his, and lifted his fingers away, unafraid of him or his anger. "We gain nothing in this battle, and could lose much. Our strength will be in unison, not conflict." Her gentleness disarmed him, her change of mood dissolved his own annoyance.

She looked up at him, her gaze clear. "Understand that I saw this vision, whether that fact pleases you or not," she whispered. "I saw Tarsuinn's wound."

He shook his head. "No, you cannot have."

"And what explanation do you offer instead?" Aileen's expression turned gloriously defiant. "I am not mad. I am not whimsical. I am not a sorceress. I am not the pawn of some traitor in your hall. I saw Tarsuinn's scar."

The Hawk could not summon a word to his lips.

"Do you call me a liar?"

He shook his head, uncertain what to think.

"I would rather that you were right in this," she asserted to his relief. "These visions are not welcome to me, but they come all the same." A tear glistened on Aileen's lashes, though she blinked it away with impatience. "Understand, my lord, that I am more afraid than ever I have been." She appealed to him, her doubts evident in her gaze, as she whispered, "What if this *is* madness? I must make sense of what is happening to me here, if I am not to share my mother's fate. I must find the source of these visions, if I am to keep my wits."

Her unexpected confession pierced his heart and he felt a strange commonality with her. Had he not been frightened when Adaira had seemed to spice his own thoughts? There was but one way to dismiss this whimsy for all time. There was but one way to protect his lady from her fears.

He had to prove her to be mistaken.

"Come." The Hawk lifted Aileen's hand in his. "Let us find Tarsuinn with all haste and prove this to be the nonsense that it is."

The Hawk and his bride found Tarsuinn in the moulting house. There must have been a dozen boys working beneath the falconer's command. Peregrines were being bathed, stroked and fed, and several boys were singing softly to their restless charges. Though it was evening, there was still labor to be done.

Tarsuinn moved from one to the next, his advice kindly but firm. His face was red from his exertions this day, for he had grown plumper on Inverfyre's fare. He secured a peregrine's tether with care, talking gently to the creature all the while. The apprentice beside him watched with keen eyes.

It was not yet time to take young birds from their parents' nests, and these were eyasses claimed at least the year before. Tarsuinn's skill was legendary, and he never relinquished a bird for sale until he was convinced that her training was flawless. The Hawk could see the admiration the boys felt for their master as they watched him. They learned a valuable trade beneath Tarsuinn's hand and learned it from one of the greatest falconers in Christendom.

It was soothing here, for the birds were all hooded and Tarsuinn would not tolerate a disturbance that might frighten his charges. Several fidgeted on their perches, and the bells affixed to their ankles rang quietly as they moved.

"Tarsuinn, might we trouble you for a moment?" The Hawk had known the falconer all of his life and his loyalty was beyond question. As a result, there was such respect between the two men that the laird refused to command Tarsuinn away from his labor on a mere whim.

The falconer turned, though his eyes widened at the sight of Aileen. He bowed hastily, but the Hawk had seen his dismay and wondered at its cause.

What fear had Tarsuinn of Aileen?

What did he know of her that the Hawk did not?

How could he know her? The Hawk thought again of treachery, of the cursed MacLaren clan and their endless schemes. Uncertainty gnawed within him and he feared that he might have claimed this bride with too much haste.

"At your service, my lord and lady," Tarsuinn said.

The Hawk nodded to Aileen. "My lady has a question for you."

Tarsuinn smiled encouragingly.

"Forgive me, Tarsuinn, but I would ask a bold favor of you."

The falconer's gaze flicked to his laird's who nodded approval. He bowed to Aileen again. "Whatsoever my lady desires, of course."

"Did the wound on your shoulder heal without a scar?"

Tarsuinn paled and he almost took a step back. When he spoke, his words were thick. "What wound would that be, my lady?"

"The one you sustained in the siege of Inverfyre."

The Hawk looked to his bride in surprise. From whence had she learned such a detail? Even he had not known that Tarsuinn had been wounded in aiding Evangeline to escape burning Inverfyre.

Aileen's tone was firm with her conviction. "The one which Adaira stitched for you, while Evangeline of Inverfyre watched."

The Hawk's blood chilled.

Tarsuinn stepped forward, though his discomfiture was clear. "See for yourself, my lady," he said unevenly, and pulled his tabard and chemise down from his neck. A fine white line was evident there, though none would have noted it in passing. "Nigh forty years have faded it much, I fancy."

The scar was older than the Hawk's bride, perhaps older than her mother would have been. The hair began to stand on the back of his neck.

Aileen could have no memory of this!

The Hawk watched as his bride touched Tarsuinn's scar with a shaking finger, running her fingertip along its length with a familiarity undeserved. Her voice was surprisingly deep when she spoke, as if it was not her own.

Indeed, she spoke with a surety even beyond that she had already shown. "Inverfyre, under all its names, has long been a contested land, and the combatants of each epoch have oft had much in common with the combatants of the past. It is a place of some witchery, a place that casts a light into the heart of all those who pass its threshold, a place that condemns many of them to return again and again."

Tarsuinn had the pallor of fresh milk now. The Hawk guessed the falconer had heard these words afore, though he still refused to accept how his bride knew them.

Aileen nodded with the resolve of one much older than her own years. Indeed, her posture was more bent, like that of an old woman, and he noted that her eyes were closed.

"One hears of ghosts in this land, of souls condemned to haunt a locale or rest uneasy," she intoned. "Mine is a tale of ghosts, if you will. Two souls I speak of, two souls whose fates are entwined like two plies of a rope. And like the plies of that rope, neither can be strong or complete without the other."

The Hawk looked between the two of them, uncertain what to do about his wife's odd manner. Would he injure her by forcing her to awaken? Would she be more wounded if she continued? She had already confessed fear that she became mad beneath his care and he was keenly aware of his responsibility to her.

The boys who aided Tarsuinn lingered around the perimeter, their eyes wide. Tarsuinn perspired freely, but he did not step away from the lady. Indeed, he did not seem to breathe.

Aileen nodded again, as slowly as a sage. Her finger worried Tarsuinn's wound, sliding back and forth, guided by some compulsion. "Magnus Armstrong was drawn to Inverfyre to meet his fated partner, to put an ancient crime to rest, to release these two souls from the confines of Inverfyre. It is the fate of these two to return time and again to Inverfyre. By divine compensation, they have the chance to set an old wrong to right, to seek each other anew each time their souls don a cloak of flesh."

She shook her head and the Hawk suppressed a shiver. "But the gods are not kind. No, they are tricksters, each and every one of them. They give with one hand while stealing with the other. The chance of winning eternity together was what they offered to this pair, but memory of the tale was what they stole. By the time Magnus understood the price of his own ambition, he had betrayed his destined lover yet again and lost her companionship for yet another mortal life."

Aileen tapped her fingertip on the Hawk's arm without glancing at him. Goosepimples rose on his flesh, as if a shade had stepped among them.

"Evangeline's son is Magnus Armstrong in new guise, as well as all the other men Magnus was afore. The wheel turns, the soul takes flesh again, and each course through the world is destined to teach some morsel of a higher truth."

Enough! The Hawk seized his wife's shoulder, not liking this fey mood a whit. "Aileen!" Her pupils were so tiny as to be invisible and she stared at him unseeingly. "Lady mine, what claims your wits?" He shook her, his voice rising when she did not respond. "Aileen, answer me!"

Her eyes rolled back, her lips parted and she fell limp. The Hawk caught her as she fainted, then looked to Tarsuinn, seeking an explanation.

"I knew it was her," the falconer muttered. "I knew from the first glimpse of her that she walked among us again." He crossed himself with vigor and licked his lips. "Upon my soul, my lord, those were the very words uttered by Adaira when she tended this wound. I swear it to you."

The Hawk shivered then in truth. The alarmed boys crossed themselves and more than one took a step back.

"That cannot be so," he insisted. "She cannot know such a detail. You must be in error, for it cannot be true."

"But still it is." Tarsuinn swallowed, then took a shuddering breath. His normal garrulousness returned now that Aileen was silent. "It was nigh thirty-eight years ago, my lord, when Malachy and I led your mother away from burning Inverfyre. She only left her home for the sake of the child in her womb; she left that you might survive. The MacLarens would have killed her to ensure that no blood heir of Inverfyre could ever be born. She was the last of your lineage, the last afore you."

"Just as I am last," the Hawk murmured, with no intent of doing so. He stared down at Aileen, his very flesh creeping. The old crone's words, just repeated by his lady wife, echoed in his thoughts. He fought the wild claim, even as his heart whispered that it was time enough he saw the truth.

It seemed that he, too, fell prey to madness. It was not the trait he had hoped he and his bride would have in common.

It was not a trait men sought in their leader. It was imperative that the Hawk not lose the support of his men in these last days afore his triumph was complete.

Tarsuinn looked at Aileen, and shook himself visibly. "Adaira found us in the woods and spoke those very words, my lord, as she stitched my wound. I never forgot them. Adaira even sounded thus, her voice low and thick, my lord. This was most uncommon! How your lady could have known such details, I cannot say, but I have gooseflesh." Tarsuinn shivered, then forced a laugh and waved the curious boys back to work with a chiding jest.

He halted then and glanced back at his lord, his voice falling low so that only the Hawk could hear his words. "I knew it was her, my lord. When I first saw your bride, I had the strange conviction that Adaira had taken flesh to walk among us again."

"It is madness to make such a claim, Tarsuinn, madness in defiance of all the church's teachings."

"I know. I know." Tarsuinn licked his lips and glanced about himself, then leaned closer. "But sometimes I recall the tales my father told and I cannot dismiss them so readily as that. Sometimes I fear there is truth in these old tales, truth that many would prefer not to heed."

With a last significant glance and a pat on the Hawk's arm, he turned away.

The Hawk studied Aileen, her visage pale, and could not summon a reasonable explanation for what he had witnessed.

Save the one he struggled against.

Tarsuinn gestured to his apprentices and the Hawk spoke to the boys, though his thoughts churned. His lady limp in his arms, he made excuses for the strain she had recently faced, the words sounding as thin as old soup even to his own ears. He spoke with surety and tried to halt rumor afore it started. All the same, he knew that the tale of his lady's fey manner would be whispered through the kitchens and stables in a matter of moments.

He cared less for that than for the lady herself. The fact remained that his wife's affliction was both his fault and his responsibility, though he had not an inkling of what he could do to heal her.

And that was worrisome indeed.

VIII

The Hawk carried Aileen to her chamber and laid her upon the bed, his thoughts in chaos and his doubts growing.

He called for a brazier, a jug of wine, some cold victuals in case she awakened with a hunger. Nissa showed great consternation for Aileen when she brought these things, and the Hawk marveled that the two women could have forged such a bond so quickly. Old Gunna, too, fairly shed a tear in her concern, though the Hawk had never seen the competent servant show any emotion at all. The hall seemed uncommonly clean, though he would have readily confessed that was not a matter that concerned him overmuch.

What magic had his wife wrought in his home?

Aileen slept like a child through all of the bustle. The Hawk dismissed the servants, locked the portal and stood beside the bed, staring down at his wife.

Was she mad? If so, then so was he, for he had had a similar experience with Adaira years past. Was she a sorceress? He was astonished by how little he cared. Perhaps his lady wife had cast a spell upon him.

If nothing else, she was an enigma that he was tempted to solve.

The shadows were deep at this hour, but the light from the brazier touched Aileen's features with gold. She looked soft and sweet as she slept and he wondered how any man could have called her plain of face.

She was not an obvious beauty, but there was dignity in her stance and intelligence in her eyes, and kindness softened the curve of her lips. She certainly was not wrought of ice, for it was fire that leapt between the two of them when they touched. Perhaps they shared an affinity.

The Hawk paced the chamber, knowing the name of that affinity well enough. He glanced back at his bride, considering what had happened this day, and tried to find a reason beyond the one she presented. It was possible that she had met with someone in the forest, for she had not progressed far during the day. That person could have told her of Tarsuinn and his scar, but the tale seemed more fanciful than the more obvious conclusion.

Dubhglas MacLaren had been a boy at the siege of Inverfyre. The Hawk's heart clenched in acknowledgment that he would have known about Tarsuinn's scar.

But Aileen insisted that she was Adaira taken flesh again and he was tempted to believe her. The Hawk shoved his hand through his hair and paced with new vigor. He had no doubt that such a feat was possible, for he had tasted the power of a vision in Adaira's embrace. He knew how terrifying that experience could be, and could understand Aileen's utter certitude that she had seen the truth.

But was it the truth? The Hawk did not know. He paused at the side of the bed and stared down at her, wishing he could put his trepidation aside, wishing he dared to trust her fully.

In two short days, there would be nothing else to fear, for all would be resolved. In two short days, he could share the story of what Adaira had done to him. In two short days, there would be no secrets between them.

It was but a blink of an eye, in terms of a lifetime, and yet it was an eternity. It seemed too long to endure.

If Aileen was not a spy, then her woes were all his fault. Tenderness and guilt consumed him in equal measure. Though he was responsible, he would never surrender his bride.

Indeed, he could not step away from the bed. He removed the boots he had had wrought for her while she slept, and admired the graceful shape of her legs. Though his intent had been to see to her comfort, a much less innocent flame of desire kindled within him.

He unlaced Aileen's tabard and eased her out of it. He unlaced her kirtle and coaxed her limp limbs from it, as with the chemise beneath. She was long and slender, her flesh fair, her nipples dark in contrast. Her breasts were high and firm—she was young and strong. There were freckles on her shoulders and her chest, the sight of them making him smile. He unbraided her hair as she dreamed and fanned it across the linens. The light danced within it and over her curves, gilding her more richly than any adornment he could have given her.

He pulled the pelts over her, reluctant to hide her from sight but not wanting her to be chilled. These dozen pelts were from wolves the Hawk had killed himself at Inverfyre. They had tormented the group of conquerors during the first years, wily predators that they were, and he alone had hunted them with success.

He had killed them to protect the people sworn to his service. It was his duty to these souls to see them safe, regardless of the risk to himself. He had had the hides tanned and kept for the bed of the bride he would ultimately take, hoping that the lady in question would understand that he meant to protect her as vigorously as he protected his holding and vassals.

His mother had taught him that duty could not be compromised.

Aileen nestled beneath the pelts, sighed in apparent contentment, and smiled. The Hawk's heart clenched. He bent, enchanted, and touched his lips to her brow.

And the lady awakened with a start.

She gasped, clutching the fur to her chest. He retreated, but sat at the foot of the bed, leaning against one of the bed's pillars. He cursed himself silently for so effectively ensuring her fear on the night of her abduction, and resolved to see the matter behind them immediately.

It was time enough that he began to court her in earnest.

"How do you fare?" the Hawk asked quietly.

Aileen caught her breath and glanced about herself. She peeked beneath the pelts and her cheeks flushed in a most delightful way. "Did Nissa . . ."

"I undressed you."

Aileen peered beneath the pelts at the linens, trying to be discreet, but her spouse knew what she sought.

"You are convinced that I intend to rape you."

"I cannot imagine why you would not do so. As long as our match remains unconsummated, it could be annulled."

The Hawk ensured that his tone was mild. "Would it be more fitting to earn your hatred than to await your welcome?"

She seemed surprised by his question and he sighed that she thought so little of his character.

He leaned closer. "Aileen, our match will be consummated when you come to me and not before."

She stared at him and he knew that he had astonished her. "But it is your right . . ."

"And I would have it be our mutual pleasure, as I tried to show you this very day." The Hawk smiled and she smiled in return, though neither of them spoke of her vision. When the silence stretched overlong, he tried to ease her trepidation with a teasing comment. "It would suit me well if you did not take overlong to consider the matter."

She regarded him and he fancied that she could read his very thoughts. "But you leave much risk by this choice."

"I like a measure of risk." The Hawk shrugged when she seemed unpersuaded. "And indeed, where is the joy of victory if one's opponent has no choice but to surrender?"

Her fair brow arched. "That did not seem troubling on the night you compelled me to wed you."

The Hawk felt his neck heat with guilt, though he admired that she was not afraid to rebuke him. "Winning you was of too great an import to be left to chance," he said gruffly.

She looked skeptical still and he claimed her hand. "Understand this, lady mine. However poorly they have begun, I would have these nuptials end well for both of us."

"Why did you not court me?"

"I feared you would underestimate my charms."

She looked at him quickly, as if uncertain whether he made a jest at his own expense. He smiled slightly and studied her fingertips, so delicate against his own, as he sought the words. "I apologize for not believing your claim about the visions."

"You believe me now?"

"I told you once that I learned during my childhood that

many apparently impossible marvels are oft true." The Hawk moved closer and, to his relief, she did not move away. "Your words in the falconry were an echo of what the old healer Adaira had told Tarsuinn when she mended his wound nigh forty years ago."

Aileen's eyes widened. "Truly?"

"Truly."

She looked as astonished as he felt. "Then it did happen," she mused. "I thought I had but dreamed it."

He ran his thumb across her knuckles. "It was never my intent to drive you to madness, Aileen."

She did not smile, but shivered elaborately. "These visions are most uncanny."

"I know."

Aileen turned her bright gaze upon him, as if she would rout his secrets. "Because you have seen them, too," she said with a certainty undeserved. It was his intent to deny as much, but the lady laid a fingertip across his lips. "But you would prefer to forget that any madness had ever claimed your wits."

"I would prefer that my men do not doubt my wits."

She tilted her head, her gaze piercing once again. "What happened when you met Adaira of the woods?"

Despite his urge to confide in her, his throat closed over the truth. "Nothing. She died. As I already said."

The Hawk rose and paced the chamber, feeling the weight of his wife's gaze upon him. He was not yet prepared to surrender all of his secrets to his beguiling wife. In less than a week, she had stormed his ramparts with alarming ease, and still he knew so little of her.

Two days. He braced his hands upon the sill and stared out into the falling darkness, silently cursing the flickering light on the tower of the MacLaren clan.

The last sliver of the moon sailed high in the sky, casting a feeble light across the lands that would soon be completely his own. The new moon would be the following evening, and his pulse quickened at the thought.

On the morrow, when darkness fell, they would ride out and reclaim the last vestige of traditional Inverfyre. Before the sun rose the following morn, he would enter what remained of Inverfyre's chapel. He would touch the graves of his forebears for the first time. He would claim the last morsel that was his birthright.

He scanned the walls, counting the sentries, eyeing the gates, and found all as it should have been. He surveyed the river and the forest, seeking a hint of something amiss.

It was of critical import that nothing go awry at this point. It was of critical import that he not stumble, as Alasdair had feared he would stumble, that he not let the conundrum of his bride undermine his determination.

Aileen would be his bride for many years ahead. Matters between them could wait one more day and night to be resolved. He should be walking the walls, ensuring the security of Inverfyre, not lingering in his lady's chambers.

But the Hawk found he could not summon the will to leave. What spell had Aileen cast to snare him so effectively?

What could he do to bind her loyalty to him?

He pivoted to meet her gaze. "Tell me of your skill with archery," he urged. Her expression became guarded immediately and she averted her face. "Tell me, Aileen, what happened between you and Blanche. I know that you have more skill than you showed that day in the forest."

She lifted her chin, her eyes gleaming. "How could you know such a thing, if indeed it were true?"

He smiled. "I am a warrior and not unfamiliar with a bow

myself. I saw how your hands fitted to the weapon, I saw your familiarity with it and your ease. And I saw you change your stance in the last moment afore you loosed the arrow." He held her gaze unswervingly. "I know that you deliberately made a poor shot and I do not blame you for it. I ask only for the tale."

She folded her arms across her chest. "So that you can despise me that my inclinations are not womanly?"

The Hawk let his smile broaden. "On the contrary, I can think of no skill more fitting for my bride than that of defending herself and her home. This gives us an understanding in common, Aileen."

Aileen watched her husband, her inclinations at war within her. She was filled with Adaira's conviction, the old words echoing in her ears. She and the Hawk were destined to be together and she wondered how best to persuade him of what she knew to be true.

She was much reassured by his pledges. A fighting man would live and die by his pledge, and she had believed his intent to be true. She liked that he put the choice into her hands. It was time enough that she accepted the man she was coming to know instead of simply believing his foul repute.

It was time she earned his trust.

She swallowed and looked down, stroking the pelt with her fingertips. "I trained with a bow from an early age. I suspect my father only indulged me at first, for I was persistent, but I soon showed skill with it. My mother endorsed my choice and persuaded my father to train me further." She met his regard. "I found more satisfaction in an arrow finding its mark than a spindle fat with fine thread."

He smiled that seductive half-smile. "This I understand well enough."

"And then, just over a year ago, my mother died." Aileen frowned, than hastened on. "And my father returned from the king's court with Blanche upon his arm. She did not want another woman's daughter in her abode, especially as we are nigh of an age. I suppose I can understand that she did not like my father's affection for me."

"That is the mark of a selfish soul, lady mine," the Hawk scoffed. "Affection is to be shared, for it replenishes itself in greater measure once spent."

They shared a smile across the chamber that heated Aileen's flesh.

The Hawk arched a brow. "I shall guess that she named your skill as the reason why you were not wedded, and insisted that your father compel you to cease."

Aileen sobered, and felt her anger anew. "She burned my bow." She met the Hawk's gaze. "She seized it and burned it before the company as she mocked me. It had been a gift from my mother's kin, carved to my hand. It was mine and mine alone and she had no right to destroy it."

The Hawk's eyes gleamed. "And your father? Surely he demanded at least an apology from her?"

Aileen blinked and looked away, bitterness rising within her. "He told me that Blanche had named the matter aright and that I would forgot my foolery in time."

"Then he is the fool," the Hawk said sharply, his anger warming Aileen's heart.

"I thank you for that," she said. Their gazes locked and held, and Aileen's mouth went dry with her desire for his touch.

Perhaps she could explain the force of his kisses to him in this moment when they seemed of one accord.

"Do you have a memory palace?" she asked.

The Hawk frowned and shook his head.

"It is not a possession as such, but a trick with one's thoughts." Aileen smiled, stroking a pelt as she spoke. "My father taught me to build a memory palace to better recall whatsoever one must. In your mind, you construct a palace, chamber by chamber, and in each chamber resides some detail that must be recalled, oft with some item that will prompt recollection of the whole."

"Grant me an example," the Hawk said, and he looked to be intrigued.

Aileen closed her eyes, sitting up straighter. "My palace is much like Abernye, but beyond its gates and the hall and the kitchen is a walled garden. I can see the stones in the wall, I can feel the sun upon my back, I can smell the roses in blossom in the very center of the garden. They reach for the sun, their blooms of richest red. There are three plants and, in their midst, I always find my mother sitting and waiting for me." Aileen smiled and felt herself flush slightly.

"You must mean your blood mother, of whom you are clearly fond."

Aileen nodded. "My mother loved roses, you see, so she is in the garden of my memory palace. She labored long to persuade them to grow at Abernye, but with limited success. This is how I recall her features, as clearly as if I saw her just moments past." Her tone turned fierce. "I will never forget her, whatever my father and Blanche would prefer."

"And so you should not."

Aileen eyed her spouse, but he smiled.

Crinkles appeared around his eyes, making him look less harsh. "No one has the right to tell you where to grant your heart, lady mine."

Did he refer to himself? Aileen could not guess. She held his gaze and continued her account, liking how intently he listened. "There are three rosebushes because my mother had three sisters, and they always surrounded her similarly when they visited Abernye." She smiled in recollection. "Within those blossoms, I see their faces as well. Around the roses are smaller plants, daisies and such, one for each of their children and named for them in my memory palace."

"This seems a most useful tool." The Hawk sat beside her on the bed again.

"But more than that. I tell you of this only so I can explain what happens when you kiss me." She took a deep breath, sensing that he would resist her notion. "It seems that some unseen hand opens doors in my memory palace, doors to chambers that I had never guessed were there."

"Chambers you had forgotten were there," he suggested cautiously.

Aileen considered this, then nodded in agreement. "Yes. Chambers I did not know were there but which seem familiar once I spy them. It is most curious. And when I laid my hands upon the walls of Adaira's hut, the doors flew open with such force that you might have been summoned to my side by the sound of them crashing back on their hinges."

She glanced up before the Hawk could school his expression and she saw that he knew this sense all too well. Then he looked down at her fingertips, a slight frown between his brows, and she could not fathom his thoughts.

But then, had she not been fearful of the import of her visions? She had drunk more deeply of the well and was reassured by that draught, but the first sip had been terrifying. What had the Hawk seen when Adaira kissed him? Silence stretched between them for a moment, a silence filled with a thousand uncertainties.

Then Aileen knew that she would have to guide her spouse on this path, just as he had guided her in the unfamiliar land of passion this very day.

She tentatively touched the Hawk's hand, then, emboldened, stroked his flesh. His was a strong hand, his fingers long and tanned, a minute scar upon one knuckle. She marveled at how much larger his hand was than hers, appreciated then how gentle he was with her. "Do you think that it will always be thus when we embrace?" she asked.

"What do you mean?"

Aileen met his gaze unswervingly. "The visions descend into my thoughts when you kiss me. Do you think there is a certain number of them that must appear, or will there always be another?"

Something flickered in his eyes, then he granted her that crooked smile that made her heart leap. "There is but one way to know, lady mine," he murmured. "Are you as bold as your words oft are?"

"Would you rather I was meek and silent?"

"No." His gaze roved over her as if he found her to be a marvel. "Even when you vex me, I like that you have thoughts of your own."

"Even when I cast the dogs from the kitchens and insist the rushes be replaced?"

His smile broadened. "Even then."

"I suppose Gregory sought your disapproval of my scheme."

He chuckled slightly and kissed her knuckles. "You suppose aright. He was most flustered, but you showed good sense. I did not challenge your edict."

Aileen felt curiously pleased by this. She dared to ask yet more of him. "Would I not irk you even if I were to ask you to find a priest to live at Inverfyre?"

His gaze flicked away as he considered this. "It is true that no priest has come from Stirling since Malcolm . . ." His words faded and his frown deepened.

"Malcolm?"

He met her gaze steadily. "The last priest who came to Inverfyre never made it to our gates alive. His death was not a kind one. I vowed never to send for another until the roads were clear of brigands."

Aileen stifled a shiver, for she understood that there was more to this tale than he would tell her. "Are they not safe yet?"

He shook his head, his gaze lifting to the window again. "Far from it. So long as the MacLaren clan survive and wish ill upon those at Inverfyre, the road to our gate will be treacherous."

"But within the walls?"

The Hawk's expression turned fierce. "It is safe within my walls for all I pledge to protect."

Aileen knew herself to be within this company and found his conviction more than reassuring. She dropped her gaze to their entwined hands and knew she dared not lose this moment to ask his favor.

"I would ask you then, as I have promised to ask, whether a priest might come to live at Inverfyre," Aileen said, her words tumbling forth in their haste to be heard. "I understand that the mass has not been sung within these walls for several years and that there are children unchristened in the village. It is unseemly to consign one's vassals to hellfire by denying them the sacraments . . ."

The warmth of the Hawk's thumb landed upon Aileen's lips, silencing her. "And you would have me see to their salvation, as a lord should do."

Aileen nodded.

"You understand that my concern lies in risking the life of any man summoned to sing the services here. It is not fitting to have the blood of priests upon one's hands."

"What of Father Gilchrist in my father's hall? Would you or your men not have killed him?"

The Hawk smiled. "I had hoped you would be so readily persuaded of the wisdom of wedding me that such a deed would not be necessary." There was something hard in his eyes, though, something that told Aileen that the Hawk did not suffer obstacles to his desires easily.

She looked to their hands again. "Your tactics were not encouraging."

"I strive to improve them," he murmured, then kissed her behind one ear with such languor that Aileen shivered. "You must report diligently upon my progress."

"You seem to fare well enough," she acknowledged, then pulled away. "But you evade the matter of a priest."

"The matter will be resolved in its own time," the Hawk said, his voice low but firm.

Aileen stared at him. "What manner of answer is this?"

"The best one that you shall have on this night."

Aileen parted her lips to argue with him, then noted how avidly he watched her. Was this a test of her trust in him?

"Fair enough," she murmured. "I shall be patient, for a time."

A smile touched the Hawk's lips at this and Aileen found herself smiling in return. Indeed, it seemed suddenly warm in her chambers, though she could not avert her gaze from the bright gleam of his eyes.

"You should kiss me," she whispered.

The Hawk shook his head slowly, though his intent manner told Aileen that he did not spurn her. "Do we not have an agreement? I fear that you must kiss me first."

Aileen caught her breath. Her hand stilled within his grasp and she expected that he could feel the race of her pulse. He sat so still that he might have been wrought of stone.

Aileen watched her husband for a moment that seemed to endure through eternity.

And then she squared her shoulders, letting the wolf pelt fall from her breasts. The Hawk caught his breath even as she rose to her knees and closed the distance between them.

"You show your mettle, Aileen," he whispered with approval.

Aileen smiled, encouraged, pleased to hear him use her name. She lifted his hand in hers, and placed it upon the indent of her waist. She framed his face in her hands and fairly leaned her breasts against his chest.

He swallowed and she watched, her own breathing quick.

"We could consider this solely a test of the power of the visions," she whispered.

"We could."

"Although, it appears that you have some desire for me," she mused playfully. "It is possible that the test itself could become forgotten . . ."

"And entirely likely that it should do so." The Hawk's brow arched and his thumb stroked her waist. "For I have a most unholy desire for you. Are you prepared to take such a risk?"

Aileen sighed in mock concern. "I suppose for the sake of knowing the truth, some risk must be incurred."

"Indeed."

"But I know so little of granting kisses."

"Even those that begin badly oft end well, perhaps not unlike nuptial nights." He smiled encouragement, the sight making her feel invincible. "That is all you have need of knowing."

"It can only be so if both parties are willing," she teased.

He chuckled then. "I assure you that this party is most willing."

Aileen smiled, then sobered anew. She leaned against him and heard him catch his breath. She framed his face in her hands and half-feared he had ceased to breathe. She pressed her lips to his and his warm scent inundated her. He parted his lips, letting her proceed as she desired, and his deed snared her fully.

Aileen arched demandingly against him, loving how he groaned when she slid her tongue between his teeth. He caught her closer and deepened their kiss as if he could do naught else. Desire roared within her and she closed her eyes, surrendering her all to this consuming embrace.

A heat flooded through the Hawk beneath Aileen's caress, his heart swelling as his bride embraced him willingly. He restrained himself with an effort, granting her time to conquer her uncertainty. His thumb worked back and forth against the softness of her flesh, for he could not hold back fully.

Indeed, he clenched his other fist in the linens. He let her taste him, felt her tremble, let her fingertips dance over him. Like butterflies, they seemed hesitant to land fully upon him.

Then she pressed her lips to his more firmly. She was innocent, but she warmed to her task. She slipped her fingers into his hair, then tightened her grip. She pulled him against her, loosing the restraints he had wrought for himself. Her tongue slipped between his teeth, dueling with his own, and he could not help but catch her closer. They rolled across the bed, limbs entangled, passion enflamed.

The moment was upon them, and to the Hawk's thinking, it came not a heartbeat too soon.

Then, in his mind's eye, he suddenly saw again the image that Adaira had once conjured. Two plies of a rope twined through his thoughts, intruding in a most unwelcome manner, the plies twisting like a Celtic tattoo. Aileen's kiss grew more bold and he could see the rope, see the plies entwined, see that it was stronger with the two plies than with one.

Then the Hawk saw that the plies were two serpents in truth, their sinuous lengths entwined, their forms writhing about each other. He shivered in revulsion and a serpent seemed to slide down his spine, cold and wet.

A serpent awakened by his lady's embrace.

The treachery he had feared was within Inverfyre's own walls.

Nay, it was within this very chamber!

He broke their kiss and leapt from the bed. His breathing was heavy, his entire being disheveled. He certainly was not flushed with pleasure as Aileen seemed to be. She smiled at him and his innards clenched.

She was triumphant.

He had taken a sorceress to his bed, a viper to his breast, and she had treacherously slipped dark poison into his thoughts. With the oldest wiles known to mankind, she distracted him from his vigilant guard of the prize of Inverfyre. That Aileen was so pleased only fed the fear that had seized him.

Who had told him of Aileen of Abernye? The Hawk could not recall, though he could not forget who other than Tarsuinn would know of Adaira.

Dubhglas MacLaren had been at the siege of Inverfyre. He had lurked on the borders for years now, seeking a chance to steal back what his family had stolen afore. And how had Aileen run all the day long but gone no further than Adaira's old hut? Had she met with one of the MacLaren clan? Had she learned details that could be used against him? Why did she seduce him in this moment? The Hawk lunged to the window, seeking a hint of some dark event he had missed.

All was tranquil.

His gaze rose to the distant keep of the treacherous MacLaren clan, the last bit of Inverfyre's soil that he had yet to reclaim. Though all appeared calm, he knew that there was a taint in the air. He did not trust the evidence before his eyes. He had to walk the walls, he had to discern the breach that he knew must be there.

Aileen sighed contentment, seemingly oblivious to his distress. "There was no vision," she whispered, her eyes sparkling in a most fetching way. "Can you command them so readily as that?"

"This dark force is not beneath my command," he snapped.

Her eyes widened slightly at his harsh tone. Her gaze darted to his clenched fists and she must have misunderstood the reason for his anger.

"Was I too bold?"

"We will not speak of it."

She swallowed, then rose to her knees, letting the pelts fall to the mattress. "You are right. This is no time for chatter." The flickering candlelight caressed her glorious curves again and she smiled so fetchingly that he was tempted. "I would welcome you to my bed this night, my lord."

The Hawk's pulse leapt, but duty made him take a step back. He would not make an error guided by passion alone. If he consummated this match, it would be with full trust of his lady wife.

Trust he did not possess in this moment.

"I fear I have demanded your passion too soon," he said

with resolve, pivoting so that he would not have to see her response. The lady could melt his resistance with a glance, and he was too unsettled by her potent kiss to risk as much.

He dared not be seduced to a fatal error. He could nigh feel the serpent within him, feel its cold slime, and he wanted naught other than to scrub himself fiercely from head to toe. He marched to the portal and paused there without looking back. He took a deep breath, though it did little to slow his raging pulse.

Solitude would grant him time to muster his thoughts, to reclaim his sense, to assess what had just occurred. It would allow him the chance to be certain whether she was part of a conspiracy to distract him in a critical moment.

And the frivolity of a hunt might coax the confidence of the MacLaren clan yet higher.

"I shall hunt on the morrow," the Hawk said crisply, deciding as much in that very moment. The hunt would give his party a chance to confirm that the borders were secure. "You need not concern yourself with my presence. Nissa will show you the keep. I ask that you do not leave the hall before my return."

Silence filled the chamber and the Hawk knew that his rejection of his bride's charms had stung. Still he could not force the serpents from his thoughts, nor could he quell his revulsion of them.

"Of course," Aileen said finally, sharpness creeping into her tone. "My lord's will is my command."

He glanced back. She still sat upon the mattress, her nipples pert in the evening's chill. She was a fetching sight, particularly as her lips were set and her eyes snapped with anger.

"I would not have matters so formal between us," he suggested, not liking that he was responsible for her mood but unable to return to the bed as she clearly desired. "You need not address me as your lord when we are alone."

"Shall I call you Magnus?" She tossed her hair over her shoulder. "Or Michael?"

His smile was thin. "The choice is yours, lady mine."

"Then I shall call you Hawk," she said with a defiance that nigh dismissed his trepidation. She folded her arms across her chest and held his gaze stubbornly. "For your repute seems to fit your nature well. Does the hawk not tear out the heart of what it kills, then leave the rest as carrion?"

That the lady was vexed with him was most clear.

"I would not know," the Hawk said with a temperance he did not feel. "I do not hunt with hawks, but with peregrines."

"Are they not the same manner of predator?"

The Hawk shook his head. "The peregrine is said to hunt with rare grace." The lady snorted, but before she could speak, he left her chamber.

He hesitated but a moment before he turned the key in the lock behind him. Indeed, he dared do naught else. He heard her swear in a most unladylike manner at the audible tumble of the lock and his own frown deepened.

Had he erred in this? The Hawk could not be certain, but he dared not risk trusting Aileen too much too soon.

Even if he felt a cur for rejecting the feast she offered.

He descended the stairs, feeling a weight settle over his shoulders. He would dream this night and he knew it well. He would dream of the carnage that had accompanied his claiming of Inverfyre, he would dream of bloodshed, he would be tormented that it had not yet been enough. He would be haunted by a vision of the original site of Inverfyre's keep, of the burned foundation stones, of the soil his forebears had walked and of the turf he had yet to make his own.

All of those he had cut down would visit him this night, point their rotted fingers at him and remind him that he had failed.

Had he been so foolish as to slumber with his bride this night, she would have found the horror of Inverfyre, of his violent nightmares, abed with her. There are men who might have found that a fitting punishment for her Jezebel's kiss, but the Hawk still could not so convict his bride. She might be a treacherous spy, but he could not make her suffer the presence of the demons she had roused.

Morning would find him tired and surly, he knew. Woe to any prey that dared to cross his path on the morrow's hunt, woe to any spy of the MacLaren clan fool enough to be caught. The Hawk would not be merciful—it was better that he hunt in such a mood. It would be a long day and the board in the kitchens would groan from his labors. He would eat none of the meat—he never did, for he was always repulsed by the darkness the nightmares summoned from deep within him.

Perhaps his lady's moniker for him was a fitting one, after all.

Liar and scoundrel! Knave and blackguard!

Aileen could think of no accusation base enough to suit her spouse.

Indeed, she nigh wore a trough in the floor of her chamber, so agitatedly did she pace. How dare he encourage her to behave as a wanton, then reject what she offered? If that was his manner when he was amenable to intimacy, she should have hated to try to seduce him when he was reluctant to meet abed.

What did he want of her? Surrender was not enough. Compliance was not enough and defiance did not suit him either. Aileen fairly spat in her frustration. The man deserved every foul thing that was rumored to be true of him. How could she burn with desire for such a man?

How could she be so persuaded that they were destined for each other, when the Hawk clearly did not share her conviction?

How could she be so certain that his ardor alone would sate her?

How could she convince him to join forces with her and see an old wrong redressed?

Aileen thumped the pillows, she tossed and turned. She stared out the window at the thirteen ghostly trees, then at the beacon of the keep far beyond. She slept nary a wink, unable to fathom either his mixed messages or her own similarly muddled response.

What could she have done, in this life or another, to earn the fate of being wedded to such a vexing man as this?

IX

The Hawk stands in the woods of Inverfyre, listening, his footsteps halted by the sounds of a creature fleeing through the bush. It is dark, darker than dark, the shadows ominous and deep. He realizes that he stands near Adaira's hut in the same moment that he sees a flicker of movement in its portal.

He pursues his prey, stepping with care so as to not make a sound.

Silence accosts his ears, silence heavy with portent. He reaches the portal and eases around it, hoping to surprise whatever or whoever is within.

His efforts are to no avail.

The maiden awaits him, she of the dark hair and blue blue eyes, she who held the heart of Magnus Armstrong in thrall. She smiles in greeting, unsurprised by his appearance despite his efforts to be stealthy. The Hawk knows that he wears Magnus' skin, for he feels the heat of his forebear's ardor for this woman as keenly as if it were his own.

She steps toward him, her ardent expression kindling the fire in his blood.

"No, Anna, I am betrothed," he protests, knowing that his forebear's words fall from his lips, knowing that Magnus yet hopes to persuade this woman to his cause. He relives a moment that was lived by Magnus, though he knows not why. "There can be naught between us, not any longer."

She slaps him with astonishing vigor.

He takes the blow, feeling it is her due to be angered.

"You vowed you would wed me," she whispers, the thrum of fury in her words.

"I would have, were you not cursed to be barren."

"You cannot know that to be true."

"All know it," he reminds her as gently as he can.

She averts her face, but this answer will not suffice.

"Do you deny what is whispered?" he asks, his tone more forceful. "Grant me evidence that it is not true, Anna."

Her lips purse, granting him all the answer he needs. He makes to leave but she seizes his chin with alarming speed and holds him in an unholy grip. "How much will you sacrifice for Inverfyre?" she demands, her eyes narrowing. "What price will you find to be too high?" She half-laughs. "I doubt there is one."

"I have to wed her," the Hawk argues, mouthing the words Magnus had uttered long afore.

The maiden shakes her head. "You are not so compelled. You choose to wed her for your own advantage. You abandon your pledge to me because it no longer suits you to keep it. Do not fatten your crime by lying to me as well."

He bows his head, guilty yet not prepared to change his plans. The Hawk understands that Magnus believes himself to be right. "It was a mistake to meet you here," he says and turns again to leave.

"You will not depart so readily as that," she mutters, but he ignores her.

She cries a word that he does not know. The walls of Adaira's hut writhe, the branches alive as they were not in the Hawk's time. He halts to stare. It seems not only that these walls are wrought of living trees, nor even that they are verdant; the trees grow with unholy vigor. They spread before the Hawk, winding their greenery across the portal and sealing him within the chamber.

Forever.

He pivots to find the maiden's eyes bright.

"Have you underestimated the potency of your foe?" she whispers.

A blossom erupts in the wall beside her, the hut filling with the sweet perfume of its scent. The smell is heavy, exotic, intoxicating and wicked. He stares at it, dumbfounded that it could sprout so quickly, even as autumn's chill wind stirs the deadened leaves outside the hut.

Anna smiles knowingly as his blood runs cold.

The blossom withers, the flower distorting as it changes to fruit with horrifying speed. An apple forms as he watches: it grows rounder and plumper, bends the branch upon which it hangs, blushes red on one side.

All within a dozen heartbeats. He takes a step backward, troubled by this uncanny event.

The maiden plucks the fruit, her gaze locking with his as she bites into it. Juice beads on her lower lip, and she touches it with her tongue, enflaming him with a single gesture. His body knows that she is the only one who will ever fire his yearning with such haste, his soul knows that she was wrought for him and he for her.

Yet he will wed another. He knows that he dare not squander all he has earned, all he has wrought. Magnus needs a son and Anna cannot give him one. It is not her fault, just as the madness that glints in her eyes is not her fault. Neither change his affection for her; neither change his decision; neither make him blame her for her bitterness.

To Magnus' thinking, she should not blame him for his good sense.

She silently offers the fruit to him and he thinks it a gesture of peace. The Hawk feels an uncommon urgency to make amends with this woman, feels Magnus' yearning to couple with her one last time, even as uncertainty roils within him. There is a force between them, one that he will deny by wedding another, and he cannot fully shake himself of the notion that he errs.

He stares at the bite she has taken of the apple. The skin of it is brilliantly red against the white of inner flesh, making him think of blood on snow. He sees it clearly, drops of blood as bright as rubies on pristine snow, though he cannot imagine why.

She pushes the fruit closer, coaxing him to partake, though she remains silent. She draws the lace from her garment with her other hand, her eyes filled with sensuous promise. He seizes the apple with Magnus' impatience, anxious to couple with her even if it is to be the last time.

He bites into the fruit and she laughs with such triumph that his ardor chills. The fruit seems to take life in his mouth, its sweet juice summoning potent visions. Before his own eyes, she is the maiden Anna, she is Adaira, she is a red-haired Celt in crude garb, she is the Hawk's own Aileen. Her eyes alone remain the same—fathomless blue, tinged with distrust and disappointment.

He has seen them filled with passion and knows that he alone is responsible for the change.

Before he can speak, something stirs in his mouth. He spits out the piece of apple, horrified to see the tail of a serpent slithering within it. He spies the rest of the vile creature in the apple itself and flings it across the hut in disgust. He spits with a vengeance and wipes his mouth, recoiling from what wickedness she has wrought.

The maiden laughs all the while. She is Adaira then, the old hag Adaira with her bewitching kiss. She reaches for him, offering her sagging breasts and withered charms, clutching at him with her yellowed nails.

She laughs and he sees that her teeth are long gone, sees the wildness that has claimed her eyes.

He tries to flee, but the portal is sealed against him. The branches that grew across it are too stout to be snapped. He shouts and beats his fists upon the walls. He bellows with all his might.

But Adaira corners him readily. She pins him

against the wall, not nearly so frail as she might appear, her strength that of a hundred men.

And she smiles as she shoves the viper-filled apple back between his teeth.

"Eat what you have wrought, Magnus Armstrong," she whispers, holding his jaw closed with fingers like talons. He is powerless to spit out the fruit, even as the serpent writhes anew.

The Hawk awakened with a shout, sweat coursing down his back. His fists were clenched, his heart racing, his breath coming in great gasps.

His chamber was silent and dark; there was no apple in his mouth.

He spat into the rushes all the same.

He rose with a shudder and poured himself a cup of wine. The richness of it was wondrous balm to his throat. He stood nude, welcoming the chill of the floor through his feet, and stared out the window at the silent forest.

He had been right about his dreams, though not about their content. He shivered again, though not because of the cold. What had summoned this dark vision? He tipped his head back and stared at the ceiling, wishing he could see through the wooden beams and into the heart of the lady he had taken to wife.

Worse than awakening his demons, she had breathed life into the seed that Adaira had buried in his thoughts all those years ago.

The Hawk shivered and bent to feed the last glowing coal in the brazier.

He recalled the maiden's features melting into Aileen's and quaffed another cup of wine to quell his revulsion. If nothing else, his dream offered a warning. He should be wary of whatever temptation his wife offered until he could be certain of her motives.

Like Eve in the garden, her gift could lead to the Hawk's downfall, even if she offered it unaware of its price.

Aileen dreams that she is in that verdant corridor again. She lays her hand upon the wall of entwined vines, knowing full well what they are. She avoids the thorns of the hazel and takes care not to crush the blossoms of the honeysuckle as she follows the course of the path, running her hand along the thick wall of growth.

She approaches the bend she had spied. It is impossible not to note that the vigorous growth falters as she draws nearer to this corner. Both plants are unhealthy, both have dark marks upon their bark. Both emerge from the corner as mere shoots, defying an illness that should have caused their demise.

Aileen pauses to examine them more closely. Here, just before the corner, the hazel grew with such lust that its roots nearly consumed the space occupied by the roots of the honeysuckle. And similarly, here the honeysuckle twined so tightly around the hazel that it nearly choked its partner.

"Their true natures were nearly their undoing," counsels a woman's voice. Aileen peers around herself, but sees no one. "Each showed concern only for itself, disregarding the partnership already forged and nigh destroying a mutually beneficial union."

"I do not understand," Aileen says.

"The hazel claims turf with a vengeance, but must cede some ambition to allow the honeysuckle to survive."

"And the honeysuckle?" she asks when the voice falls silent.

"You know what the honeysuckle must battle," advises the voice, its tone warm with affection. "Balance is the key, child."

"Mother?" Aileen spins in the leafy corridor, seeking her mother's familiar form. There is no other soul near her, no movement other than the leaves lifting in the breeze. "Mother!" she cries, her voice rising. "Reveal yourself to me, please!"

But no woman steps from the shadows, and the voice does not carry to her ears again. Aileen shouts and shouts, knowing that it is to no avail but unable to stop herself.

In the darkest hour of the night, Aileen heard a male roar of satisfaction echo in the chamber below her own. There was no mystery as to its import.

Guinevere! Aileen leapt to her feet, furious and frustrated, her dream scattering like pollen in the wind. How dare the Hawk spurn his wife only to take a whore to his bed?

Aileen paced her chamber, vexed as she had not been before. There was no question of her sleeping again. Indeed, she tired of the Hawk's game. As with the hawk and the hare, her husband's jest was at her own expense. Why had he feigned rape, then rejected her welcome to her bed? Why had he wed her, then refused to consummate their match?

Worse, she feared these visions and dreams. What whimsy conjured her mother's voice, after all this time, even in her sleep? To see visions was one matter; to speak with the voice of the dead was quite another.

What if she *was* mad?

Long hours later, the horns blew and Aileen watched the hunting party stream through Inverfyre's gates. Her husband was garbed in leather and wool as dark as the midnight sky, but he did not ride his black destrier. He and all of his men rode smaller palfreys, perhaps to ensure greater agility in the woods, though Aileen heard the stallions stamping with displeasure in the stables.

A hooded peregrine perched upon the Hawk's fist and his mail gleamed. Alone in the company, he looked neither merry nor sleepy. His countenance was grim, Aileen could see as much even from this distance, and she fancied that he spared a hot glance for the high tower.

Did his whore wait abed for his return? Or had she too left him unsated?

In her irked mood, Aileen did not move from the window. Let him see that she watched him. Let him realize that she too was awake, that she too met the morn with a sour visage. Let him know that she had heard his triumphant roar abed and that she knew what he had done.

The Hawk looked to Aileen's window, as if he could hear her accusations.

She thought for a moment that he might halt, that he might turn back and come to her side, and she very nearly raised a hand to him in salute.

Then he spurred his horse and urged it to greater speed. The palfrey leapt the river and galloped into the forest, away from Inverfyre, away from their cold marital bed, away from Aileen.

She turned her back upon the morning, her eyes stinging with unwelcome tears. Aileen heard a footstep on the stairs and cast back her braid, brushing the tears from her eyes, just as Nissa rapped on her door.

She knew with sudden clarity what she must do. She

must solve the riddle of Anna and Magnus herself, using her wits and the evidence of this world to better understand the mysteries presented to her in the visions. She was Lady of Inverfyre; no door should be closed to her.

In the end, she could neither ignore the visions nor dismiss them. Interpretation was her only chance to save herself from madness.

It might well be her chance to win the Hawk's respect, not to mention the legendary love promised by the visions.

Aileen could only try.

The Hawk found small consolation in the fact that he had predicted his morning mood aright.

The dawn had seemingly taken a lifetime to pinken the eastern sky. He had considered a hundred times whether he should ascend to his wife's chamber, whether Aileen might offer him solace, whether he cared at her motivation for doing so.

In the end, he sat alone and watched the stars fade, loathe to awaken her, loathe to confide his secrets in her, loathe to give voice to his nightmares.

He might not spurn risk, but there were dangers a wise man knew were best left unexplored.

He summoned his men early to the hunt, earlier than they might have preferred. He was impatient to undertake some deed and hunting would have to suffice.

Ewen and Alasdair he left in command of the gates, Reinhard was left to guard the prisoner. Fernando was elusive, and the Hawk assumed some urgent business regarding his moustache was at root.

Ahearn was sitting downcast in the bailey, doubtless having been less successful in amorous pursuit the night before than was his wont, and was quickly recruited.

Sebastien was brushing down his steed in the stables and more than amenable to joining the hunt, though a mischievous twinkle seemed to dawn in his eye when he spied Ahearn. Tarsuinn and his boys brought a number of peregrines, including the Hawk's favored huntress which he carried upon his fist.

His men did not trouble themselves overmuch with him—even Ahearn was uncommonly silent—but no doubt they had discerned his mood. Over the years, even the most simple of them would have come to understand that little could change the Hawk's foul temper on those rare days that it claimed him.

The beaters ran faster than usual, perhaps in an effort to please their laird, and as a result, the hunting party took partridge and quail in astonishing quantity in the morning. The Hawk found himself amazed yet again at the wealth of his lands and the bounty of its wildlife. The dogs barked and circled the party, well pleased with the excursion and gleeful to have such a run. The day was overcast after the rosy smudge of the dawn, so the peregrines did not cast shadows. By midday, as a result, they had a brace of rabbits and ducks, as well.

It was all empty for the Hawk. He should have been jubilant that they found such success and he knew it, for they would have meat in both hall and village for more than a week. It would be more than welcome in the village so late in the winter when the meat of the pigs and chickens had been long eaten. It should always be a triumph to feed the men beneath one's hand well, but on this day, the Hawk found no joy in his accomplishment.

He found no joy in the quietude of his borders, either. The MacLarens would seem to be yet asleep for the winter.

The Hawk dispatched men in every direction, suspicious but finding nothing to justify his trepidation.

He thought of Aileen. The recollection of her consumed him. He thought of the tear upon her lashes, so quickly blinked away, when she confessed her fear of madness. He thought of her dismay when he had rejected her, and again he felt a cur.

His courtship made a poor beginning, by any measure.

He thought of his responsibility to her, for he had compelled her to come to Inverfyre. He considered her potential treachery and found the evidence against her cursedly thin.

But what of the warning of his dream?

He acknowledged that a lack of sleep did little to improve either his reasoning or his mood. His gut warned him, but he could not determine of what it would advise him to beware.

They hunted longer and farther from the hall, as a result. The men became tired, the hounds panted, but the Hawk pressed on, driven by some compulsion he could not name. He suspected that he merely avoided another troubling confrontation with his lady wife, for he knew not how to proceed, but he refused to give credence to that prospect.

No, he would hunt, as was his right and his responsibility, and leave his lady to her own resources for the moment. How much trouble could she find or make within the walls of Inverfyre?

"My lady?" Nissa's voice was clearly recognizable through the wood. "I have brought hot water, if you would care to rise."

Aileen crossed the floor with purpose. "I would indeed, Nissa, though the portal is locked from your side."

"But the key is here, my lady." The lock complained as the key was turned, then Nissa's friendly smile appeared in the opening. The maid bustled into the chamber, setting down her various burdens. She cast a gown of glorious green samite across the bed, the fabric glistening with the luster of silk. Aileen fairly gaped at the wealth of it.

Nissa then pulled fine stockings and an embroidered belt out of her own belt. She heaved a sigh and smiled pertly. "Those stairs are steep! I brought you a fine tabard, as well, my lady, and I hope it suits your favor."

Aileen shook her head in wonder. "It is beautiful."

"My lord's mother has been bringing silken garments upon her visits here. She has filled two chests with finery, and always comments that my lord should take a wife afore the moths eat them to ribbons." Nissa giggled and Aileen managed to smile. "But then, I suppose a mother is always concerned with nuptial matters. My own mother sent word to me last Yule asking when I would wed and have bairns of my own."

Aileen caught the maid's quick glance and wondered at its import. "And what did you tell her?"

Nissa sighed elaborately. "What could I tell her, my lady? Ours is a hall filled with knights and warriors, who take their pleasure where they may and never intend to wed. A maiden must be clever to maintain her purity here." She mixed the pail of hot water with cold and ran her hand in the water to check it. "I believe it is just warm enough, my lady." She hastened to help Aileen out of her chemise, then offered the cloth.

"You learn your tasks quickly," Aileen commented with a smile.

Nissa flushed. "Gunna told me what to do, although I would do otherwise if you preferred, of course."

"This is more than fine, Nissa." Aileen washed herself,

then recalled the thread of their conversation. "And have you managed to be sufficiently cunning?"

"Of course! There are several of us who barricade ourselves in a storeroom in the kitchens when the men revel overmuch."

"Surely you jest!"

The maid shook her head. "It is safer to sleep this way, and there are whores enough to sate the men in the hall. Oh, let me comb your hair. I can braid it high so that it holds your veil and circlet better."

"Veil and circlet?"

Nissa clicked her tongue. "My lady, even I know that only a maiden may leave her hair unbound. I found a fine veil for you and a silver circlet. Look. Is it not pretty?"

Aileen accepted the circlet and studied it as Nissa braided her hair. It was wrought of two strands of silver, each fashioned to look like a vine or plant. One was adorned with flowers, the other with thorns.

Aileen smiled. "The honeysuckle and the hazel," she murmured, tracing the endless loop of the circle with her fingertip.

"I suppose," Nissa acknowledged with a shrug. "Now, I cannot wait to see this hue of emerald upon you and then, you can tell me what you would see of the keep this day. My lord bade me show you all of it, or whatsoever you wished to see of it . . ."

"Where did you find the circlet?"

Nissa halted her chatter and glanced up with surprise. "It was within the trunk of goods destined for my laird's lady wife, whosoever she might prove to be." The girl smiled. "Is it not pretty enough?"

"No, it is a marvel. I wondered only where such finery

might have been crafted," Aileen lied, unable to cease running her fingers over the ornate design.

"Sicily, no doubt!" Nissa declared. "Oh, Lady Evangeline brings the finest marvels! She will arrive at midsummer this year, and Lord Gawain at her side, of course. They come each year, though this year, she will be delighted to discover your presence here." The maid winked. "Especially if you are round with child by then!"

Nissa smiled sunnily and Aileen suppressed a tremor of uncertainty. Would the Hawk's mother approve of her? Who could say? And how could she conceive an heir if the man lavished his attentions upon his whore?

Annoyed anew, Aileen donned the chemise and kirtle with Nissa's aid, then smiled approvingly at the lowered hem. "Your needle has been busy again, Nissa." Aileen spun for the maid's benefit and found her own spirits rising, as she delighted that her ankles were gracefully covered.

The girl beamed with pride. "I lengthened the hem for you, my lady. I am almost done with the first trunk, though I slept little last night. It seemed right to me that as you are the Lady of Inverfyre, these garments are for you, and I know how disappointing it is when garb does not fit. The laird agreed."

"Nissa! This is uncommonly kind of you."

Nissa flushed scarlet, then dropped to her knees before Aileen. "You can barely discern the mark of the old hem on this one, and there is a good bit of cloth on most of them. There are several that will need a band of embroidery or some other frippery to lengthen them fully."

"Do you not think this garb too fine for a day without guests or festivities?"

The girl smiled. "They are all so fine, my lady." She flicked at the hem again, frowning at a fold.

"Nissa!" Aileen seized the girl's busy hands to still them. "This is a marvelous gift and I thank you for your kindness. Let me aid you with the others and let me grant you some favor in gratitude. What would you have of me?"

The girl sighed as if she could not believe her fortune. Then she clasped her hands together in her lap and gazed up at Aileen. "I would be honorably wed, my lady, to a good man. I would have a small house and bairns of my own, though still I would serve you well. Would you find me a man of merit?"

Aileen smiled. "Have you a particular man in mind?"

Nissa's gaze clouded and she looked away before she shook her head. Aileen would have wagered that the girl lied. "I would trust your judgment, my lady."

"Then I shall look for a man just as you desire, and perhaps, when a priest comes to live at Inverfyre, your nuptials will be among the first celebrated here."

"Oh, but they cannot be," Nissa said hastily. "The first ceremony that must be celebrated at Inverfyre is the investiture of the relic in the chapel."

Aileen frowned in confusion. She knew that a church could only be sacred if graced by a holy relic, but she assumed that Inverfyre's chapel already had such a relic. Had Nissa not said that there *was* no chapel? "Is the relic not already in the chapel?"

"Of course not!" Nissa shook her head at this foolish notion. "For then, the MacLaren clan would have possession of it!"

"I do not understand."

"The chapel of Inverfyre, the old chapel, is on the original site of the keep. That is the land held by the MacLaren clan."

"Then, where is the relic?"

Nissa flushed and studied the hem again. "It is said to be a secret."

"But you know."

She straightened and met Aileen's gaze. "I found it within the trunk of the garments destined for you. The Hawk bade me work upon one trunk, but I opened the other when I was done. I meant no harm! The *Titulus* was there, wrapped in silk at the bottom. I left it be, of course, though I did touch it with my fingertips."

"And asked for a husband?" Aileen teased.

The maid flushed. "It seemed an opportunity that would be folly to waste."

Aileen pursed her lips and considered this. She stared out the window at the distant MacLaren keep. Was it possible that the Hawk waited to summon a priest until he held that old chapel? Was it possible that he counseled patience because he meant to claim that land soon?

Or did she grant him more noble motives than he possessed?

"And what would you see of Inverfyre this day?" Nissa asked, apparently convinced that all was resolved.

"The village, and then the dungeon," Aileen said firmly, holding up a finger when the girl might have protested. "It is the solemn duty of the lady of the keep to ensure that all beneath the laird's care are treated with justice and compassion."

"But my lady . . ."

"None will oppose me, Nissa. I am the Lady of Inverfyre and I mean to do this."

"But the laird . . ."

"Has ridden to hunt and left me free to go wheresoever I will within Inverfyre's walls. You told me as much, did you not?" Aileen paused while Nissa nodded, the maiden clearly displeased with the lady's choice. "We will visit the village first, to ensure that none of the laird's vassals are in need of care, then we will confirm that the prisoner is well." She offered the band of worked silver with a smile. "Might you aid me in donning the circlet, please?"

The Hawk felled a buck in the late afternoon but found no triumph even in that kill. The sky was darkening with ominous clouds, the snow beginning to fall. The Hawk took the deer with a single arrow, his squires cheering when the magnificent beast tumbled to earth.

The Hawk dismounted and cast aside his reins, handing off his falcon to one of Tarsuinn's boys. His horse stood its ground, nostrils quivering at the scent of blood as the Hawk gutted the deer with quick gestures. There were foragers in the forest who would welcome the offal and the cook would have enough labor this day without the gutting as well.

He pulled the sweetmeats from the entrails and granted them to the boy from the kitchens, except for the liver. He took his peregrine back upon his fist, noting the brightness of her gaze as he held the warm meat in his other gloved hand.

This was her reward for a day of diligence. It had been she who had spotted the buck and flown above it, and she who had killed a dozen rabbits. She was tired but yet restless, for she had not fed.

The Hawk began to hum the feeding song chosen specifically for this bird and she became even more tense in expectation. She devoured her reward greedily, tearing at it with her talons and spattering her feathers with blood in her haste to consume it. The Hawk permitted her solely a portion, for too much of its richness would make her ill. She expected as much and ate with undue haste, snatching after the flesh with an anguished cry when he took the bulk of it away from her.

She screamed outrage and flapped her wings, fighting her tethers as Tarsuinn accepted the rest to divide it among the other peregrines. The Hawk hooded her and held her tethers fast. He spoke to her quietly, stroked her with his fingertip and she settled, then groomed herself with undisguised satisfaction.

Meanwhile, his men trussed the buck's feet to a stake and hefted its weight. A pair of them carried it back toward the hall, all of the party discussing the better moments of the hunt.

"Do you tire of our excursion yet, my lord?" Ahearn demanded with a smile.

"Ah, yes, Ahearn would hasten back to the keep to coax the affections of a reluctant maiden," Sebastien teased. "Every moment gone is a moment lost, is it not?" He laughed uproariously at his own apparent jest, though Ahearn only scowled.

"I think only of our responsibilities at the gates," that man retorted.

Even the Hawk raised a brow. "How uncommon that you should be fretful for our security. This reluctant demoiselle must be a rare prize."

Ahearn colored as the company looked to him in curiosity and Sebastien laughed.

"I ask only if we return," Ahearn said stubbornly. "I vowed to relieve Ewen at midday, which is long past."

"Ah, Ewen," Sebastien mused, his eyes dancing with mischief. "There is a man who might steal a maiden's heart. He is not hard upon the eyes, he is tall and broad of shoulder. Indeed, does he not hail from the same land as your fair maiden? They might have so much in common that even our quiet Ewen might find much to say."

Ahearn's eyes flashed, but whatever he might have replied was silenced by the echo of a clarion call. The men paused and glanced back toward Inverfyre as one. The call came again, a signal not of attack but of guests arrived at Inverfyre. The snowflakes began to tumble in earnest from the sky as the Hawk and his men swung into their saddles again.

Sebastien's merry manner was dismissed. "Did you expect guests, my lord?"

"Yes and no." The Hawk nodded to the company, who began to herd the dogs homeward, then lowered his voice to speak to his cohorts. "It would have been most uncommon if my lady's father had not taken exception to the manner of her departure. I would have been surprised if Nigel Urquhart of Abernye had not demanded an explanation of me."

Ahearn's smile flashed. "Do you mean to surrender the lady, my lord?"

The Hawk let his quelling glance be the sole answer he granted.

Sebastien snorted. "A prize hard won is not casually surrendered." The Sicilian's expression turned wry. "But then, you know little of keeping women, let alone of keeping them content, Ahearn. Your attention is so fleeting that you have never so troubled yourself. Is that this tempting damsel's concern?"

"While your manner has so little appeal that you must scheme to capture any woman's affection," Ahearn retorted. "Save your barbs, Sebastien, for I know that they come from thwarted desires of your own."

The Hawk understood that there was some matter between these two. A woman's charms were at root of this trivial rivalry, no doubt. It had happened before and would undoubtedly happen again.

In truth, he was more concerned with the prospect of guests. The timing of their arrival could not have been worse—or more suspect.

Yet, the Hawk's greatest fear was not that his scheme for this very night might be foiled. Nay, he feared that his decision to leave Aileen's bed the night before had been poorly timed. Might she insist upon leaving Inverfyre with her father? Might she confide in her kin that their match had not been consummated?

Might she be lost to him?

The Hawk spurred his steed, making all haste back to Inverfyre, his heart pounding as it had upon his awakening in the early hours of the morning.

Aileen found little but curiosity in Inverfyre's village. Children ran to meet her, their garb simple but clean and their cheeks rosy with good health. The brewster was the first to bow before her, though he was quickly followed by the baker and the miller. The miller's adult son cast shy but appreciative glances at Nissa, glances that the maid did not notice. Aileen found this intriguing, as the maid professed to be seeking a spouse.

It was yet more evidence that Nissa's heart was already captured.

The women came hesitantly behind these men of the village, their manner warming as Aileen greeted them kindly. A small girl touched Aileen's samite kirtle with wonder and Aileen touched her hair. The child flushed, then ran to hide in her mother's skirts. A crowd gathered as word spread that the lady had come to meet them.

They were good people, friendly and hard-working. The

village was clean and well-organized, small gardens behind each of the houses and a trough for slops carved down the middle of the path. Aileen heard more than one pig in the gardens and chickens scattered before her as she walked.

The brewster took it upon himself to petition her earnestly for more pasturage and better guard of what few fields were tilled beyond the walls. It seemed that what little they tilled at Inverfyre was precious, though much grain was purchased by the Hawk at the market in Edinburgh. Aileen learned that the MacLarens had raided crops in the past, diverted the river, stolen sheep and killed chickens. She asked the brewster to consider what lands might best be cleared so that he would have firm suggestions by the time she discussed the matter with the Hawk.

The people were amenable to this and greeted Aileen's counsel with approval. She asked after the capture of fish, as it was Lent and she had only been served meat in the hall. She learned that there were some fish in the river, but that they were not so plentiful here, perhaps because the river ran so fast. She considered the prospect of creating a pond where eels might be raised and the miller vowed to ask his brother for advice.

One father asked her whether his son might be apprenticed to the falconer, another if his boy could learn the arts of war. Aileen carefully gathered names into her memory and vowed to present their requests to her spouse.

Overall, Aileen was impressed. The people seemed content with the Hawk's leadership, if vexed with the continuing state of war. They had regular courts and fair tithes, though there was more that she could do. If she could have taken maidens into the keep for service without risking their virginity, the bonds betwixt vassal and laird would be much improved.

Nissa hovered beside Aileen, ensuring that she learned the names of every vassal she met. The maid's assistance was invaluable. Aileen met Gunna's young niece and repeated her pledge to that child's mother that she hoped to install a priest at Inverfyre. This notion was met with approval, though many recalled the tragedy of Malcolm's death. Aileen did not dare ask for details, as it was assumed she knew more of the matter than they.

"They seem healthy indeed," Aileen murmured to Nissa as they strolled back toward the gates.

The maid nodded. "Praise be to the Hawk's demons, for he always hunts after they visit him." She smiled at Aileen's confusion. "There will be meat for all on the morrow, upon that we can rely."

His demons?

X

*A*ileen had no chance to ask what Nissa meant, for the girl clutched her arm. "Look! It is Margery."

A young woman with a long tawny braid over her shoulder was retching into the ditch. Aileen would not have troubled her, but clearly she and Nissa were friends. Nissa called out to the other woman, then embraced her and clucked over her embarrassment. Margery turned crimson when she realized that the Lady of Inverfyre was directly at hand, then she bowed low.

Margery, Aileen noted, was rounding with child, though her ring finger was barren. Her eyes were reddened, as if she had been weeping, and Aileen guessed that the man responsible for her state had refused to wed her honorably.

They spoke only briefly, for the other woman was clearly uncomfortable. No doubt she was shamed amongst her fellows. Aileen's determination to see a priest at Inverfyre—and the warriors answer for their pleasures—was redoubled.

"Is there any soul within these walls with a talent for mixing herbs?" Aileen asked when they left Margery, thinking of that woman's discomfort.

Nissa was wary. "Perhaps."

"Then, I would have you fetch him or her and ask for a potion for Margery. Though I recall little of the herb itself, I believe there is a concoction that could ease her illness without injuring her child."

"Perhaps another soul might fetch him," Nissa fairly growled.

Aileen halted, surprised that the maid was not helpful in this matter. "Is Margery not your friend? Do you not wish to aid her?"

"Of course I do!" Nissa's lips set and her eyes flashed. "But I would sell my soul afore I ask a favor of Ahearn."

"Ahearn?" Understanding dawned within Aileen but she gave no outward sign of it. "Is he not the mischievous one in the Hawk's company?"

"He is none other." Nissa tossed her hair with a vigor that fed Aileen's suspicions. "Perhaps you might send another to coax him to use his healing skills, my lady. I know well enough what his price will be and I will surrender no kiss to Ahearn O'Donnell, even for Margery."

"You are without compassion," Aileen observed, biting back a smile.

"Is her illness not wrought of her own deed?"

"Nissa! Do not speak so unkindly!"

Nissa flushed and Aileen knew the girl had lost her heart. "It will avail nothing to avoid the man and indeed, it is not possible to do so in a keep such as this. You will fetch Ahearn this very day and entreat him to aid Margery, regardless of his price."

"But, my lady . . ."

Aileen smiled and patted the girl's arm. "And while you speak with Ahearn, I see no reason not to mention that the miller's son means to court you."

Nissa's eyes widened in surprise. "Does he?"

"By the way he watched you, he could be encouraged with but a crook of your finger. A miller's son might be the perfect match for you, after all," Aileen said, watching the unhappy maid carefully. "His trade pays good coin in any year and he never travels far from home, as he must tend the stones. I think you could find your reliable spouse in a miller's son, no less your little house and wee bairns."

Nissa showed a telling lack of enthusiasm for this notion. "I thank you for your good counsel, my lady," she said, her tone so flat that Aileen knew Ahearn would not be forgotten so readily as that.

Perhaps he was similarly plagued by thoughts of Nissa, though only time would tell.

"Hasten yourself, Nissa." Aileen picked up her skirts and left the village. "The midday meal is upon us, then we must visit the dungeon afore the Hawk returns."

"Oh no, my lady!"

"Oh *yes*, Nissa."

The Hawk's cohort, Reinhard, was disinclined to grant Aileen admission to the dungeons. The Bavarian mercenary made a formidable obstacle, filling the portal with his body as he crossed his arms and braced his feet on the ground. His hair was a dark auburn, his eyes a green that approached brown, and his manner both taciturn and inflexible. Aileen despaired of slipping past him, much less of winning his agreement to her scheme, but she would not surrender so readily as this.

"It is no place for a lady, my lady," the warrior said, polite but firm. "I could not countenance your entry."

"It is the duty of the lady of any holding to ensure that prisoners are not poorly treated," Aileen insisted. She indicated the basket over her arm. "I have brought him only bread, a quaff of ale and a piece of cheese. All of it is cut in pieces and I have no knife upon my person. I welcome your perusal of it all."

Reinhard did not so much as blink. "There is no point in doing so, my lady, as you will not proceed beyond me."

Aileen straightened. "I assure you that I performed this duty often in my father's abode. At times, a prisoner has need of care, a wound stitched or a boil lanced. Although many men would leave their prisoners to rot, compassion oft earns greater gains than a lack of mercy."

"I have no doubt of your capabilities, my lady, but I cannot let you pass, all the same."

"If you fret for my person, know that Nissa shall accompany me."

Reinhard granted her a knowing glance. "Neither of you shall proceed past me."

Aileen disliked having to argue on the basis of her rank alone, but the man left her little choice. "Surely you do not defy the will of the Lady of Inverfyre?"

Reinhard shook his head slightly. "Surely I am not so foolish as to defy the will of the Laird of Inverfyre." He leaned down and winked unexpectedly, dropping his voice to a confidential tone. "He will have my liver if harm comes to you, my lady, and I am overfond of my liver being in its rightful place."

"Then grant my will and ensure no harm comes to me in the process."

"It cannot be done." Reinhard fixed his gaze on the middle distance and Aileen could not think of how she might win this argument.

Nissa tapped the mercenary on his forearm. "We saw Margery this day, Reinhard."

Ruddy color blossomed on the back of Reinhard's neck and he seemed slightly discomfited. "You did? Is she well?"

Aileen glanced between the pair, mystified as to the maid's intent.

Nissa sniffed. "She was hale enough, for a woman retching into a ditch."

"No!" The mercenary looked as if he might have said more, but then he shook his head and fell silent.

"Do you not court her affections still?"

"Indeed, but, I . . ." Reinhard fell silent, his gaze fixed upon the ground.

Aileen cleared her throat. "It seems that Margery's belly rounds, and not with fat. Is it your babe she carries?"

Reinhard colored even more deeply. "Aye, but . . ." He sputtered as he tried to explain himself, then fell silent.

Aileen straightened in disapproval. "You have got a child upon one of the laird's vassals? I do not suppose that you have considered wedding her? Although many in this household seem to believe that men should take their pleasure where they would, and women should bear the consequences alone, I do not countenance this view. I expect better of the Hawk's comrades, Reinhard."

Reinhard appeared to be ashamed. "I would wed her. I understand your concerns, my lady. I believe . . ." He halted and swallowed forcibly. "It is impossible to wed Margery, thus I will not promise what I cannot see done. It is not honorable."

"Yet it was honorable to get a child upon her?" Aileen demanded, outraged. "Are you wedded already?"

Nissa shook her head. "No, my lady. Reinhard means that it would be dishonorable to make an offer of marriage unless there was a means to be wedded."

"I would not pledge to her what I cannot see done," Reinhard said, his manner vexed. "And without a priest to bless the match, what honorable offer can I make to her?"

Nissa leaned against the wall beside Reinhard with such a confident manner that the man looked both cornered and deeply suspicious of her motives. "Reinhard, what you have failed to understand is that we can aid you."

The mercenary looked between the two women in surprise. Aileen kept her expression composed, even as she wondered at Nissa's scheme.

"My lady has made it her task to ensure that a priest comes to live at Inverfyre," Nissa confided, every word heavy with import. "I have no doubt that she will succeed, for we all have seen how our laird favors his lady's will."

"If there is a priest, we can be wed!" Reinhard's eyes widened. "I implore you, my lady, to make every effort to see this done."

Nissa dropped her voice to a whisper. "Yet even if there is a priest, there are details to be observed, details that consume time. And it may take some weeks or even months for the laird to not only agree but to find a priest."

Reinhard frowned even as he nodded woeful agreement.

"But imagine if our lady urged the priest to forgo the banns for your nuptials when he arrives? You and Margery might wed more hastily, perhaps even afore the child makes its first cry?"

"You would do this for me?" Reinhard demanded of Aileen, his excitement evident.

Aileen could not hold his gaze, for she was far less certain of her eventual success than Nissa. "There is not a decent soul in Christendom who would not return a favor willingly granted." She pointedly hefted the basket of provisions for the prisoner.

Reinhard glanced from side to side, then nodded once,

his decision made. "You will not utter a word of this visit to the Hawk."

"Nor will you," Aileen agreed with a smile.

"But I shall speak with Margery this very night. Her mother is most distressed with me and all will be relieved to know that matters can be resolved. I thank you, my lady. It was not my intent that our match should begin this way."

"I shall do my best to ensure it continues more honorably," Aileen vowed.

The mercenary bowed deeply, then stepped away from the barred portal. He struck a flint and lit a candle, leading the way down the stairs to Inverfyre's cold dungeon. The darkness closed around them and Aileen clutched her basket even as she lifted the hem of her skirts.

Reinhard took a key from his belt, granting Aileen a stern glance as he turned it in the lock. "You have only to call if you need me. Recall, my lady, that he is dangerous."

"You need not wait directly outside the cell for me," Aileen said, her spirit quailing with the boldness of what she meant to do. "I shall summon you when I am prepared to leave."

"But my lady . . ."

"No man would confide the weakness of an injury while in your presence, Reinhard, for all know you to be a warrior at the laird's command. And Nissa will accompany me to ensure that no improprieties occur."

Aileen granted the pair no time to argue with her choice. She ducked into the dungeon cell, Nissa on her heels, and confronted the man there as the door clanged shut behind them. He was young, sandy of hair and green of eye, and he was shackled to the wall. His forlorn expression brightened.

"And good day to you," he said with astonishing cheer. "Am I dead then, that angels have come to visit me?"

*   *   *

Nigel Urquhart, Lord of Abernye, paced the Hawk's hall, his agitation more than clear. He was armed as he had not been in his own hall, his hauberk falling to his knees, his helmet still under his arm. He was as large and burly a man as the Hawk recalled, red of face and round of chest.

The very sight of him awakened every possessive urge within the Hawk. He knew that he would have to be slaughtered himself afore he would willingly relinquish his wife.

Despite his suspicions of her.

How could Magnus have chosen to live without Anna, even if he had known her to be barren? The Hawk could not understand his forebear's choice.

The Hawk advanced into the hall, shedding his gloves as he walked. He felt rather than saw that his cohorts had moved to secure the doors and had quietly surrounded the men accompanying Aileen's father. This was a matter of some delicacy: he would not be challenged by another within his own hall, yet he did not wish to make an enemy of Aileen's father. Beneath the watchful gazes of nearly a hundred souls, the Hawk chose his course.

Abernye noted the moves of the Hawk's men, his gaze flicking left and right. He met the Hawk's gaze again and snorted under his breath. He had not exhibited such confident skepticism in his own hall, but then, his new wife had kept him upon a short rein. In her absence, he seemed more vigorously alive.

Indeed, he drew himself taller, then brandished a fist at the Hawk. "Where is my daughter?" he roared. "How dare you so insult my hospitality? I treated you as my guest!"

The Hawk refused to answer in kind lest matters grow more hostile. An angry man cannot make a fight alone.

He smiled slightly. "Against your daughter's counsel, if I recall well enough. I thank you for teaching her well."

Abernye reddened. "I will have redress for your insult . . ."

"Where is the insult?" the Hawk demanded. "I wedded your daughter before your own priest."

The Hawk's men smiled and put their hands upon the hilts of their blades. Abernye's men belatedly realized that they were surrounded and tried to hide their dismay.

Abernye fumed. "Aileen did not come to this match willingly!"

"Surely, that was not your priest's recollection. I distinctly recall that the lady agreed." He indicated that his guest should be served a cup of wine. "I cannot imagine that your priest tells a falsehood about this matter."

"My priest does not lie!" he thundered. "He knows well what she said and he knows well what little choice she had. It was nuptials or dishonor, two poor choices." He pointed a shaking finger at the Hawk. "You soiled my daughter in my own home, sir, in my own lady's chamber . . ."

At least, the consummation of their nuptials was not in doubt.

Thus far.

"Do you have proof of that?" the Hawk asked, nodding approval of the cask of wine his castellan would order to be opened.

"Of the deed, you left enough!"

"I confess to supplying evidence of the deed, but have you evidence of the location of the deed?" The Hawk slapped his gloves against his palm. "Or of your daughter's lack of interest in it? Perhaps she welcomed me."

His guest glowered. "Do not cast aspersions upon my daughter's character."

"I would not dream of doing so base a deed. I simply acknowledge the force of passion between us, and would ask you to do the same."

Abernye breathed heavily, no little discontent in his expression.

The Hawk smiled. "I intend no dishonor in admitting that the lady claimed my heart with a glance. You cannot argue that Aileen is a pearl, no less that she is now rightly set amidst finery."

Abernye cast a covert glance around the hall, just as Gregory, the castellan, paused before him, offering a cup of wine.

The Hawk accepted his own cup of wine. "And surely, you do not protest my uninterest in any dowry you might offer. I assure you that the lady's charms are sufficient prize for me."

Abernye sputtered. "You would insult me again by dismissing my charges . . ."

The Hawk spoke firmly, having no fear of using blunt speech to end this argument. "And surely you do not argue with my choice to make matters come aright by wedding the lady, once passion had had its due?"

"Still, you should not have . . ."

"And you should not have let your maiden daughter reach eighteen summers of age with neither suitor nor spouse," the Hawk interrupted curtly. "You might consider yourself fortunate that I am not of more lawless character than I am."

"That cannot be possible," Abernye muttered and with this, finally, he provoked his host.

The Hawk cast down his gloves and crossed the floor to stand toe to toe with his guest. "Indeed? I could have taken her and abandoned her," he retorted, his voice rising. "You could have had a soiled daughter to wed and no compense for my deed, and you know the truth of it well!" He dropped his voice when Abernye looked away. "You might have considered that it would be prudent to court my alliance, rather than make accusations against me in my own hall. Did you intend to coax me to reject your daughter now?"

Abernye straightened, eyes wide. "You would not!"

"No, I would not, but that says more of my character than of your strategy." The Hawk pivoted and strode back across the hall.

"You rendered insult to my house," Aileen's father insisted.

"And now you offer insult to mine." The Hawk indicated the cup still proffered by the patient Gregory to his guest. "Let us speak plainly. I resolved the matter of your daughter remaining unwed, did so in a manner that left no argument between us and cost you no coin. Indeed, I consider this matter most amiably concluded."

Abernye eyed the cup, knowing that accepting it implied that he was the Hawk's guest. As such, there were customary restraints upon his behavior in Inverfyre.

They were restraints that the Hawk had ignored at Abernye.

"It is a long ride from Abernye," the Hawk said softly. "Surely you would like to quench your thirst? Surely we might put a matter poorly begun but happily ended behind us? Will you not raise a cup to your daughter's newfound status?"

Abernye studied the hall with dissatisfaction, clearly noting that his men were outnumbered and older than the military men of Inverfyre. It was evident that the Hawk's men were more accustomed to negotiating with their blades.

Abernye looked and considered, then accepted the cup.

"Wound Aileen and I will kill you myself," he muttered by way of salute, lifted the cup high, then drained it.

"I doubt you could," the Hawk murmured as he sipped from his own cup.

The Hawk savored his wine while Abernye choked upon his.

It was an excellent wine, brought from the south by the Hawk's parents the year before and certainly far finer than any swill that might have previously crossed the lips of Aileen's father.

If nothing else, he had learned something of his father-in-law by this exchange. The Hawk could see how Abernye had found a wife when he had not been seeking one: the older man was impulsive in his speech, betrayed by his passions to make poor plans. He was much concerned with honor, so concerned that the tale the Hawk had concocted of the defloration of Aileen might have actually been true of Abernye's meeting with Blanche.

Blanche, who had seemed most cunning, would have perceived the man's traits and used them against him to further her own ambitions.

The Hawk arched his brow as his guest recovered from his coughing.

"It is a fine wine you serve at Inverfyre," the older man finally managed to say.

"Indeed."

Abernye looked a third time at the hall, more leisurely in this perusal. There was a hearty blaze upon the hearth, and the smells of roasting meat and fresh bread filled the air. The whores were young and alluring, and indeed, Guinevere winked boldly at the guest when his gaze fell upon her.

Abernye cleared his throat and met the Hawk's gaze. "I

visited Inverfyre as a squire, but I do not recall the hall being so rich."

"The old timber hall was burned afore I was born," the Hawk said. "And indeed, this is not the same site as that old Inverfyre."

Abernye held out his cup to a serving girl, pragmatism taking the place of his annoyance. The wine had mellowed him, apparently, and made him realize that he could not have made a better match for his daughter. "It is poor luck to rebuild upon destruction," he said with a nod, "for it makes the gods think a man above his place."

"I apologize for the lack of adornment in the hall as yet," the Hawk said. "But such are matters better suited to a woman's eye."

Abernye straightened. "I assume that you mean a lady's eye."

"Who else would have such authority than my lady wife?"

The older man looked again at the company of comely whores and his lips thinned. "Who else, indeed," he muttered, then lifted a finger, belligerent again. "Your tower is tall and your walls long. Your horses black enough to be spawned from hell."

"From Lucifer himself," the Hawk jested, though none understood his reference to the stallion he had brought here from Sicily save Fernando and Sebastien. The Hawk sobered. "Surely you will agree that Inverfyre is a prize worth defending."

His guest glared at him. "It has long been said that Satan himself has command of fathomless riches such as these you possess."

The Hawk smiled coolly. "How sad, then, that Satan does

not tithe to me. It is cursedly expensive to raise such walls as these."

The company chuckled at this jest, though Aileen's father did not.

The Hawk sobered, then closed the space between himself and his guest. "I assure you, Lord Abernye, that the richest prize in all of Inverfyre, if not in all of Christendom, is the lady so recently come to my side. Surely upon this matter, we can agree. Let us drink to the health of Lady Aileen of Inverfyre."

The entire company raised their cups to this sentiment, though Abernye remained grim after he had drained his cup.

"Then, let me see her." His voice rose in challenge. "Should all be well, as you indicate, you have naught to fear in letting me converse with my daughter." He held the Hawk's gaze in challenge. "Alone."

The Hawk liked a risk, though it seemed he liked risk less in association with his lady wife. All the same, he would die afore he let Aileen's father so much as sense his uncertainties.

"Of course," he said smoothly. "It is only natural to expect a doting father to anticipate as much." To his credit, the older man flushed slightly when the Hawk emphasized "doting."

The Hawk began to cross the hall, then paused to glance back. "Tell me, does Blanche miss the company of her stepdaughter? Any woman of merit would undoubtedly be dismayed by the loss of such a fine companion."

Abernye's flush deepened in a most satisfactory way. The Hawk held his gaze for a telling moment, then pivoted. He handed off his cup and might have made his way to the stairs had Guinevere not touched his elbow. The Hawk brushed off the weight of the whore's hand, but Guinevere seized his arm again.

"Do not despise one who does you a favor," she counseled, her voice low and luscious.

"Guinevere, you know that there will never be affection between us," the Hawk said with undisguised impatience. "Leave the matter be."

"Perhaps I do, perhaps I do not," she said with a smile. "What I do know, though, is that your lady is not to be found in her chambers with her spindle."

The Hawk's heart leapt with fear that Aileen had been injured.

Or worse.

"What is this? Where is she?"

Guinevere smiled coldly. "Your lady visits the spy, and one can only wonder why." She examined her nails. "No less, one must wonder why she descended to that hole in such finery. Green samite from Sicily!" Guinevere whistled under her breath, then looked up knowingly. "What could a prisoner do to merit such attention from the lady of the keep?"

"Cease your poisonous whispers," the Hawk bade her, but Guinevere only chuckled.

"Call truth poison if you will, Hawk, but one has to consider whether you erred in choosing a bride."

The Hawk spared her a glance that spoke clearly of his thoughts. "Be gone by the morrow, Guinevere. I have tolerated you in my hall overlong. You and your 'sisters' can find accommodation in the village from this night forward."

The whore's lips tightened with anger, but the Hawk had no care for her response. He turned and strode out to the bailey, intent upon finding his wife.

What folly did Aileen make? It was regrettable, to be

sure, that they had parted poorly the night before, even more regrettable that her every choice fed his suspicions of her intentions. Sebastien and Ewen fell into step behind the Hawk, though they said nothing.

The Hawk had questions enough of his own. Was the Laird of Abernye in league with the MacLaren clan? The Urquhart holding had not been an affluent one, yet the new Lady Abernye clearly had a tendency to spend coin. How much would Abernye do to ensure the happiness of his new bride? Would he make an alliance with the MacLarens against the Hawk?

The timing of Abernye's arrival was uncanny and made the Hawk restless: did the conspirators close their trap just when he was on the verge of his final triumph?

And how much did Aileen know of such a scheme?

The prisoner devoured the food Aileen had brought with unholy haste, then glanced up guiltily. He must have spied her horror afore she tried to hide it, for he smiled ruefully and dropped his gaze again. "I beg your pardon, my lady, but it has been two days since I ate."

There was a pleasant roll to his speech, his vowels tinged with the fact that Gaelic was clearly his mother tongue. Aileen felt an immediate affinity with him, for she spoke the same way, as did all in her father's hall.

Accents were many in her husband's hall, and oft unfamiliar.

"They have not fed you in this dungeon?"

He shook his head and though she was outraged at this harsh treatment, he showed a surprising lack of bitterness. "I expected no less when I was seized," he said, then summoned a smile for her. He drank the ale and sighed with contentment as he leaned back against the stone wall.

His eyes twinkled now and she felt the urge to return his smile. "I thank you from the bottom of my heart, my lady. I am much restored."

"You are welcome." Aileen hesitated, knowing that she should leave. But she would learn nothing if she did not prompt a conversation and she had not simply come to be charitable. "Even a spy is entitled to a meal afore his guilt is proven."

The prisoner granted her a knowing glance. "Is that what they declare me to be?" Aileen nodded. He chuckled to himself, seemingly finding great amusement in this.

"Are you not one?"

His chuckles faded and he fixed her with a suspicious glance. "Were you sent by the Hawk to coax my secrets from me?"

"No, he does not know I am here," Aileen said hastily, then regretted confiding so much information. "I came because it is the role of the lady of the keep to show compassion for prisoners and ensure that they have decent care. Were you injured, before your capture or since?"

The prisoner studied her with new curiosity. "The lady of the keep?"

"Indeed. I am Lady of Inverfyre."

The man's eyes widened. "The Hawk has wed?"

Aileen smiled. "Clearly. I am not of an age to be his mother."

The prisoner did not smile at her jest. He rubbed his chin, his gaze flicking over the cell. "That is portentous news." His bright gaze landed upon her so suddenly that Aileen nearly jumped. "Do you carry the fruit of his seed?"

Aileen straightened and stepped back, feeling her color rise as she did so. Nissa gasped outrage at his audacity. "You have no right to ask a lady such a question!"

"Though the answer would be most intriguing," he murmured. He cleared his throat and smiled so abruptly that Aileen almost wondered whether she had imagined the comment and his sly manner. "I suppose your beloved spouse has regaled you with his scheme to reclaim all of his birthright, sworn that all of Inverfyre is his legacy, and vowed that the MacLaren clan must be ousted from his lands."

Aileen smiled, letting the man think what he would.

"It is not a mere tale . . ." Nissa began, but Aileen put a hand upon her arm to silence her.

The prisoner granted the maid a hot glance. "Aye, it is the simple folk who believe such foolery."

Nissa inhaled sharply, taking umbrage at his comment, but Aileen tightened her grip upon the girl's arm. "There is oft a rift between the truth and the tale that all hear," she said in a conciliatory tone.

"There is indeed! I suppose the Hawk has told you of his own heroic deeds and his noble destiny," the prisoner snorted, showing some anger now. "What man would not wish to so impress such a pretty bride?" He spat into the rushes in the corner. "I suppose he told you that the MacLarens are no better than vermin, and that it is his duty to rid this fair land, his rightful domain, of their pestilence."

Aileen kept her expression carefully composed. "You would not happen to be of the MacLaren clan?"

His gaze was sharp. "What do you think?"

Aileen shrugged.

The man lifted his chin, and his eyes glinted in his anger. "No doubt your fine spouse omitted many details from his tale. There are two sides to every story, of that you can be certain."

"My mother oft said as much," Aileen agreed. "Tell me your side."

"Did he tell you how he and his men arrived here eighteen years past and proceeded to slaughter our kin for no reason but his own greed for our land?"

"But I thought Inverfyre to be his legacy?"

"And whence does sovereignty begin, my lady?" The prisoner rattled his chains. "Answer me this, my lady: who held these lands when Magnus Armstrong came, just as the Hawk came, and claimed them for his own?"

"I do not know. Perhaps Inverfyre was mere wilderness."

He snorted with vigor. "These were MacLaren lands, stolen once and now stolen again."

"I do not think so!" Nissa protested.

"Believe what you must, peasant, but I know the truth of it. Righteousness rides with the MacLaren clan: why else do we hold the original site of Inverfyre? Why else does the chapel itself remain in our hands, if not for God's favor of our cause? I know who is thief and who is rightful owner, even if the Hawk would tempt his lady's ardor with fulsome lies."

"What did you hope to achieve by coming here?" Aileen asked softly. "I doubt there are weaknesses in these stout walls."

He regarded her for such a long interval that Aileen did not think he would speak again. His implication was clear to her: the weaknesses of the Hawk's keep would be found *within* its walls, in people who would betray their lord.

She held his gaze, knowing he believed wrongly in this. Never had she seen such loyalty granted to a lord by his men as she had witnessed here, and Aileen knew it was because the Hawk was fair. Instinctively, she trusted him and believed in his cause.

What if this man planned some treachery? What if she could uncover the truth of it?

Surely that feat would encourage the Hawk to trust her?

What if she could persuade him that she was the weak link?

"Even if your cause is righteous, you can achieve nothing in this cell," she said with apparent idleness. "It would seem your efforts were a waste."

The prisoner glanced around the dungeon again, then to his shackles. "Especially as I am to be executed on the morrow."

Aileen caught her breath, having known no such thing.

He watched her assessingly. "You did not know."

Aileen shook her head, not disguising her horror. "Executed!" Surely he was mistaken. Surely the Hawk would not pronounce a fate so cruel.

But she suspected that the Hawk would do so, if he believed this man to be a threat to Inverfyre's security. He had told her time and again that he took no risks with the lives of those beneath his hand.

The prisoner reached out and caught Aileen's hand in his own. She jumped, but forced herself to leave her fingers in his grip. "I never guessed that he could be so cruel," she whispered, feigning dismay.

The prisoner's eyes narrowed. "It is not every noblewoman who would have made her way to this cell."

Aileen smiled sadly. "Then, the world has come to a sorry crossroads indeed."

His grip tightened upon her hand. "I suspect that you are one much enamored of justice."

"We would be as brute beasts without it," Aileen agreed.

The prisoner looked to Nissa pointedly.

"Nissa, go to the portal and call for Reinhard, if you

will," Aileen advised, guessing that the prisoner wished to confide in her alone.

"But, my lady—"

"Do as I bid you, Nissa, and do it immediately."

The girl rose with reluctance and crossed to the door.

The prisoner leaned close and dropped his voice to a whisper. "For the sake of justice, I would beg a favor from you."

"A dangerous favor," she guessed.

"My kin will welcome you and see to your future, whatever happens, if you aid their cause. You risk naught in this endeavor."

"Reinhard!" Nissa called and shook the portal in her anxiety.

Aileen felt her eyes narrow even as she whispered. "In what endeavor?"

"If the Hawk rides out from Inverfyre, my kin must be warned. Our sole hope of survival is if we are forewarned and survive until the king responds to our summons for his aid. My task here was to alert my kin if the Hawk rode out, regardless of the hour." He glanced up at Nissa. "I was caught, but I have heard whispers from within this cell that the Hawk plans a final assault soon."

"Reinhard! Make haste!" Nissa shouted, for Reinhard did not come.

"Should the king not decide whose claim to sovereignty is the most compelling?" the prisoner demanded, his eyes flashing. "Do you, a woman enamored of justice, deny the righteousness of this? We will stand by the decision of the king, but we will not willingly be slaughtered for the sake of a foreigner's ambitions. If the Hawk kills us, though, the king will hear no protest."

Aileen dropped her gaze to his grip upon her hand. He

was lying and she knew it well. If the MacLaren clan truly had cause to dispute the Hawk's claim, they would have appealed to the king sooner: the Hawk had been at Inverfyre for eighteen years.

The prisoner lied, but he must not know that she knew as much.

Aileen nodded carefully. "It is not easy to betray one's husband," she said, her voice low. "But you speak aright when you argue for justice. This decision lies with the king alone." She looked up and met his gaze. "Tell me how I might aid your mission."

His smile was immediate and bright. "Yours is a valiant heart!"

"Reinhard, hasten yourself!" Nissa cried.

The prisoner whispered in haste. "Three flaming arrows, fired high in quick succession, will serve as the warning." He looked about himself, despondent to be acknowledging his failure. "They snared me while I slept. They took my quiver and bow, they broke my arrows." He closed his eyes. "They laughed when they destroyed what was precious to me."

Aileen's heart clenched, for she felt a kinship with him over this destruction. A tear spilled from his lashes and he steadfastly looked away in his shame. "We may be impoverished," he said, his voice husky. "We may be weakened, we may be hungry, but our cause is righteous. Do we not still avenge our kinswoman?"

Aileen did not understand this last comment but she nodded anyway. "Indeed, you are a most steadfast clan."

The key tumbled the locks.

"Pray for me, my lady," the prisoner whispered, his words nigh swallowed by the creak of the opening door.

Aileen felt her own compassion rise. She spun to greet Reinhard, but her words froze on her lips.

The Hawk stood in the portal, Nissa behind him. His expression was impassive but Aileen felt the anger that emanated from him. His gaze flicked from her to the prisoner, though he made no comment upon her presence here.

Indeed, he offered his hand to her, as courteously as if he had found her at her spinning. "Your father has arrived, my lady, and awaits your greeting."

XI

*W*hat had Aileen been doing in the dungeon? What secrets had she and the prisoner been sharing? The Hawk's heart thumped with uncertainty but he dared not grant voice to his doubts. She could abandon him too readily in this moment, and his instincts told him that he would regret her departure.

He silently escorted Aileen from the dark dungeon and across the bailey, while Nissa hastened ahead of them. The shadows were drawing long, the sky painted bright with the last banners of the setting sun. He held the portal so that she could precede him into the corridor that led to the hall, his innards writhing with doubts all the while.

"Must he die?" she asked quietly when he matched his pace to hers.

"At some point," the Hawk said, no mercy in his tone. The threat of death was the sole chance of gaining some truth from this spy, though the Hawk doubted that even that would be effective. He had no intent of releasing him to share details of the keep with the MacLarens. He took a deep breath, not wanting to trouble Aileen with such details. "It is for the best."

"Whose best?" she demanded sharply. "Surely, it cannot be the best fate for him?"

"Death or torture are the two choices for coaxing the truth from a spy. He will not speak, and I will not tolerate torture in my hall. There is no other choice."

"You could release him."

"And find my hall set to fire beneath me the next night," the Hawk said grimly. "I owe better to my vassals, Aileen, and I owe better to you." He granted her a sharp glance. "What did he tell you?"

"Little."

"You lingered long for no reason, then."

She granted him a cool glance that he could not interpret. "He was anxious to ensure that I understood you to be the thief of Inverfyre, not his own people. I could hardly argue your cause, as you have not confided it in me."

Her implied accusation pushed his temper too far. He halted to face her, knowing that his words thrummed with anger. "You wish to know my side of the tale, is this the meat of it? You wish to decide for yourself whether I am innocent or guilty of the charges a spy has wrought against me?"

"I did not say that I believed him—"

"I shall tell you of the MacLaren clan and their deeds," he interrupted, not interested in her appeasement. "You have seen their tower from your chamber window, no doubt. That tower is built upon the original site of Inverfyre, upon the burned ruins of the old keep which was built by my forebear Magnus Armstrong. The MacLarens tried to steal Inverfyre from my mother, they tried to kill me within her womb so that there would be never be another Armstrong to challenge them. They tried to kill her, to ensure that she could never bear fruit again, for the same reason."

She tried to say something but the Hawk shook a finger at her, not prepared for an interruption. "And when these devious schemes failed, they assaulted the family keep during my parents' nuptials, when all were gathered for the celebration, and razed it to the ground. Hundreds of innocent vassals died, either cut down by bloodthirsty warriors or left to be burned alive when the gates were locked against them. This was the work of the MacLarens, and they perch upon their meager gain, like a dragon drooling over his stolen hoard."

Aileen's features were ashen. "That was when your mother fled, with you in her belly, and Tarsuinn took his wound defending her."

The Hawk knew his anger showed and did not care. "For the sake of my survival, my mother left Inverfyre, the only home she had ever known, and traveled all the distance to Sicily. For her, I returned to rout the MacLarens, but like any pestilence, they are not so readily dismissed."

"They must have built that tower, if the keep was destroyed."

"And a sorry piece of construction it is. They linger there, harassing my borders, stealing from my couriers, putting spies in my hall whenever they can. They stop at naught, they have not a moral among them, and they breed like hares. No matter how many are killed, a dozen more appear to take their places." He shoved a hand through his hair, his annoyance spent. "These are my neighbors, Aileen. These are the people who make accusations against me."

She bit her lip and he hated that he could not guess her thoughts. "Did they kill the priest? What happened to Malcolm?"

"He was beset upon the road that passes the land they have claimed." The Hawk fell silent, unwilling to continue the gruesome tale.

Aileen stepped forward and touched a fingertip to his arm. "Tell me," she urged.

The Hawk held her gaze. "They tied his ankles beneath the saddle and his wrists to the pommel. We heard his cry for aid and rode out with all haste. They slit his throat, but not so fully that he died in that moment, then beat the steed so that it would run. We saw him galloping toward us, the blood flowing like a river." The Hawk swallowed. "He died shortly after we brought him back here. There was nothing that we could do, for he had bled much and his wounds were grievous."

She caught her breath and looked away. "Was he not accompanied?"

"We found his three squires left dead by the road."

"A priest," she whispered unevenly and crossed herself. "They are barbarians!"

He nodded but once, his agreement heartfelt.

"And this is why you will summon no priest to Inverfyre."

"As yet."

She lifted her gaze to his, her own expression shrewd. "But you let me believe it your fault that the priest died."

"It *was* my fault!" The Hawk flung out his hand. "I should have ridden to Stirling to accompany him. I should have guessed what fate awaited him. I, better than anyone, should have known the blackness of their hearts."

Aileen laid her hand upon his arm and she shook her head slightly. Her gaze was warm, her voice soft. "You cannot anticipate the evil of another, Hawk. The blame is not yours in this, but that of the one who wielded the blade."

He took a deep breath and frowned. "No, lady mine. I have witnessed the wickedness of Dubhglas MacLaren. I should have protected the priest."

She granted him a beguiling smile and her grip tightened slightly on his arm. "Would you protect every soul in Christendom, my lord?"

He stiffened. "Do you mock me?"

She shook her head, her eyes shining so bright a blue that the Hawk had to look away. He stared down at her fingers upon his arm, and covered them with his other hand. A lump rose in his throat when she eased closer. Never had he felt such kinship with his bride. Her fingers were soft beneath his own, feminine and a marked contrast to his own calloused hands. Her grip was firm, though, and he liked well that she had neither fainted nor trembled before the horror of this tale.

Her fingers tightened upon his. "Are there spies within your hall, Hawk?"

He abandoned any inclination to lie. "I do not know."

The silence hung heavily between them, and neither uttered a word.

She spied something in his expression, though, for she sighed and granted him a sad smile. "You do not trust me."

"I dare not trust any soul."

"Save your men," she amended tartly.

"They have served me faithfully for years."

Aileen studied him, clearly unpersuaded. "Am I condemned solely for my recent arrival? Or do you believe me to be the spy in your hall for another reason?"

He said nothing, for he would neither lie to her nor wound her with careless accusations. The moment of understanding between them had passed, though he wished heartily that he could have coaxed it back.

Aileen muttered something beneath her breath and might have turned away, but the Hawk caught her hand more firmly within his own. "Your father would speak with you alone," he admitted, his words terse.

She considered this for a moment then inclined her head to watch him. "And this concerns you."

"I do not know what you will tell him."

"What would you have me tell him?" the lady demanded with some annoyance. "Shall I confess the truth, that my husband has never possessed me and appears to have no desire to do so? Shall I tell him that I am not trusted? Would you not be glad to be rid of me, potential spy that I am?"

"You know that I would not be."

"I know no such thing!" she retorted, then turned to enter the hall. Her chin was high and she walked like a queen, her spine as straight as a newly honed blade. He realized belatedly the import of the veil and circlet she wore, that she supported his ruse that their match was consummated, and his heart softened. She raised a hand to wave to her father, but the Hawk could not let this matter be.

He seized her elbow and pulled her to a halt, flicking his wrist so that she pivoted to face him. She gasped and flushed but she did not pull away. Indeed, her eyes sparkled with either defiance or delight.

The Hawk did not care which.

He caught her other elbow in his grip and held her fast, letting her see the desire that burned within him. "I would not have you leave my side," he said with quiet resolve. "Let me persuade you of the truth of it."

A smile touched her ruddy lips. Her gaze dropped to his mouth, her cheeks flushed in anticipation and he spied the flicker of her pulse at her throat.

"I thought the task was mine to invite your ardor," she

whispered mischievously, the twinkle that danced in her eyes making the Hawk's blood heat.

"I suggest you make your invitation with haste," he murmured, feeling the attention of the hall land upon them. He smiled slightly. "For I would not willingly break my pledge to you, lady mine."

"Then kiss me, Hawk," she whispered. Her fingers gripped his upper arms as she rose on her toes, pressing her breasts against his chest as her lips parted. "Kiss me now and kiss me lingeringly. Persuade me that you are not displeased with your bride."

The Hawk needed no second invitation, and indeed, he granted his lady wife no chance to offer one.

Nissa found Ahearn in the stables, brushing down a palfrey. He spoke gently to the beast as he worked, and she heaved a sigh at the soft burr of his speech. When he was alone and unobserved, she could almost believe he had a heart. He had shed his tabard and cloak, and worked with the sleeves of his chemise rolled up. His hair was a dark tangle upon his brow, and she could see how finely wrought he was.

She cleared her throat sharply before she lost her resolve and stepped pertly into the stables, enjoying how he jumped with surprise. His expression brightened at the sight of her and she softened toward him, then reminded herself not to be a fool.

"I come only because I was commanded to do so," she said. "Do not imagine that I sought you out of my choice."

His brow darkened and he returned to his labor. "And is that not a charming greeting?" he muttered. "If you mean to ask a favor from me, you make a poor beginning, Nissa."

"The favor is not for me, but for my lady." Nissa eased

closer, liking the smell of the horses and leather harnesses. Her father had been an ostler and she felt comfort around these familiar scents and routines. Ahearn spared her a glance and she caught her breath at the clear sparkle of his eyes. "She seeks someone with a knowledge of herbs to ease the suffering of Margery in the village."

"What ails her?"

"She carries Reinhard's child, and the lady thought there was a potion that might alleviate her retching."

Ahearn frowned as he finished brushing the steed, then he straightened and cast the brush aside. He stroked the great beast's rump, then turned to regard Nissa. "And my compense for this is to be solely the pleasure of aiding another?"

Nissa folded her arms across her chest, knowing full well what he would ask of her. "That should be compense enough for a man of merit."

Ahearn's survey of her was so intent that Nissa yearned to fidget. "Since when have you had an interest in men of merit?" he asked quietly.

Nissa felt herself flush. She studied the horse with feigned interest as her cheeks burned. "Since my mother asked when I would wed, when I would have bairns of my own."

"And a single question changed all between us?"

Nissa took a breath. "I would wed a man who will see me clothed and in good care, a man who will provide a hearth and home, and children." She met his gaze again, her own heart leaping with the hope that he would pledge as much to her. "The time for a merry jest is passed, Ahearn. I grow no younger."

He scowled and turned away from her. "Life is not worth the living if one has no time for a jest, Nissa," he said, his tone fierce. "I can clearly be of no aid to Margery, as I am no man of merit."

"But what shall I do? What shall I tell my lady?" Nissa asked, astonished at the change in his manner.

"Tell her nothing. Ask Guinevere for aid," Ahearn said tightly. "She knows more of womanly concerns than I." He spared her a hard glance. "After all, a man such as myself might be more inclined to grant Margery a potion that saw her rid of the child."

Nissa felt her lips part in amazement.

He snorted and turned back to his steed, his manner telling her that matters had changed between them forever. It was devastating to realize how shallow their friendship had been.

He had not even demanded the boon of a kiss for his favors.

Nissa supposed she saw the matter clearly now, and not a moment too soon.

She straightened, pride coming to her aid. "Your counsel is good. I will halt at the miller's abode this night, as well," she said as carelessly as she could. "My lady believes the miller's son would make a good match for me, no less that he would willingly pursue my hand."

"Then, you should grant him encouragement soon, Nissa. I understand that you grow no younger," Ahearn snapped.

Nissa was shocked by the rare sight of his anger. "You might wish me well," she said, guessing that this would be their final conversation.

He turned to her, his gaze softening along with his tone. "I have always wished you well, Nissa. Perhaps that was my error." Before she could ask for an explanation, he smiled mischievously, winked and turned back to his horse.

As if it did not matter that their friendship had ended.

Nissa picked up her skirts in her fists, sparing him a last word afore she left. "So, Ahearn, you are as heartless and selfish a cur as I so oft was warned. I imagined otherwise, but then, my mother always said that I was overly fanciful and saw matters as they were not."

He turned, astonished, but Nissa did not linger to savor his surprise. She marched toward the hall, where she would surely find Guinevere, her lips set as she fought her tears.

The Hawk's kiss was powerful and splendid. Aileen closed her eyes as his lips captured hers and surrendered to his ardor. He caught her close and kissed her deeply. Her hand landed upon his neck and she felt the thunder of his racing pulse.

Encouraged by this sign, she opened her mouth to him and abandoned herself to pleasure.

The vision unfurled in her thoughts, as potent as the Hawk's kiss though it was more fleeting. She saw Anna, dark-haired Anna with her ripe bosom and flashing eyes, her leather jerkin and high boots, a dagger with an odd hilt hanging from her belt.

No, Aileen *was* Anna, inside Anna's skin with alarming speed, seeing through Anna's eyes, feeling the fury of Anna at Magnus' rejection, sensing the many wounds this woman bore. Anna stood beneath a tall tower with a broad dark lake at its base, and the moon was waxing full.

Aileen saw her hand, Anna's hand, rise before her. She saw Anna's fingers twist into the ancient hex gesture and she heard the viciousness in Anna's tone as she began to speak.

Then the vision dispersed and there was only the Hawk, only his embrace, only his kiss. A thousand questions would fill Aileen's thoughts later, but for the moment, she cared little for Anna and her woes. She wanted the Hawk's kiss to never end. She wanted him to caress her as he had before. She wanted him to carry her to his bed and love her all the night long.

Aileen vaguely heard the hoots and whistles of the company, but she did not care. Indeed, she had nigh forgotten who awaited her in the hall, so lost was she in the Hawk's embrace.

When he lifted his head, she tingled from head to toe. She could have melted into him, so languid did she feel, and she had no doubt that he could see how aroused she was. His green eyes glittered and he arched a brow, seemingly asking if she was persuaded of his desire.

"Come to my bed this night, my lord," Aileen whispered, her words hot. "There is a matter left unfinished between us that I would see resolved with all haste."

"As would I," he murmured, his words husky. He released her, then claimed her hand and pressed a kiss upon its back, his eyes dancing wickedly. "Though haste was not within my scheme for seeing this deed resolved."

Aileen gasped, then smiled, knowing that she flushed scarlet. The Hawk smiled, clearly well pleased with her response. He tucked her hand into his elbow, leading her courteously toward her father even as Aileen struggled to regain her composure. She had been thoroughly kissed and right beneath her father's eye.

Her father, she immediately realized, was not so pleased as the Hawk.

Indeed, he scowled, and cast his cup of wine onto the board as they approached. "Have I come to a keep or a brothel?" he demanded gruffly. "Do you keep my daughter as your wife, or merely another of your whores?"

The whores in question giggled. Aileen glanced their way

in time to see luscious Guinevere blow a kiss to the Hawk. He remained impassive, but Aileen's heart sank to her toes.

How could she have forgotten that he had taken a whore to his bed the night before instead of his wife?

"How good to see you, Father," she said with a tranquillity she did not feel. She kissed her father upon one whiskered cheek and then the other and smiled for him. He wavered slightly on his feet and Aileen wondered how long he had been left alone to indulge in the Hawk's wine. "It is too kind of you to journey this far to ensure my welfare."

"What else could I do?" her father demanded with a bluster characteristic of him when he was in his cups. He touched her cheek with a rough fingertip, a rare sign of affection that further illustrated his state. "I feared for your life."

"Yet despite expectations, I am well."

Her father studied her with care, his voice dropping low. "Are you, Aileen?"

She felt the Hawk bristle behind her, insulted by the query and no doubt anxious to hear her reply. Every soul in the hall seemed to hold his or her breath, waiting for her reply.

Aileen turned and took her husband's arm, smiling fully for her sire. "I am well, Father, and content with my new abode."

She felt the tension ease from the Hawk, though doubted that any other would have noted a change in his stance. His gaze was fixed upon her, though, and Aileen knew his expression thawed slightly. Her father glanced between the two of them, then he finally nodded with resolve.

He lifted his cup and turned to the company. "Time it is then to toast the bride!" he cried. "This wedding feast is late, but no less heartfelt for all of that. Join me, all of you, in a salute to Aileen Urquhart, the new Lady of Inverfyre!"

The company cheered and lifted their cups, then drank heartily. They settled at their tables and began to chatter anew, the hall soon filling with laughter and the smell of the meat paraded from the kitchens.

Aileen took her seat and accepted a cup of wine, though she did not taste its richness. She felt the Hawk's attention turn away, as one of his men came to ask something of him, and felt immediately bereft of his attention.

Her father seized the opportunity, leaning close and dropping his voice to address her alone. "We will speak in solitude, Aileen, and I will have the truth of your ordeal from your own lips. You shall have the chance then to speak freely."

"On the morrow will suffice," Aileen said with a smile more confident than she felt. "Let us savor the evening feast this night and leave such serious matters for another day." Her father was reassured and turned to his meal with gusto.

Indeed, one would think he had not eaten in a week. He was more jubilant than Aileen had seen him since her mother's death, outspoken and lavish in his praise of the comforts of Inverfyre even as his speech grew more slurred. He insisted upon singing a tribute to the roast venison when it was paraded from the kitchens and to Aileen's mortification his men-at-arms encouraged him.

The Hawk and his men remained reserved, quiet and watchful. Aileen noted that although the Hawk oft lifted his cup to his lips, he never needed his wine refilled from the decanter. His men loitered in the shadows around the perimeter of the hall, making a pretext of joining the merriment by each holding a cup, but their eyes were as bright as cut glass.

There were two she did not know, though she guessed that the dark-haired warrior with the enormous moustache was Fernando. He seemed to be of an age with Sebastien and the Hawk. There was a grim Scotsman in the same dark garb, whose eyes flashed with suspicion despite any friendly comments made to him. He seemed restless, even more restless than the Hawk's other cohorts.

Was some matter afoot?

There were a surprising number of women in the hall, and worse, most of them were young and fetching. Their chemises gaped to display ripe cleavage and when they bent to serve meat or wine, Aileen feared their breasts would tumble from their garb.

The fighting men in the hall had similar expectations and watched avidly when the women bent near them. The women's buttocks swayed as they eased between the rows of trestle tables and they squealed at intervals as they were evidently pinched. They laughed and teased as no lady of merit would have the shame to do. One even settled upon her father's lap to feed him morsels from his own trencher.

Aileen watched the whores in the hall and the joy she had felt in the Hawk's embrace diminished. Had he only kissed her thus to prove his possession before her father? His lack of interest now that the crisis was behind them said little good about his true feelings.

What if he did not desire her at all? She did not know if she had the audacity to offer herself to him again, and did not know how she would hold up her chin if he rejected her once more. She caught Guinevere's gaze unwittingly and that woman granted her a smile so knowing that Aileen's blood fair boiled.

No, she would not falter before this challenge.

As the meal was served and noise erupted on all sides of

her, Aileen found fortitude in her wine. Her visions had told her that her destiny was tied to that of the Hawk, even if he chose to ignore such counsel. She knew that she had to persuade him to make this a marriage in truth and she could not dismiss that pulse of urgency that tormented her.

The answer was to force the man to consummate their match. It should not be impossible, though she knew little of such intimacy; Aileen knew he could not feign the enthusiasm she felt in his chausses when he kissed her.

She did not doubt that Guinevere with her languid grace and low laughter offered more abed than virginal Aileen could. Aileen drank deeply of her wine. She would have to seduce the Hawk, there was nothing else for it, and she would need fortitude and fortune in considerable measure to ensure her success.

Aileen decided that she would ensure that the Hawk had no choice but to meet her abed this very night. And if he did not, she would depart with her father on the morrow. That would show him the import of this matter.

Perhaps, though, a measure of encouragement was in order.

Aileen cleared her throat and glanced pointedly between the two men on either side of her. They regarded her with polite curiosity, though she expected the Hawk's expression at least would shortly change.

"I have had an idea, Father, that would increase the comfort of your visit to Inverfyre."

"Indeed? Truly all is most hospitable."

"Ah, but I can improve your slumber this night. The Hawk has seen fit to grant me a lady's chamber at the top of the tower, with a fine bed within it."

"Ooooo!" the whore squealed with delight. "A bed, Nigel!"

"Aileen . . ." the Hawk murmured, but Aileen continued undeterred.

"I insist that you use my chamber this night, and however many nights you remain our guest," she said cheerfully. She laid a hand upon her husband's arm and took warning from his stillness. Her pulse quickened, for he was surely angry, but she intended to be certain that they shared a bed this night.

"I shall be slumbering in my husband's bed at any rate," she said, feeling herself flush. "It would be a waste of a good plump mattress for you to sleep on a pallet in the hall."

"I thank you for your generous offer," her father said, clearly pleased by the notion. "But what of your ladies?"

"This lady will be pleased indeed to share your bed, Nigel," purred the whore, then kissed his ear. She whispered something that made Nigel chortle.

Aileen ignored the exchange. "I have few ladies as yet, Father. As you have doubtless noted, Inverfyre has been a warrior's hall." Aileen slid a fingertip down the Hawk's arm, knowing she tempted his wrath but not caring. "My husband has granted me the duty of making a proper hall of Inverfyre, but one cannot force change in haste, particularly in the face of such numbers."

"Indeed not," her father concurred. The whore upon his lap gave Aileen a poisonous glance. "The Hawk has told me of his ambitions for a noblewoman's touch upon his hall."

"Indeed?" Aileen was surprised by this and looked to her spouse.

His expression was grim, his hot glance boding ill for Aileen's scheme. "Indeed," he said flatly. "I would have a word with you, lady mine. Immediately, if it suits your convenience."

The Hawk's wife was a madness in his blood.

He knew that he was bewitched and beguiled, and the worst of it was that he did not care. He was consumed with the prospect of claiming his bride abed, when he should have been ensuring that all was in order for this evening's assault upon the MacLaren clan.

Instead he tasted her kiss upon his lips and felt her thigh pressed against his own and feared he would not be able to wait until the meal was completed.

He was a fool and he knew it. He had never probed her reasons for visiting the prisoner, much less what she had learned from the man. He thought of meeting her abed, and naught else, not even the battle before him this night.

And while he sat and boiled with lust, she gaily offered her bed to her father. His intellect argued with his desire over her plans—was she genuinely concerned for her father's comfort, or was there a darker scheme at work?

The Hawk could not say. His wits were addled, of that there was no doubt, and he guessed that there could be but a single cure: he had to utterly exhaust his desire for his bride, for this alone would clear the fog of lust from his thoughts.

But first, he had to ensure she understood the folly of what she had just done.

If she did not know it already.

If she had not conjured this scheme apurpose to foil his own ambitions.

He claimed her elbow in silence and walked her from the hall, simmering even as she smiled and charmed every blessed soul in his company. They adored her, each and every one of them, and if ever he decided to put her aside for

treachery, the Hawk had no doubt that he would have a re-
volt upon his hands.

They made the bailey, the sky overhead glittering with
early stars, before she turned upon him. Her manner was
markedly less sweet. "What complaint do you have with
me?" she demanded, her eyes flashing.

"Can you not guess the truth of it?" he retorted. "How
could you grant your chamber to your father?"

"How could I not? He is aged, and unaccustomed to a
hard pallet upon a cold floor! He has ridden hard to ensure
my welfare." She propped her hands upon her hips and
glared at the Hawk, clearly unafraid of his temper. "Would
you have my father shown poor hospitality, simply so that
you can bed your whore more readily?"

The Hawk blinked in confusion. "My whore?"

Aileen scoffed. "Play no jest with me! I heard you roar
when your whore sated you early this morn. I know you left
my bed to find someone sweeter to warm your own." She
shook a finger at him as he gaped at her in astonishment.
"Do not imagine that I am so slow of wit that I do not understand why Guinevere beckons to you across the hall."

The Hawk smiled, for he could not help himself. She was
jealous! This was no small triumph in winning the lady's
loyalty! "I have no whore, Aileen."

Her eyes flashed like lightning, a most delightful sight.
"Do not worsen your crime with a lie! I know the truth of it,
and if I have to force you to my bed to ensure that I am not
shamed before my father, then you may be certain that I will
do so." Tears glittered then and he felt a cur for feeding her
doubts. She averted her face, proudly hiding her dismay, and
his heart swelled.

She had feared that he did not desire her and he could not
blame her, not after his abrupt departure from her chamber

the night before. She had meant to compel him to meet her abed, by removing his choice of bedding another elsewhere. And what harm in ensuring that their match could not be readily dissolved? His suspicions faded once again.

He touched her cheek with a fingertip, not surprised when she did not turn to meet his regard. "I have no whore, Aileen, I swear it to you."

"Your hall is filled with whores."

"Their presence keeps the men from making trouble in the village. In truth, I had forgotten their presence as their charms do not beguile me."

Aileen snorted and granted him a sharp glance. "I heartily doubt that you do not notice those breasts fairly spilled in your face. Such women have no place in a decent hall."

"Indeed they do not." The Hawk smiled at her skeptical expression. "I have already bidden them to depart by the morrow, despite Fernando's protests. I am encouraged that our thoughts are as one in this."

The lady was clearly surprised. "You would rid your hall of them so readily as that?"

He nodded, noting that her wariness did not entirely diminish.

"You shouted," she insisted. "Last night, you shouted, as a man in pleasure. Do not deny this, for I know it to be true."

"I did shout."

"Ha!"

"But for another reason than the one you suspect. I am oft visited by nightmares, as I was last night. I awakened, raging at invisible assailants." He grinned, liking the hopeful light in her expression. "I was quite alone, save for the flask of wine which I soon emptied."

"Your demons," she mused inexplicably. "This is the truth?"

"I will never lie to you, lady mine."

She held his gaze for a long moment, then heaved a sigh. Concern lit her blue eyes then, concern that warmed his heart. "What manner of nightmares do you have, Hawk?"

He watched his fingertip as he stroked her cheek. "Nightmares of past deeds, with which I will not burden you. It has been an ugly matter, reclaiming these lands."

She leaned her cheek into the palm of his hand. "The prisoner said that you were the thief and the MacLarens the rightful lairds of Inverfyre."

The Hawk's finger stilled. "Do you believe him?"

"No." She heaved a sigh and frowned. "But I fear he has an ally in your hall, Hawk. He alluded to weakness *inside* the walls when I told him that Inverfyre's walls are too newly wrought to be breached."

The Hawk's heart clenched. "Did he name a man?"

She shook her head and folded her arms across her chest, though she did not move away from his touch. "He solicited my aid in his cause, no more than that."

The Hawk's thoughts flew. Who could be scheming to betray him? Had he rejected Guinevere once too often? Was some servant in his hall discontent? What of those in the village? Aileen had said that the women were discontent to not have a priest, but surely that was not cause enough for treachery?

Aileen shuddered then and glanced up at him. "I confess that I did not trust him. You cannot intend to let these people harass your lands forever."

"No, I do not." Though he was tempted to confide in her, the Hawk could not help but note the timing of her query.

On the morrow, he would trust her with his every secret: on this night, silence was imperative.

She watched him, then looked to her toes. "Why are you so angered with my offer? A mere bed should not have vexed you so."

"Turn and look," he urged. He indicated the tower, catching her shoulders in his hands as she pivoted to study it. He pulled her back against him, though the scent of her rose to torment him. "Where is your chamber?"

"At the top, of course," she said with impatience, then caught her breath in sudden understanding. The Hawk smiled, for he had known she would see the truth of it. "From whence you can see all of Inverfyre."

"And the final refuge of the laird in a siege. With the summit claimed by another and the hall filled with his men, my chamber is betwixt the two."

"Besieged, you would have to defend yourself from both sides," she concluded, then turned to glance up at him. "But, Hawk, my father will not assault you."

He smiled, proud that she had readily understood his concerns. "I do not know him as well as you do. He is displeased with me, that much is true, but I suspect you speak aright. It is his alliances that concern me, though I cede that I am suspicious of all in these times."

"And so you will be until the MacLaren clan are ousted from the original site of Inverfyre," she murmured, looking to the light atop that distant tower. Her fingers tightened upon his and she spoke with vigor. "I would have them routed this very night, Hawk, if the deed would allow your trust of me."

He caught her chin in his hand even as her words made his heart jump. He could find no deception in her gaze, save a desire that echoed his own.

He chose to take her at her word, to follow his instinct and trust his wife.

Aileen must have guessed his intent, for she smiled that slow smile as she turned in his embrace. She rose on her toes, her arms twining around his neck, her fingers winding into his hair. Her lips parted and she reached for his kiss, as tempting an invitation as he had ever been offered.

He caught her close and claimed her lips, lifting her against him without restraint. She arched her back and pulled him closer, demanding more of him with her ardor. He nigh forgot the many guests in his hall. He caught her buttocks in his hands and lifted her off her feet as she slipped her tongue between his teeth.

The serpent bared its fangs in his thoughts and he recoiled from vision and kiss in one vehement gesture. He stepped away from his startled bride and wiped her kiss from his lips with the back of his hand. His heart raced in fear and he could not meet her gaze.

What warning did his instincts grant him?

"Our guests wait overlong for our presence," he said flatly and turned to stride back to the hall.

He took a dozen steps afore he heard Aileen follow him, but still he could not look back at her.

Terror had him in its clutch. What had she done to him? From whence did she conjure this dark power?

And why?

XII

$\mathcal{A}$ileen had no doubt that she had erred. The Hawk's eyes had glittered with distrust when he ended their kiss, and his gesture of wiping away her embrace had been almost disdainful.

What had happened? She knew full well that even if she asked, he would not tell her. Did the Hawk not like a bold woman?

Aileen doubted that audacity alone could have put that flicker of fear in his eye. Though it had been quickly hidden, she had seen it and she had heard its echo in his terse words.

What did the Hawk fear?

What could such a warrior fear from *her*?

She stumbled after him, fighting to make sense of what had just occurred. The company greeted them with a cheer. Aileen managed to flush as she touched her swollen lips. They roared approval that the newly wed couple could apparently not restrain their ardor. The Hawk took his seat grimly and quaffed two cups of wine with a speed that set most of the men to chuckling.

They thought his passion frustrated, though they did not

guess the half of it. Aileen sat in silence, thinking furiously. Had she not seen as much of the Hawk's character as she had, she might have thought him mad or impetuous or rude. She knew though that something had startled him.

He had been startled the moment she had slid her tongue between his teeth. Aileen caught her breath, covering her reaction by taking a sip of wine herself. Whenever the Hawk kissed her, when he initiated and commanded their embrace, she invariably had a vision of the past.

What if the inverse was also true? What if her meager attempts at seduction inflicted visions upon the Hawk? She knew that Adaira had granted him a vision deliberately on his arrival at Inverfyre, for she had experienced that in her own visions and tasted the Hawk's response. She knew her enthusiasm the night before had sent the Hawk from their marital bed. Twice she had attempted to join his loveplay and those were the very two instances when he had spurned her touch.

Because she had inflicted visions upon him, however unintentionally. Aileen was not so simple that she could not discern the pattern. This man was not so bloodless that a bold wife would prompt such a vehement rejection. No, he did not fear her passion.

He feared madness. It was his intellect that had kept him alive and had brought Inverfyre to his grasp. It was the Hawk's cleverness that had kept the MacLarens cornered and would ultimately see them evicted.

Aileen felt a sudden affinity with her taciturn spouse. All the same, she knew that their match must be made whole. How could she encourage him to couple with her?

With passivity, it was clear, though she was cursedly poor at being passive. With Fortune's grace, intimacy would dispel the power of the visions. Though Aileen might choose passivity abed for one night, she would not welcome a life-time of passionless coupling.

She slanted a sidelong glance at her spouse. She did not imagine that he would welcome an uninterested partner abed either. She smiled at him, and ran her fingertip down his thigh. He caught his breath and granted her a look so hot that she inhaled sharply in her turn.

"Patience, lady mine," he muttered as his hand closed over her own. Aileen thrilled with the certainty that he had not been dissuaded from meeting her abed this night.

She liked the resolve of her warrior spouse and his lack of fear. Indeed, the hours could not pass quickly enough for her taste.

Viper in his mind's eye or no, the Hawk knew that he had little choice. On this night, he must claim Aileen or risk losing her on the morrow. He was impatient with the meal, yet did not wish to offend his wife's father. In the end, he could not resist the weight of Aileen's fingers on his thigh. He stood as soon as the meat had been removed from the board and lifted his cup high.

The company fell immediately silent.

"I salute our guest, Nigel Urquhart of Abernye, and bid him to always be welcome in my hall."

The assembly roared approval of this sentiment and Abernye patted his daughter's shoulder. Aileen granted her father a sunny smile, as if to reassure him, and it seemed to work.

"And I salute the bride that Fortune chose for me," the Hawk said, meeting Aileen's shy smile. Abernye snorted under his breath, as if to say that Fortune had no hand in his daughter's abduction. "May our match prosper long."

"May it, indeed," the lady said, rising to her feet to sip from his cup. The company stamped their feet and applauded as he sipped from the same place on the cup.

"Come, lady mine," he said. "Inverfyre has need of an heir."

Aileen smiled and her eyes sparkled. "At least two, my lord, for the world is filled with uncertainty."

The Hawk found himself smiling at her suggestion and she flushed in a most charming manner. "Another cask of wine, if you will, Gregory," he said to his castellan. "The company has a rare thirst this night."

The Hawk kissed his lady's hand and escorted her from the high table to the accompanying cheers of his household. He paused to grant direction to three of his men to guard the outside of his door, those men nodding as Aileen said nothing.

They ascended the stairs alone together, silence claiming them as the raucous merrymaking in the hall faded behind them. Aileen carried a lantern that she had lit before departing the hall and the light cast long shadows on the fitted stones.

The Hawk was aware of her as he had seldom been before. He could smell her flesh, he could see the play of the golden light upon her skin, he could feel the softness of her fingers within his own. The straightness of her spine before him made him think of her rare resolve, the curve of her neck heated his blood with awareness of her femininity. Yet she was no foolish beauty and he found her intellect as alluring as her curves. Were it not for the visions, he would have no fear of confiding his every secret to this woman.

Perhaps that should have frightened him more than it did, but the Hawk could think only of the deed before him. He heard footsteps behind him, heard Ewen's muttered comment to Alasdair, and was reassured that he would not be assaulted while abed.

Aileen preceded him into his chamber and lit a number of fat candles in the chamber. She paused once the room was lit, and glanced about herself, no doubt noting the differences between this chamber and her own.

"You will want to put a woman's touch upon this chamber, no doubt," he said gruffly.

Aileen smiled. "I like it as it is. I miss only the wolf pelts." She regarded him, her sapphire gaze bright. "Did you kill them?"

He nodded but once, awkward with an accounting of his own deeds in this situation. "Ewen can fetch them, if you prefer."

She nodded. "I would. I sleep more soundly with evidence of my husband's prowess beneath my chin."

They shared a smile that warmed the Hawk to his toes. He strode back to the door and sent Ewen to do the lady's bidding, filling his gaze with her as he waited. She removed her circlet and cast aside her veil. She untied her braid and shook the wavy length of her fair hair over her shoulders. The candlelight seized the opportunity to dance within those tresses, gilding each strand. She paused, her hand upon the laces at her throat, and met his regard.

"My lord?"

The Hawk jumped when Ewen spoke behind him. He accepted the pelts with a gruff word of thanks, then closed the portal, ignoring Alasdair's knowing wink. He turned the key in the lock, making it clear that intruders would be unwelcome this night.

When he glanced back to Aileen, she wore only her chemise and her stockings. She bent to untie her garters and he could see the curve of her breast through the thin linen. Her slender strength fired his blood and he said a silent prayer that the visions would abandon him for these few hours.

She cast him a playful smile. "I cannot unfasten the knot."

"A man of honor can only offer his aid," the Hawk murmured. He crossed the chamber, poured the pelts onto the bed, then knelt before her. He loosed the knot and eased the garter from beneath her knee. His mouth went dry when she lifted her foot, indicating that he should remove her stocking.

He slid his hands over her silken skin as he pushed down the stocking, then repeated the task with its mate. She whispered his name, her voice trembling with mingled uncertainty and desire, and he knew that he must reassure her this night.

He caught her chemise upon his wrists and slid his hands up her legs. She caught her breath as he stood slowly, lifting the garment as he did so. When they stood facing each other, she lifted her arms, a silent plea in her eyes. He lifted the chemise over her head and cast it aside, smiling when she stood nude before him.

"Beautiful," he whispered, running his fingertips over her lean strength.

"Blanche said that archery had wrought me too much like a man," she whispered, doubt in her magnificent eyes. "She said that I was made too tall for any man to desire me."

"She was wrong, though that should not surprise you." The Hawk shook his head and caressed the strength evident in Aileen's upper arms. "I like that you are wrought with grace and purpose both, like a skillfully forged blade."

She smiled and blushed, her eyes widening as his hand closed over her breast. He regretted then that she had not yet had the courtship he had hoped to grant her, and made a silent vow to himself to address the matter upon the morrow.

Her talk of archery granted him an idea of what might please his lady.

First, though, there was a more immediate pleasure to be savored. He bent and kissed her nipple, loving how it tightened beneath his caress. His bride murmured his name, her voice uneven and filled with awe. He smiled and captured her nipple in his mouth, teasing it to turgid peak, and caught her close when she arched against him.

There were still several hours afore the night was utterly dark, and the Hawk intended to make the most of every moment before he was compelled to leave his lady wife.

Aileen surrendered to the pleasure that the Hawk conjured with his touch. She clutched his shoulders as her knees threatened to buckle and he lifted her smoothly in his arms. He carried her to the bed and buried her in the wolf pelts. He stepped back and shed his garb, his gaze fixed hotly upon her all the while.

His bed was no less enormous than her own. Its coverings were of boiled wool, thick and warm but plain. Four or five trunks were scattered around the perimeter of the chamber. They were wrought of dark wood, their fronts carved. Aileen looked upon them as the Hawk undressed, modesty compelling her to glance away despite her curiosity.

He pulled his tabard over his head with undisguised impatience and cast it aside, leaving his dark hair tousled. She had been curious enough to steal glimpses of the men sworn to her father's hand over the years, and truly no maiden could live in an abode like Abernye without glimpsing a shepherd without his shirt or surprising a sentry who took a plunge in the Nye river on a summer's afternoon.

She knew how men looked, but Aileen was curious to see how *this* man looked.

His chemise followed his tabard and Aileen could no longer resist her urge. She studied her spouse covertly through her lashes, even as her color rose.

He was muscled and taut, a thicket of hair in the midst of his tanned chest, and he moved as one at ease with his body. There was more than one scar gracing his flesh, but then, she supposed she should have expected no less. He had a rare vigor that made Aileen's mouth go dry. He shed his boots and his hand fell to the lace of his chausses.

That vestige of a smile touched the Hawk's lips as he turned his gaze upon her, and Aileen guessed that he knew she watched him. He worked the lace loose as he crossed the chamber, pulled them over his buttocks as he sat on the edge of the mattress, then kicked them across the floor. He lay back and turned so that they were shoulder to shoulder, lying on their backs. His eyes glimmered with humor and the heat of desire and Aileen smiled.

She reached to caress his jaw with her fingertips, savoring the roughness of stubble. She felt the tension in him then and knew he held himself back.

"How many times must I invite you to partake of your due, Hawk?" she teased and was gifted with a smile.

"Perhaps this shall be the last time," he murmured. He rolled to his side and caught her chin in the warm breadth of his hand, his smile fading as he looked into her eyes. He ran his thumb across her lips, as if marveling at their softness. Aileen yearned to touch him, but she dared not take the chance of granting him a vision. She waited, as if shy, and prayed that this burden would abandon them soon enough.

Then he kissed her with such tender deliberation that she forgot her concerns.

The weight of the Hawk's hand slid over Aileen's breasts, then over her belly, leaving languorous heat in its wake. His fingers slipped between her thighs even as his kiss became more demanding. Aileen gasped at the surety of his touch and parted her thighs, welcoming his caress. She caught his shoulders in her hands and felt the vision gathering strength in the periphery of her thoughts, but she ignored it.

For this night, she wanted to think only of the Hawk.

He kissed her ear, her throat, her neck. He kissed her breasts again, then traced a burning path of kisses to her navel. He piled the furs atop her, rubbing their softness against her pert nipples, then framed her waist in his hands as he eased between her thighs.

He kissed her there, with a gentle boldness that made Aileen catch her breath. He wrought magic with his tongue and she could do naught but savor the pleasure he granted. Heat built within her, a simmering in her very veins that rivaled any sensation she had felt before. An inferno was conjured by the Hawk's sure caress, and though Aileen writhed, he held her fast beneath his questing kiss. She heard herself moan as she felt a throb of desire begin deep within herself. She arched upon the great bed, she caught his hair in her hands, she begged him for release. The heat raged within her, building relentlessly, growing hotter and greater than she had ever imagined possible.

Then the fire exploded. Aileen shouted with her release, even as she was certain she would be burned to a cinder. She clutched at the Hawk, she locked her legs around his shoulders, and they rolled across the mattress as she found her pleasure.

She was breathless and faint when she opened her eyes, though the Hawk smiled up at her. He looked reckless and mischievous, as seldom he did, and Aileen's heart melted fully.

She had rare fortune indeed to have been wed by this man. She admired his resolve and his fairness, his sense of justice and the honor with which he treated her.

"I love you," she whispered, only realizing it to be true in that moment.

The Hawk arched a brow. "A dangerous confession for a new bride," he murmured, his expression yet diabolical. He eased closer, leaning upon his elbow at her side. He wound a tendril of her hair around his fingertip, his expression pensive.

"You should smile more often," she said, running an affectionate fingertip down his cheek.

He smiled then, just for her. "Were you pleased?"

"Could you not tell?"

His chuckle warmed Aileen to her toes and she wished fervently that their nights abed together would be plentiful. She let her fingertip slide down his chest, through the tangle of hair there to playfully encircle his navel. He sobered, and his emerald gaze brightened as he became very still.

"I know enough to know that the deed is not done," Aileen said as her fingers brushed across his erection. The Hawk caught his breath as she caressed him. "I thought we had agreed to see this matter resolved."

"And so we had," he whispered, his words hoarse. He rolled atop her and Aileen hesitated but a moment before she wrapped her legs around his waist. "I will try not to injure you, lady mine."

He braced himself upon his hands, holding his weight above her, his gaze piercing. Aileen kissed his temple and closed her eyes, preparing for the worst, for she had heard fearsome tales of this moment's pain. The Hawk was large but gentle, however, and she was surprised at how readily they two became one.

He waited when he was within her fully, and Aileen opened her eyes to regard him. She saw his uncertainty and smiled. "We must be wrought each for the other," she said and he smiled in his turn.

Aileen rolled her hips and he inhaled sharply. She saw him clutch the linens in his fists, then his gaze darkened as he began to move within her.

"Put your hand upon yourself," he said through gritted teeth. "Thus we can find pleasure together." Aileen followed his instruction and realized that her fingers were pushed against her own tenderness with each move the Hawk made.

She gasped with pleasure and he held her gaze, his own filled with satisfaction. He moved deliberately and she did not doubt that he delayed his own release to ensure her own. Once again, she felt the heat rise within her. A thousand prickles launched over her flesh and her blood seemed to boil beneath her skin.

She arched to meet him, her nails digging into his arms and her breasts brushing his chest. She watched the tension rise within him, watched him flush, watched his eyes brighten, and knew a power in her own allure.

Then the eruption within her made her cry out his name.

The vision thrust itself into her thoughts with cruel vigor. Aileen gasped at the wickedness of what she spied, fighting against the knowledge inflicted upon her, even though she knew it must be true.

What had she done in Anna's skin?

Then, she heard the Hawk's bellow of satisfaction and smiled to herself that it was utterly unlike the cry she had heard from his chamber the night before. They collapsed onto the bed, limbs entangled and breathing hastened, and she welcomed his weight atop her. He pushed her hair back from her face and kissed her with a possessive ardor that made her heart race anew.

"Never betray me, Aileen," he whispered into her ear. "Never dare to be so foolish, for I know not what I would do." He kissed her again, but Aileen closed her eyes as if languorous with sleep.

In truth, her heart raced and she stifled the urge to shiver. The vision had granted her a truth she did not welcome and she hoped with all her heart that the Hawk never learned of it.

She had already betrayed him.

She had heard the curse that she herself had pronounced upon him in Anna's life. And worse, Anna had been Anna MacLaren. The kinswoman that the MacLarens avenged by assaulting Inverfyre was none other than herself in a former life.

Aileen rolled to her side and feigned sleep, taking solace from the Hawk's heat behind her as she considered what she might do to remedy a betrayal she had made centuries before.

The Hawk awakened when the sky was as dark as it would be. The moon was new, though still a thousand stars lit the cloudless sky. He rose, restless, intent upon seeing this last challenge resolved.

He dressed in hasty silence, watching Aileen's silhouette as she dreamed. On impulse, he took the dagger that Adaira had granted them so many years before and tucked it beneath his tabard. He fetched the treasured bow he had been granted years past but seldom used: his skill was with a blade, though he had never been able to part with this fine weapon.

Until now. Perhaps he had never known an archer deserving of it. Perhaps some part of him had known that he had to keep it for the bride he would take to his hand.

The thought made him smile. He caressed the strong arch of the finely crafted bow, and felt the tautness of the bowstring. A quiver of arrows had accompanied the gift, each as strong and true as when they had first come to his hand.

This was a courtship gift his lady would well appreciate. He had a notion that she would be much pleased to have a fine bow in her hands again, though he also recognized that she might be obliged to defend herself, if matters went awry.

He would not leave his most precious prize without a weapon.

The Hawk laid both upon the bed beside Aileen, already imagining her delight when she awakened, and she stirred slightly at his presence. He smiled when she reached across the mattress, seeking his heat, then bent to kiss her brow. He stroked her hair, unable to resist its golden splendor, then touched her cheek with his fingertip.

"Sleep deeply, lady mine," he whispered, his heart clenching when she burrowed her cheek in the palm of his hand. "I leave you only to ensure that Inverfyre is fully ours when you awaken." He gave her cheek one last lingering caress, then pivoted and strode to the door. On the morrow, there would be no cause for distrust between them.

The Hawk could scarcely wait.

Anna walks through the forest of Inverfyre, despondent that Magnus has cast her aside. Cruel Rumor whispers that Anna cannot bear a child, but Anna knows the truth is far darker than that. Shame has sealed her lips, shame has kept her from telling Magnus the truth, and now she has lost her sole chance of escape.

How she wishes he could have asked her for the truth.

How she wishes she had been brave enough to tell him.

But now, now it is too late.

As if summoned by her thoughts, Anna's cousins slip from the forest to walk alongside her. Her brother joins their ranks, a leer upon his face. They are three against her and well practiced in this wickedness. Anna quickens her pace, though she knows it to be of no avail.

Her heart thunders in her fear as they match their steps to hers.

"No tryst with your fine lover this day, Anna," chides her brother.

"On the morrow," she lies, desperately wishing that their fear of Magnus still protected her.

She should have guessed that they would know the very moment that she was defenseless again.

Her taller cousin laughs. "Naughty Anna, to tell us such a lie."

"Have you need of a lesson, Anna?" demands the other cousin.

"Not I!" she declares, her steps lengthening to a run.

"Liar, Anna!" cries her brother. "Your fine Magnus has cast you out. Every soul knows that he will take Margaret for his bride."

"Were you too dirty for him, Anna?" whispers her cousin.

"Dirty slut, Anna," chides the second.

"We shall have to teach her a lesson," her brother threatens. Anna flees, but one cousin trips her.

She cries out as she falls, but the other shoves a rag into her mouth. She is struck across the face and held down in the wet undergrowth of the forest. She struggles, her tears blurring her vision, and screams despite the rag. She feels the chill air of spring upon her thighs and rages as the first climbs atop her.

Aye, she is barren, barren because of the wicked things done to her to ensure that her own family's seed never bore fruit. She weeps at the pain, knowing there will be blood, just as the first time there was blood on the snow. She is trapped forever, ensnared in this wickedness, because she was too proud to ask the only man who could save her for his aid.

She was too ashamed to tell him the truth.

And now Anna will pay time and again for her folly.

A cool hand touches Aileen's brow, easing away her fear. "There are deeds no soul should be doomed to recall," that kind voice whispers and the memory of Anna's assault fades away. Aileen's heart still races with terror, but the familiar feminine voice speaks soothingly. "What could make you hate a man enough to curse him? This is all you have need of knowing, this is the sole reason that you remember any of this."

"Magnus was Anna's chance of escape."

"Indeed, and by spurning her, he condemned her to a life of abuse. Ambition on his side made him fear truth in the rumor that she could not bear a child, a rumor begun by her tormentors."

"And pride on her side kept her from confessing

the truth to him," Aileen murmurs. "She feared to lose him with the truth, but lost him all the same with the lie."

"Indeed." Those cool fingers stroke Aileen's brow again and a fog seems to clear from a vision before her eyes. "Look again, and see how Anna's vengeance was wrought."

Aileen sees Anna utter her curse, sees the company watching her deed, feels Anna's anger. Aye, she hates Magnus as one can only despise what one has loved. But Anna is not content with otherworldly vengeance—Aileen sees her mixing herbs, tainting the water of Inverfyre with her brew, ensuring that Magnus is denied the heir he so desires.

"She knew the herbs well," that kindly voice advises. "For she had used them oft herself."

She sees Anna disguising herself, presenting potions to Magnus' pregnant bride. Then she sees a coffin in the chapel and Magnus himself planting a tree to mark the burial spot of his wife.

And the cycle repeats, Anna's fury burning through her reason.

Aileen is sickened. "What happened to her?" she asks and the voice hesitates.

"But a glimpse will suffice," that woman advises, those fingertips touching Aileen's brow again. Aileen has a fleeting glimpse of flames surrounding her, licking high, scorching her skin. She smells the smell that has always made her bile rise and she gasps in anxiety. She sees the cousins and brother jeering, feels the tightness of her bonds, hears the crowd chanting that she is a witch.

Yet she feels Anna's relief that this torment will end the woes of her days.

"Come, come," the voice coaxes. "Enough of such old pain." Laughter dances in the next words. "Meet me at your memory palace, child."

Aileen is cheered, knowing who she will find there. She summons the recollection of her memory palace and winds her way to the garden. The sun is shining, as always it is, but the rose bushes with their red red blossoms in the midst of the garden are gone.

Instead an older woman stands there, a smile curving her lips and affection lighting her eyes.

"Mother!" Aileen runs to her mother and is caught in a tight embrace. Though she knows this to only be a dream, she is relieved and tearful. "I knew you were not mad."

Her mother strokes her hair, tucking a strand of it behind her ear. "And what is madness, but a differing perception of the world around us?" she asks gently. "Who is to say what is truth from a divine source, what is revelation, and what is madness?" She takes Aileen's hand before Aileen can respond and leads her to a corner of the garden that Aileen had never examined before.

She is no longer surprised to discover things in her memory palace that she had not placed there.

Two plants grow there, a shrub with hardy branches and many thick thorns, and a vine that twines around it like a garland. The vine is graced with white flowers that have a beguiling scent.

"The honeysuckle and the hazel," Aileen says, with certainty.

Her mother smiles. "Aye, for none other could

grace the garden of your soul. Look upon them, daughter mine, and learn something from their growth."

"The honeysuckle adorns the hazel, while the hazel defends the honeysuckle."

"More than that, child. The honeysuckle gains support from the hazel, and stability." She untangles one of the honeysuckle vines and lets Aileen hold its fine length. *"See how narrowly wrought it is; a strong wind would uproot it, or tear it to shreds."*

"But the hazel clings to the earth, granting support."

"Indeed, but the hazel is plain and attracts no bees to its own humble flowers. The honeysuckle gives it beauty while aiding in the fulfilling of its responsibilities. They grant each other purpose, but only when they trust each other fully."

"They are partners in truth, better together than apart."

"And the garden benefits from their combination. Left to itself, the hazel will spread most ambitiously, while the honeysuckle will wind so tightly around other plants as to choke the life from them. They are vigorous plants and both require a strong companion to muster their best." Her mother grants her a shrewd glance. *"They must contain the darker impulses of their nature to nurture each other."*

"The hazel must be less ambitious."

"The honeysuckle less inclined to climb where it is treacherous to pass."

"Anna should not have used the Sight for vengeance," Aileen guesses and her mother smiles.

"And had Magnus compromised his ambition, they might have found happiness together in that life."

Aileen considers the entwined pair of plants. "They require each other, and no others," she says, understanding that her mother speaks more of Aileen and the Hawk than of these two plants.

There is no reply. Aileen turns, but her mother is gone. She gasps and pivots, then her gaze falls upon the red red rose in the middle of her memory garden. As she watches, the bush grows taller, summons a hundred buds, then bursts into glorious bloom. Tears come to Aileen's eyes, for she perceives this to be her mother's blessing of her match.

Then her mother's voice comes from everywhere and nowhere. "Learn your lessons from your past, daughter mine, and the future is yours to claim."

And Aileen knows then that she will always find her mother's clear voice in her memory garden. She has only to dream to find wise counsel.

That is a gift beyond expectation.

Aileen awakened with tears wet upon her cheeks. She reached across the bed, but the Hawk was not there. Her fingers grazed something wrought of polished wood, but Aileen ignored that. She sat up, expecting that he would be watching her as he sipped a cup of wine. The last embers gleamed in the brazier, casting a glow across the chamber.

But the Hawk was gone.

Had she displeased him? Had she unwittingly inflicted another vision upon him? Aileen's breath caught as she scanned the chamber. His garb was gone, as was his blade and his mail.

Had Inverfyre been attacked?

She glanced down to whatever had been left on the mattress and a lump rose in her throat. It was a bow, a beautifully wrought bow, its finish as smooth as silk and its wood the hue of fine honey. Aileen caressed it with a fingertip, noting the quiver of arrows beside it. This was a weapon wrought for a prince, and she understood that her husband had left it for her.

She blinked back her tears of delight and lifted the bow, noting how it fit into her grip. It could have been made for her, the way it nestled into her shoulder, the way the bowstring hummed taut against her hand. Aileen understood that it must have been a gift to her spouse in his youth, for the Hawk was tall enough and strong enough to need a deeper draw.

It was perfect for her, though, and far finer than the bow Blanche had seen destroyed. Aileen smiled to herself, pleased beyond compare that her spouse not only understood how she loved to practice this skill but that he endorsed such a practice in his wife.

She thought of her dream, of the errors they had made in the past and were in danger of repeating, and considered that they two might manage to achieve happiness together this time.

Honesty was a critical part of that potential success, and a need to put one's pride aside. Aileen dressed in haste, wanting only to find the Hawk and express her thanks.

She heard the heavy echo of hoofbeats and hastened to the window, but they faded from earshot, too far for her to see the steeds. The night was darker than dark, the moon new, and she could discern little. The keep appeared to be quiet, as if all slumbered the night away.

But Aileen had heard the hoofbeats of destriers, she knew it well. She knew there were solely seven such warhorses in

Inverfyre, and she knew who rode those beasts. She peered in the direction of the stables, and could see nothing in the deep shadows there.

Uncertainty and fear rose within her. She wondered whether the Hawk had had a particular reason for leaving her bed, or even for leaving her the bow. Had he suspected an assault?

Had he ridden out from the gates?

There was but one way to be certain.

Aileen opened the portal, her fears confirmed by the absence of any guard posted there. Alasdair and Ewen were gone, as doubtless was the Hawk. Nissa was curled as tightly as a cold hound upon her pallet, as if she feared assault in the night.

Aileen touched the maid's shoulder and the girl jumped. "Nissa, the Hawk is gone, as I suspect are his men."

"But where have they gone, my lady?" Nissa blinked as she wakened. "It is the midst of the night!"

The two women's gazes met and Aileen saw the fear in the younger maiden's eyes. She did indeed care for Ahearn.

"I am certain they will return hale enough," she said calmly. "But I would have you join me in my chamber."

The maid swallowed and nodded, then rose quickly. She was yet fully garbed. "I sleep uneasily in the hall, at any rate," she said with forced cheer.

"Did my father retire to the chamber above?" Aileen asked as they entered the chamber and she turned the key in the lock behind them.

Nissa nodded, stooping to stir the coals in the brazier. "With two of his men and a pair of whores." She grimaced even as she coaxed the flames to burn more lustily. "Never have I seen such a drunken lot as your father brought to Inverfyre! Meaning no disrespect, of course, my lady, but one would think that they had never partaken of decent fare."

"There never has been wine of this caliber at Abernye," Aileen admitted. "My father's wealth is far less than that of the Hawk, it is evident."

Nissa's tone softened. "Then, perhaps their gluttony is not so unexpected. They will suffer on the morrow, though, my lady, upon that we can rely."

It was true enough. Aileen realized it was also true that none in this hall would be aware that the Hawk and his cohorts were gone.

Had his generosity with the wine been part of a scheme?

The sound of hoofbeats made both women hasten across the chamber.

"Who is it?" Nissa whispered as the horse drew ever nearer.

Aileen shook her head as she tried to peer into the darkness. She saw the silhouettes of sentries as they clustered at one point on the wall. The hoofbeats changed in speed and in sound, as if the horse left the road, and the steed whinnied. The sentries gathered closer and one shouted.

"Look!" Aileen whispered. On the opposite side of the wall from where the sentries huddled, a shadow slipped over the wall. It was in the same place that Aileen had imagined seeing an intruder on her first night at Inverfyre. There was no doubt that the man was truly there this time though, for Nissa put her hand over her mouth and stared.

"He let the horse run alone," Aileen guessed. "He ensured thus that the sentries would be distracted from their labor."

"Fools! The Hawk would not have been so readily deceived," Nissa whispered loyally, though Aileen knew it was true.

As they watched, the man unslung a bow from his back. He fitted an arrow to the bowstring, then touched it to the flaming torch on the inside of the wall there. The tip of the arrow blazed as he launched it skyward.

"The signal!" Nissa cried in dismay even as Aileen's heart stopped in understanding. Her husband had ridden out to dispatch the MacLaren clan.

And far worse, the Hawk had been betrayed.

XIII

$\mathcal{A}$ileen had no doubt that this arrow was but the first of three. Her heart clenched in fear for the Hawk, who could not know that the surprise would be his, not theirs. The MacLaren clan surely would rather see the Hawk dead than alive.

Perhaps the bowman could be stopped before loosing all three arrows.

"Intruder!" Aileen shouted, even as the sentries pivoted. They shouted and began to race toward the bowman. He launched a second burning arrow in quick succession to the first.

"They will never reach him in time!" Nissa cried.

Aileen pivoted and snatched up the bow the Hawk had left for her. It fitted to her hand as if wrought for her and she savored the tautness of the bowstring as she drew it back.

She doubted she could kill the intruder from this distance in such poor lighting. Perhaps she could wound him so that he was readily identified later—or even injure him so severely that he would bleed beyond salvation.

She took her aim with care, fixing her sight upon his exposed throat. It was a narrow mark, but he wore a mail tabard. He had cast aside his helmet, doubtless because it impaired his vision. His head and throat were the only flesh unprotected, so she had little choice of where to injure him.

Nissa began to pray softly beside Aileen, her plea for aid fervent. Aileen felt her gaze sharpen in the familiar way that foretold that she would hit her mark. When the intruder leaned back to fire his third burning missile high, Aileen loosed her own arrow with vigor.

It whistled through the air, a dark missive fitting for a traitor. The bowman's arrow took flight and Nissa swore softly. He spun, turning to leap from the wall. All the same, Aileen's arrow caught him in the shoulder before he could disappear.

He cried out, in shock and pain, then turned. He sought the arrow's origin, even as he tried to worry the arrow from the wound.

He faced the tower, his features wreathed in shadows. He fitted another arrow to his bow, and took his aim.

Aileen realized that they must be cast in silhouette by the light of the brazier.

"Down to the floor!" She clutched Nissa's shoulder and pushed the girl away from the window.

"But . . ."

An arrow whistled over their heads, so close that it fairly stirred their hair. It planted in the mortar of the far wall, quivering there with malicious intent. Nissa crossed herself, but Aileen peered over the sill.

It was clear why the intruder had not feared the sentries.

The sentries shouted with dismay and despair. Hundreds of shadows slipped over the walls, as plentiful as vermin. They overwhelmed the sentries as the women watched in horror, spilled into the bailey, and claimed Inverfyre for their own. The village must be occupied, as well, for there was no aid forthcoming from that settlement.

"They attacked this holding, knowing that the Hawk had ridden to claim the chapel," Aileen murmured. "But they could only make such a plan, if someone in the Hawk's company confided his scheme." She turned to the maid. "Who knew of it, do you think?"

"I heard not a whisper," Nissa confessed. "But I would wager that his six companions knew the truth. There are no secrets within that company, but many between them and the rest of the household."

Footsteps and shouts echoed from the hall below and Nissa clutched Aileen's hand so tightly that she nigh broke the bones. "What will happen to us, my lady?"

"We shall use our cunning, Nissa," Aileen said with a confidence she did not quite feel. Revulsion rose within her as she guessed what scheme these men would have for herself and Nissa. "We shall survive until the Hawk's return."

Nissa began to pray again.

Aileen raced across the chamber and pushed a trunk against the locked door. Her thoughts flew as she tried to determine what prize these felons might seek. The only thing of value she could recall was the relic Nissa had mentioned, aside from the wealth of the holding itself. "What is said of this relic you found?"

Nissa blinked. "It is the *Titulus Croce*, the sign that was hung above Jesus when he was crucified, and a most holy relic indeed. It was surrendered to the care of the first Laird of Inverfyre."

"Magnus Armstrong?"

"None other. The laird's good care and protection of it ensures God's favor for Inverfyre."

"And it is not in the chapel, because the chapel is held by

the MacLaren clan," Aileen mused. "The Hawk awaits this last triumph before he invests the chapel with this prize."

"I suppose as much. It would fulfill the old tale, for the rightful laird possesses the *Titulus*."

"So, any man who would claim Inverfyre in the Hawk's stead would have need of it," Aileen concluded, remembering the prisoner's insistence that the Hawk was the thief and Dubhglas MacLaren the rightful laird. He would need the *Titulus* to legitimize his claim. "Where is it, Nissa? We must ensure that the *Titulus* is secured for the Hawk."

"But how, my lady? It is nigh as round and large as a loaf of bread!"

Aileen smiled. "Have you a needle and thread? If you sew quickly, we can see it concealed where no man would look."

The forest was dark and silent as a tomb.

The Hawk's company closed from all sides upon the stronghold of the MacLaren clan and his sense of foreboding grew with every step. They saw no soul. They heard no soul.

But he smelled roasting meat. The scent was strong enough that he was tempted to retreat, the aroma of burning flesh and singed hair enough to make his innards churn.

"They cannot be far," he muttered to Sebastien. "Not if they have cooked meat this day."

Sebastien looked to him in confusion. "What do you mean?"

"Do you not smell the meat?"

Sebastien shook his head. "There is no scent of food that I can discern, my lord, no smell of fire or meat or horses." He peered into the darkness. "It is as if we approach an abandoned keep or even the wilderness itself."

"But the smell. Surely you smell it!"

Sebastien shook his head.

"And look!" The Hawk pointed through the thick growth of the forest to a bonfire that crackled far ahead of them. "There are the flames themselves! The fire must burn in the old holding itself."

Sebastien regarded him as if he had gone mad. "I see no flames, my lord," he said softly.

"I do," the Hawk insisted and lunged toward the bonfire with purpose. He suspected no trap, for the MacLarens had no knowledge of this assault. All the same, the Hawk drew his sword and moved stealthily through the forest.

The flames crackled as he drew closer and he felt their heat. They cast dancing lights onto the silent forest, and still he saw no soul. There was no one tending the blaze, evidently, and no one gathered close to its warmth. This puzzling fact made him pause and consider his surroundings.

Was it a trap? He looked down and saw by the light of the fire that the ruins of the old stone walls were directly before him, though the forest had nearly reclaimed them. The fire crackled, the scent of sizzling skin tormented him, but he stepped over the walls and approached the bonfire.

It was built as high as a pyre and a dark shadow was consumed in its midst. What did the MacLaren clan burn? What did they destroy of his birthright?

The Hawk rounded the fire with quick steps, his blade at the ready, and nigh vomited at what he finally saw.

A woman was bound in the middle of the fire. It was her burning flesh he smelled, her singed hair. He shouted and lunged toward the fire, thinking to save her afore it was too late, and she lifted her agonized gaze to him.

It was the maiden Anna, her blue blue eyes filled with torment. "Be not deceived, my love," she whispered hoarsely, then lifted her hand toward him. A serpent writhed in her palm, then bared its fangs.

And the vision was gone, as surely as if it had never been.

The Hawk raced forward, touched the ground where the fire had been. It was damp and cold, as if there had never been flames kindled here. The shadows were dark and silent on all sides, and the Hawk spun in place, that cursed scent still filling his nostrils.

"Did you see it?" he demanded of Sebastien, who had hung back.

That man shook his head once again. "I see nothing," he said, kicking at the loose stones in what had been the bailey as he approached the Hawk. "They are not here," he continued with disgust. "They knew we would assault them this night and have taken to the forest."

"That makes little sense. Why would they so willingly cede the last portion of Inverfyre to me?"

Their gazes met in horror as they guessed in the same moment where the MacLaren clan had gone. "They could not seize the keep!" Sebastien whispered, his tone by no means certain.

"They could, if they had surprise within their ranks," the Hawk said grimly. He thought of Aileen and feared mightily for her fate. "But who could have told them? Only we seven knew of the scheme."

Sebastien's lips tightened to a thin line. "Then one of your most trusted cohorts must have betrayed you, my lord."

Indeed. The answer was unassailable.

"Someone advised the MacLarens that we had ridden out," the Hawk mused. He watched as his men appeared from other points of entry. Reinhard and Ahearn came from the MacLarens' sorry hall, shaking their heads and sheathing their blades as they crossed the clearing.

"They have left only the breadcrumbs," Ahearn said.

"They have been gone at least a day," Reinhard concurred.

"Were you two together every moment since leaving Inverfyre?" the Hawk demanded and the pair sobered, understanding immediately the portent of his question.

Ahearn nodded. "We left you at the first fork in the road, as you recall, and have been inseparable since."

Reinhard nodded agreement.

The other three men came from the ruins of the chapel, Ewen's disgust nearly tangible. "Gone!" he cried with undisguised frustration. He swung his blade. "Fled like chickens! Grant the word, my lord, and we shall hunt them down with the hounds."

"You need not hunt them, for it is clear where they are," the Hawk said, watching the three men.

"A clever ruse," Fernando said, obviously seeing the Hawk's meaning. "Though one that requires a traitor in your ranks."

"Have you all remained together?"

Alasdair nodded, though the other two men were not so hasty to agree. "We were," he insisted.

"Except when your horse threw its shoe," Fernando said quietly.

Alasdair scoffed. "I followed fast behind you though on foot, you know as much."

"We know no such thing," Ewen argued quietly. "Save by your own tale."

"You were fair out of breath," Fernando commented.

Alasdair grinned. "I have not run sufficiently of late, it is clear."

Fernando abruptly touched Alasdair's upper arm and that man flinched. Fernando caught his sleeve and tore the cloth away. Alasdair had bound a length of linen around his arm, though it was stained with blood. "And you favored your arm. How did you sustain a wound, when we faced no attack?"

"I fell when my steed stumbled and impaled it upon some dead tree," Alasdair said crossly. "What is the root of this suspicion? Have you need of some soul to blame for this failure, and I have been chosen?" He sauntered toward the Hawk, challenge in his eyes. "Have I not served you well these years?"

The Hawk studied him, not wanting to be unfair and knowing that he had no evidence against this man. Fernando's suspicion, though, was never roused without cause. He flicked away the length of linen and revealed that Alasdair's tattoo was that of two entwined serpents.

And the wound, curiously like that wrought by an arrow, marred the head of one serpent.

Here was Anna's signal to him.

Something must have gleamed in the Hawk's eyes at his realization, for Alasdair suddenly lunged forward with a snarl. The Hawk ducked but Alasdair's blade caught his cheek, drawing blood. Alasdair kicked the Hawk's sword from his hand, then caught the Hawk around the neck and tucked his blade beneath the Hawk's chin.

"All of you shall back away, or I will kill him," he declared, gesturing to the other five men.

"You will never conquer the Hawk," snorted Sebastien.

Alasdair stiffened and the Hawk knew to expect more trickery from this man. "Tell us of your brilliant scheme," the Hawk urged softly. "I had no reason to suspect you."

"Because you are not so clever as I," Alasdair said. "I came to serve you, seeking adventure. I yearned to follow a brave and lawless man, but you, you wish only to be a landholder." He pulled the Hawk to one side and sneered in his very face.

The Hawk remained passive even as he considered his choices.

"You wished only to feed your vassals and hold fair courts and collect your tithes and bed your wife," Alasdair continued with disdain. "What manner of life is this for a man whose blood runs red?" He drew the blade across the Hawk's throat, and the Hawk did not flinch as he felt his blood trickle down his flesh.

Ahearn stepped forward to intervene, but Alasdair waved him off. "Assault me and I will kill the Hawk."

"Then we will kill you!" said Ewen.

Alasdair smiled. "You will never manage it. I vowed to kill the Hawk, even if it is the last deed I do, and God favors my cause."

"And what did Dubhglas MacLaren offer you in return for this deed?" the Hawk asked mildly.

"Silver! Enough coin that I could claim a ship myself and commandeer a crew, enough riches that I could seek that adventure upon the seas."

"My coin, I suppose," the Hawk mused.

Alasdair shrugged. "What do I care of its source? The bounty will be mine, for I will not fail at this deed." He gave the Hawk a shove. "Hasten yourselves, for Dubhglas insisted you must die in the chapel."

The Hawk gave his men a minute nod. He did not doubt that some trap had been contrived in the chapel that would see his men disabled while Alasdair fled.

He had to outwit Alasdair before his men were injured. Despite his hope, there was no opportunity to surprise the warrior, who was keenly observant of every detail. The men were backed into the chapel, predictably concerned for their leader's fate. When Alasdair demanded that they retreat further and punctuated his demand with a jab at the Hawk's throat, they stepped back of one accord.

And the floor gave beneath their feet. The five men tumbled with a shout into one of the old crypts and the Hawk was left alone with his assailant. He did not doubt that they could free themselves, but Alasdair would have time enough to steal a steed and escape.

"How wickedly clever!" The Hawk spoke with an admiration he did not feel. "You have cornered us most cunningly. I salute your intellect." He withdrew slightly, letting the warrior preen. "I must confess, Alasdair, that I never guessed at the full power of wits and sorely misused your abilities."

"Indeed you did."

"Then, let me apologize, afore I die." As Alasdair gloated, the Hawk bowed deeply and seized the dagger hidden beneath his tabard.

He straightened with the weapon in his hand. The Hawk would have the chance to land only one blow, and he made it count. He slashed at Alasdair's throat while that man was still surprised. He drove the old blade into the other man's throat, so deep that the wound was fatal. Its blade was honed so sharply that his flesh might have been wrought of butter.

Alasdair crumbled at the Hawk's feet, his blood running in a torrent, an expression of surprise still upon his face. He gurgled as he claimed his last breath and the Hawk watched to ensure that he died.

Then he aided his men to escape the hole, all five of them upon their feet in no time at all. They all treated Alasdair's body with disgust, nudging him with a foot or spitting upon him.

Sebastien looked upon him with scorn. "No wickedness

goes unpunished," he muttered, then crossed himself. "And there is honor even among thieves. Rosamunde would never suffer a traitor like this one in her service."

The Hawk was already striding back toward his steed. "Into the forest!" he commanded. "We will hide ourselves, as they have hidden themselves, so they can find no trace of us if they seek us out."

"What of Alasdair's body?" Reinhard asked.

"Leave it for carrion," the Hawk said with resolve. "A traitor deserves no better fate than that."

Especially as that man had endangered the Hawk's lady wife.

"But what of these lands?" Ewen demanded. "Should we not defend what we have won?"

"Leave it," the Hawk counseled. "The MacLaren clan are welcome to this shred of Inverfyre, for the price they have set upon its acquisition is too high." He swung into his saddle and gathered the reins in his fist. "Come. It is of greater import to learn the fates of the rest of Inverfyre."

By the time Aileen and Nissa heard heavy boots upon the stairs, they were as prepared as they could be. Nissa was suddenly pregnant, the *Titulus* cleverly sewn into her chemise so that she looked to be round with child. She hid behind the draperies of the bed at Aileen's commanding glance and clutched her weapon of choice.

Aileen faced the door when the men began to pound their fists upon it. She wore only a chemise and had left her hair unbound. The linens of the bed she had rumpled, as if she had just been roused from sleep by the unholy noise in the hall. She took a deep breath as the wood shattered around the lock and the portal swung open. She held her ground when they kicked it in so hard that it hit the wall.

And she was heartily glad that she and Nissa had not exchanged places—for she had considered the merit of such a scheme—once she saw the sorry excuse for a man who shouldered his way through the portal. His hair was a ruddy thatch, his complexion reddened by exertion, though he was as broad as an ox. He was missing at least one tooth and sported a scar across his brow. The flesh puckered where one of his eyes had been, though the other gleamed with malice when his glance landed upon her.

He gave Aileen the sense that she faced an angry, hungry hound and she suppressed a shiver with an effort.

"The Lady of Inverfyre, I assume?" he said.

Aileen inclined her head. "None other. And you?"

"Dubhglas MacLaren," he said with satisfaction. "Chieftain of the MacLaren clan and soon to be the Laird of Inverfyre." His smile was evil. "But first, I intend to become your worst nightmare."

Aileen raised a hand to her lips, as if she was a demure maid, and let her eyes widen. "Oh my," she whispered and he chuckled darkly.

Half a dozen rough men crowded the door behind Dubhglas. He grinned as he brazenly assessed Aileen, and his hand fell to the lacings of his chausses. "The Hawk has finer taste than I had dared to hope," he said, his voice rough with threat. He waved his men away. "Open the Hawk's casks of wine and take every whore in his hall that tempts you. This one shall be mine alone."

One man behind him protested, but Dubhglas shook his head. "On the morrow, lads, on the morrow you can all sample her, once the Hawk is securely in our hands." He could not restrain his laughter. "I would not have him miss the witnessing of such an event."

He kicked the door closed and shoved a trunk against it.

He fixed his gaze upon Aileen, and crossed the floor, unlacing his chausses with unholy haste.

A man bellowed upon the stairs and Aileen heard booted feet descending. She felt herself pale at the bellow of her father's battle cry, though she knew there was nothing she could do to aid him. A struggle ensued as Dubhglas watched her keenly and she had to close her eyes when bodies thumped against the wall.

"An acquaintance, perhaps?" Dubhglas inquired.

"My father," Aileen admitted, uncertain whether the truth would aid her father or harm him.

"Ah!" Dubhglas rapped his knuckles upon the portal. "Do not kill him yet," he cried, watching Aileen all the while. "The father of the Lady of Inverfyre may yet prove useful."

A rumble of assent carried through the oaken portal and Aileen's mouth went dry as Dubhglas strode toward her again. "And now," he said. "You may show your gratitude for my kindness. Indeed, you may be so sweet that you save your father's life."

Aileen nodded, though she did not believe a word he said. For all she knew, her father was already dead. Certainly, there were no sounds from the corridor and her father would not let himself calmly be captured.

She retreated, sitting on the edge of the bed with apparent meekness. "Oh, I hope you are a man who knows a woman's desire," she whispered.

"Does the Hawk not sate you?"

"He cannot come close to seeing the task done," Aileen murmured, then slid back across the bed. She patted its plumpness, inviting him to join her. "I have yearned for a true warrior between my thighs."

"You need yearn no longer," Dubhglas declared. "Indeed,

should we please each other, I might let you live, as my lady wife."

Aileen licked her lips, wishing he would make haste.

He roared and leapt upon her, seizing her hair in his fist before he kissed her brutally. He was heavier than she had anticipated and rougher than she had hoped. She rolled him toward Nissa's hiding place with an effort, fighting against her revulsion and her own desire to do him damage. He was harsh enough to ensure that she felt a welt rise upon her lip.

When he lifted his head and fingered the swelling with satisfaction, he had only long enough to smile before Aileen spied Nissa. The maid lifted the brass candlestick high. Aileen kept her expression demure so that her assailant would not be warned, then Nissa brought it down upon his head with a loud crack.

He groaned and Aileen shoved his weight from her. He bled slightly, but he raised his head and fixed his baleful glance upon her. "Bitch!" he cried, and Aileen seized the candlestick herself. She swung it hard into his face and heard a bone crack. She struck him again upon the head, Anna's thirst for vengeance hot within her. He collapsed across the bed and the two regarded each other shakily.

"We must bind him fast," Aileen said. "And hastily."

They trussed him like a lamb meant for the slaughter and gagged him tight in case he awakened too soon. He began to struggle when they shoved him under the bedlinens and Aileen hit him again without remorse. Fortunately, the ruckus of men celebrating that rose from the hall below was enough to hide many sounds of struggle.

Aileen donned some of her husband's clothing with haste, then handed Nissa a knife. "Cut my hair and cut it short," she commanded.

The wide-eyed maid did as she was bidden, and Aileen

made another bundle in the bed beside the trussed Dubhglas. She fanned her hair across the pillow, as if the bundle was her body and her hair spread loose in sleep. When she turned away, Nissa lifted a handful of ash from the brazier and rubbed it into her lady's short hair, disguising its fair color.

"My lord?" a man demanded suddenly from the other side of the portal. "Is all well?"

The women's gazes met in alarm.

"Grunt," Aileen bade Nissa in a whisper, then raised her voice in a gasp that sounded as if she was finding her pleasure. Nissa grinned in understanding, then grunted in a low voice, her rhythm unmistakable.

"Oh!" Aileen wailed. "Oh, oh!"

The man on the other side of the door laughed heartily. "Far be it for me to interrupt such merriment," he said, then a thump echoed as if he settled his weight against the door.

Aileen and Nissa turned as one, and Aileen fastened a rope that had been stored in one of the trunks to the bedpost. She flung it over the sill and the maid swallowed.

"I am afeared, my lady."

"You should fear what will happen in this chamber more than a broken bone," Aileen counseled. She laced the Hawk's bow across her shoulders and seized the quiver. "Go!"

The maid licked her lips with trepidation, then seized the rope. She climbed over the sill, her feet scrabbling for some grip upon the smooth walls.

"Quickly!" Aileen bade her. "They are not so drunk as to be completely blind!"

Nissa lost her grip in that moment and slid down the rope with astonishing haste. She landed with a thump upon her buttocks, and uttered a gasp of surprise that none but Aileen could have heard. She glanced up then, nodded to her lady, then picked up her skirts and hastened into the shadows.

Aileen spared a glance for the high walls, but the few sentries there were watching the road, undoubtedly for the Hawk's return. She slipped over the sill and made haste down the wall, then hastened through the bailey.

Nissa, she knew, would make her way to the miller's abode, as they had agreed. The girl had so glib a tongue that Aileen did not doubt that she would persuade the guards on the gates of the inner wall to let her proceed. She smiled from her hiding place in the shadows when she heard Nissa weep in a most emotional manner, crying that her husband would be vexed with her. Aileen hoped that those guards had no desire to despoil a woman so clearly pregnant, so she watched until Nissa was successfully through the gates.

The maid even waddled like a woman round with child, her ruse utterly convincing. Though the miller knew nothing of the tale, he and his son would protect Nissa, this Aileen knew without doubt.

She herself hid in the shadows of the stables, watching the gates for her opportunity to slip through to the village. She would seek out the sole person remaining within Inverfyre's walls whom the Hawk trusted without reservation.

She would seek refuge and counsel from the falconer, Tarsuinn.

The Hawk and his men lurked in the forest outside Inverfyre's gates, merging with the shadows even as the sun rose high the following day. The snow was melting with a vengeance and mud churned on the road.

"There are too many of them," Sebastien muttered for the hundredth time. "They must have hired mercenaries."

"With what coin would they pay such men?" Ewen demanded.

"My coin," the Hawk muttered. "You may be certain that my treasury is empty by now."

"As are your wine cellars," murmured Sebastien, as another drunken sentry tried to walk the wall. Even with the high number of besotted men, the Hawk and his men were still vastly outnumbered, the gates were still barred against them, and the Hawk had no doubt that many of these men would sober in haste if attacked.

A mercenary owed his survival to his quick wits, after all.

His gaze flicked repeatedly to the high tower, but he had yet to see any sign of life in any of its windows. Dread gripped his heart and he feared mightily for his lady's fate.

It did not seem, however, that there was much he could do.

A clarion call was blown, albeit raggedly, and the men in the woods straightened silently. The gates began to groan as they were opened. Every man dropped his hand to the hilt of his blade, and fixed his gaze upon the rising portcullis. The silhouette of a horse and rider came into view, then the horse was slapped from behind. The horse took the bit in its teeth and ran, while the man in the saddle toppled back and forth as if powerless.

"What folly is this?" Ahearn demanded in a whisper.

"It is Nigel," the Hawk declared, and indeed it was.

"He is tied to the saddle," said Sebastien.

"Like Father Malcolm!" Fernando muttered.

The six men sprang into their own saddles, fearful but determined to do what they could. Ahearn whistled to the horse, then ran alongside it, coaxing it to a halt, even as the others rode to block the road. Jeers rose from the high walls of Inverfyre, and several arrows buried themselves in the muddy road, but they were far enough from the gates to escape injury.

Nigel had not been so fortunate. He was weeping openly and one of his eyes had been put out. His wrists were trussed to the pommel and his feet to the stirrups, and a burden had been laid in his lap. The blood still running from his wound was what had made the horse so skittish.

They released him despite the beast's frenzied prancing and carried him into the protective shadow of the forest. Ahearn remained with the horse, striving to calm it with his soothing murmur as he walked it. Nigel wept so copiously that it was difficult to understand what he tried to say.

"How badly are you injured?" the Hawk demanded. "What else have they done to you?"

"Just the eye." Nigel took several gulping breaths and steadied himself. "They put out my eye so that you would know from whom I came."

"Dubhglas MacLaren," the Hawk growled.

Nigel sighed. "I least I still have one, that I might have vengeance from the one who did this foul deed."

"And why do you weep? What is amiss in my hall?" The Hawk gritted his teeth when Nigel shook his head and began to sob again, then shook the man's shoulders with vexation. "What of Aileen?" he shouted.

"I have betrayed her," Nigel confessed, his words sending a chill through the Hawk's heart. "I tried to defend her when they assaulted your chamber. I did not realize you were not there." He shook his head, tears still rolling down his cheeks. "They were so many and in the end, I fell." He met the Hawk's gaze with pain in his own. "I failed my only daughter, for she was left alone with Dubhglas."

"That fiend has no heart," Sebastien whispered but the Hawk turned away.

"I shall hope that the lady's uncommon resilience aided her," he said, his voice husky.

"I fear that hope is not enough," Nigel said. "Look at the missive they have sent to you." He unfurled the bundle that had been in his grasp and the men stepped back from the stench of it.

It was the banner of Inverfyre, the banner of the Hawk, and it had been torn from its place of honor above the gates. The intruders had defecated upon it and the smell was unbearable.

But the Hawk did not step away. For there, in the middle of the mired banner, lay the length of his lady's hair. It gleamed golden, shorn cruelly from her head, and he could not draw a breath at the sight of it.

His men swore softly, but the Hawk gently picked up Aileen's hair. This must be all of it, from the quantity, and he recoiled from what must have happened for her to have allowed this to be done.

"They want the seal of Inverfyre and the relic called the *Titulus Croce*," Nigel said. "For they say that neither are within your treasury."

"They lie," Ahearn said bluntly. "I have seen the *Titulus* there myself."

"They say that they will exchange Aileen for relic and seal," Nigel continued.

"They lie!" Sebastien said hotly. "She is probably dead already, or close to it!"

Ahearn and Fernando silenced him with a glance, but the Hawk barely noted the exchange. He saw only the length of her hair cradled in his hands and remembered caressing it the night before.

But hours before he had left her and unwittingly abandoned her to a cruel fate.

"I will be at the river," he said tersely, and left to see the soil washed from the hair.

While he did so, he prayed with all his heart that she had avoided torment. He prayed that she could forgive him, for like his forebear Magnus Armstrong, he had sacrificed his sole desire for the sake of his earthly ambition. Despite all the warnings the lady had granted to him, he had walked precisely the same path again.

He coiled her hair with care and put it into his purse, as a talisman, and his fingers brushed the other item secured there.

It was the seal of Inverfyre, which he had carried upon his person since it had first been entrusted to him by his father, almost twenty years before. He turned it in the light, noting the carving of the peregrine and the residue of red wax caught upon its edges.

The Hawk knew that the true prize Dubhglas desired of him was not this seal. It was the Hawk's own life that was the issue, for so long as the Hawk drew breath, Dubhglas would not sleep soundly. So long as the Hawk drew breath, his vassals would defend his interests—upon his death, they would probably scatter for lack of leadership and protection, abandoning Dubhglas' every desire to his hand.

Perhaps he and Dubhglas could make a wager.

The Hawk glanced back through the trees and saw that his men were aiding Nigel. Ahearn wore a frown as he treated the wound, his saddlebag laid open at his side, and Ewen offered Nigel a flask of *eau de vie*. The horses loitered beyond them, nibbling at the undergrowth and quietly nickering.

They would never notice his departure. He would take no horse, for he would offer Dubhglas no other chance to make a creature suffer.

That man had souls enough to torment behind Inverfyre's walls. The Hawk slipped through the shadows of the forest on silent feet, and emerged on the road just outside Inverfyre's gates.

The sentry shouted and a crowd gathered atop the walls as the Hawk walked steadily toward the portcullis. A dozen bowmen trained their arrows upon him, but none loosed a shot. He heard a shout behind him as his men undoubtedly realized what he did, then he paused and unbuckled his scabbard with deliberate gestures.

"I come to parley with Dubhglas MacLaren," he said, his voice carrying clearly to the sentries arrayed before him. "And I come unarmed." He laid his scabbard and belt upon the road, then walked toward the gates as the portcullis slowly rose.

XIV

*A*lthough Tarsuinn recognized Aileen immediately and quickly stepped back from his portal to invite her inside, she realized that she was not alone in seeking his hospitality.

Guinevere sat at the small table, her cloak and hood nestled tightly around her neck. She granted Aileen a wry glance which told Aileen that she was not fooled and turned back to the fire without comment.

"I did not mean to interrupt," Aileen said quietly, assuming that the whore pursued her trade here.

Tarsuinn snorted. "You interrupt nothing but two old friends comparing knowledge of poultices."

Aileen's surprise must have shown for the old falconer smiled.

"We each offer our share of healing, in my case to peregrines, in Guinevere's case to women who seek her aid."

"I thought Ahearn was the one with healing gifts at Inverfyre," Aileen said, daring to take one of the other seats at the table.

Guinevere shrugged. "It was not Ahearn who granted Margery aid, at your dictate."

"I thought Nissa went to Ahearn."

"She came to me when he refused." Guinevere arched a brow. "Perhaps he knows less of women, or at least of their woes, than he would like all to believe."

"I would have thanked you, had I known," Aileen said. "And though it is belated, I would thank you now."

Guinevere looked up, not troubling to hide her bitterness. "I wondered why I was cast from the keep immediately after following the Lady of Inverfyre's bidding. The Hawk bade all the whores be gone by first light, but at least Tarsuinn has a shred of compassion in his heart."

"It is not a lack of compassion that persuades a man that his children should not be raised in the company of whores," Aileen argued.

Guinevere chuckled. "No, it is his new wife that so persuades him."

Silence stretched between the pair, until Aileen laid her hands upon the table. "And what am I to do? Surely you can see that this hall has to change from one of fighting men and their whores to one of respectability? My mother never had to tolerate whores in the hall of Abernye."

"So, you are the one who lacks compassion," Guinevere mused.

"I do not! I know what is proper—"

"You know nothing," Guinevere sneered. "You do not know what it is to have your father die and your brothers offer you to their friends for coin. You do not know the shame of losing every item in your possession, even your dignity. You do not know what a refuge Inverfyre has been for me and others who have shared my sorry path. You do not know what it is to be a woman undefended amongst rogues. Condemn me if you will, and I have no doubt that you will, but I have survived. I will not be compelled to agree with your petty notions of propriety."

She sat back and sipped her ale, her eyes filled with malice.

"I did not know," Aileen said, ashamed of her hasty assumptions.

"You did not ask."

Tarsuinn sighed and sat down heavily beside Guinevere. He touched her shoulder in a paternal gesture that she did not avoid. Indeed, she spared him a sad smile, as if to reassure him that her anger was not aimed at him. "It is better always to have the truth told," he said, then turned to Aileen. "Guinevere's father was a baron in Wales, who died young and left insufficient coin to sate his four sons."

"No amount of coin would have sated them," Guinevere muttered.

Belatedly, Aileen saw a lesson that was hers to learn. With power of any kind—not just that of the Sight—comes the burden of responsibility. As Anna, she should not have used her gift against her love, however Magnus had vexed her. And here, at Inverfyre, she should not have shunned Guinevere and the other women without first asking for their tales.

As Lady of Inverfyre, she had power to aid them, and the responsibility to do so.

Aileen leaned across the table and touched Guinevere's hand. "I am sorry that I spoke in haste. If we triumph, know that I will teach you and any of the women from the Hawk's hall to serve noblewomen. And I shall endeavor to make good matches for them, as the lady of any abode should do. I ask them and you only for honesty and a desire to learn."

Guinevere inclined her head. "It may be too high a price

for some," she said with a smile. "But your wager is fair, my lady."

The two women shared a tentative smile, the first mark of a truce that Aileen hoped would only grow stronger.

She cleared her throat, for there was one matter yet that she did not understand. "But you have the healer's gift, Guinevere. Why do you earn coin upon your back?" Aileen asked, not flinching from the other woman's sharp look. "People willingly offer coin for potions and healing counsel."

"So I have told her, many a time," Tarsuinn agreed.

"It is wicked to take payment for such a gift," Guinevere insisted.

"Hardly that," Aileen said. "And surely it offers a better chance for your future. A healer's price only increases as she ages and gains wisdom, though the same can hardly be said of a whore."

"What of Fernando?" Tarsuinn asked kindly and Guinevere flushed.

"What of him? He speaks with me, as if my sole asset is not between my thighs." She lifted her chin, her eyes bright with challenge. "I like him well, but what of it?"

Tarsuinn smiled. "I think he likes you more than well, Guinevere, and I think this admiration is mutually shared. Have you had this same argument with him?"

"He is always vexed when I take a lover, but men are possessive."

"Yet you have never taken Fernando as a lover," Tarsuinn observed.

"I would not sacrifice the friendship we share. And it is true that he coaxes me with pretty words to do his bidding, to leave my lovers for all time, even to abide with him." She looked into her cup, her expression bleak and her voice soft.

"I dare not believe him, Tarsuinn. I could not bear to learn that he is just as fickle as all the others."

Aileen reached across the table and seized the other woman's hand. "But what if he is not? What if you have a chance of happiness, yet you are spurning it for no good reason?"

Guinevere looked up, hope dawning in her eyes.

A heavy knock came on the door in that moment, then the portal was kicked open. "Surrender your weapons!" bellowed one of the MacLarens' mercenaries.

All three of the occupants stood in fear.

The mercenary glanced over them without interest. "Where is your sword, old man?"

"I have none. I am but a humble falconer."

The mercenary kicked over a barrel of oats, disregarding that the contents spilled onto the dirt floor. Indeed, he walked through it, as if to ensure that the oats would be of no value. "And you, pretty boy?"

Aileen shook her head and the mercenary's eyes narrowed.

"Oh no, he is mine!" Guinevere purred. She closed her hand over the place where Aileen's jewels should have been and Aileen was so clearly surprised that the mercenary laughed.

"Aye? And when you are done with the boy, why not lie with a man?" He gave her breast an impudent squeeze and Guinevere managed to smile, as if she was encouraging.

"Do you know where I might find one?" she asked with a smile, her manner flirtatious.

The mercenary laughed, then caught her roughly against him. He kissed her with vigor, then cast her back toward her stool with such force that she stumbled. "I know the weapons that your kind wield," he said with a sneer. "I shall remember this abode this night, that much is for certain."

He kicked over the jug of cream as he left the hut and none of them protested. "And what is in here?" he roared, no doubt at the moulting house beside Tarsuinn's house.

The old falconer ran after him then. "The peregrines must have silence to preserve their value as hunters," Tarsuinn insisted.

"Let me see them. I am bidden to examine every structure for weapons and women."

"I would not suggest . . ."

The women winced when they heard Tarsuinn grunt in pain. The moulting house door opened and the birds began to protest as the mercenary obviously checked the hut. Tarsuinn grunted again and the mercenary laughed.

"Let that teach you to not defy me, old man," he said. "I will be back, and you will be more compliant, I trust." And with a whistle, he continued upon his way.

Tarsuinn returned to the hut, nursing an eye that was rapidly swelling and a sore midriff where he had been punched. Guinevere fussed over him, the affection between them more than clear.

"Fernando's promises are of no import now," Guinevere said, as if the conversation had not been so rudely interrupted. "The Hawk and his men have ridden out, Inverfyre is lost, and we shall be on our backs, my lady, afore the week is complete."

"No," Aileen insisted. "We must aid the Hawk somehow."

"We are outnumbered," Guinevere argued. "Even if the Hawk and his men return, there must be a hundred mercenaries in the hall. I was there. I counted them."

"And how many villagers have we? How many ostlers

and squires and sentries and millers and wives and children? We are more than them in total, though they count only the fighting men. Can you not wield a knife, Guinevere? Could a peasant not wield his scythe? Could we not overwhelm the attackers, if we all rose in defiance together?"

"Vassals will be killed," Tarsuinn said with a shake of his head. "It is not their place to fight for this very reason."

"They will be killed beneath the MacLarens' hand, at any rate," Aileen insisted. "I, for one, would rather die fighting, than die however and whenever some cur decides my fate. I would fight for Inverfyre, even if I risk dying in the fray. We owe no less to the Hawk."

"She is right," Guinevere said unexpectedly. "I, too, will fight for the Hawk and for Inverfyre, though my contribution may be small."

Tarsuinn glanced between the two women, noted their determination, then nodded. "Fair enough. I will wield my blade in turn."

"What blade?" Guinevere demanded.

The falconer grinned. "My sword is secured in the wall. I would not surrender such a noble blade willingly to such a felon." He savored the women's surprise, then winked at Aileen. "Choose the time, my lady, and we shall send word through the village. You speak aright when you say that they do not trouble themselves overmuch with the common people."

"I shall fire the first arrow," Aileen said with conviction, and touched the Hawk's bow with her fingertips. "I shall try to set it aflame first. Let us scheme to attack once they have retired to the hall for the night, for they will be drowsy with wine and not anticipating an assault."

Guinevere smiled. "Aye. Villagers all retire with the sun,

the better to rise with the sun. The MacLarens will not anticipate us."

Word traveled through the village more quickly than a fire and Tarsuinn reported that more than one household were surreptitiously sharpening their hoes and scythes. Aileen chafed to see the evidence of support for the Hawk herself, but Tarsuinn had insisted that she remain hidden in the moulting house. Small knives abounded in every household and Aileen imagined that whetstones were busy. She had forgotten about the stonemasons with their chisels and hammers, though there were still a number of them in the village. Guinevere reported with satisfaction that all were easily roused to defend the Hawk and Inverfyre.

But at midday, a ruckus carried from the bailey. Aileen heard hoofbeats and men shouting and curiosity made it nigh impossible for her to remain hidden. The ensuing silence had her pacing the confines of the moulting house. Though it made the hooded peregrines most anxious, she could not be still in the face of such uncertainty.

Tarsuinn appeared finally, his expression grim. "They have sent a missive to the Hawk," he said, his words thick.

"What kind of missive? What do you mean?"

He granted her a solemn glance. "You will hear the truth from some soul, I suppose." He sighed. "It was your father, bound to his steed, with his eye put out."

Aileen cried out in anguish but Tarsuinn patted her shoulder paternally. "He is alive, lass, and Dubhglas himself is proof that loss of an eye does not kill a man."

"I should not have fled the tower and left him there."

"Do not blame yourself!" He let her weep upon his shoulder, though his voice was stern. "There was nothing you might have done to halt their wickedness, lass. The Hawk will be pleased beyond all that you escaped, for you would have borne the brunt of their wrath against him."

"But my father . . ."

"Has been dispatched to the Hawk, who will find him. Remember that Ahearn is in the Hawk's company and if any soul can tend your father's injuries in this moment, it is Ahearn."

Aileen wept for a moment, then straightened when Guinevere came to the moulting house in haste.

"The Hawk has surrendered!" Guinevere said, astonishment and fear in her eyes. "He means to exchange his life for ours."

"No!" Aileen cried and would have run to witness his foolery.

Tarsuinn seized the back of her tabard and Guinevere caught her shoulders even as she blocked the door. "You cannot aid him," Tarsuinn said sternly.

"You must not draw their eyes to yourself," Guinevere insisted.

"But they will kill him!" Aileen took a deep breath and forced her galloping heart to slow. "No. We will aid him before they have the chance to injure him."

"Disguise yourself," Tarsuinn counseled, then cast a homespun cloak over Aileen's shoulders. "Remember that weapons were confiscated early this morn. You must hide the bow with care."

Guinevere pulled up the hood with a wry smile. "You are a woman in man's clothing," she said with a smile. "Anyone with eyes to look will guess the truth of it."

"So you drew the mercenary's eye to yourself, this morn," Aileen realized belatedly. The other woman smiled and Aileen touched her shoulder, her determination to wrest a better fate for this woman redoubling. "Thank you, Guinevere."

A considerable crowd had gathered between the gates of inner and outer wall. The villagers were held back by a number of armed mercenaries, who did not let the commoners approach too closely. They created a circle of barren space, and the Hawk stood alone in its center.

Aileen noted that his sword and scabbard were gone and feared mightily for his fate. All waited, apparently, for Dubhglas, who descended from the hall for the Hawk's surrender. When that man appeared, he did not walk with the confident swagger he had the night before and Aileen noted with satisfaction that a wound upon his head was bound.

"The portcullis in the outer gate must remain open," she told Guinevere, who nodded once, then disappeared into the crowd. She did not doubt that the Hawk's men would appear, and wanted to ensure that they were not trapped outside the gates. Tarsuinn remained beside her, her bow and his sword between them so that no other would feel their shape. She let the crowd jostle her, and waited impatiently for a chance to reveal itself.

To her delight, Dubhglas' entire company came through the bailey with him to witness this moment. The sentries upon the walls watched events below avidly. The Hawk did not move and the villagers were silent with expectation. There was not a single flame alight in the village at this hour of the day, and Aileen despaired of sending her signal.

Then she spied Nissa and had a thought. The mill wheel was turning in the waters of the river, which meant the millstones would be grinding.

And there would be sparks thrown by the stones. In addition, the miller's abode was one of the tallest in the village: she would have a good vantage from the upper windows.

Aileen eased toward the miller's abode, Tarsuinn keeping beside her with such casual ease that she knew he had had more adventures in his days than the training of falcons.

"You are slow to claim what you declare is your desire!" the Hawk called to Dubhglas. "Could it be that you are not so bold as you would have all believe?"

"There is no need for haste," Dubhglas retorted. "Indeed, vengeance is better savored cold than devoured in haste."

The Hawk scoffed. "I owe you no vengeance. Yours is a theft, no more and no less. There is not a soul within these walls who does not know the truth of it."

Dubhglas halted and glared at the Hawk, men on his every side. "Yet you surrender to me all the same."

"Because you are evil of intent, not because your cause is righteous," the Hawk retorted. "I would surrender my life for that of my wife. Where is she? Or have you killed her so quickly as this?"

Aileen and Tarsuinn reached the mill. The miller and his family stood before the door in a row, with their hands clasped behind their backs. The miller's eyes widened slightly when he recognized Aileen. He nodded minutely when she eased closer to the door, and Tarsuinn followed. Nissa, looking ripe and benign, stood beside the miller's son like a dutiful wife. Aileen saw, though, that the maid held a wicked little knife behind her back, her grip fast upon it. They all held weapons and stood straight with resolve.

Dubhglas laughed. "The whore sleeps so soundly that she could not be roused in haste. I suppose she has finally been sated. I found her lusty indeed, Hawk. Tell me, have you bedded her at all?"

Aileen raced up the steps to the upper floor of the mill,

the heavy grinding of the millstones hiding the sound of her footsteps. She looked out across the lower bailey and saw the Hawk straighten, though he said nothing.

"I thought it would be fitting if I took her as my wife in your stead," Dubhglas taunted. "Either by me or my men, she would conceive a child with MacLaren blood in its veins, which would be a fine legacy for the future."

"You have killed her," the Hawk said flatly.

Tarsuinn appeared at Aileen's side, a flame kindled in his hand. He hovered in the shadows as she fitted an arrow to the bowstring. "Make it count, my lady," he whispered.

Aileen nodded and lifted the bow, trembling inside at the import of this single shot.

"Not yet." Dubhglas raised a finger and his men took a step toward the Hawk. "There will be no wager, Hawk. I have anticipated too long the sweet joy of you watching your lady wife despoiled."

"No!" the Hawk cried.

"No!" Aileen cried, tipped the arrow into the flames, then loosed it directly at Dubhglas. He turned at the sound of her voice, his movement ensuring that the arrow caught him in the other eye. He screamed, even as the village erupted in chaos. At every point, villagers raised their weapons and assaulted the mercenaries in their proximity. Surprise served them well, for a number of men fell before they realized what was happening. Dubhglas roared with fury and lunged toward the Hawk.

The Hawk pulled a dagger from beneath his tabard and stabbed Dubhglas. Aileen watched him split the other man from gullet to groin, then kick aside his corpse in satisfaction.

"Lady mine!" he roared, pivoting in the empty space as he sought Aileen.

Aileen took her aim and loosed an arrow. It felled the mercenary who lunged at the Hawk from his blind side. The Hawk spun and laughed, then granted a fleeting glance to the millhouse.

It was enough that more than one mercenary followed his gaze and began to fight closer.

Hoofbeats echoed on the road beyond the gate. Seven black stallions raced through the gates, then reared above the chaos of the crowd. One had an empty saddle and Aileen saw with delight that her father rode another. She could not immediately discern who was missing from the Hawk's company of cohorts.

She saw Ahearn cast the reins of the one with the empty saddle to the Hawk. Her husband swung into the saddle and Sebastien handed him his unsheathed blade. He galloped toward the millhouse, cutting a path through the crowd with his blade and his steed, Ahearn riding fast behind.

Her position known, Aileen loosed as many arrows into the fray as possible. She would do what she could to aid the Hawk's cause, though she could not guess her own fate.

The Hawk cut down two mercenaries on the very steps of the millhouse, but two others lunged inside. Tarsuinn pivoted, his blade at the ready as footsteps sounded on the stairs. Aileen did not know where to look first.

She saw a fifth mercenary battling with the miller's son, who valiantly tried to defend Nissa and his parents. He was poorly equipped though, his small blade a poor match for his assailant's larger sword. The mercenary forced him back, cutting his face, then hooking the knife out of his hand. That man laughed, though Nissa's expression revealed that she tightened her grip on her own still-hidden blade.

Ahearn rode out of the crowd abruptly and shouted. He dispatched the surprised mercenary with a fatal stroke, then dismounted with the Hawk. He guarded the portal, while the Hawk took the stairs. Nissa bent over the miller's son with concern.

Tarsuinn shouted and Aileen spun to find the first assailant upon them. She cast aside the bow, which was useless in such close proximity, and pulled the small eating knife from her belt. She heard the clash of steel upon steel as the Hawk attacked the other mercenary below.

Tarsuinn was unexpectedly agile, though once he had surprised his attacker, that advantage was lost. They battled fiercely, back and forth across the floor, the mercenary larger and younger than the falconer.

But not perhaps as wily. Tarsuinn took a blow and bent over in pain. The mercenary stepped closer to make his kill, even as silence rose from the floor below.

"Praise be!" Tarsuinn cried with delight. "The Hawk comes for you!"

The mercenary glanced over his shoulder for the barest moment. It was long enough for Tarsuinn to recover from his feigned injury and lunge toward his assailant. Their blades clashed, but the mercenary was off balance. Tarsuinn landed a blow and the mercenary fell backward, shouting once before his head cracked upon the stone stairs. The Hawk hailed Tarsuinn's triumph with a cry and Aileen stepped away from the wall to congratulate them.

But a man's gloved hand closed harshly over her mouth, shoving her back against the cold stone wall.

"Not so hastily," he muttered in Aileen's ear as his knife touched her chin. "I will see some gain from my journey this far."

Aileen realized belatedly that he had scaled the wall of the millhouse and slipped through the large window while her attention was diverted. This mercenary was large and bearded, pungent and determined.

"I never had my pay," he declared when the Hawk and Tarsuinn approached with caution. He drew the knife across Aileen's throat. "Make me an offer, and perhaps the lady will live another day."

The Hawk smiled with confidence and rested the tip of his bloody blade on the floor. He folded his hands atop the hilt and regarded the mercenary with undisguised amusement. "You expect a ransom for a dirty boy? I have a village full of them."

"But you called for your lady."

"Ah yes. She is the pregnant one, who stands defended outside these walls."

Tarsuinn chuckled and turned as if to leave. "Fool! You have erred in truth."

"But you defended . . ."

"Myself," Tarsuinn said wryly. "I defended myself. The boy simply happened to be here." He turned his back upon the mercenary and sighed. "Come, my lord, battle awaits." Tarsuinn began to descend the stairs.

"Indeed, you speak aright. We shall have no rest on this day."

Aileen could nigh hear the mercenary thinking. There was no doubt that he was not keen of wit, though she guessed his blade was lethal enough. She met the Hawk's gaze and knew he was not as much at ease as he would have this mercenary believe.

He whistled as he caught up his blade, as if indifferent to the fate of Aileen or the military power of the man who held her captive. The mercenary gasped in amazement and his grip loosed slightly upon her.

Aileen grasped his wrist, pushing his blade away from

her throat, in the same moment that she drove her heel up into his crotch.

The mercenary howled in pain. Aileen ran. The mercenary snatched after her with a bellow. The Hawk leapt up the stairs and pushed Aileen behind him to safety. The mercenary swung his blade and the Hawk leapt over the strike, landing on the lip that kept the millstones confined. The mercenary lunged after him and the Hawk jumped out of the way, catching the back of the mercenary's tabard and hurling him over the lip of stone.

He screamed but not for long. The stones continued to churn, though their passage became more labored. Aileen had to look away as the flour coming out of the mill ran red, but then the Hawk's arms closed around her. He pushed one hand through her shorn hair, then cupped her chin in his hand.

"Are you well?" he demanded urgently, uncertainty in his eyes.

Aileen smiled for him. "Now that you are returned, I am well indeed," she said, then welcomed his kiss.

They descended hand in hand to find that the villagers had fought with vigor. Many of the attackers had been injured or killed, and the vast majority of them had chosen to depart from Inverfyre's gates.

"But why?" Aileen asked her husband.

"Without Dubhglas and his pledge to see them paid, these mercenaries' lust for battle quickly waned," he said. "It is the weakness of hiring men to fight, as they have no loyalty to leader or cause. Their loyalty is solely to their own advantage."

Aileen's father embraced her with undisguised relief.

Ewen had been slightly injured and one of the black stallions had sustained a cut upon its flank. Reinhard had sought out Margery and her family, and Aileen was pleased to note that Margery's mother was clearly enchanted with that warrior. The pledge of nuptials had gone far to mend that rift.

Guinevere was already busy setting bones and binding wounds, Fernando fast by her side to aid her. The flush on the woman's cheeks told Aileen that if this pair had not agreed upon some course together thus far, then they shortly would do so. The villagers seemed to bear their wounds as marks of valor, and worthy of pride. None of them had been killed. Gregory the castellan was flustered but busy ensuring that pitchers of ale were distributed among the villagers.

Only Ahearn was vexed and he was vexed indeed. He tended to the injured stallion with gentle fingers but his brow was furrowed with annoyance. When he finished and turned back to the company, Nissa confronted him. "Are you so determined as that to evade me?" she demanded. "I would thank you for your aid, as would Ruardh."

Ahearn scoffed. "Is that whose babe rounds your belly? The miller's son's?"

Nissa's surprise was evident, then she touched her belly as she laughed. "This is what has irked you so?"

Ahearn shook his finger beneath the nose of the miller's son. "What manner of man are you to take your pleasure with a maiden and not offer to wed her? Do you not know that Nissa desires a man of honor as her husband and a house of her own, as well as children? You would seem to have ensured that she had a child, but what of the rest?"

Aileen began to chuckle at Ahearn's outrage. Nissa was laughing so hard that she could barely stand and even the miller and his family seemed to be amused.

"What manner of place is this?" Ahearn demanded in a

roar. "Is it so amusing that I would see you treated with honor?"

"Indeed it is," Nissa said pertly. She reached beneath the folds of her robe and removed the *Titulus Croce* from its hiding place. Her apparent pregnancy disappeared and even the Hawk began to chuckle as she granted the relic back into his care.

"There is not a man alive whose seed ripens so much as that in a day or two, Ahearn," Nissa chided Ahearn with a smile.

Sebastien began to laugh uproariously. "Did love cloud your vision, friend of mine?"

"Of course not!" The back of Ahearn's neck turned crimson and he was sorely discomfited.

"Perhaps you should name the matter aright," Sebastien teased. "This is the first time that I have ever seen you fall victim to a prank, though you scheme to trick others often. Perhaps little Nissa is the woman you should take to wife."

Ahearn glanced up, his expression hopeful.

Nissa tapped her toe with mock impatience. "And all these years, Ahearn, I thought you were keen of wit." She tossed her hair. "I should need much persuasion to wed a man who is such a fool."

The Irishman grinned, pure mischief in his eyes once again. "Persuasion is it then? How about that kiss, Nissa?"

"Oh!" Now it was Nissa who flushed, much to Aileen's delight. The maid still shook a finger at her would-be suitor. "We shall only have a kiss if you pledge to wed me."

"I do," Ahearn said as he strode closer to her. "Sebastien will keep me to my word, for he dreads the prospect of competing with me still."

They all laughed as Ahearn kissed Nissa soundly, leaving

the maid dizzy when he lifted his head and his smile filled with satisfaction.

"It seems that all ends well at Inverfyre," Aileen murmured to the Hawk.

He smiled down at her, sensual intent gleaming in his eyes. "But I still believe there are matters left unfinished between us. Our wedding night was celebrated in such haste." He kissed her then and Aileen sighed contentment in his embrace.

"It is so long to wait until the evening," she whispered and was rewarded by his wicked grin.

"The Laird of Inverfyre pronounces that his lady shall not wait," he declared, then caught her in his arms. He carried her toward the hall, ignoring the whistles that echoed after them.

They both would have preferred to ignore the sounds of a party arriving at the gates, but the Hawk spared a backward glance.

"Oh no," Aileen whispered, recognizing her father's banner before a familiar voice carried over the bailey.

"Nigel? Nigel! *Eh bien*, look at your garb! Your daughter has come to live, how do you say, among the pigs!" Then Blanche screamed, apparently seeing Nigel's wound. They watched as she fainted and Nigel caught her, then her entourage clustered closer to revive her.

Aileen and the Hawk exchanged a glance, then he pivoted and strode toward the tower without a backward look, his lady wife laughing all the while.

It was comparatively quiet in their chamber. The trunks had been dumped and all was in shambles. The Hawk hesitated on the threshold, his grip tightening upon his bride as he guessed that she must have faced Dubhglas here.

"Would you prefer elsewhere?" he asked.

She surveyed the chamber somberly, then met his gaze. "It is our chamber, for now and always. The sooner we fill it with happy memories, the sooner the poor ones will weaken and fade."

Pride bloomed within him that his bride was not readily daunted. The Hawk closed the door with his boot and she turned the key in the lock, her smile turning playful. He laid her upon the bed, pleased to see that the wolf pelts were yet there and intact. Their gazes held as they undressed impatiently, each casting their soiled garments aside with haste. Aileen rose on her knees and pulled the drapes closed on the bed, hiding the disarray from sight and creating a quiet haven for them both. The Hawk was honored indeed to share that haven with her.

He noticed the difference as soon as she kissed him. This time, she was not shy; this time she returned his kiss with passion. Visions unfurled in his thoughts—tangled vines and ripened fruit, what must have been past lives and deeds—but he gave them no heed, choosing instead to concentrate upon pleasing his lady. They wove a potent spell between each other that afternoon, as the sun slanted through the window and gilded the drapes, a spell that bound their hearts and souls together for all time.

And when they reached their culmination together, the Hawk did not close his eyes. He watched Aileen, watched passion take her over the summit, watched an understanding dawn in her blue blue gaze.

The vision tumbled into his thoughts, alien and yet familiar, and he was certain that she saw it in the same moment as he. He followed the course of the entangled vines with increasing haste, as if he raced down a corridor. His sight plummeted along their length until he reached the roots and the entwined stems dove into the ground.

He was in a meadow, waist-high with wildflowers with the summer sun heating his back. The sky was blue beyond blue, as were the eyes of the red-haired maiden whose hands he held fast within his own. She whispered a spell in some old tongue, one that he knew he had agreed to join. Though he could not understand the words, he knew their import well enough.

They two agreed to become one. They two agreed to meet again and again, to draw flesh across their souls, to live and breathe and grow in wisdom, to do so together. They vowed to remind each other of their shared past, of their bonds, of their love, all to ensure that neither would never be alone again.

It was a memory that brought tears to the Hawk's eyes, and made him clutch Aileen close when they lay together on the linens. Their limbs were entangled, he noted with a smile, like the honeysuckle and the hazel, and that delighted him.

Aileen propped herself up on her elbow to look down at him. "Did you see it?" she whispered.

The Hawk smiled and stroked her cheek. "I saw it, lady mine. I saw that we are each wrought solely for the other, from that day through all time." He ran his thumb across her smooth flesh and made a confession long overdue. "I love you, lady mine, with all my heart and soul."

Her smile was all the answer that he needed, though her kiss was a marvel he would not refuse.

Epilogue

The Hawk's family gathered at Inverfyre for Midsummer and the Feast of the Nativity of Saint John the Baptist on the following day, as was their wont.

Horns were sounded from the high walls of Inverfyre when the party was spied upon the road. The villagers clustered along the roadway, intent upon seeing the finery of the visitors. The Hawk and Aileen stood at the portal of the keep, the Hawk's cohorts standing to his either side. Tarsuinn the falconer stood with them, then the ladies Aileen had taken into the household to train arrayed themselves on either side. Those who labored in the kitchens and the hall stood in a row behind.

All were garbed in their best and a sense of festivity filled the air. Smiles were plentiful and eyes were sparkling, even as the merry sun herself glinted on gems and polished buckles. Aileen caught her breath at the splendor of the company that spilled through the gates.

Their horses were fine beasts with long tails and manes, and they pranced as if they knew the import of the occasion. Two banners were carried before the company, a dark banner that the Hawk told Aileen was that of Ravensmuir, and a one with a burning orb which he said to be of Kinfairlie.

Squires flanked the first noble couple in the party: a dark-haired knight and a red-haired lady rode larger steeds than the company surrounding them. They were of an age with her father, though handsome. Their horses had silver bells hanging from their harnesses, and the bells tinkled merrily as the company advanced. Their harnesses were finely wrought of colored leather and Aileen thought that gems glistened, both on the saddle and on the lady's fingers. They were dressed in silk, this pair, their garb lavishly embroidered and embellished, the fur-lined cloak of each held on the shoulder with a large ornate brooch.

They held hands as they rode, and Aileen noted that the lady cast many uncertain glances at her steed.

"My aunt and uncle, Ysabella and Merlyn, Lady and Laird of Kinfairlie," the Hawk murmured in her ear. "Ysabella has never had a fondness for riding."

Aileen could not imagine why, for the older woman looked most elegant upon her steed and rode with grace.

Behind this pair rode a dark-haired man alone. He seemed more sober than most, his smile thin as he glanced over Inverfyre's high walls and its villagers.

He smiled when he spied the Hawk, the expression taking years from his manner. "You have made many changes since last I rode this way!" he called to the Hawk by way of greeting.

Aileen watched her husband smile in his turn as he waved in acknowledgment. "My cousin, Tynan, accompanied me when first I came to Inverfyre, then was obliged to return to the administration of Ravensmuir. When he reached his eighteenth summer, Merlyn relinquished the lairdship of Ravensmuir to his son, then bent his attention upon rebuilding Kinfairlie."

"Why?"

"Ravensmuir would ultimately become Tynan's holding and Merlyn wished him to learn his responsibility while he had recourse to good counsel. By then, the damage from Ravensmuir's fire had been repaired, while Kinfairlie was still in ashes. It had been razed to the ground when Ysabella was but a glimmer in her mother's eye and is her ancestral holding."

Aileen granted her husband a wry glance. "You are much vexed by fires in this clan."

The Hawk smiled. "A timber keep, even if faced with stone, is most susceptible. The new walls of all these keeps are built to withstand such treachery."

She indicated Tynan with a lift of her chin. "Your cousin appears to be a most sober man."

The Hawk seemed to fight his laughter. "He has traveled in the company of Rosamunde. I have no doubt that he has been sorely vexed by her."

"They do not like each other?"

The Hawk shrugged. "They infuriate each other. I suspect, in truth, that Rosamunde vexes Tynan apurpose. Look! Roland, my milk cousin, has come with his wife and children!"

"God in heaven, how many children do they have?" Aileen whispered as the large party came into view. There were many children, all dressed splendidly as if they were the progeny of a nobleman.

"Eight," the Hawk said with a wink.

"And there is not a one of them even old enough to earn his spurs!"

"I hear 'tis cold in Kinfairlie in the winter," the Hawk

jested. "Though I do not doubt that Roland welcomes his father's aid with the administration of that estate."

Though finely dressed, the children were clearly restless. Roland waved heartily and was the first to dismount. He aided his wife from her saddle, then loosed his children. He laughed as they scattered. Two scampered directly for Ahearn, who was clearly a favorite. He swung them high and teased them, as Nissa watched with a smile. Roland crossed the bailey to the Hawk, and Aileen liked the merry twinkle in his eyes.

One of the children shrieked, another shouted and Roland's wife shook her finger in the direction that the majority of them had disappeared. "Mind your new garb!" she cried so good-naturedly that Aileen knew she was well accustomed to such foolery. "Remain out of both millpond and stables, if you please, at least until you meet your new cousin."

There was no reply to her command, merely more giggles. She spared a glance for her husband and rolled her eyes, her expression making him chuckle.

"By the time we depart, you will be persuaded to remain chaste all your days and nights," he teased, sparing a wink for the Hawk.

The Hawk's grip tightened over Aileen's fingers, for their lovemaking had already conjured results. They had agreed to tell his mother the news first, so they held their tongues at this moment.

Boys from the village who had been trained for this moment leapt forward as the company dismounted to lead the horses to the stables. They would see the beasts brushed and tended, under the ostler's stern eye.

Introductions were made and greetings exchanged, a

warmth lighting around Aileen's heart that the Hawk's family accepted her so readily into their brood.

Carts and maids and palfreys crowded into the bailey as the family spoke, then another banner was carried in triumph through the gates. Aileen began to fret about the amount of food prepared in the kitchens, for she had not anticipated so large a company.

"Do you think we will have sufficient fish for the meal this day?" she asked her husband in a whisper. "The eels are not so prolific as yet though the miller's son has labored hard."

The Hawk caught her close against his side. "What we have will suffice. I knew my family would arrive in full this year, so fear not, lady mine."

"Because the capture of all of Inverfyre is worthy of celebration?" she asked, letting him see her pride in him.

"Indeed." He smiled slowly. "Though my mother will be as intent upon meeting my new bride as visiting the chapel once again. Fear not—they come for the company more than the fare."

The clarion sounded again and another party rode through the gates. The villagers began to cheer and Aileen guessed why. "This is the Lammergeier banner, then?" she asked.

"It is no other. Come and meet my parents." The Hawk caught her hand in his and led her to meet the pair that had ridden through the gates.

Their steeds were as dark and as large as the stallions favored by the Hawk and his men, and Aileen understood from whence this magnificent lineage had come. The woman's hair was dark, like the Hawk's, but threaded with silver, while the man was tall and fair. The man dismounted, then aided his wife to do so, and Aileen saw that there were tears in the older woman's eyes.

"Aileen, meet my father, Gawain, and my mother, Evangeline."

Gawain granted Aileen a crooked smile that reminded her of the one the Hawk could conjure when he so chose. He bent over her hand with a flourish and kissed her knuckles. "It is a delight to make your acquaintance," he said. There was devilry in his eyes and Aileen imagined that the children would be smitten with him as well.

"The Lady of Inverfyre," Evangeline murmured, smiling through her tears. She was a beautiful woman, her features strong, and she moved with grace. "I am delighted to meet you, Aileen." She kissed Aileen's cheek, her touch as light as a brush of a feather though it warmed Aileen to her toes.

"You asked us to accompany Inverfyre's new priest," Gawain said, then turn and gestured to the simply garbed man who slipped from his saddle when indicated. His name was Father Gilchrist, the same as the priest at Abernye, and Aileen smiled at the coincidence. She greeted him warmly, as did her husband.

"I hope you have slept well these past weeks," Aileen told the priest. His brows rose in silent query. "You have much labor awaiting you here, for there are children to be christened and marriages to be blessed and many confessions to be heard afore we celebrate the mass on the morrow."

He smiled with confidence. "I welcome the challenge, my lady. Surely I will not be forsaken in doing God's work?" He chuckled along with Aileen, and she liked his manner. The Hawk had chosen well when he had journeyed to Edinburgh in the spring to find a priest and she gave him a smile that showed her pleasure.

"Michael!" shouted a woman who rode last through the gates, in defiance of protocol, her steed galloping with haste. Her hair was long and as fair as gilded sunlight, and though she must have bound it neatly that morn, tendrils escaped her braid. She leapt from the saddle with astonishing agility and Aileen thought she heard Sebastien catch his breath. "You have made a millpond in this wretched wilderness! And there are walls built around the old chapel now! Zounds, but you are becoming a respectable laird, little brother!"

With that, she threw herself upon the Hawk, landing a tempest of kisses upon his cheeks while he laughed. "Rosamunde, you will persuade my new wife that my mistress has arrived."

She laughed in her turn. "To couple with one's sister would be disgusting beyond belief. I do not believe you capable of such a foul deed," she chided cheerfully, then turned a bright smile upon Aileen. "So, you are the woman who finally captured the Hawk's reluctant heart?" she demanded, an approving light in her eyes. "I can see why, for it is clear the match favors both of you."

Before Aileen could summon a word, Rosamunde seized her shoulders and kissed her heartily upon both cheeks. "Be happy, Aileen, that is my wish for you both," she whispered, then winked as she stepped back.

Sebastien clutched at his heart and feigned a swoon. Rosamunde watched him and laughed merrily. "What a woman!" he cried, and she laughed louder.

Tynan shook his head and turned away, his manner grim. Aileen watched Evangeline note Tynan's response, then exchange a thoughtful glance with her spouse. Clearly there was some old tale at root of this, though Aileen did not dare to ask after it as yet.

"We have brought you gifts, Aileen," Evangeline said. "For any lady has need of a garden to take a repose, and we knew full well that Inverfyre's garden was long destroyed."

"Indeed," Ysabella said with resolve, quickly pointing out the box that she wished to have brought before them. It was more like a cage, its sides and top wrought with holes, and Aileen could not imagine what it contained.

Ysabella unfastened the buckles and threw back the lid. "I brought you a hazel, from my own garden," she said, her tone crisp. "It is a most practical tree, for it will bear nuts in time, which one can eat in harsh times."

Evangeline laughed with affection. "Ysabella is always certain that dark times could lie ahead."

"And so they could," that woman agreed, though she smiled at Merlyn. "Though some of us are better at keeping them at bay."

"And I brought you a honeysuckle," Evangeline declared. "Also from Ysabella's garden, for I feared that her gift was too pragmatic. You have need of beauty and scent in a garden, and so you will have both from this vine. Look, it has made a blossom even as we journeyed!"

Rosamunde stepped forward and gestured to the third plant nestled in the box. "And I have brought you the plant without which no lady's garden can be complete. My mother and aunt insist it will die in this clime, and that it is no gift to bring something so ill-fated, but my heart is more merry than theirs."

"It is a rose," Aileen whispered despite the lump in her throat.

"You know it?" Rosamunde demanded with delight. "I thought you were raised even further north than Inverfyre?" A wicked gleam lit her eyes. "Could it be that my aunt and mother are mistaken?"

Aileen smiled. "My mother grew them, though not easily, at Abernye." She reached out and touched the green leaves of the plant and was pleased with its vigor.

"Its roses are as red as blood," Rosamunde confided. "And smell more sweetly than the finest perfume in Constantinople."

"I thank you," Aileen said hoarsely. "The red blooms were my mother's favorites." She turned to the other women and smiled. "I thank you all for your kindness. I have yearned for a garden and these gifts will begin it well."

She knew the Hawk understood that she was thinking of the garden in her memory palace, as well as the honeysuckle and hazel that had appeared in her visions. Her chest was tight with emotion, for these guests had unwittingly chosen the perfect gifts for her, and she was deeply touched.

But there would be time aplenty for expressing her gratitude more fully. Their guests were tired, hungry and thirsty. It was time to show the Hawk's hospitality.

"I bid you all welcome to Inverfyre," Aileen said, encompassing the entire company with a gesture. "And heartily anticipate the chance to know you all better. Come, come into the hall and partake of the meal that has been prepared."

The grass was wet with dew on the morning of the Nativity of Saint John the Baptist, but the ladies lifted their skirts and walked to the chapel. The way was not short, but a path had been cut through the woods, and they made a procession to the chapel high on the hill. There were those in the company, without doubt, who had an aching head this morning, but Aileen was filled with joy. She carried a blessed burden fast against her left side and her heart pounded in anticipation of this day's events.

The sunlight danced through the leaves of the trees, casting bright patches of light upon the forest floor. They walked in pairs, the priest leading the company with his censer swinging. Aileen and the Hawk followed behind him, followed by the Hawk's parents, his aunt and uncle, his cousins and their uncommonly subdued children. Those of the Hawk's cohorts destined to be wed this day—Reinhard and Margery, Ahearn and Nissa, Fernando and Guinevere— were next in the procession. (Aileen wondered whether she alone found it amusing that Guinevere was the sole bride who was not obviously pregnant.) The Hawk's remaining cohorts strode after them, his household followed, then their remaining guests and their households, and finally, the villagers of Inverfyre. All were dressed in their richest finery; all wore their best gems; all weapons and mail were polished to a gleam.

Their procession moved with a purposeful rustle, solely the brush of silken robes and their footfalls on the path disturbing the quiet of the forest. Birds called to each other and the stream gurgled alongside their course. Smoke and a sweet scent rose from the censer as the priest swung it from side to side.

The chapel itself was astonishingly bright in comparison, for the walls and roof had yet to be rebuilt. The altar had been replaced, however, and an embroidered cloth graced it on this day, the hem flicking in the breeze. The cross and chalice upon the altar shone. A dozen waiting boys began to sing a hymn as the company crossed the threshold, their music as sweet as that of the birds.

Aileen looked as they walked down the aisle, feeling the past in close proximity. They stepped first upon the stone that marked the grave of Magnus Armstrong, then each successive son of the lineage. The last space before the altar was devoid of carvings, a place left for the seventh son of Magnus' bloodline. She and the Hawk halted upon that stone, her right hand held fast in his left at shoulder height, as Father Gilchrist sang the mass.

The tang of blessed wine was still upon their tongues when Aileen turned to face the Hawk. She took her burden in both hands and unfurled the undyed silk that surrounded it. The wooden *Titulus Croce* had been broken once, and now was graced with a red leather harness, adorned with gilt crosses, that held its two halves together.

On impulse, Aileen turned and offered the relic to Evangeline. A flush stained that lady's cheeks, though she stepped quickly to accept its burden in her hands. She caressed it slightly as she took Aileen's place afore the altar and held it out to her son.

The Hawk laid his hands upon it. "I swear by all that is holy to defend the *Titulus Croce* entrusted to our forebear Magnus Armstrong, to protect the holding of Inverfyre granted by God to that same forebear, and to defend all those souls pledged to my blade and my household. This vow I do swear to uphold for as long as there is blood in my veins and breath in my body, so help me God."

Evangeline surrendered the relic to the Hawk, who then entrusted it to the priest. Father Gilchrist kissed it and murmured a prayer over it. Evangeline kissed her son's cheeks in succession, then stepped back, blinking back her tears.

Aileen then resumed her place. She took the seal of Inverfyre, which had been fashioned into a ring, and slipped it onto her husband's finger. They shared a smile as the priest blessed them, then turned to face the company.

Aileen held the Hawk's be-ringed hand high. "Praise be to God," she cried, so all could hear the truth of it. "The rightful Laird of Inverfyre is restored!"

The company cheered and the sunlight seemed to sparkle a little brighter. "And from this day forward, there shall be two strongholds upon the lands of Inverfyre," the Hawk declared. "One here, where the chapel and relic will be guarded." He offered a scroll to the priest with a flourish. "As you know, I have made an endowment to support a monastic house and granted these lands, including the chapel, for their sustenance in exchange for holy services."

"Praise be," Father Gilchrist said with a smile. "I trust you will see the outer walls protected with men of greater military might. There is nothing like a rare prize, my laird, to tempt the ambitions of others."

"I have entrusted that burden to my comrade, Ewen. He shall be the marshal of the priory of Inverfyre."

Ewen bowed, his neck reddening at this honor. "I shall do my best, my laird."

"And that will more than suffice," the Hawk said. He raised his voice when he continued. "And still there shall remain the second keep of Inverfyre, where my wife and I will abide."

The company turned as one to view the distant keep and Aileen smiled as a banner was unfurled over its gates. It was a replacement for the one destroyed by the MacLaren clan, wrought by Nissa and Aileen in stolen hours these past months. Aileen saw that she had surprised her husband and knew she did not imagine the sheen of tears in his eyes.

"You did this for me?" he murmured.

"It was only fitting." She smiled as she held his gaze. "Though I must confess that I have added a hazel and honeysuckle to your insignia."

The Hawk laughed. "So long as they are entwined forevermore, lady mine, I have no complaint."

They looked back together and Aileen caught her breath.

Somehow the sunlight danced in the leaves of those thirteen silver-barked trees and for a heartbeat, the leaves appeared to be blood red.

Then they were green again, rustling slightly in the breeze. Aileen looked up and the Hawk regarded her so solemnly that she knew he too had seen it, whatever it had been. She smiled and touched his jaw.

"The old injustices have been resolved then," she had time to whisper before the Hawk caught Aileen close and kissed her soundly. He let his hand curve over her rounding belly as he did so, revealing its ripe shape to the company. Evangeline gasped with delight. The assembly stamped their feet and hooted, immediately understanding, and Aileen was flushed scarlet when her husband raised his head.

"Perhaps we should make a dozen heirs," he whispered mischievously. "As you so keenly observed, lady mine, the world is most unpredictable."

Aileen laughed, but Nissa began to sing, and the Hawk could only read her assent in her eyes as the company joined the song.

> "When the seventh son of Inverfyre,
> Saves his legacy from intrigue and mire,
> Only then shall glorious Inverfyre,
> Reflect in full its first laird's desire.

Tarsuinn released a trio of peregrines as they left the chapel and the birds cried overhead. Aileen smiled to herself, letting her husband guide her steps on the descent. The hawk had captured the hare, the hazel had twined with the honeysuckle, and against all odds, both partners were happier together than apart.

That was a good portent for their future, indeed.

Dear Reader,

How can star-crossed lovers ever change their fortune? Do people really learn from their mistakes? In *The Warrior*, I wanted to explore a reincarnation theme, with the ill-fated lovers learning from their mistakes. When the Hawk and Aileen changed their choices, they changed their future and ensured that they could be together for all time. I hope you enjoyed the book as much as I enjoyed writing it.

At the end of *The Warrior*, you met the Hawk's eight busy nephews and nieces. My next trilogy follows the adventures of three of these children. Alexander, the eldest son and abruptly Laird of Kinfairlie, is more accustomed to playing tricks on his sisters than finding suitable husbands for them. In *The Bride Auction*, his eldest sister Madeline refuses to wed. With the help of his aunt Rosamunde, Alexander concocts a scheme to see Madeline married quickly—you can read more about it in the excerpt included here. Of course, the best laid plans oft go awry, though you can be sure that Madeline finds true love in the end. *The Bride Thief* tells of Alexander's attempt to do better in finding a suitable spouse for his next sister, Vivienne. Though his intentions are good, Alexander just doesn't anticipate these determined heroes! Finally, the two sisters get even with Alexander in *The Bride Wager*. I'm having a wonderful time writing these books and hope you enjoy reading them too.

Visit my website for news and review quotes, and the chance to win a free book every two weeks! Château Delacroix is at http://www.delacroix.net.

Until next time, happy reading!

Prologue

*Kinfairlie, on the east coast of Scotland—April
1421*

Alexander, newly made Laird of Kinfairlie, glowered at
his sister.

There was no immediate effect. In fact, Madeline granted
him a charming smile. She was a beautiful woman, dark of
hair and blue of eye, her coloring and comeliness so striking
that men oft stared at her in awe. She was fiercely clever and
charming, as well. All of these traits, along with the score of

men anxious to wed her, only made Madeline's refusal to wed more irksome.

"You need not look so annoyed, Alexander," she said, her tone teasing. "My suggestion is wrought of good sense."

"It is no good sense for a woman of three and twenty summers to remain unwed," he grumbled. "I cannot imagine what Papa was thinking not to have seen you safely wed a decade ago."

Madeline's eyes flashed. "Papa was thinking that I loved James and that I would wed James in time."

"James is dead," Alexander retorted, speaking more harshly than was his wont. They had had this argument a dozen times and he tired of his sister's stubborn refusal to accept his counsel. "And dead these ten months. Though I appreciate a wound to the heart takes long to heal, you grow no younger, Madeline."

Madeline laughed. "Nor do any of us, brother mine, but it is not my age that troubles you."

Her playful manner made him feel all the more grumpy. Alexander knew that he sounded like a man fifty years older than he was, but he could not help himself—though Madeline's refusal to take him seriously did not aid his mood.

He glared at her, again to no avail. "I ask only that you wed, that you do so out of regard for your five younger sisters, that they too might wed."

Madeline lifted one slender shoulder in a shrug. "I do not halt their nuptials."

"They will not wed afore you and you know it well. So Vivienne and Annelise and Isabella and Elizabeth have *all* informed me. The lot of you are in league against me!" Alexander flung out his hands and rose to his feet, pacing the chamber in his frustration.

Madeline—curse her!—laughed. "It is no small burden

to become laird of the keep," she teased, though the expression in her eyes was knowing when he spun to face her.

"It is hell!" he shouted, feeling better for it. "And not a one of you makes it any easier for me! I am not mad to demand that you wed! I am trying to assure your future, yet you all defy me at every step!"

Madeline tilted her head, her eyes sparkling merrily and a smile lifting the corner of her lips. "Can you not imagine that it is a sweet kind of vengeance for all the pranks you have played upon us over the years? How delicious it is to foil you, Alexander, now that you are suddenly stern and proper!"

"I will not be foiled!" he roared and thudded his fist upon the table between them.

Madeline clucked her tongue, chiding him for his show of temper. "And I will not be wed," she said softly. "Not so readily as that. At any rate, you have not the coin in the treasury to offer a dowry, so there is no need to discuss the matter afore the tithes come in."

Alexander spun to look out the window, hoping to hide his expression from his confident sister. There might have been a steel band around his heart, for he knew a detail that Madeline did not. The tithes would be low this year, so the castellan had confided. There had been torrential rains this spring and what seed had not been washed away had rotted in the ground. He marvelled that he had never thought of such matters until this past year and marvelled again at how much he had yet to learn.

How had Papa managed all these concerns? How had he laughed and been so merry with such a weight upon his shoulders? Alexander's gaze trailed over the sea that lapped beneath Kinfairlie's towers and mourned their loss anew. He knew Madeline and the others defied him as a way of defying the cruel truth of their parents' sudden death, but he also knew that he could not feed all those currently resident in this keep in the winter to come. The castellan had told him so, and in no uncertain terms.

His sisters had to be wed, and at least the two eldest had to be wed this summer. They were all of an age to do so, ranging as they did from twenty-three summers to twelve, but Madeline was the sole obstacle to his scheme.

He pivoted to regard her, noting the concern that she quickly hid. She must know what it cost him to so change his own nature, to abandon his recklessness in favor of responsibility; she must know that he shouldered this burden for the sake of all of them.

Yet still she defied him.

"You could at least feign compliance," he suggested, anger running beneath his words. "You could try to make my task lighter, Madeline, instead of encouraging our sisters to vex me."

She leaned closer. "You could at least ask," she retorted, the sapphire flash of her eyes showing that this would be no easy victory. "In truth, Alexander, you are so demanding that a saint would defy you simply for the pleasure of foiling your schemes."

"I am making choices for the best of all of us," he insisted, "and you only vex me."

Madeline smiled with confidence. "You are not vexed. You are irked, perhaps."

"Annoyed," contributed another feminine voice. Vivienne tipped her head around the corner, revealing that she had been listening to the entire exchange. Vivienne's hair was of a russet hue and her eyes were a dark green. Otherwise, she shared Madeline's virtues.

Three shorter women peeked around the edge of the portal, their eyes bright with curiosity. Annelise was sixteen with auburn tresses and eyes as blue as cornflowers; Isabella was fourteen with eyes of vivid green, orange-red hair and freckles across her nose; Elizabeth was ebony-haired like himself and Madeline, her eyes an uncanny green. The sight of all those uncovered tresses—the mark of unmarried maidens—made Alexander's innards clench.

"But you are certainly not vexed, Alexander," Vivienne continued with a smile.

Madeline nodded agreement. "When Alexander is vexed in truth, he shouts. So know this, Annelise, Isabella and Elizabeth, you have not truly vexed Alexander until he roars fit to lift the roof." The five women giggled and that was enough.

"I am indeed vexed!" Alexander bellowed, the result of his anger solely that the three younger women nodded.

"Now he *is* vexed," said Annelise.

"You can tell by the way he shouts," Elizabeth agreed.

"Indeed," said Madeline, that teasing smile curving her lips again. "But still he is a man of honor, upon that we can all rely." She rose and gave a simmering Alexander a peck of a kiss upon each of his cheeks.

She smiled at him with a surety that made him long to throttle her, for she was right. "Still he will not raise a hand against a woman." Madeline patted his shoulder, as if he were no more threatening than a kitten. "I shall wed when I so choose, Alexander, and not one day before. Fear not—all will be resolved well enough in the end."

With that, Madeline left the chamber, easily gathering their sisters about her. They chattered of kirtles and chemises and new shoes as their voices faded to naught.

Alexander sat down heavily and put his head in his hands. What was he going to do?

Alexander was still there, though the sky was darker, when his visitors arrived.

"He does indeed look glum enough," a familiar voice said, laughter beneath her tone. "So we were warned."

Alexander looked up as his Aunt Rosamunde cast herself upon the bench Madeline had abandoned. She shook the pins from her hair with characteristic impatience. The sunlit tresses fell loose over her shoulders and she sighed with relief.

She winked at him, though spoke to the other visitor. "I would wager that sisters are his woe, Tynan."

"That is not much of a wager," Uncle Tynan said grimly, shaking out his cloak before he leaned upon the lip of the window. "They are too merry not to have recently triumphed over Alexander." The older man smiled slightly at his beleaguered nephew. "You are outnumbered and further encumbered by honor. Those five will use any means against you."

This pair had made an unlikely alliance these past years, since it had been revealed at the Hawk's wedding that they were not blood cousins, after all. Rosamunde, it seemed, had been adopted by Gawain and Evangeline and was not of Gawain's seed in truth. None had been more surprised by the revelation than this pair. Sparks still flew between them as they always had, but Alexander sometimes had a sense that there was more between his aunt and uncle than others suspected.

Who knew what had happened at his uncle's keep of Ravensmuir when Rosamunde's ship was docked in its bay? Alexander knew better than to ask.

He shook his head now and grimaced. "I could strangle Madeline."

Rosamunde shook her head, dismissive of the notion.

"But then you would have to face a court and the king's justice, and some misery of incarceration."

"Not to mention purgatory, if not hell itself," Tynan added.

"Hardly worth it," Rosamunde said sagely, then winked at him again. "What has she done—or refused to do—this time?"

"She refuses to wed. She thinks she does me a favor, but saving coin in the treasury." Alexander sighed, then lowered his voice. "But there is no coin and there will be none soon. The castellan says the harvest will be bad, and I fear I will not be able to feed all within these walls this winter."

"The others?" Tynan demanded, leaning forward in his interest.

"I would guess that they refuse to wed afore Madeline," Rosamunde said softly.

Alexander nodded glumly. His guests exchanged a glance, then Rosamunde cleared her throat. "Do you not miss the old days, Alexander, when your deeds were the most outrageous of all?"

"I have duties now, and an obligation to Papa's trust," Alexander said, his very tone dutiful beyond belief.

"And so all the spark has gone from your days and your deeds." Rosamunde sat back and shook her head, her eyes dancing wickedly. "I think you should surprise Madeline. You have tried to reason with her, after all, and without success."

"Rosamunde . . ." Tynan said, the single word filled with warning.

Rosamunde leaned toward Alexander, undeterred. "We came this day to tell you of our agreement to be rid of all the relics at Ravensmuir. Tynan will not suffer them beneath the roof any longer, for he tires of my nocturnal visits to plunder his treasure."

Tynan snorted, but said nothing.

"Surely you cannot mean to abandon your trade in relics?" Alexander asked in surprise.

Rosamunde shrugged, her gaze sliding to Tynan. A beguiling color touched her cheeks, then she met Alexander's gaze again. "I grow no younger, Alexander, and the risk of the seas holds less allure than once it did. Perhaps I shall become a nun."

Both men laughed uproariously at this prospect, and Rosamunde chuckled in her turn.

"We are agreed that the trade will halt," she continued more soberly. "And also that the last of the relics must leave Ravensmuir to ensure Tynan has his peace."

"But what will you do with them?" Alexander asked. "Surely you do not mean to grant them as gifts?"

Tynan chuckled darkly. "I would be a generous donor indeed."

"We intend to auction them, in the middle of May, when all are anxious for a diversion," Rosamunde declared, her eyes bright. "We will invite noblemen, bishops and knights from all of Christendom to bid against each other for these prizes. It will be a grand fête and a fitting end to my trade."

"Madeline might find a spouse there," Alexander mused, but his aunt laughed aloud.

"Be more bold than that, Alexander!" she declared. "You sound like a man three times your age."

"Rosamunde," Tynan warned again, but was heeded no more closely than the first time.

Indeed, Rosamunde's voice dropped low and she tapped a finger upon Alexander's knee. Mischief emanated from her every pore. "Perhaps, Alexander, you should auction the jewel of Kinfairlie. You said you were in need of coin."

Alexander glanced between the pair of them. Tynan had dropped his brow to his hand and shook his head in apparent despair. Rosamunde looked so delighted with herself that he knew he had missed some critical detail.

"But there is no jewel of Kinfairlie," Alexander began cautiously. Rosamunde laughed and understanding dawned. "Oh! But Madeline would loathe me forever if I auctioned her off!"

"Shhhh!" counselled Rosamunde. Tynan, with obvious resignation, closed the portal and leaned against it.

Alexander looked between the pair of them, his blood quickening at the prospect. Oh, he could well imagine how vexed Madeline would be—and truly the prospect gave him some pleasure. "I should not dare," he said carefully.

Rosamunde laughed. "There was a time when you would have dared far more than this to best Madeline." She braced her elbows upon her knees. "Do not tell me that I have to dare you to do this deed? Alexander, what has become of you? Surely the ruffian we knew and loved is yet within your heart?"

And that was all it took.

Alexander raised a finger. "We will do this upon one condition. I will compile a list of those I deem suitable matches, and only those men will be advised that the jewel of Kinfairlie is for sale."

"There is nothing amiss with a private auction, provided all those invited have weighty purses," Rosamunde conceded.

"I cannot believe that I am a part of this," Tynan grumbled good-naturedly.

"Of course you are a part of it," Rosamunde said crisply.

"It is you who must pass the word along." She patted his arm and a spark danced between the two of them, one so hot that Alexander felt obliged to glance away. "Who better to quietly and competently ensure that our niece's needs are met?"

A ghost of a smile touched Tynan's lips. "I came also with a proposition for you, Alexander, and one you may find timely. I have need of an heir, as I have never wedded. If you are desirous of it, I will take your brother Malcolm to Ravensmuir, for he is old enough to be groomed for such a task."

"You would make him your heir?" Alexander asked.

"Indeed."

"You are too kind, Uncle. And I know that Malcolm would welcome this trust. He has great fondness for you both as well as for Ravensmuir."

"And should you desire it," Tynan continued, "I could send word to the Hawk of Inverfyre. I do not doubt that he would take Ross beneath his care, and train him as a warrior, though the Hawk has heirs enough of his own."

"It would see another mouth from your board this winter," Rosamunde said quietly.

Alexander felt his burden lighten. "You are too kind to aid me in this."

"We are family," Rosamunde said firmly. "It is our solemn duty to aid each other, and you have need of more aid than most in these times."

"I thank you for your counsel and your aid," Alexander said, knowing his gratitude showed.

"You must contrive to bring Madeline to Ravensmuir for the auction," Rosamunde said with resolve. "For if she guesses the truth afore the nuptials are complete, there will be trouble. We must act with haste and daring to succeed."

"Woe may come of this particular scheme," Tynan said darkly.

Rosamunde laughed. "You always say as much. I have a feeling, though, that Madeline might well meet her match."

For the first time in many months, Alexander felt himself begin to smile. With such a scheme, much could be resolved, and a mischievous part of him looked forward to irking Madeline as he had for decades. He would not have been her elder brother otherwise.

"I mean to ensure that she does meet her match." Alexander imagined Madeline's outrage and chuckled, even as he compiled a list of suitors he knew would treat her well. More than one of them annoyed her mightily and every one of them had snared her gaze at one time or another.

Within a year, Madeline would forget about her lost betrothed James and the wound in her heart would heal. He knew with utter certainty that she would be happy once she was wed and had a babe in her belly. Within a year, Madeline would thank him mightily for his daring deed.

Truly, this was the best possible solution.

"But I have been remiss," Alexander said with a heartiness he could not have imagined he would soon feel again. "You are my guests, yet you have neither wine nor ale in your hand. Come to the hall, come and make merry with all of us. Your presence at Kinfairlie is welcome. I thank you, Aunt and Uncle, for you have brought good tidings and welcome counsel indeed."